"I can't go home," I whispered, holding him to me. "Not now. I can't bring this madness home to my family. I stared at the house for a moment more, then shut my eyes. "The false king won't stop here. He'll keep sending things after me, and my family will get caught in the middle. I can't let that happen. I...I have to leave. Now."

I opened my eyes and stared at the place where the Iron fey had fallen, at the slivers of metal glinting in the weeds. The thought of such monsters stealing into my room, turning their murderous eyes on Ethan or my mom, made me cold with rage. *All right,* I thought, clenching my fists in Ash's shirt, *the false king wants a war? I'll give him one.*

* * *

Buzz about The Iron Fey novels

If y   rough

ns

"   of...

SUMMER FADES.
ICE MELTS.
HERE'S WHAT'S LEFT.
THE IRON FEY

THE IRON QUEEN

JULIE KAGAWA

HARLEQUIN®TEEN

Recycling programs
for this product may
not exist in your area.

ISBN-13: 978-0-373-21018-3

THE IRON QUEEN

Printed in U.S.A.

To Erica and Gail, Ash's biggest fans. And to Nick, always my inspiration.

PART ONE

CHAPTER ONE

THE LONG ROAD HOME

Eleven years ago, on my sixth birthday, my father disappeared.

One year ago, on the very same day, my brother was taken from me, as well. But that time, I went into Faery to take him back.

It's strange how a journey can change you, what you can learn from it. I learned that the man I thought was my father wasn't my father at all. That my biological dad wasn't even human. That I was the half-breed daughter of a legendary faery king, and his blood flowed in my veins. I learned that I had power, a power that scares me, even now. A power that even the fey dread, something that can destroy them—and I'm not sure I can control it.

I learned that love can transcend race and time, and that it can be beautiful and perfect and worth fighting for but also fragile and heartbreaking, and sometimes sacrifice is necessary. That sometimes it's you against the world, and there are no easy answers. That you have to know when to hold on…and when to let go. And even if that love comes back, you could discover something in someone else who has been there all along.

I thought it was over. I thought my time with the fey, the impossible choices I had to make, the sacrifices for those I loved, was behind me. But a storm was approaching, one that would test those choices like never before. And this time, there would be no turning back.

My name is Meghan Chase.

In less than twenty-four hours, I'll be seventeen.

Déjà vu, right? Shocking how quickly time can pass you by, like you're standing still. I can't believe it's been a year since that day. The day I went into Faery. The day that changed my life forever.

Technically, I won't actually be turning seventeen. I've been in the Nevernever too long. When you're in Faery, you don't age, or you age so slowly it's not worth mentioning. So, while a year has passed in the real world, I'm probably only a few days older than when I went in.

In real life, I've changed so much I don't even recognize myself.

Beneath me, the tatter-colt's hooves clopped against the pavement, a quiet rhythm that matched my own heartbeat. On this lonely stretch of Louisiana highway, surrounded by tupelo trees and moss-covered cypress, few cars passed us, and the ones that did flew by without slowing down, tossing leaves in their wake. They couldn't see the shaggy black horse with eyes like hot coals, walking along the road without reins or bit or saddle. They couldn't see the figures on its back, the pale-haired girl and the dark, beautiful prince behind her, his arms around her waist. Mortals were blind to the world of Faery, a world I was a part of now, whether I'd asked for it or not.

"What are you afraid of?" a deep voice murmured in my ear, sending a shiver up my spine. Even in the humid swamps of Louisiana, the Winter prince radiated cold, and his breath was wonderfully cool against my skin.

I peered at him over my shoulder. "What do you mean?" Ash, prince of the Unseelie Court, met my gaze, silver eyes gleaming in the twilight. Officially, he was no longer a prince. Queen Mab had exiled him from the Nevernever after he refused to renounce his love for the half-human daughter of Oberon, the Summer King. My father. Summer and Winter were supposed to be enemies. We were not supposed to cooperate, we were not supposed to go on quests together and, most important, we were not supposed to fall in love.

But we had, and now Ash was here, with me. We were exiles, and the trods—the paths into Faery—were closed to us forever, but I didn't care. I wasn't planning to ever go back.

"You're nervous." Ash's hand stroked the back of my head, brushing the hair from my neck, making me shiver. "I can feel it. You have this anxious, flickering aura all around you, and it's driving me a little nuts, being this close. What's wrong?"

I should've known. There was no hiding what I felt from Ash, or any faery for that matter. Their magic, their glamour, came from human dreams and emotions. So Ash could sense what I was feeling without even trying. "Sorry," I told him. "I guess I am a little nervous."

"Why?"

"Why? I've been gone almost a year. Mom will hit the roof when she sees me." My stomach squirmed as I imagined the reunion: the tears, the angry relief, the inevitable questions. "They didn't hear anything from me while I was in Faery." I sighed, gazing up the road to where the stretch of pavement melted into the darkness. "What am I going to tell them? How will I even begin to explain?"

The tatter-colt snorted and pinned its ears at a truck that roared by, passing uncomfortably close. I couldn't be sure, but it looked like Luke's battered old Ford, rattling down the road and vanishing around a curve. If it was my stepdad, he definitely wouldn't have seen us; he'd had a hard time remembering my name even when I'd lived in the same house.

"You tell them the truth," Ash said, startling me. I wasn't expecting him to answer. "From the beginning. Either they accept it, or they don't, but you can't hide who you are, especially from your family. Best to get it over with—we can deal with whatever happens after."

His candor surprised me. I was still getting used to this new Ash, this faery who talked and smiled instead of hiding behind an icy wall of indifference. Ever since we were banished from the Nevernever, he'd been more open, less brooding and angst-ridden, as if a huge weight had been lifted from his shoulders. True, he was still quiet and solemn by anyone's standards, but for the first time, I felt I was finally getting a glimpse of the Ash I knew was there all along.

"But what if they *can't* deal with it?" I muttered, voicing the concern that had been plaguing me all morning. "What if they see what I am and freak out? What if they don't… want me anymore?"

I trailed off at the end, knowing I sounded like a sullen five-year-old. But Ash's hold on me tightened, and he pulled me closer against him.

"Then you'll be an orphan, just like me," he said. "And we'll find a way to get by." His lips brushed against my ear, tying my stomach into about a dozen knots. "Together."

My breath hitched, and I turned my head to kiss him, reaching back to run my hand through his silky dark hair.

The tatter-colt snorted and bucked midstep, not enough to throw me off, but enough to bounce me a few inches straight up. I snatched wildly for its mane as Ash grabbed my waist, keeping me from falling off. Heart pounding, I shot a glare between the tatter-colt's ears, resisting the urge to kick it in the ribs and give it another excuse to buck me off. It raised its head and glared back at us, eyes glowing crimson, disgust written plainly on its equine face.

I wrinkled my nose at it. "Oh, excuse me, are we making you uncomfortable?" I asked sarcastically, and it snorted. "Fine. We'll behave."

Ash chuckled but didn't attempt to pull me back. I sighed and gazed at the road over the colt's bobbing head, looking for familiar landmarks. My heart leaped when I saw a rusty van sitting in the trees off the side of the road, so ancient and corroded a tree had grown through the roof. It had been there for as long as I could remember, and I saw it every day on the bus to and from school. It always told me when I was nearly home.

It seemed so long ago, now—a lifetime ago—that I'd sat on the bus with my friend Robbie, when all I had to worry about was grades and homework and getting my driver's permit. So much had changed; it would feel strange return-ing to school and my old, mundane life like nothing had happened. "I'll probably have to repeat a year," I sighed, and felt Ash's puzzled gaze on my neck. Of course, being an immortal faery, he didn't have to worry about school and licenses and—

I stopped as reality seemed to descend on me all at once. My time in the Nevernever was like a dream, hazy and ethereal, but we were back in the real world now. Where I had to worry about homework and grades and getting into college. I'd wanted to get a summer job and save up for a car. I'd wanted to attend ITT Tech after high school, maybe move to the Baton Rouge or New Orleans campuses when I graduated. Could I still do that? Even after everything that happened? And where would a dark, exiled faery prince fit into all of this?

"What is it?" Ash's breath tickled the back of my ear, making me shiver.

I took a deep breath. "How is this going to work, Ash?" I half turned to face him. "Where will we be a year from now, two years from now? I can't stay here forever—sooner or later, I'm going to have to get on with my life. School, work, college someday..." I broke off and looked down at my hands. "I have to move on eventually, but I don't want to do any of those things without you."

"I've been thinking about that," Ash replied. I glanced up at him, and he surprised me with a brief smile. "You have your whole life ahead of you. It makes sense that you should plan for the future. And I figure, Goodfellow pretended to be mortal for sixteen years. There's no reason I can't do the same."

I blinked at him. "Really?"

He touched my cheek softly, his eyes intense as they gazed into mine. "You might have to teach me a little about the human world, but I'm willing to learn if it means being close to you." He smiled again, a wry quirk of his lips. "I'm sure I can adapt to 'being human,' if I must. If you want me to attend classes as a student, I can do that. If you want to move to a large city to pursue your dreams, I will follow. And if, someday, you wish to be married in a white gown and make this official in human eyes, I'm willing to do that, too." He leaned in, close enough for me to see my reflection in his silver gaze. "For better or worse, I'm afraid you're stuck with me now."

I felt breathless, not knowing what to say. I wanted to thank him, but those words didn't mean the same in faery terms. I wanted to lean in the rest of the way and kiss him, but the tatter-colt would probably throw me into the ditch if I tried. "Ash," I began, but was saved a response as the tatter-colt abruptly came to a full stop at the end of a long gravel driveway that stretched away over a short rise. A familiar green mailbox balanced precariously on its post at the end of the drive, faded with age and time, but I had no trouble reading it, even in the darkness.

Chase. 14202

My heart stood still. I was home.

I slid off the tatter-colt's back and stumbled as I hit the ground, my legs feeling weird and shaky after being on horseback for so long. Ash dismounted with ease, murmuring something to the tatter-colt, which snorted, threw up its head and bounded into the darkness. In seconds, it had disappeared.

I gazed up the long gravel road, my heart pounding in my chest. Home and family waited just beyond that rise: the old green farmhouse with paint peeling off the wood, the pig barns out back through the mud, Luke's truck and Mom's station wagon in the driveway.

Ash moved up beside me, making no noise on the rocks. "Are you ready?"

No, I wasn't. I peered into the darkness where the tatter-colt had vanished instead. "What happened to our ride?" I asked, to distract myself from what I had to do. "What did you say to it?"

"I told him the favor has been paid and that we're even now." For some reason, this seemed to amuse him; he gazed after the colt with a faint smile on his lips. "It appears I can't order them around like I used to. I'll have to rely on calling in favors from now on."

"Is that bad?"

The smile twitched into a smirk. "A lot of people owe me." When I still hesitated, he nodded toward the driveway. "Go on. Your family is waiting."

"What about you?"

"It's probably better if you go alone this time." A flicker of regret passed through his eyes, and he gave me a pained smile. "I don't think your brother would be happy to see me again."

"But—"

"I'll be close." He reached out and tucked a strand of hair behind my ears. "Promise."

I sighed and gazed up the driveway once more. "All right," I muttered, steeling myself for the inevitable. "Here goes nothing."

I took three steps, feeling the gravel crunch under my feet, and glanced over my shoulder. The empty road mocked me, the breeze stirring up leaves in the spot Ash had been. *Typical faery.* I shook my head and continued my solitary trek up the driveway.

It wasn't long before I reached the top of the rise, and there, in all its rustic glory, was the house I'd lived in for ten years. I could see lights on in the window, and my family moving about in the kitchen. There was Mom's slender frame, bent over the sink, and Luke in his faded overalls, putting a stack of dirty plates on the counter. And if I squinted hard enough, I could just see the top of Ethan's curly head, poking over the kitchen table.

Tears pricked my eyes. After a year of being away, fighting faeries, discovering who I was, cheating death more times than I cared to remember, I was finally home.

"Isn't that precious," a voice hissed.

I spun, looking around wildly.

"Up here, princess."

I looked straight up, and my vision was filled with a thin, shimmering net an instant before it struck me and sent me tumbling back. Cursing, I thrashed and tore at the threads, trying to rip through the flimsy barrier. Stinging pain made me gasp. Blood streamed down my hands, and I squinted at the threads. The net was actually made of fine, flexible wire, and my struggles had sliced my fingers open.

Harsh laughter caught my attention, and I craned my neck up, searching for my assailants. On the lone set of power lines that stretched to the roof of the house perched three bulbous creatures with spindly legs that glinted under the moonlight. My heart gave a violent lurch when, as one, they unfurled and leaped from the lines, landing in the gravel with faint clicking sounds. Straightening, they scuttled toward me.

I recoiled, tangling myself even further in the wire net. Now that I saw them clearly, they reminded me of giant spiders, only somehow even more horrible. Their spindly legs were huge needles, shiny and pointed as they skittered over the ground. But their upper bodies were of gaunt, emaciated women with pale skin and bulging black eyes. Their arms were made of wire, and long, needlelike fingers uncurled like claws as they approached, their legs clicking over the gravel.

"Here she is," hissed one as they surrounded me, grinning. "Just as the king said she would be."

"Too easy," rasped another, peering at me with a bulbous black eye. "I'm rather disappointed. I thought she would be a good catch, but she's just a skinny little bug, trapped in a web. What is the king so afraid of?"

"The king," I said, and all three blinked at me, surprised I was talking to them instead of cringing in fear, perhaps. "You mean the false king, don't you? He's still after me."

The spider-hags hissed, baring pointed teeth. "Do not blaspheme him so, child!" one screeched, grabbing the net and pulling me forward. "He is not the *false* king! He is the Iron King, the true monarch of the Iron fey!"

"Not from what I heard," I retorted, meeting the blazing black eyes full on. "I've met the Iron King, the real Iron King, Machina. Or have you forgotten him?"

"Of course we haven't!" hissed the hag's sister. "We will never forget Machina. He wanted to make you his queen, queen of all the Iron fey, and you killed him for his trouble."

"He kidnapped my brother and was planning to destroy the Nevernever!" I snapped in return. "But you're missing the point. The king you serve, the one who took over the throne, is an imposter. He isn't the real heir. You're supporting a false king."

"Lies!" the hags screeched, crowding in, grabbing me with pointed needle claws, drawing blood. "Who told you this? Who dares blaspheme the name of the new king?"

"Ironhorse," I said, wincing as one snatched my hair, shaking my head back and forth. "Ironhorse told me, Machina's lieutenant himself."

"The traitor fey! He and the rebels will be destroyed, right after the king takes care of you!"

The spider-hags were shrieking now, shouting curses and threats, tearing at me through the wire net. One of them tightened her grip in my hair and lifted me off my feet. I gasped, tears of pain flooding my eyes as the faery hissed in my face.

A flash of cold blue light erupted between us. The Iron faery gave a shriek and...*disintegrated,* becoming thousands of tiny slivers that rained down around me. They glimmered in the darkness, needles and pins catching the moonlight as the spider-hag departed the world in the manner of her kind. The other two wailed and drew back as something tore the net off me and stepped between us.

"Are you all right?" Ash growled as I staggered to my feet, his gaze never leaving the hags in front of him. My scalp burned, my fingers still bled, and a dozen tiny scratches covered my arms from the hag's claws, but I wasn't badly hurt.

"I'm fine," I told him, a slow anger building in my chest. I felt my glamour rise like a tornado, swirling with emotion and energy. When I'd first met Mab, the Winter Queen had sealed my magic away, afraid of my power, but the seal had been broken and I could feel the pulse of glamour once more. It was everywhere around me, savage and wild, the magic of Oberon and the Summer fey.

"You killed our sister!" the hags screeched, tearing at their own hair. "We'll slice you to pieces!" Hissing, they scuttled toward us with raised claws. I felt a ripple of glamour from Ash, colder than the fiery magic of Summer, and the Winter prince swept his arm forward.

A burst of blue light, and one of the hags skittered into a hail of ice-daggers, the pointed shards ripping through her like shrapnel. She wailed and fell apart, scattering into thousands of glittering pieces in the grass. Ash brandished his sword and charged the last one.

The remaining spider-hag screamed her fury and raised her arms. Ten shimmering lengths of wire seemed to grow from her needle-tip fingers. She sliced them toward Ash, who ducked, and the wires cut a nearby sapling into pieces. As he danced around her, I knelt and buried my hands in the dirt, calling up my glamour. I felt the pulse of living things deep in the earth and sent a request into the ground, asking for aid in defeating the iron monster on the surface.

The spider-hag was so busy trying to slice Ash to ribbons, she was taken completely by surprise when the ground erupted at her feet. Grass and weeds, vines and roots wrapped around her spindly legs and crawled up her torso. She shrieked and flailed with her deadly wires, slicing vegetation like an angry weed-whacker, but I poured more glamour into the ground, and the plants responded like they were growing in fast-forward. Panicked, the spider-hag tried to flee, ripping through vegetation as it twined around her legs, dragging her down.

A dark form blurred the air above her as Ash dropped from the sky, his blade pointed straight down. It struck the faery's bulbous torso, pinning her to the earth for a split second, before she shivered into an enormous needle pile and scattered over the ground.

I sighed with relief and stood, but suddenly the ground tilted. The trees began to spin, all feeling left my legs and arms, and the next thing I knew the ground rushed up at me.

I woke lying on my back, feeling breathless and faint as if I'd just run a marathon. Ash was peering down at me, silver eyes bright with concern.

"Meghan, are you all right? What happened?"

The dizziness was fading. I took several deep breaths to make sure my gut stayed where it was supposed to, and sat up to face him.

"I...don't know. I used my glamour, and just...passed out." Dammit, the ground was still spinning. I leaned into Ash, who held me cautiously, as if afraid I would break. "Is that normal?" I muttered against his chest.

"Not that I know of." He sounded troubled, worried but trying not to show it. "Perhaps it's a side effect from having your magic sealed for so long."

Well, that was another thing I'd have to thank Mab for. Ash stood, carefully drawing me up with him. My arms stung, and my fingers were sticky from where I'd sliced myself on the wire net. Ash tore strips from his shirt and wrapped them around my hands, silent and efficient, though his touch was gentle.

"They were waiting for me," I murmured, gazing at the thousands of needles scattered through the yard, glittering in the moonlight. More problems the fey had brought to my family. Mom and Luke would probably have a fit, and I desperately hoped Ethan wouldn't accidentally step on one before they had a chance to disappear. "They know where I live," I continued, watching the slivers wink at me in the grass. "The false king knew I'd be coming home, and he sent them..." My gaze rose to my house, and my family moving about through the windows, unaware of the chaos outside.

I felt cold. And sick. "I can't go home," I whispered, feeling Ash's gaze on me. "Not now. I can't bring this madness home to my family." I stared at the house for a moment more, then shut my eyes. "The false king won't stop here. He'll keep sending things after me, and my family will get caught in the middle. I can't let that happen. I...I have to leave. Now."

"Where will you go?" Ash's steady voice broke through my despair. "We can't go back to Faery, and the Iron fey are everywhere in the mortal world."

"I don't know." I covered my face with my hands. All I knew was that I couldn't be with my family, I couldn't go home, and I couldn't have a normal life. Not until the false king gave up looking for me, or miraculously keeled over and died.

Or *I* keeled over and died. "It doesn't matter now, does it?" I groaned through my fingers. "No matter where I go, they're going to follow me."

Strong fingers wrapped around my wrists and gently tugged my hands down. I shivered and looked up into glittering silver eyes. "I will keep fighting for you," Ash said in a low, intense voice. "Do what you must. I'll be here, whatever you decide. If it takes one year or a thousand, I will keep you safe."

My heart pounded. Ash released my wrists and slid his hands up my arms, pulling me close. I sank into his embrace and buried my face in his chest, using him as a shield against disappointment and grief, against the knowledge that my wandering wasn't over yet. The choice loomed clear before me. If I ever wanted this endless running and fighting to stop, I would have to deal with the Iron King. Again.

I opened my eyes and stared at the place where the Iron fey had fallen, at the slivers of metal glinting in the weeds. The thought of such monsters stealing into my room, turning their murderous eyes on Ethan or my mom, made me cold with rage. *All right,* I thought, clenching my fists in Ash's shirt, *the false king wants a war? I'll give him one.*

I wasn't ready. Not yet. I had to get stronger. I had to learn to control my magic, both Summer and Iron glamour, if it was actually possible to learn both. And for that, I needed time. I needed a place where the Iron fey couldn't follow. And there was only one place I knew that was safe, where the false king's servants would never find me.

Ash must've sensed the change. "Where are we going?" he murmured into my hair.

I took a deep breath and pulled back to face him. "Leanansidhe's."

Surprise and a flicker of alarm crossed his face. "The Exile Queen? Are you sure she'll help us?"

No, I wasn't. The Exile Queen, as she was called among other things, was capricious and unpredictable and, frankly, quite terrifying. But she had helped me before, and her home in the Between—the veil separating the mortal world from Faery—was the only potentially safe haven we had.

Besides, I had a score to settle with Leanansidhe, and more than a few questions I needed answered.

Ash was still watching me, his silver gaze concerned. "I don't know," I told him truthfully. "But she's the only one I can think of who can help, and she hates the Iron fey with a fiery passion. Besides, she *is* Queen of the Exiles. That means we qualify, right?"

"You tell me." Ash crossed his arms and leaned against a tree. "I haven't had the pleasure of meeting her. Though I have heard the stories. Terrifying as they are." A tiny furrow creased his brow, and he sighed. "This is going to be very dangerous, isn't it?"

"Probably."

A rueful smile quirked his lips. "Where to first?"

A cold resolve tightened my stomach. I looked back at my home, at my family, so very close, and swallowed the lump in my throat. *Not yet,* I promised them, *but soon. Soon, I'll be able to see you again.* "New Orleans," I replied, turning to

Ash, who waited patiently, his eyes never leaving my face. "The Historic Voodoo Museum. There's something there I have to take back."

CHAPTER TWO

OF TOKENS AND CHURCH GRIMS

Any tour guide worth his badge in New Orleans will tell you not to go gallivanting around the city streets alone in the middle of the night. In the heart of the French Quarter, where street lamps and tourism had a firm hold, it was fairly safe, but just outside the district, the dark alleyways hid thugs and gangs and predators of the night.

I wasn't worried about the human predators. They couldn't see us, except for one white-haired homeless man who cringed against a wall and chanted "Not here, not here," as we went by. But the darkness hid other things as well, like the goat-headed phouka who watched us from an alley across the street, grinning madly, and the redcap gang who trailed us through several neighborhoods until they got bored and went looking for easier prey. New Orleans was a faery city; mystery, imagination and old traditions blended perfectly here and drew scores of exiled fey to this spot.

Ash walked next to me, a silent, watchful shadow, one hand resting casually on his sword hilt. Everything, from his eyes, to the chill in the air as he passed, to the calm lethality on his face, was a warning: this wasn't someone you wanted to mess around with. Even though he had been exiled and was no longer a prince of the Unseelie Court, he was an imposing warrior, still the son of Queen Mab, and few dared challenge him.

At least, that's what I kept telling myself as we ventured deeper into the back alleys of the French Quarter, moving steadily toward our goal. But at the mouth of a narrow alley, the redcap gang I thought had given up appeared, blocking the exit. They were short and stout, evil dwarves with bloody red hats, their eyes and jagged fangs shining in the darkness.

Ash stopped and in one smooth motion eased me behind him and drew his sword, bathing the alley in flickering blue light. I clenched my fists, drawing glamour from the air, tasting fear and apprehension and a hint of violence. As I drew the glamour to me, I felt the nausea and dizziness and fought to remain steady on my feet.

For a moment, no one moved.

Then Ash gave a dark, humorless chuckle and stepped forward. "We can stand around looking at each other all night," he said, locking gazes with the biggest redcap, who had a stained red bandana on his head and was missing an eye. "Or would you like me to start the massacre?"

One-Eye bared his fangs. "Keep your pants on, prince," he spat, his guttural voice like a dog's snarl. "We got no quarrel with you." He sniffed and brushed his crooked nose. "Just heard the rumor you was in town, see, and we'd like to have a few words with the lady before you go, that's all."

I was instantly suspicious. I had no love for redcaps; the ones I'd run into were trying to kidnap, torture, or eat me. They were the mercenaries and thugs of the Unseelie Court, and the exiled ones were even worse. I wanted nothing to do with them.

Ash kept his sword out, his eyes never leaving the redcaps, but his free hand reached back and gripped mine. "Fine. Say what you came to say and get out of here."

One-Eye sneered at him, then turned to me. "Just wanted to let you know, *princess*—" he emphasized the word with a toothy leer "—that there's a bunch of Iron faeries sniffing around the city looking for you. One of them is offering a reward for any information concerning your whereabouts. So I'd be really careful if I were you." One-Eye pulled off his bandana and gave me a ridiculous, mocking bow. "Just thought you'd want to know."

I tried to hide my shock. Not that the Iron fey were looking for me, that was a given, but that a redcap would take it upon himself to warn me about it. "Why are you telling me this?"

"And how can I be certain *you* won't run to them with our location?" Ash chimed in, his voice flat and cold.

The redcap leader gave Ash a half disgusted, half fearful look. "You think I want these Iron bastards on my turf? You really think I'd want to *bargain* with them? I want every one of them dead, or at least out of my territory. I sure as hell ain't going to give them exactly what they want. If there's any way I can throw a wrench in their plans, I'll take it, even if that means warning *you* to spite *them*. And if you manage to kill them all for me, hey—that'll make my evening."

He stared at me with a hopeful expression. I squirmed uncomfortably. "I'm not going to promise anything," I warned, "so you can stop threatening me."

"Who said I was threatening you?" One-Eye held up his hands with a quick glance at Ash. "I'm just giving you a friendly warning. I thought, hey, she's killed the Iron bastards before. She might want to do it again."

"Who told you that?"

"Oh, please. It's all over the streets. We know about you— you and your Unseelie boyfriend here." He curled a lip at Ash, who stared back stoically. "We heard about the scepter, and how you killed the Iron bitch who stole it. We know you returned it to Mab to stop the war between Summer and

Winter, and that they exiled you for your trouble." One-Eye shook his head and gave me a look that was almost sympathetic. "Word travels fast on the streets, princess, especially when the Iron fey are running around like chickens with their heads ripped off, offering rewards for 'the daughter of the Summer King.' So, I'd watch my back, if I were you."

He snorted, then turned and spat on one of his flunky's shoes. The other redcap snarled and cursed, but One-Eye didn't seem to notice. "Anyway, there it is. Last time I checked, the bastards were nosing around Bourbon Street. If you do manage to kill them, princess, tell them One-Eyed Jack says hello. Let's go, boys."

"Aw, boss." The redcap who was spit on smiled at me and licked his fangs. "Can't we chew on the princess, just a little?"

One-Eyed Jack slapped the offending faery upside the head without looking at him. "Idiot," he snapped. "I have no desire to pick your frozen guts off the pavement. Now move, you stupid lot. Before I lose my temper."

The redcap leader grinned at me, gave Ash one last sneer, and backed away. Snapping and arguing with each other, the redcap gang ambled into the darkness and vanished from sight.

I looked at Ash. "You know, there was a time I wished I could be so popular."

He sheathed his sword. "Should we stop for the night?"

"No." I rubbed my arms, dropping the glamour and the queasiness that came with it, and peered into the street. "I can't run and hide just because the Iron fey are looking for me. I'd never get anywhere. Let's keep moving."

Ash nodded. "We're almost there."

We reached our destination without further incident. The New Orleans Historic Voodoo Museum looked exactly how I remembered it, faded black doors sunk into the wall. The wooden sign creaked on its chains overhead.

"Ash," I murmured as we walked quietly to the doors. "I've been thinking." The encounter with the spider-hags and the redcaps had strengthened my convictions, and I was ready to voice my plans. "I want you to do something for me, if you would."

"Whatever you need." We reached the doors, and Ash peered in the window. The interior of the museum was dark. He scanned the area around us before turning to place a hand on one of the doors. "I'm still listening, Meghan," he murmured. "What do you want me to do?"

I took a breath. "Teach me how to fight."

He turned back, his eyebrows raised. I took advantage of the moment of silence and plunged on before he could protest. "I mean it, Ash. I'm tired of standing on the sidelines doing nothing, watching you fight for me. I want to learn to defend myself. Will you teach me?" He frowned and opened his mouth, but before he could say anything, I added, "And don't give me any crap about defending my honor, or how a girl can't use a weapon, or how it's too dangerous for me to fight. How am I going to beat the false king if I can't even swing a sword?"

"I was *going* to say," Ash continued in what was almost a solemn voice, if it wasn't for the faint smirk on his lips, "that I thought it was a good idea. In fact, I was going to suggest picking up a weapon for you after we're done here."

"Oh," I said in a small voice. Ash sighed.

"We have a lot of enemies," he continued. "And as much as I hate it, there might be times when I won't be there to help you. Learning to fight and use glamour will be crucial now. I was trying to think of a way to suggest teaching you without having it blow up in my face." He smiled then, a tiny twitch of his lips, and shook his head. "I suppose I was doomed either way."

"Oh," I said again, in an even smaller voice. "Well…good. As long as we understand each other." I was glad the darkness

hid my burning face, though knowing Ash, he could probably see it anyway.

Still smiling, Ash turned back to the door, placing a hand
on the faded wood and speaking a quiet word under his
breath. The door clicked and slowly swung open.

The interior of the museum was musty and warm. As we
eased through the door, I tripped over the same bump in
the carpet that had been there a year ago and stumbled into
Ash. He steadied me with a sigh, just like a year ago. Only
this time, he reached down and touched my hand, moving
close to whisper in my ear.

"First lesson," he said, and even in the darkness I heard
the amusement in his voice. "Always be aware of where you
put your feet."

"Thanks," I said dryly. "I'll remember that."

He turned away and tossed a ball of faery fire into existence. The glowing, blue-white sphere hovered overhead,
illuminating the room and the macabre collection of voodoo
items surrounding us. The skeleton in the top hat and the
mannequin with the alligator head still grinned at us along
the wall. But now, an ancient, mummylike figure had been
added to the duo, a shriveled old woman with hollow pits
for eyes and arms like brittle sticks.

Then the withered face turned and smiled at me, and I bit
down a yelp.

"Hello, Meghan Chase," the oracle whispered, gliding
away from the wall and her two ghastly bodyguards. "I knew
you would return."

Ash didn't go for his sword, but I sensed muscles coiling
beneath his skin. I took a deep breath to calm my pounding heart and stepped forward. "Then you know why I'm
here."

The oracle's eyeless gaze peered at my face. "You seek to
take back what you gave away a year ago. That which did not
seem so important then has become very dear to you now.

Such is always the case. You mortals do not know what you have until it is gone."

"The memory of my father." I moved away from Ash, closing the distance between me and the oracle. Her hollow gaze followed me, and the smell of dusty newspapers clogged my nose and mouth as I approached. "I want it back. I need it if...if I'm going to see him again at Leanansidhe's. I have to know what he means to me. Please."

The knowledge of that mistake was still painful. When I was first searching for my brother, we'd come to the oracle for help. She'd agreed to help us, but asked for a memory in return; it had sounded insignificant at the time. I had agreed to her price, and afterward had had no clue which memory she took.

Then, we'd met Leanansidhe, who kept several humans in her home in the Between. All her humans were artists of some sort, brilliant, talented, and slightly mad from living in the Between so long. One of them, a gifted pianist, had taken quite an interest in me, though I hadn't known who he was. I found out only after we had left the manor and it was too late to go back.

My father. My human father, or at least the man who'd raised me until I was six, and he disappeared. That was the memory the oracle had taken: all recollections of my human dad. And now, I needed them back. If I was going to Leanansidhe's, I wanted the memory of my father intact when I demanded to know why she had him in the first place.

"Your father is Oberon, the Summer King," the oracle whispered, her thin mouth pulled into a smile. "This man you seek, this human, is no blood relation to you. He is a mere mortal. A stranger. Why do you care?"

"I don't know," I said miserably. "I don't know if I *should* care, and I want to be sure. Who was he? Why did he leave us? Why is he with Leanansidhe now?" I broke off and stared at the oracle, feeling Ash come up behind me as silent support. "I have to know," I whispered. "I need that memory back."

The oracle tapped glittering nails together, considering. "The bargain was fair," she rasped. "One exchange for another, we both agreed to this. I cannot simply give you what you seek." She sniffed, looking momentarily indignant. "I will have something in return."

I figured. Can't expect a faery to do you a favor without naming a price. Squashing down my annoyance, I stole a glance at Ash, and saw him nod. He'd expected it, too. I sighed and turned back to the oracle. "What do you want?"

She tapped a nail against her chin, dislodging a few flakes of dead skin or dust. I wrinkled my nose and eased back a step. "Hmm, let us see. What would the girl be willing to part with. Perhaps…your future chi—"

"No," Ash and I said in unison. She snorted.

"Can't blame me for trying. Very well." She leaned forward, studying me with the empty holes in her face. I felt a presence brush lightly against my mind and recoiled, shutting her out.

The oracle hissed, filling the air with the smell of decay. "How…interesting," she mused. I waited, but she didn't elaborate, and after a moment she drew back with a strange smile on her withered face. "Very well, Meghan Chase, this is my request. You are loathe to give up anything you hold dear, and it would be a waste of breath to ask for those things. So, instead I will ask that you fetch me something someone else held dear."

I blinked at her. "What?"

"I wish for you to bring me a Token. Surely that is not too much to ask."

"Um…" I cast a helpless glance at Ash. "What's a token?"

The oracle sighed. "Still so naive." She gave Ash an almost motherly frown. "I trust you will teach her better than this in the future, young prince. Now, listen to me, Meghan Chase, and I will share a bit of faery lore. Most items," she continued, plucking a skull from a table with her bony talons, "are just that. Mundane, ordinary, commonplace. Nothing special. However..." She replaced the skull with a *thunk* and carefully picked up a small leather bag, tied with a leather thong. I heard the rattle of pebbles or bones within as she held it up. "Certain items have been so loved and cherished by mortals that they become something else entirely—a symbol of that emotion, whether it be love, hate, pride, or fear. A favored doll, or an artist's masterpiece. And sometimes, though rarely, the item becomes so important that it grows a life of its own. It's as if a bit of the human's soul was left behind, clinging to the once-ordinary article. We fey call these items Tokens, and they are highly sought after, for they radiate a special glamour that never fades away." The oracle stepped back, seeming to fade into the paraphernalia lining the walls. "Find me a Token, Meghan Chase," she whispered, "and I will give you back your memory."

And then she was gone.

I rubbed my arms and turned to Ash, who bore a thoughtful expression. He stared after the vanished oracle. "Great," I muttered. "So, we need to find a Token thing. I suppose they're not just lying around for the taking, huh? Any ideas?"

He roused himself and glanced down at me. "I might know where we can find one," he mused, suddenly solemn again. "But it's not a place humans like to visit, especially at night."

I laughed. "What, you don't think I can handle it?" He raised an eyebrow, and I frowned. "Ash, I've been through Arcadia, Tir Na Nog, the Briars, the Between, the Iron Realm, Machina's tower, and the killing fields of the Nevernever. I don't think there's a place capable of freaking me out anymore."

A trace of humor touched his eyes, a silent challenge. "All right, then," he said, leading me out. "Follow me."

THE CITY OF THE DEAD stretched away before me, stark and black under the swollen yellow moon, steaming in the humid air. Rows upon rows of crypts, tombs, and mausoleums lined the narrow streets, some lovingly decorated with flowers, candles, and plaques, others crumbling with age and neglect. Some of them looked like miniature houses, or even tiny cathedrals, spires and stone crosses raking the sky. Statues of angels and weeping women peered down from rooftops, looking stern or in the throes of grief. Their hollow eyes seemed to follow me down the tomb-lined alleyways.

I really have to learn to keep my mouth shut, I thought, trailing Ash through the narrow streets, my skin crawling with every noise and suspicious-looking shadow. A warm breeze whispered between crypts, kicking up dust and causing dead leaves to skitter along the ground. My overactive imagination kicked into high gear, seeing zombies shuffling between the rows, the tomb doors creaking open as skeletal hands reached out for us. I shuddered and pressed closer to Ash who, damn him, seemed quite unfazed about walking through a New Orleans cemetery in the dead of night. I sensed his secret amusement at my expense, and so help me, if he said anything along the lines of *I told you so* I was going to smack him.

There are no ghosts here, I told myself, my gaze flickering between the rows of crypts. *No ghosts, no zombies, no men with hook-hands waiting to ambush stupid teenagers who come to the cemetery at night. Stop being paranoi—*

I caught a shimmer of movement between the crypts, a flutter of something white and ghostly, a woman in a blood-stained hood and cowl, floating over the ground. My heart nearly stopped, and with a squeak, I grabbed Ash's sleeve, tugging him to a halt. He turned, and I threw myself into his arms, burying my face in his chest. Pride be damned; I'd kill him later for bringing me here.

"Meghan?" His grip tightened in concern. "What's wrong?"

"A ghost," I whispered, frantically pointing in the direction of the specter. "I saw a ghost. Over there."

He turned to look in that direction, and I felt him relax. "Bean sidhe," he murmured, sounding like he was trying to stifle his amusement. "It's not unusual to see them here. They often hang around graveyards after the dead have been buried."

I peeked up, watching the bean sidhe float away into the darkness. Not a ghost, then. With an indignant huff I pulled back, but not enough to let go. "Aren't bean sidhes supposed to be off wailing somewhere?" I muttered, scowling at the ghostly look-alike. "Why is she hanging around here?"

"Plenty of glamour to be found in old cemeteries. You can feel it, can't you?"

Now that he mentioned it, I could. Grief, fear, and despair hung like a thin gray mist over everything, clinging to the stones and crawling along the ground. I took a breath, and the glamour flooded my nose and mouth. I tasted salt and tears and raw, festering grief, mixed with a black fear of death and the dread of the unknown.

"Awful," I managed, gagging.

Ash nodded. "I don't much care for it, but several of our kind prefer grief and fear over anything else. So graveyards tend to attract them, especially at night."

"Like the bean sidhe?"

"Bean sidhe are portents of death and sometimes hang around the site of their last mark." Ash still hadn't released his grip. He seemed content to hold me, and I was content to stay there. "But there are others, like bogies and galley beggars, whose sole purpose in life is to frighten mortals. We could see a few of them here, but they won't bother you if you're not afraid."

"Too late," I muttered, and felt his silent chuckle. Turning, I glowered at him and he stared back innocently. "Just so you know," I growled, poking his chest, "I *am* going to kill you later for bringing me here."

"I look forward to it."

"You wait. You'll be sorry when something grabs me and I scream loud enough to wake the dead."

Ash smiled and let me go. "They'll have to get past me first," he promised, a steely glint in his eye. "Besides, most things that would grab you are just nursery bogies—irritating but harmless. They only want to scare you." He sobered, and his eyes narrowed, peering around the cemetery. "The real threat will be the Grim, assuming this cemetery has one."

"What's a Grim?" I immediately thought of Grimalkin, the smart-mouthed talking cat who always seemed to pop up when least expected, demanding favors in return for his help. I wondered where the cat was now, if he had returned to the wyldwood after our last adventure. Of course, being in a cemetery, a Grim might also be a grinning skeleton in a black cowl, gliding down the aisles with a scythe in hand. I shivered and cursed my overactive imagination. So help me, it didn't matter if Ash was here or not, if I saw *that* coming, people on the other side of the city would hear me scream.

An eerie howl cut through the night, making me jump. Ash froze, lean muscles tightening beneath the fabric of his shirt. A lethal calmness entered his face: his killer's mask. The cemetery went deathly still, as if even the ghosts and nursery bogies were afraid to move.

"Let me guess. *That* was a Grim."

Ash's voice was soft as he turned away. "Let's go."

We continued down several more aisles, stone mausoleums flanking us. I peered anxiously between the tombs, wary of bogies and galley beggars and anything else that might jump out at me. I searched for the mysterious Grim, my creeped-out brain imagining werewolves and zombie dogs and scythe-toting skeletons following us down the streets.

Finally, we came to a small stone mausoleum with an ancient cross perched on the roof and a simple wooden door, nothing fancy or extravagant. The tiny plaque on the wall was so faded it was impossible to read. I would've walked right past it, if Ash hadn't stopped.

"Whose tomb is this?" I asked, hanging back from the door as if it would creak open to reveal its grisly contents. Ash walked up the crumbling granite steps and put a hand against the wood.

"An older couple, no one important," he replied, running his fingers down the faded surface as if he could sense what was on the other side. Narrowing his eyes, he glanced back at me. "Meghan, get up here, now."

I cringed. "We're going *inside?*"

"Once I open the door, the Grim will know we're here. Its duty is to guard the cemetery, and the remains of those in it, so it's *not* going to be happy about us disturbing the dead. You don't want to be out here alone when it comes, trust me."

Heart pounding, I scurried up the steps and pressed close to his back, peering out over the graveyard. "What is this thing, anyway?" I asked. "Can't you just slice your way past it, or turn us invisible for that matter?"

"It's not that easy," Ash explained patiently. "Church Grims are immune to magic and glamour—they see right through it. And even if you kill one, it doesn't die. To destroy a Grim, you have to dig up and burn its real body, and we don't have the time." He turned back to the door, murmured a quiet word, and pushed it open.

A blast of hot air wafted out of the open crypt, along with the musty scent of dust and mold and decay. I gagged and pressed my face into Ash's shoulder as we eased inside, shutting the door behind us. The tiny room was like an oven; I was almost instantly covered in sweat, and I pressed my sleeve to my mouth. Gasping into the fabric, I tried not to be sick at the scene in the middle of the floor.

On a raised stone table lay two skeletons, side by side. The room was so small that there was barely enough room to skirt the edges of the table, so the bodies were quite close. Too close, in my opinion. The bones were yellowed with age, and nothing clung to them—no skin, hair, or flesh—so they must've been here awhile.

I noticed that the skeletons were holding hands, long bony fingers wrapped around each other in a gruesome parody of affection. On one knobby, naked digit, a tarnished ring glinted in the shadows.

Curiosity battled revulsion, and I looked at Ash, who was staring at the couple with a grave expression on his face. "Who are they?" I whispered through my sleeve. Ash hesitated, then took a quiet breath.

"There is a story," he began in a solemn tone, "about a talented saxophone player who went to Mardi Gras one night and caught the eye of a faery queen. And the queen bid him come to her, because he was young and handsome and charming, and his music could set one's soul on fire. But the sax player refused, because he already had a wife, and his love for her was greater than even the beauty of the faery queen. And so, angry that he spurned her, the queen took him anyway, and held him in the Nevernever for many long days, forcing him to entertain her. But no matter what the young man saw in Faery, and no matter how much the queen tried to make him her own, even when he forgot his own name, he could not forget his wife back in the mortal world."

Watching Ash's face, the shadows in his eyes as he spoke, I got the feeling this wasn't a story he'd heard somewhere. This was a tale he'd watched unfold before him. He knew of the Token and where to find it because he remembered the sax player from the queen's court; another mortal caught up in the cruelty of the fey.

"Time passed," Ash went on, "and the queen finally released him, because it amused her to do so. And when the young human, his head filled with memories both real and imagined, returned to his beloved wife, he found her aged sixty years, while he had not changed a day since he vanished from the mortal world. She still wore his ring, and had not taken another husband or suitor, for she always believed he would return."

Ash paused, and I used my free hand to wipe my eyes. The skeletons didn't seem so creepy now, lying motionless on the table. At least I could look at them without my stomach churning. "What happened after that?" I whispered, glancing at Ash hopefully, pleading for this faery tale to have a happy ending. Or at least a nonhorrible one. I should've known better by now. Ash shook his head and sighed.

"Neighbors found them days later lying in bed, a young man and a shrunken old woman, their fingers intertwined in an unbreakable grip and their faces turned toward one another. The blood from their wrists had already dried on the sheets."

I swallowed the lump in my throat and looked at the skeletons again, fingers interlocked in death as they had been in life. And I wished that, for *once,* faery tales—*real* faery tales, not Disney fairy tales—would have a happy ending.

I wonder what my ending will be? The thought came out of nowhere, making me frown. I looked at Ash over the table; his silver gaze met mine, and I felt my heart swell in my chest. I was in a faery tale, wasn't I? I was playing my part in the story, the human girl who had fallen in love with a faery prince. Stories like that rarely ended well. Even if I did finish this thing with the false king, even if I did go back to my family and live out a normal life, where would Ash fit

in? I was human; he was an immortal, soulless faery. What
kind of future did we have together? I would eventually grow
old and die; Ash would live on forever, or at least until the
mortal world became too much for him and he simply ceased
to exist.

I closed my eyes, my heart aching with the bitter truth. He
didn't belong here, in the mortal world. He belonged back in
Faery, with the other creatures of myth and nightmares and
imagination. Ash was a beautiful, impossible dream: a faery
tale. And I, despite my father's blood, was still human.

"Meghan?" His voice was soft, questioning. "What is
it?"

Suddenly angry, I cut off my bleak thoughts. No. I would
not accept that. This was my story, *our* story. I would find
a way for us both to live, to be happy. I owed Ash that
much.

Something landed on the roof overhead with a hollow
thud, and a shower of dust filtered over me. Coughing, I
waved my hand in front of my face, squinting in the sudden
rain of filth.

"What was that?"

Ash glanced at the roof, eyes narrowing. "Our signal to
leave. Here." He tossed something at me over the table. It
glimmered briefly as I caught it—the tarnished gold ring
from the skeleton's finger. "There's your Token," Ash muttered, and I saw his hand dart into his coat pocket, almost
too quick to be seen, before he stepped away from the table.
"Let's get out of here."

He pulled the door open, motioning me out. As I ducked
through the frame, something dripped onto my shoulder from
above, something warm and wet and slimy. I put my hand
to my neck, and it came away covered in frothy drool.

Heart in my throat, I looked back and up.

A monstrous shape crouched atop the mausoleum, silhouetted against the moonlit sky, something lean and muscular

and decidedly unnatural. Trembling, I gazed up into the burning crimson eyes of an enormous black dog, big as a cow, lips pulled back to reveal fangs as long as dinner knives.

"Ash," I squeaked, backing away. The monster dog's eyes followed me, their burning glare fastened on the hand where I clutched the ring. "Is that—?"

Ash's sword rasped free. "The Grim." The Grim glanced at him and snarled, making the ground tremble, then swung its terrifying gaze back to me. Muscles rippled under its slick coat as it crouched lower, drool hanging in glistening ribbons from its teeth. Ash brandished his sword, speaking to me though he never took his eyes from the Grim. "Meghan, when I say 'go,' run *forward,* not away from it. Understand?"

That sounded very much like suicide, but I trusted Ash. "Yeah," I whispered, clenching the ring tighter, feeling the edges dig into my palm. "I'm ready."

The Grim howled, an earsplitting bay that split my head open, making me want to cover my ears and close my eyes. It leaped, and I would've been frozen to the spot if Ash hadn't snapped me out of it by yelling, *"Go!"* Spurred into action, I dove forward, beneath the dog hurtling over my head, and felt the crushing impact as the Grim hit the spot where I had been standing.

"Run!" Ash yelled at me. "We have to get off the cemetery grounds, now!"

Behind us, the Grim roared in fury and attacked.

CHAPTER THREE

MEMORY

A hail of glittering shards erupted from Ash's direction, pelting the Grim with frozen daggers and stinging bits of ice. They shattered or glanced off the Grim's muscular hide, not injuring the beast, but it was enough to buy us a few seconds' head start. We fled down the aisles, dashing between crypts, ducking around statues of angels and saints, the hot breath of the Grim at our heels. If we had been in the open, the monstrous dog would've run me down and used me as a chew toy in three seconds flat, but the narrow streets and tight corridors slowed it down a bit. We zigzagged our way through the cemetery, staying one step ahead of the Grim, until the white concrete wall that marked the cemetery grounds loomed ahead of us.

Ash reached the barrier first and whirled to help me up, positioning himself as a step stool. Expecting to feel teeth on my back at any moment, I stepped onto his knee and launched myself for the top, clawing and kicking. Ash leaped straight up, like he was attached to wires, and landed on the edge, grabbing my arm.

A deafening howl made my ears ring, and I made the mistake of looking back. The Grim's open maw filled my vision, breath hot and foul in my face, spraying me with drool. Ash yanked me backward just as those jaws snapped inches from my face, and we fell off the wall together, hitting the ground with a jolt that knocked the breath from my lungs.

Gasping, I looked up. The Grim crouched at the top of the wall, glaring at me, fangs bared and shiny in the moonlight. For a moment, I was sure it would leap down and rip us both to pieces. But, with one last snarl, it turned and dropped out of sight, back to the cemetery it was bound to protect.

Ash let out a breath and let his head fall back to the grass. "I will say this," he panted, his eyes closed and his face turned toward the sky. "Being with you is never boring."

I opened my shaking fist and looked down at the ring still lying in my palm. It glowed with its own inner light, surrounded by an aura of glamour that shimmered with emotion: deep blue sorrow, emerald hope, and scarlet love. Now that I saw it clearly, I felt a stab of remorse and guilt; this was the symbol of a love that had endured for decades, and we had taken it from the grave with barely a second thought.

I swallowed the lump in my throat and stuck the ring in my jeans pocket. Wiping disgusting Grim drool off my face, I glanced down at Ash.

He opened his eyes, and I suddenly realized how close we were. I was practically lying on top of him, our limbs tangled together and our faces inches apart. My heart stuttered a bit, then picked up faster than before. Ever since our exile from Faery and my journey home, we had never *been together,* really been together. I'd been so preoccupied with what I would say to my family, so anxious to get home, that I hadn't given it much thought. And Ash never went any further than a brief touch or caress, seeming content to let me set the pace. Only I didn't know what he wanted, what he expected. What did we *have,* exactly?

"You're worried again." Ash narrowed his eyes, and the

nearness of him made me catch my breath. "It seems you're always worried, and I can't do anything to help."

I scowled at him. "You could stop reading my emotions every time I turn around," I said, feigning irritation, when in reality my heart was beating so hard I knew he had to feel it. "If it bothers you so much, you could find something else to focus on."

"Can't help it." He sounded annoyingly cavalier, completely self-assured and comfortable, lying there on his back. "The more we're connected to our chosen someone, the more we can pick up on what they're feeling. It's instinctive, like breathing."

"You can't hold your breath?"

One corner of his mouth twitched. "I suppose I could block it out, if I tried."

"Uh-huh. But you're not going to, are you?"

"No." Serious again, he reached up and ran his fingers through my hair, and for a moment I forgot to breathe. "I want to know when you're worried, when you're angry or happy or sad. You can probably do the same to me, though I'm slightly better at shielding my emotions. More practice." A shadow crossed his face, a flicker of pain, before it was gone. "Unfortunately, the longer we're together, the harder hiding it will become, for both of us." He shook his head and gave me a wry smile. "One of the hazards of having a faery in love with you."

I kissed him. His arms slid around me and drew me close, and we stayed like that for a while, my hands tangled in his hair, his cool lips on mine. My earlier thoughts in the crypt came back to haunt me, and I shoved them into the darkest corner of my mind. I would not give him up. I would find a way to have a happy ending, for both of us.

For a few seconds, my world shrank down to this tiny spot, with Ash's heartbeat under my fingers, me breathing in his breath. But then he grunted softly and pulled back, his expression caught between amusement and caution. "We have an audience," he murmured, and I jerked upright, looking around warily. The night was still and quiet, but a large gray cat sat on the wall with his tail curled around himself, watching us with amused golden eyes.

I leaped up, my face burning. "Grimalkin!" I glared at the cat, who regarded me blandly. "Dammit, Grim! Do you plan these things? How long were you watching us?"

"So nice to see you as well, human." Grimalkin blinked at me, sarcastic, unruffled, and completely infuriating. He glanced at Ash, who'd gotten to his feet with barely a sound, and twitched an ear. "And it is good to know the rumors are entirely true."

Ash wore a blank expression, nonchalantly raking leaves from his hair, but I felt my face heat even more. "Why are you here, Grim?" I demanded. "I don't have any more debts you can collect on. Or did you just get bored?"

The cat yawned and licked a front paw. "Do not flatter yourself, human. Though it is always amusing to watch you flounder about, I am not here for my own entertainment." Grim scrubbed the paw over his face, then carefully cleaned the claws, one by one, before turning to me again. "When Leanansidhe heard why you were banished from the Nevernever, she could not believe it. I told her humans are unreasonable and irrational when it comes to their emotions, but to have the Winter prince exiled as well…she was sure it was a false rumor. Mab's son would never defy his queen and court, to be banished to the mortal world with the half-blood daughter of Oberon." Grimalkin snorted, sounding pleased with himself. "In fact, we made a rather interesting bet on it. She will be terribly annoyed when she hears she has lost."

I glanced at Ash, who was keeping his expression carefully neutral. Grimalkin sneezed, the feline equivalent of a laugh, and continued. "So, naturally, when you disappeared from the Nevernever, Leanansidhe asked me to find you. She wishes to speak to you, human. Now."

My stomach contracted into a tiny knot, as Grimalkin stood and leaped gracefully from the wall, landing in the grass without a sound. "Follow me," he ordered, his eyes becoming floating golden orbs in the dark. "I will show you the trod to the Between from here. And human, there are rumors of Iron fey hunting you as well, so I suggest we hurry."

I swallowed. "No," I told him, and the orbs blinked in surprise. "I'm not done here. Leanansidhe wants to talk to me? Good, I have some things to talk to her about, as well. But I am not going into her mansion, knowing my dad is *right there,* and still having no idea who he is. I'm getting my memory back. Until then, she can just wait."

Ash touched the back of my arm, a silent, approving gesture, and Grimalkin stared at me as if I'd grown three heads. "Defying Leanansidhe. I had no idea it was going to be so interesting." He purred, narrowing his eyes. "Very well, human. I will accompany you, if only to see the Exile Queen's face when you tell her the reason she had to wait."

That sounded faintly ominous, but I didn't care. Leanansidhe had a lot to answer for, and I *would* get those answers—but first I needed to know what I was asking about.

THE MUSEUM DOORS WERE still unlocked as I eased my way inside, followed by Ash and a continuously purring Grimalkin, who disappeared as soon as he slipped through the door. He didn't creep away or hide in the shadows; he simply vanished from sight. It didn't surprise me in the least—I was used to it by now.

A withered figure waited for us near the back, leaning against a glass counter, turning a skull over in her hands. She bared her needlelike teeth in a smile as I approached, raking her nails along the skull's naked cheekbones.

"You have it," she whispered, her hollow gaze fastened on

me. "I can smell it from here. Show it to me, human. What have you brought old Anna?"

I pulled the ring from my pocket and held it up, where it glimmered in the musty darkness like a firefly. The oracle's smile grew wider.

"Ah, yes. The doomed lovers, separated by age and time, and the hope that kept them alive. Futile though it was, in the end." She coughed a laugh, a wisp of dust billowing from her mouth into the air. "Went to the graveyard, did you? How brazen. No wonder I kept seeing a dog in your future. You did not, by chance, get the mate of this ring, did you?"

"Um...no."

"Ah, well." She held out a withered hand, like a bird opening its talons. "I guess I shall have to be content with the one. Now, Meghan Chase, give me the Token."

"You promised," I reminded her, taking one step forward. "The Token for my memory. I want it all back."

"Of course, child." The oracle seemed annoyed. "I will relinquish the memory of your father—the memory you freely gave up, may I add—in exchange for the Token. As our bargain dictates, so shall it be done." She flexed her claws impatiently. "Now, please. Hand it over."

I hesitated a moment more, then dropped the ring into her palm.

Her fingers closed with such speed that I took a step back. The oracle sighed, holding the ring to her sunken chest. "Such longing," she mused, as if in a daze. "Such emotion. I remember. Before I gave them all away. I remember how it felt to *feel*." She sniffed, coming out of her trance, and floated back, behind the counter, her voice suddenly brittle and sour. "I don't see how you mortals do it, these feelings you must endure. They will ruin you, in the end. Isn't that right, prince?"

I started, but Ash didn't seem surprised. "It's worth it," he said quietly.

"Yes, you tell yourself that now." The oracle slipped the ring over a talon and held up her hand, admiring it. "But see how you feel a few decades from now, when the girl has grown withered and weak, slipping farther from you with each passing day, and you are as ageless as time. Or, perhaps—" she turned to me now "—your beloved prince will find the mortal realm is too much for him to stay, to *be*, and he will fade into nothingness. One day, you will wake up and he will simply be gone, only a memory, and you will never find love again, because how can a mere mortal compete with the fair folk?" The oracle hissed, lips curled into a sneer. "Then you will wish you were empty inside. Like me."

Ash remained calm, expressionless, but I felt a stab of fear twist my stomach. "Is this...what you see?" I whispered, a band tightening around my heart. "Our future?"

"Flashes," the oracle said, waving her hand dismissively. "The far-future is a constantly changing wave, always in motion, never certain. The story changes with every breath. Every decision we make sends it down another path. But..." She narrowed her hollow eyes at me. "There is one constant in your future, child, and that is pain. Pain and emptiness, for your friends, the ones you hold dearest to your heart, are nowhere to be seen."

The band around my chest squeezed tight. The oracle smiled, a bitter, empty smile, and broke eye contact. "But perhaps you will change all that," she mused, gesturing to something I couldn't see behind the counter. "Perhaps you will find a happy ending to this tale, one that I have not seen. After all—" she held up a long finger, where the ring glimmered brightly against the gloom "—without hope, where would we be now?" She cackled and held out her hand.

A small glass globe floated up from behind the counter, hovering in the air before it came to rest in the oracle's palm.

Her nails curled over it, and she beckoned to me with her other hand.

"Here is what you seek," she rasped, dropping the globe into my hand. I blinked in surprise. The glass felt as light and delicate as a bubble resting in my palm, as if I could crush it just by flexing my fingers. "When you are ready, simply shatter the globe, and your memory will be released.

"Now," she continued, drawing back, "I believe that is everything you need, Meghan Chase. When I see you again, no matter what you choose, you will not be the same."

"What do you mean by that?"

The oracle smiled. A breath of wind stirred the room, and she dissolved into a swirling cyclone of dust, sweeping through the air and stinging my eyes and throat. Coughing, I turned away, and when I was able to look up again, she was gone.

Trembling, I looked down at the globe in my hand. In the flickering faery light, I could see faint outlines in the reflective surface, images sliding across the glass. Reflections of things not there.

"Well?" came Grimalkin's voice, as the cat appeared on another counter amid several jars containing dead snakes in amber liquid. "Are you going to smash it or not?"

"Are you sure it'll come back to me?" I asked, watching a man's face slide across the glass, followed by a girl on a bike. More images rippled like mirages, too brief and distorted to recognize. "The oracle just told me they'd be released—she didn't specifically say that they would come back. If I break this now, my memory won't dissolve into thin air, or get soaked up by some hidden faery memory-soaker, will it?"

Grimalkin sneezed, echoing Ash's quiet chuckle in the corner. "You've been around us too long," Ash murmured, and I thought I heard a trace of sadness in his voice. I didn't know if he meant I was being too suspicious, looking for loopholes in a faery bargain, or that he thought that was exactly what I should be doing.

Grimalkin snorted, giving me a disdainful look. "Not all fey seek to deceive you, human," he said in a bored voice. "As far as I could tell, the oracle's offer was genuine." He sniffed and thumped his tail against the counter. "Had she wanted to entrap you, she would have wrapped so many riddles around the offer that you would never have a chance of untangling the true meaning."

I looked at Ash, and he nodded. "Okay, then," I said, taking a deep breath. I raised the globe above my head. "Here goes nothing." And I flung it to the floor with all my might.

The fragile glass shattered against the carpet with an almost musical chime, shards spiraling up to become fragments of light that spun around the room. They merged and coalesced into a thousand images, fluttering through the air like frantic doves. As I watched, breathless, they swirled together and descended like a flock of birds in a horror movie. I was bombarded by an endless stream of images and emotions, all trying to rip into my head at once.

I put my hands to my face, trying to block them out, but it didn't help. The visions kept coming, flitting through my head like a strobe light. Of a man with lank brown hair, long gentle fingers, and eyes that were always smiling. The images were all of him. Him...pushing me on the park swing. Holding my first bike steady as I wobbled down the sidewalk. Sitting at our old piano, his long fingers flying over the keys, as I sat on the couch and watched him play.

Walking into a tiny green pond, the water closing over his head, as I screamed and screamed until the police arrived.

When it was over, I was kneeling on the floor with Ash's arms around me, holding me to his chest. I was panting, my hands clenched in his shirt, and his body was rigid against mine. My head felt too full, throbbing like it was about to explode, ready to burst open at the seams.

But I remembered. Everything. I remembered the man who'd looked after me for six years. Who'd raised me, thinking I was his only daughter, not knowing my real heritage. Oberon had called him a stranger, but to hell with that. As far as I was concerned, Paul *was* my father in everything but blood. Oberon might be my biological dad, but he was never around. He was a stranger who had no interest in my life, who called me *daughter* but didn't know me at all. The man who'd read me bedtime stories in a singsong voice, put unicorn bandages on my scraped elbows, and held me on his knee while he played the piano—*he* was my real dad. And I'd always think of him as such.

"You okay?" Ash's cool breath tickled my cheek.

I nodded and pulled myself upright. My head still hurt, and there would be many long hours trying to sort out the torrent of images and emotions, but I finally knew what I had to do.

"All right, Grim," I said, looking up with a new resolve. "I have what I came for. *Now* I'm ready to see Leanansidhe."

But there was no answer. Grimalkin had disappeared.

CHAPTER FOUR

GLITCH'S RESISTANCE

"Grimalkin?" I called again, looking around the room. "Where are you?" Nothing. This was a bad sign. Grimalkin often disappeared when there was trouble, with no explanation and no warning for the rest of us. Of course, sometimes he disappeared just because he felt like it, so there was no telling what was going on, really.

"Meghan," Ash said, looking out the window with narrowed eyes, "I think you'd better see this."

A figure stood in the road outside the museum. Not human, I could tell that much. Though he wore ripped jeans and a studded leather jacket, the sharp, angular face and pointed ears gave him away. That, and his wild black hair, spiked up like a punk rocker, had neon threads of lightning flickering between the strands, reminding me of those plasma globes found in novelty stores. From his stance, it was obvious he was waiting for us.

"An Iron faery," Ash muttered, dropping his hand to his sword. "Do you want me to kill it?"

"No," I said, laying a hand on his arm. "He knows we're here. If he was going to attack us he would've done it by now. Let's see what he wants first."

"I would advise against that." Ash glowered at me, a hint of exasperation in his eyes. "Remember that the false king is still after you. You can't trust the Iron fey, especially now. Why would you want to speak with this one? The Iron Kingdom and everything in it are your enemies."

"Ironhorse wasn't."

Ash sighed and took his hand off the sword hilt. "As you wish," he murmured, bowing his head. "I don't like it, but let's see what the Iron faery wants. Though if he makes any threatening move at all, I will cut him down faster than he can blink."

We slipped out the doors into the humid night, crossing the road to where the Iron faery waited for us.

"Oh, good." The Iron fey smiled as we walked up, a cocky, self-confident grin, much like a certain redhead I knew. "You didn't run. I was afraid I'd have to chase you through the city streets before we could talk."

I scowled at him. Up close, he looked younger, almost my age, though I knew that meant nothing. The fey were ageless. He could have been centuries old for all I knew. But despite that, and despite his obvious fey beauty, he looked like nothing more than a seventeen-year-old punk kid.

"Well," I said, crossing my arms, "here I am. Who are you, and what do you want?"

"Brief and to the point. I like that." The faery smirked. I didn't return his smile, and he rolled his eyes, which were a shimmering violet, I noticed. "Fine, allow me to introduce myself, then. My name is Glitch."

"Glitch." I furrowed my brow, looking at Ash. "That sounds familiar. Where have I heard that name before?"

"I'm sure you've heard it before, Meghan Chase," Glitch said, and the grin on his face stretched wider, showing teeth. "I was King Machina's first lieutenant."

Ash drew his sword in a flash of blue light, filling the air with cold. Glitch's eyebrows shot up, but he didn't move, even as the tip of the sword hovered inches from his chest. "You *could* hear me out instead of jumping to conclusions," he offered.

"Ash," I said softly, and Ash backed off a step, not sheathing his sword but not aiming it at Glitch's heart anymore, either. "What do you want with me?" I asked, holding his gaze. "Do you serve the false king, now? Or did you just come by for introductions?"

"I'm here," Glitch said, "because I want the false king stopped as much as you do. In case you haven't heard, princess, the war with Iron isn't going so well. Oberon and Mab have united to stop the false king, but their armies are slowly being crushed. The wyldwood grows smaller every day, as more and more territory is absorbed into the Iron Kingdom, expanding the false king's realm. He needs only one more thing to be completely unstoppable."

"Me," I whispered. It wasn't a question.

Glitch nodded. "He needs Machina's power, and then his claim to the throne will be irrefutable. If he can kill you and take that power for himself, it will be over."

"How does he know I have it? I'm not even sure, myself."

"You killed Machina." Glitch looked at me soberly, all cockiness gone. "The power of the Iron King passes to the one who defeats him. At least, that's how I understand it. That's why the false king's claim to the throne is a sham. That's why he wants you so badly." He grinned then, evil and mischievous. "Thankfully, we're making it a bit difficult for him, both in the war effort, and now with you."

"Who's 'we'?"

Glitch sobered. "Ironhorse was a friend of mine," he murmured, and I felt a sharp pang at the mention of the noble faery. "He was the first to denounce the false king, and after him, more followed his example. We're few in number, and we've been reduced to guerilla tactics against the false king's army, but we do what we can."

"You're the resistance the spider-hags were talking about."

"Spider-hags?" Glitch looked confused. "Ah, you must mean the king's assassins. Yep, that's us. Though like I said, we're too small to really strike a blow against the false king. But we can do one very important thing that will keep him off the throne forever."

"And what's that?"

Glitch gave me an apologetic smile, and snapped his fingers.

Movement all around us, as dozens of Iron fey melted out of the shadows. I felt the cold pulse of Iron glamour, gray and flat and colorless, as they surrounded us in a bristly ring. I saw dwarves with mechanical arms and elves with huge black eyes, numbers scrolling across their pupils like glowing green ants. I saw dogs with bodies made of ticking clockwork, green-skinned fey with computer wires for hair, and many more. All of them had weapons—blades of iron, metal bats and chains, steely fangs or talons—all deadly to regular fey. Ash pressed close to me, his face grim, muscles coiled tight as he raised his sword. I spun and glared at Glitch.

"So, this is your plan?" I snapped, gesturing to the ring around us. "You want to kidnap me? That's your answer to stopping the false king?"

"You have to understand, princess." Glitch shrugged as he backed away from me, into the circle of fey. "This is for your own safety. We cannot allow you to fall into the false king's hands, or he'll win and everything will be lost. We have to keep you hidden, and safe. Nothing else matters now. Please, come quietly. You know there's too many of us to fight. Even the Winter prince cannot defeat this many."

"Really?" called a new voice, somewhere behind and above us all. "Well, if that's the case, why don't we level the field a bit?"

I whirled around, gazing up toward the rooftops, my heart leaping in my chest. Silhouetted against the moon, with his arms crossed and his red hair tousled by the wind, a familiar face grinned down at us, shaking his head.

"You," Puck said, locking eyes with me, "are extremely difficult to track down, princess. Good thing Grimalkin came and found me. As usual, it looks like I have to rescue you and ice-boy from something. Again. This is starting to become a habit."

Ash rolled his eyes, though his attention didn't leave the fey surrounding us. "Stop yapping and get down here, Goodfellow."

"Goodfellow?" Glitch stared at Puck nervously. "*Robin* Goodfellow?"

"Oh, look at that, he's heard of me. My fame grows." Puck snorted and leaped off the roof. In midair, he became a giant black raven, who swooped toward us with a raucous cry before dropping into the circle as Puck in an explosion of feathers. "Ta-daaaaaaaaaa."

The rebels backed off a step, though Glitch held his ground. "There's still only three of you," he said firmly. "Not enough to fight us all. Princess, please, we only want to protect you. This doesn't have to end in violence."

"I don't need your protection," I said. "As you can see, I have more than enough."

"Besides," Puck said, grinning his evil grin, "who says I came alone?"

"You did," called another Puck from the rooftop he just left. Glitch's eyes bugged as the second Puck grinned down at him.

"No, he didn't," said a third Puck from the opposite roof.

"Well, I'm sure they know what he meant," said yet another Puck, sitting atop a street lamp. "In any case, here we are."

"This is a trick," Glitch muttered, as the rebels shot

nervous glances at the three Pucks, who waved back cheerfully. "Those aren't real bodies. You're screwing with our heads."

Puck snickered. "Well, if that's what you think, you're welcome to try something."

"It won't end well for you, either way," Ash broke in. "Even if you manage to beat us, we'll make sure to decimate your little band of rebels before we fall. Count on it."

"Get out of here, Glitch," I said quietly. "We're not going anywhere with you or your friends. I'm not going to hide from the false king and do nothing."

"That," Glitch said, narrowing his eyes, "is exactly what I'm afraid of." But he turned and signaled his forces to back off, and the Iron fey melted into the shadows again. "We'll be watching you, princess," he warned, before he, too, turned and disappeared into the night.

Heart racing, I turned to see Puck staring at me, lopsided smirk firmly in place. Tall and gangly, he looked the same as always, eager for trouble, forever ready with a sarcastic quip or witty comeback. But I saw the flicker of pain in his eyes, a glint of anger he couldn't quite conceal, and it made my gut clench. "Hey, princess."

"Hey," I whispered, as Ash slipped his arms around my waist from behind, drawing me close. I could feel his glare aimed at Puck over my head, a silent, protective gesture that spoke louder than any words. *Mine. Back off.* Puck ignored him, gazing solely at me. In the shadow of his gaze, I remembered our last meeting, and the ill-fated decision that brought us here.

"MEGHAN CHASE!"

Oberon's voice cracked like a whip, and a roar of thunder shook the ground. The Erlking's voice was ominously quiet, eyes glowing amber through the gently falling snow. "The laws of our people are absolute," Oberon warned. "Summer and Winter share many things, but love is not one of them. If you make this choice, daughter, the trods will never open for you again."

"Meghan." Puck stepped forward, pleading. "Don't do this. I can't follow you this time. Stay here. With me."

"I can't," I whispered. "I'm sorry, Puck. I do love you, but I have to do this." His face clouded with pain, and he turned away. Guilt stabbed at me, but in the end, the choice had always been clear.

"I'm sorry," I whispered again, and followed Ash through the portal, leaving Faery behind me forever.

THE MEMORY BURNED like bile in my stomach, and I closed my eyes, wishing it didn't have to be this way. I loved Puck like a brother and a best friend. And yet, during a very dark period when I was confused and lonely and hurt, my affection for him had led me to do something stupid, something I shouldn't have done. I knew he loved me, and the fact that I'd taken advantage of his feelings made me disgusted with myself. I wished I knew how to fix it, but the barely concealed pain in Puck's eyes told me no amount of words would make it better.

Finally, I found my voice. "What are you doing here?" I whispered, suddenly grateful for Ash's arms around me, a barrier between me and Puck. Puck shrugged and rolled his eyes.

"It's obvious, isn't it?" he replied, sounding a bit sharper than normal. "After you and ice-boy got yourselves exiled, I was worried that the Iron fey were still looking for you. So I came to find out. Good thing I did, too. So, who is this newest Iron fey you pissed off? Glitch, was it? Machina's first lieutenant—you sure know how to pick 'em, princess."

"Later." Grimalkin appeared from a shadow, bottlebrush tail waving in the wind. "Human, your attempted kidnapping has set off a riot among the New Orleans fey," he announced, his golden eyes boring into me. "We should get moving before anything else happens. The Iron fey are coming for you, and I have no wish to do this entire little rescue again. Talk when we get to Leanansidhe's. Let us go."

He trotted down the street with his tail held high, pausing once to peer at us from the edge of an alley, eyes glowing in the darkness, before slipping into the black.

I slid out of Ash's embrace and took a step toward Puck, hoping we could talk. I missed him. He was my best friend, and I wanted it to be like it was before, the three of us taking on the world. But as soon as I moved, Puck slid away, as if being near me was too uncomfortable to bear. In three long strides he reached the mouth of the alley, then turned to grin at us, red hair gleaming under the street lamps.

"Well, lovebirds? You coming or not? I can't wait to see the look on Lea's face when you both come strolling in." His eyes glinted, and his grin turned faintly savage. "You know, I heard she does horrid things to those who annoy her. Here's hoping she won't rip out your guts and use them for harp strings, prince." Snickering, he waggled his eyebrows at us and turned away, following Grimalkin into the shadows.

I sighed. "He hates me."

Ash grunted. "No, I think that particular sentiment is reserved for me alone," he said in an amused voice. When I didn't answer, he motioned us forward, and we crossed the street together, coming to the mouth of the alley. "Goodfellow doesn't hate you," he continued as the shadows loomed dark and menacing beyond the street lamps. "He's angry, but I think it's more at himself. After all, he had sixteen years to make his move. It's no one's fault but his own that I beat him to it."

"So it's a competition now, huh?"

"If you want to call it that." I had started to follow Puck and Grimalkin into the corridor, but he caught my waist and drew me close, sliding one hand up my back while the other framed my face. "I've already lost one girl to him," Ash murmured, tangling his fingers in my hair. Though his voice was light, an old pain flickered across his face and vanished. "I won't lose another." His forehead bumped softly against mine, his brilliant silver gaze searing into me. "I plan to keep you, from everyone, for as long as I'm alive. That includes Puck, the false king, and anyone else who would take you away." One corner of his mouth quirked, as I struggled to catch my breath under his powerful scrutiny. "I guess I should've warned you that I have a slight possessive streak."

"I didn't notice," I whispered, trying to keep my voice light and sarcastic, but it came out rather breathy. "It's all right—I'm not giving you up, either."

His eyes turned very soft, and he lowered his head, brushing his lips to mine. I laced my hands behind his neck and closed my eyes, breathing in his scent, forgetting everything, if only for a moment.

"Oi, lovebirds!" Puck's voice shattered the quiet, bouncing through the darkness. Ash pulled back with a rueful look. "Get a room, would ya? We've got better things to do than watch you suck face!"

"Indeed." Grimalkin's voice echoed Puck's irritation, and I winced. Now even the cat was agreeing with Puck? "Hurry up, or we shall leave you behind."

We followed Grimalkin through the city, down an unusually long, curving alleyway that turned pitch-black, and suddenly we were back in a familiar dungeonlike basement with torches set into the walls and leering gargoyles curled around stone pillars.

Grimalkin set a brisk pace down several hallways, where torchlight flickered erratically and unseen things growled and scurried about in the darkness. I remembered the first time we came here, the first time we'd met Leanansidhe. Back then, there were more of us. Me, Puck, Grim, Ironhorse, and three half-breeds named Kimi, Nelson, and Warren.

We were a much smaller group now. Ironhorse was gone,

as were Kimi and Nelson, all victims of Machina's cruel lieutenant Virus. Warren was a traitor, working for the false king. I wondered who else I would lose before this was over, if everyone around me was destined to die. I remembered the oracle's grim prophecy, about how I would end up all alone, and fought down my apprehension.

Ash's fingers curled around mine and squeezed. He didn't say anything, but I clung to his hand like a lifeline, as if he could vanish at any moment. We followed Grimalkin up a long flight of stairs to Leanansidhe's magnificent foyer, with the double grand staircases sweeping toward the roof, the walls covered with famous paintings and art. Instinctively, my eyes were drawn to the baby grand piano in the corner of the room. Where I'd first seen my father, sitting at that bench, hunched over the keys, and hadn't even known him.

The baby grand was empty, but the plush black sofa near the roaring fireplace was not. Reclining against the cushions, one slender hand gripping a sparkling wine flute, was Leanansidhe, Queen of the Exiles.

"Darlings!" Pale, tall, and beautiful, Leanansidhe smiled at us with lips as red as blood, bright copper hair rippling through the air as if it weighed nothing at all. She rose with liquid grace, her ebony gown swirling around her feet, and absently handed her wineglass to a waiting satyr, trading it for a cigarette flute. With the end trailing sapphire-blue smoke, she approached us with the grin of a hungry tiger.

"Meghan, my pet, how *good* of you to drop by. When you didn't return from the last mission, I thought the worst, darling. But I see you made it out, after all." Her cold blue gaze flicked to Ash, and she raised a slender eyebrow. "*And* with the Winter prince in tow. How—" she tapped her nails together, pursing her lips "—tenacious." Her gaze narrowed, and a ripple of power shivered through the air, making the lights flicker, as Leanansidhe turned on Ash. "The last I saw of you, your highness, you were threatening to slaughter the girl's family. Be forewarned, darling, I don't care if you are Mab's favorite son. If you threaten any in *this* house, I will rip your guts out through your nose and string my harps with them."

"I'd love to see that, personally," Puck muttered, smirking. I shot him a furious glare, and he stuck out his tongue at me.

Ash bowed. "I've severed all ties to the Winter Court," he said evenly, facing the Exile Queen's glare. "I'm no longer 'your highness,' just an exile, like Meghan. And yourself. I mean no harm to you, or anyone within your house."

Leanansidhe gave him a tight smile. "Just remember who the queen is around here, darling." With a nod to the rest of my companions, she motioned us to the couches. "Sit, darlings, sit," she said in a voice that held an only thinly veiled threat. "I am afraid we have a lot to discuss."

I took a calming breath as I sank into the velvet cushions, feeling very small as the couch tried to swallow me whole. Ash chose to stand, looming behind me, while Puck and Grim perched on the arms. Leanansidhe sank gracefully into the opposite chair, crossing her long legs and staring at me over her cigarette. I thought of my dad, and anger burned, hot and furious. I had so much to ask her, so many questions, I didn't know where to start. Ash put a warning hand on my shoulder, squeezing gently. No good would come of pissing off the Exile Queen, especially since she had the morbid habit of turning people into harps, cellos, or violins when they annoyed her. I had to proceed cautiously.

"So, darling." Leanansidhe took a drag off her cigarette and blew a smoke fish at me. "You've been banished from the Nevernever, in a most spectacular show of defiance, I've heard. What are you planning to do now?"

"Why do you care?" I asked her, trying to keep my emotions in check. "We returned the scepter and stopped the war between the courts. What do you care what we do now?"

Leanansidhe's eyes glittered, and her cigarette bobbed in annoyance. "Because, darling, there are disturbing rumors circulating the streets. Strange weather is plaguing the mortal world, Summer and Winter are losing ground to the Iron Realm, and there is a new faction of Iron fey that have popped up recently, looking for you. Also…" Leanansidhe leaned forward, narrowing her eyes "…there are stories about a half-breed princess who controls both Summer magic and Iron glamour. That she has the power to rule both courts, and she is raising an army of her own—an army of exiles and Iron fey—to overthrow everything."

"*What?*"

"Those are the rumors, darling." Leanansidhe sat back and puffed out a swarm of butterflies. They flittered around me, smelling of smoke and cloves, before writhing into nothingness. "So, you can see why I would be concerned, pet. I wanted to see the truth for myself."

"But…that's…" I sputtered for words, feeling Ash's gaze on the back of my head, and Puck's curious stare. Only Grimalkin, washing his tail on the armrest, seemed unconcerned. "Of course I'm not raising an army," I burst out at last. "That's ridiculous. I have no intention of overthrowing anything!"

Leanansidhe gave me an unreadable look. "And the other claims, darling? About the princess using both Summer and Iron glamour? Are those fabricated, as well?"

I chewed my lip. "No. They're real."

She nodded slowly. "Like it or not, dove, you've become a major player in this war. You're balanced on the edge of everything—faery and mortal, Summer and Iron, the old ways and the march of progress. Which way will you fall? Which side will you choose? You'll forgive me if I'm not a little concerned with your affairs and state of mind, darling. What are your plans, exactly, for the future?"

"I don't know." I buried my face in my hands. I just wanted

a normal life. I wanted to go home. I wanted... I sat up, looking her straight in the eye. "I want my father back. I want to know why you stole him from me eleven years ago."

Silence fell. I could feel the tension mount as Leanansidhe stared at me, her cigarette flute halfway to her mouth, trailing blue smoke. Ash gripped my shoulders, tense and ready to spring into action if needed. Out of the corner of my eye, I saw that Grimalkin had disappeared, and Puck was frozen on the edge of the couch.

For a few heartbeats, nobody moved.

Then Leanansidhe threw back her head and laughed, making me jump. The lights flickered once, went out, and returned as the Queen of the Exiles swung her gaze down to me.

"Stole?" Leanansidhe sat back and crossed her long legs. "Stole? I'm quite certain you mean *saved,* don't you, pet?"

"I—" I blinked at her. "What are you talking about?"

"Oh, so you haven't heard this story. Puck, darling, shame on you. You never told her."

I glanced sharply at Puck. He fidgeted on the armrest, not meeting my gaze, and I felt my stomach sink all the way down to my toes.

No, no. Not you, Puck. I've known you forever. Tell me you had nothing to do with this.

Leanansidhe laughed again. "Well, this is an unexpected drama. How fabulous! I must set the stage." She clapped, and the lights abruptly went out, save for a single spotlight over the piano.

"Lea, don't." Puck's voice surprised me, low, rough, and almost desperate. My stomach sank even lower. "Not this way. Let me explain it to her."

Leanansidhe turned a remorseless gaze on Puck and shook her head. "No, darling. I think it's time the girl knew the truth. You had plenty of time to tell her, so this is no fault but your own." She waved her hand, and music started, dark, ominous piano chords, though no one sat at the bench. Another spotlight clicked on, this time over Leanansidhe as she rose in a billowing of cloth and hair. Standing tall, her hands raised as if embracing an audience, the Dark Muse closed her eyes and began to speak.

"Once upon a time, there were two mortals."

Her musical voice shivered into my head, and I saw the images as clearly as if I was watching a movie. I saw my mom, younger, smiling, carefree, holding hands with a tall, lanky man whom I recognized now. Paul. My dad. They were talking and laughing, obviously in love and oblivious to the world. A lump rose in my throat.

"In mortal eyes," Leanansidhe continued, "they were unremarkable. Two souls in a throng of identical humans. But to the faery world, they were fountains of glamour, beacons of light in the darkness. An artist whose paintings almost sang with a life of their own, and a musician whose soul was intertwined in his music, their love only heightened their talents."

"Wait," I blurted, interrupting the flow of the story. Leanansidhe blinked and dropped her hands, and the stream of images stumbled to a halt. "I think you have it wrong. My dad wasn't a great musician, he was an insurance salesman. I mean, I know he played the piano, but if he was *so* good, why didn't he do anything with it?"

"Who is telling the story here, pet?" The Exile Queen bristled, and the lights flickered again. "Don't you know the term 'starving artist'? Your father was very gifted, but music did not pay the bills. Now, do you want to hear this story or not, pet?"

"Sorry," I mumbled, sinking back in the couch. "Go on, please."

Leanansidhe sniffed, flipping back her hair, and the visions started again as she continued.

"They got married and, as humans do, began to drift

apart. The man took a new job, one that required him to leave home for long periods of time; his music dwindled and soon ceased altogether. His wife continued to paint, less frequently than before, but now her art was filled with longing, a yearning for something more. And perhaps that was what drew the eye of the Summer King."

I bit my lip. I'd heard this story before, from Oberon himself, but it still didn't make it any easier. Ash squeezed my shoulder.

"Not long after, a child was born, a child of two worlds, half faery and half mortal. During that time, there was much speculation in the Summer Court, wondering if the child should be taken into Faery and raised as Oberon's daughter, or if she was to stay in the human world with her mortal parents. Unfortunately, before a decision could be made, the family fled with the child, spiriting her far away and out of Oberon's reach. To this day, no one knows how they accomplished this, though there was a rumor that the girl's mother somehow found a way to hide them all, that perhaps she was not as blind to Faery as she first appeared.

"Ironically, it was the human's music that gave them away again, when the father of the girl began composing again. Six years after they fled from the courts, Queen Titania discovered the location of the child's family, and was determined to take her revenge. She could not kill the girl and risk Oberon's wrath, nor did she dare strike at the mother, the human who caught the eye of the Summer King. But the girl's mortal father had no such protection."

"So, Titania took my dad?" I had to interrupt, though I knew it would probably piss Leanansidhe off again. She glowered at me, but I was too frustrated to care. "But, that doesn't make sense! How'd he end up with you?"

Leanansidhe gave a dramatic sigh and picked up her cigarette holder, sucking on it with pursed lips. "I was just getting to the climax, darling," she sighed, blowing out a blue panther that bounded over my head. "You're probably a horror to take to the movies, aren't you?"

"No more stories," I said, standing up. "Please, just tell me. Did Titania steal my father or not?"

"No, darling." Leanansidhe rolled her eyes. "*I* stole your father."

I gaped at her. "You did! *Why?* Just so Titania couldn't?"

"Exactly, dove. I'm not particularly fond of the Summer bitch, pardon my French, since the jealous shrew was responsible for my exile. And you should be grateful it was I instead of Titania who took your father. He doesn't have a bad life, here. The Summer Queen probably would have turned him into a toad or rosebush or something similar."

"How did you even know about it? Why did you get involved?"

"Ask Puck," Leanansidhe said, waving her cigarette flute toward the end of the couch. "He was your appointed guardian at the time. He was the one who told me all about it."

I felt like someone punched me in the stomach. Incredulous, I turned to Puck, who was studiously studying the corner, and felt breathless. "Puck? *You* told her about my dad?"

He winced and looked at me, scrubbing the back of his head. "You don't understand, princess. When I got wind of Titania's plans, I had to do something. Oberon didn't care, he wouldn't have sent any help. Lea was the only one I could ask." He shrugged and offered a meek, apologetic grin. "I can't take on the Queen of the Seelie Court, princess. That would be suicide, even for me."

I took a deep breath to clear my thoughts, but my mood veered sharply to anger. Puck had known. He'd known all along where my dad was. All those years of being my best friend—of *pretending* to be my best friend—watching me struggle with the pain of losing a father, the nightmares that followed, the confusion and isolation and loneliness, and he'd known all along.

Rage flared, tinting my vision red, as eleven years of grief, confusion, and anger flooded in all at once. "Why didn't you tell me!" I burst out, making Puck flinch again. Clenching my fists, I stalked over to where he sat. Glamour flicked around me, hot and furious. "All that time, all those *years,* of knowing, and you never said anything! How could you? You were supposed to be my friend!"

"Princess—" Puck began, but fury overwhelmed me, and I slapped him across the face as hard as I could, knocking him off the armrest. He sprawled on the floor in shock, and I loomed over him, shaking with hate and tears. "You took my dad from me!" I screamed, fighting the urge to kick him in the ribs, repeatedly. "It was you all along!"

Ash grabbed me from behind, holding me back. I shook for a moment, then turned and buried my face in his chest, gasping for air as my tears stained his shirt.

So. Now I knew the truth, but took no pleasure from it. What do you say when your best friend has been lying to you for eleven years? I didn't know how I could look at Puck again without wanting to punch him in the face. I did know this, however—the longer my dad remained here in the Between, the more he would forget the real world. I couldn't let him stay with Leanansidhe. I had to get him out, today.

When I looked up again, Puck was gone, but Leanansidhe remained, watching me from the sofa with narrowed blue eyes. "So, darling," she murmured as I stepped away from Ash, wiping my cheeks with my sleeve. "What will you do, now?"

I took a deep breath and faced Leanansidhe with the last of my remaining calm. "I want you to let my dad go," I said, watching her arc one slender eyebrow. "He doesn't belong here, with you. Let me take him back to the real world."

Leanansidhe regarded me with a blank expression; no

emotion showed in her eyes or face as she puffed her cigarette and blew a coiling viper into the air. "Darling, you know your mother will likely freak out if you show up one night with her long-lost husband. Do you think she will just take him back and things will go back to normal? It doesn't work that way, dove. You will likely tear your little human family apart."

"I know." I swallowed a fresh batch of tears, but they still clogged my throat, making it hard to talk without crying. "I don't plan to take him home. Mom…Mom has Luke and Ethan now. I know…we can't be that family again, ever." Tears spilled over as soon as I said the words out loud. It had been a fantasy, yes, but it still hurt to see it crushed, knowing the family I lost back then was gone forever.

"Then what do you want with him, dove?"

"I want him to be normal, just to have a normal life again!" I threw my hands up in frustrated despair. "I don't want him to be crazy! I don't want him to wander around here forever, not knowing who he is or anything about his past. I…I want to talk to him, like a regular person, and see if he remembers me." Ash moved closer and touched my back, just to reassure me he was still there. I glanced at him and smiled.

"I want him to move on," I finished, looking Leanansidhe in the eyes. "And…he won't be able to do that here, not aging, not remembering anything of who he is. You have to let him go."

"Do I, now?" Leanansidhe smiled humorously, a dangerous edge to her voice. "And just how do you expect to convince me, darling? I'm rather loathe to give up any of my pets, relative of yours or not. So, my dove, what do you have to offer for your father's freedom?"

I steeled myself. Now came the most dangerous part, the bargaining. I could only imagine what the Dark Muse might want from me—my voice, my youth, my firstborn child were all things she could ask for. But before I could say a word, Ash took my elbow and pressed something into my palm.

Curious, I held up my hand. A small gold ring flickered in my palm, surrounded by a gently swirling aura of blue and green. It looked exactly like the one we'd taken from the tomb. I glanced at Ash sharply, and he winked at me.

"Remember when the oracle asked if you had the ring's mate?" he whispered, his breath tickling my ear. "At least one of us was thinking ahead."

"Well, darling?" Leanansidhe called before I could reply. "What are you two whispering about? Does it have anything to do with what you're going to trade for your father?"

I gave Ash a brilliant smile and turned to Leanansidhe again. "Yes," I murmured, and raised the Token so that it gleamed under the lights. Leanansidhe sat straight up in her chair. "I can give you this."

The brief, eager flash in the queen's eyes told me we had won. "A Token, darling?" Leanansidhe leaned back again, feigning nonchalance. "That might be sufficient. For now, anyway. I suppose I can trade your father for that."

I was weak with relief, but Ash stepped forward, closing his hand over the ring and my fingers. "That's not enough," he said, and I gaped at him in disbelief. "You know the Iron fey are looking for Meghan. We can't just wander around the mortal world without a plan. We need a place that will be secure from the false king's minions."

"Ash, what are you doing?" I hissed under my breath. He gave me a sideways glance and mouthed, "Trust me."

Leanansidhe pursed her lips. "You two are pressing the boundaries of my patience." She drummed her nails on the armrest and sighed. "Oh, very well, darlings. I have a quaint little hideaway that I can lend you for the time being. It's out in the middle of nowhere and fairly safe—I've got a few of the local trows keeping an eye on it. Will that be *good enough* for you, dove?"

I looked at Ash, and he nodded. "All right," I told Leanansidhe, putting the Token on an end table, where it glimmered like a stray firefly. "You have a deal. Now, where's
my dad?"

Leanansidhe smiled. Rising gracefully, she floated over to
the baby grand in the corner and sat at the bench, running
her fingers over the keys.

"Right here, darling. After you left, I'm afraid your father
became inconsolable. He kept trying to leave the manor,
so I'm afraid I had to put an end to those silly notions of
escape."

CHAPTER FIVE

THE HIDDEN SANCTUARY

"Change him back!" I cried, horror pinning my feet to the carpet.

"Oh, don't fret, darling." Leanansidhe stroked a nail over the keys, releasing a mournful, shivery note. "It's not permanent. However, you will have to take him out of the Between to change him back. The spell dictates that as long as he stays here, he remains as he is. But look at it this way, darling—at least I didn't turn him into a pipe organ.

"Now," she said, rising with a catlike stretch, oblivious to my horrified stare, "I simply insist you join me for dinner, darlings. Cook is making hippocampus soup tonight, and I'm dying to hear how you got the scepter back from Virus. And of course, your little declaration in front of Mab and Oberon and the entirety of the courts." She wrinkled her nose in an almost affectionate manner. "Ah, young love. It must be wonderful to be so naive."

"What about my dad?"

"Pish, darling. He's not going anywhere." Leanansidhe waved her hand airily. If she saw me bristle, she didn't comment on it. Ash put a hand on my arm before I could explode. "Now, come with me, dove. Dinner first, maybe a little gossip, and then you can run off if you like. I believe Puck and Grimalkin are already in the dining hall."

Anger flared again at the mention of Puck. *Bastard,* I thought, following Leanansidhe down her many red-carpeted hallways, only half listening to her chatter. *I'll never forgive him. Never. Not telling me about my dad was unforgivable. He's gone too far this time.*

Puck wasn't in the dining room with Grimalkin when we came in, which was a good thing because I would've spent the whole evening shooting him poisonous glares over my bowl. Instead, I ate an extremely fishy soup that turned everything weird swirly colors with every swallow, answered Leanansidhe's questions as to what happened with Virus and the scepter, and eventually came to the part where Ash and I were banished from the Nevernever.

"And what happened then, dove?" Leanansidhe prodded when I told her how I'd given the scepter back to Mab.

"Um..." I hesitated, embarrassed, and snuck a peek at Ash. He sat in his chair, fingers laced under his chin, pretending no interest in the conversation. "Didn't Grimalkin tell you?"

"He did, darling, but I'd much prefer to hear it firsthand. I'm about to lose a very costly wager, you see, so I'd love it if you could give me a loophole." She scowled at Grimalkin, who sat on the table, washing his paws in a very smug manner. "He'll be simply insufferable after this, I'm afraid. Details, darling, I need details."

"Well..."

"Mistress!"

Fortunately, I was saved a reply by the noisy arrival of Razor Dan and his redcaps. Still dressed in matching butler suits with pink bow ties, the redcaps filed into the dining room, every one of them scowling at me. Ash's eyes widened, and he quickly hid his mouth under his laced fingers, but I saw his shoulders shaking with silent laughter.

Luckily, the redcaps didn't notice. "We delivered the piano

to the cabin, like you ordered," Razor Dan growled, the fishhook in his nose quivering indignantly. "And we stocked it with supplies, like you asked. It's all ready for the brat and her pets." He glared at me and bared his fangs, as if remembering our last little encounter. He had been in cahoots with Warren, the bitter half satyr who'd tried to kidnap me and take me to the false king the last time I was here. Leanansidhe had punished Warren (I wasn't sure how, and I didn't want to know) but spared the redcaps, saying they were only following their base instincts. Or maybe she just didn't want to lose her free slave labor. In any case, they'd just provided me with a much-needed distraction.

I leaped from my chair, drawing surprised looks from everyone in the room. "We really should go," I said, not needing to feign my impatience. "My dad is there, right? I don't want him to be alone when he turns back from being a piano."

Leanansidhe snorted with amusement, and I realized how odd that sentence sounded, even to me. "Don't worry, dove. It will take time for the glamour to wear off. But I understand if you have to go. Just remember, my door is always open if you want to come back." She waved her cigarette at Grimalkin, sitting on the other side of the table. "Grim, darling, you know the way, right?"

Grimalkin yawned widely and stretched. Curling his tail around himself, he regarded the Exile Queen without blinking and twitched an ear. "I believe you and I still have a wager to settle," he purred. "One that you lost, if you remember."

"You are a horrid creature, Grimalkin." Leanansidhe sighed and puffed a smoke-cat into the air, then sent a smoke-hound after it. "It seems I am destined to lose bargains today. Very well, cat, you can have your bloody favor. And may you choke on it when you try to call it in."

Grimalkin purred and seemed to smile. "This way," he

told me, waving his tail as he stood. "We will have to go back through the cellar, but the trod is not far. Just be wary when we get there—Leanansidhe failed to mention that this particular spot is infested with bogles."

"What about Goodfellow?" Ash said, before I could ask what a bogle was. "Should he know where we're going, or are we going to leave him behind?"

My stomach turned, angry and sullen. "I don't care," I growled, and scanned the dining room, wondering if one of the chairs, plates, or utensils was actually Puck in disguise. "He can follow us or not, but he'd better stay out of my way if he knows what's good for him. I don't want to see his face for a long time. Come on, Grim." I looked at the cat, watching us with an amused, half-lidded expression, and raised my chin. "Let's get out of here."

BACK THROUGH THE BASEMENT we went, Grimalkin in the lead, down another maze of torchlit hallways to an old wooden door hanging crookedly from its hinges. Sunlight streamed in through the cracks, and birdsong trilled somewhere beyond the door.

I pulled it open and found myself in a dense forest glen, broad-leafed trees surrounding us on every side and a babbling stream cutting through the clearing. Sunlight dappled the forest floor, and a pair of spotted deer raised their heads to watch us, curious and unafraid.

Ash stepped through the stony mound we'd exited, and the door creaked shut behind him. He took in the forest surroundings with one smooth, practiced gaze, and turned to Grimalkin.

"There are several trows watching us from the bushes. Are they going to be a problem?"

Startled, I scanned the clearing, searching for the elusive trows, which, from what I understood, were squat, ugly fey who lived underground, but apart from the deer, we

appeared to be alone. Grimalkin yawned and scratched behind
an ear.

"Leanansidhe's groundskeepers," he said offhandedly.
"Nothing to worry about. If you hear feet moving around
the cabin at night, it is probably them. Or the brownies."

"What cabin?" I asked, gazing around the clearing. "I
don't see a cabin."

"Of course not. This way, human." Tail up, Grimalkin
trotted across the clearing, hopped the stream, and disappeared midjump.

I sighed. "Why does he always do that?"

"I don't think it was on purpose this time," Ash said, and
took my hand. "Come on."

We crossed the glen, passing very close to the deer, who
still didn't run away, and hopped over the little stream.

As soon as my feet left the ground, I felt a tingle of magic,
like I was jumping through an invisible barrier. When I
landed, I was no longer staring at empty forest but an enormous, two-story lodge with a veranda that circled the entire
upper deck and smoke writhing from the chimney. The front
of it stood on stilts, a good twenty-something feet off the
ground, and gave the front deck a fantastic view of the whole
clearing.

I gaped. "This is her 'quaint little hideaway'? I was thinking more along the lines of a one-room cabin with an out-
house or something."

"That's Leanansidhe," Ash said, sounding amused. "She
could have glamoured the outside to look like a rundown
cabin instead of hiding the whole thing, but I don't think
that's her style." He gazed up at the looming structure and
frowned. "I hear music."

My heart jumped. "Piano music? My dad!"

We raced up the steps, taking them two at a time, and
burst into the living room, where a cheerful fire crackled in

the hearth and the dark strains of piano music pounded from the corner.

My dad sat at the piano bench, his lank brown hair falling into his eyes, his skinny shoulders hunched over the keys. Slouched a few feet away, with his shoes on the coffee table and his hands behind his head, was Puck.

Puck caught my gaze and smirked, but I ignored him as I rushed to the piano bench. "Dad!" I had to shout to be heard over the music. "Dad! Do you recognize me? It's Meghan. Meghan, your daughter. Do you remember?"

He hunched even farther over the keys, pounding on them like his life depended on it. I grabbed his arm and yanked him around, forcing him to look at me. "Dad!"

His hazel eyes, empty as the sky, stared right through me, and I felt an icy spear plunge into my stomach. I let him go, and he immediately went back to playing the piano, pounding the keys as I staggered back and sank into a nearby chair.

"What's wrong with him?" I whispered.

Grimalkin leaped up beside me. "Remember, human, he has been in Faery for a very long time. Also, until just recently, he was a musical instrument, which was probably fairly traumatic. It is to be expected that his mind is a little fractured. Give him time, and he should come out of it eventually."

"Should?" I choked, but the cat had moved on to washing his back toes and did not reply.

I hid my face in my hands, then pulled them back and glared at Puck. "What are you doing here?" I asked stonily.

"Me?" Puck leered at me, smug and looking not the least bit sorry. "I'm on vacation, princess."

"Go away," I told him, rising from my seat. "Go back to Oberon and leave us alone. You've done enough damage."

"He cannot go back to Oberon," Grimalkin said, leaping to the back of the couch. "Oberon exiled him when he came after you. He disobeyed the king's orders and has been banished from the Nevernever."

Guilt now joined the swirl of angry emotions, and I stared at Puck in disbelief. "That was stupid," I told him. "Why would you get yourself banished like that? Now you're stuck here with the rest of us."

Puck's eyes gleamed, feral and menacing. "Oh, I don't know, princess. Maybe it was because I was stupid enough to care about you. Maybe I actually thought I had a chance. Silly me, thinking that one little kiss meant anything to you."

"You kissed him?" Ash sounded like he was trying to hide his shock. I cringed. Things were rapidly spinning out of control. My father seemed to pick up on the tension, and banged harder on the keys.

I stared at Puck, torn between anger and guilt. "We're not talking about that right now," I began, but he overrode me.

"Oh, I think we should," Puck interrupted, crossing his arms. I started to protest, but he raised his voice. "So, tell me, princess, when you said you loved me, was that a lie?"

Ash went rigid; I could feel his eyes on me, and cursed Puck for bringing this up now. Puck was watching me too, lips curled in a smirk, enjoying my reaction. I wanted to hit him and apologize at the same time, but anger was stronger.

I took a breath. Fine. If Puck wanted to force the issue now, I'd tell him the truth. "No," I said, raising my voice to be heard over the piano chords. "I didn't lie to you, Puck. I meant what I said—at least, I did back then. But it's not the same as what I feel for Ash, you knew that."

"Did I?" Puck's voice was ugly. "Maybe I did, but you sure led me on a merry chase, princess. Just like a pro. When were you going to tell me I didn't have a cold chance in hell?"

"I don't know!" I snapped, taking a step forward and clenching my fists. "When were you going to tell me about my father, Puck? When were you going to tell me you knew where he was all along?"

Puck fell silent, watching me with a sullen expression. The clanging of the piano filled the room, frantic and chaotic. In the corner, Ash was motionless; he could've been made of stone.

Rising from the couch, Puck swept a cruel gaze at us all and broke into a sneer.

"You know, I think I will get out of here," he drawled. "It's gotten crowded of late, and I was just thinking I needed a vacation." Glancing at Ash, he smirked and shook his head. "Not enough room in this cabin for both of us, ice-boy. You ever want that duel, you can find me in the woods. And if either one of you comes up with an actual plan, do me a favor and leave me out of it. I'm outta here."

With a last sneer, Puck walked across the room and out the door without looking back.

Guilt and anger flared, but I turned back to my dad, whose frantic banging on the piano keys had calmed somewhat. I had other things to worry about besides Puck. "Dad," I said quietly, slipping beside him. "You need to stop now. Just for a little while, okay? Will you stop?" I pried his hands away from the keys, and this time he let me, dropping them to his lap. So he wasn't completely unreachable, that was good. He still didn't look at me, though, and I studied the lean, haggard face, the lines around his eyes and mouth even though he was a fairly young man, and felt close to despair.

Ash appeared beside me, close but not quite touching. "The master bedroom is down the hall," he said quietly. "I think your father will be comfortable there, if you can get him to follow you."

In a daze, I nodded. Somehow, we got my dad on his feet and led him down the hall to the large bedroom at the end. Leanansidhe's master bedroom didn't lack anything in luxury, from the four-poster bed to the bubbling natural hot spring in the bathroom, but it still felt like a jail cell as I ushered my dad inside and shut the door behind him.

Leaning against the door, I shook with exhausted tears, feeling stretched in several directions at once. Ash hovered nearby, just watching. He looked uncomfortable, like he wanted to pull me close, but there was a barrier between us now, the admission with Puck hanging in the air like barbed wire.

"Come on," Ash murmured, finally brushing my arm. "There's nothing you can do for him now. You're exhausted, and you can't help anyone like this. Get some rest."

Feeling numb, I let him lead me away, down the hall and up a flight of stairs to the loft overlooking the main room. A rustic log railing barred the edge, where you could peer down on the living room below, and a queen-size bed with a grizzly-bear rug complete with head and claws crouched under the eaves.

Ash dragged the awful bear rug off the bed and motioned for me to get in. In a daze, I settled on top of the covers. Without the piano chords, the cabin seemed unnaturally quiet, the silence thudding in my ears. Ash loomed over me, strangely formal and unsure. "I'll be downstairs," he murmured. "Try to get some sleep." He started to pull away, but I reached up and grabbed his hand, holding it tight.

"Ash, wait," I said, and he went perfectly still. It might've been too soon, reaching out for him, but I was drowning in an overload of emotion: anger at Puck, worry for my dad, fear that I'd just sabotaged my relationship with Ash. "I can't be alone right now," I whispered, clinging to his hand. "Please, just stay with me for a little while. You don't have to say anything, we don't have to talk. Just…stay. Please."

He hesitated. I saw the indecision in his eyes, the silent battle, before he finally nodded. Sliding onto the bed, he leaned back against the headboard and I curled up beside him, content just to feel him near me. I heard his heartbeat,

despite the rigid way he held himself, and caught a glimmer
of emotion surrounding him like a hazy aura, a reaction he
wasn't able to hide.

I blinked. "You're…jealous," I said in disbelief. Ash, former
prince of the Unseelie Court, was jealous. Of Puck. I didn't
know why I found that so surprising; maybe Ash seemed
too calm and self-assured to be jealous. But there was no
mistaking what I saw.

Ash shifted uncomfortably and gave me a look from the
corner of his eye. "Is that so wrong?" he asked softly, turning
to stare at the far wall. "Is it so wrong to be jealous, when I
heard that you kissed him, when you told him…" He trailed
off, raking a hand through his hair, and I bit my lip. "I know
I was the one who left," he continued, still staring at the wall.
"I said we were enemies and that we couldn't be together.
I knew it would break your heart, but…I also knew Puck
would be there to pick up the pieces. Whatever came of that,
I brought on myself. I know I have no right to ask…" He
stopped, taking a short breath, as if that confession had been
difficult. I held my breath, knowing there was more.

"But," he went on, finally turning to me, "I have to know,
Meghan. I can't wonder about this, not with him. Or you.
It will drive me crazy." He sighed and suddenly took my
hand, staring at our tangled fingers. "You know what I feel
for you. You know I'll protect you from whatever comes at
us, but this is the one thing I can't fight."

"Ash—"

"If you're torn about whether you want to be with Goodfellow, tell me now. I'll step down, give you space, whatever
you want me to do." Ash trembled, just a little, as he said
this. I felt his heart speed up as he turned to meet my gaze,
his silver eyes intense. "Just answer me this today, and I'll
never ask you again. Do you love him?"

I took a breath, ready to deny it immediately, but stopped.
I couldn't give him a short, flippant answer, not when he was

looking at me like that. He deserved to know the truth. All of it.

"I did," I said softly. "At least, I thought I did. I'm not so sure now." I paused, choosing my words carefully. Ash waited, his whole body tense like a coiled wire, as I gathered my thoughts. "When you left," I went on, "I was hurt. I thought I wouldn't see you again. You told me we were enemies, that we couldn't be together, and I believed you. I was angry and confused, and Puck was there to pick up the pieces, like you said. It was easy to turn to Puck because I knew how he felt. And, for a little while, I thought I might... love him, too.

"But," I continued, as my voice started to shake, "when I saw you again, I realized what I felt for Puck wasn't the same. He was my best friend, and I'd always have a spot for him in my heart, but...it was you, Ash. I didn't really have a choice. It's always been you."

Ash didn't say anything, but I heard his faint sigh, as if he'd been holding his breath, and he drew me close, wrapping his arms around me. I lay my head on his chest and closed my eyes, shoving thoughts of Puck and my dad and the false king to the back of my mind. I would deal with them tomorrow. Right now, I just wanted to sleep, to sink into oblivion and forget everything for a little while. Ash was still quiet, thoughtful. His glamour aura glimmered once, then flickered out of sight again. But all I had to do was listen to his heart, thudding in his chest, to know what he was feeling.

"Talk to me," I whispered, tracing his ribs through his shirt, making him shiver. "Please. The silence is driving me crazy. I don't want to hear myself think right now."

"What do you want me to say?"

"Anything. Tell me a story. Tell me about the places you've been. Anything to keep my mind off...everything."

Ash paused. After a moment, he started humming a soft, slow melody, drowning out the silence. It was a haunting, peaceful tune, reminding me of falling snow and hibernating trees and animals huddled in their dens, sleeping the winter away. I felt his hand running the length of my back, a gentle rhythm in time with the lullaby, and sleep crept over me like a warm blanket.

"Ash?" I whispered, as my eyelids began to drift shut.

"Yes?"

"Don't leave me, all right?

"I already promised that I would stay." He stroked my hair, his voice dropping to a near whisper. "For as long as you want me."

"Ash?"

"Mmm?"

"…I love you."

His hands stilled; I felt them tremble. "I know," he murmured, bending his head close to mine. "Get some sleep. I'll be right here."

His deep voice was the last thing I heard before I drifted into the void.

"Hello, my love," Machina whispered, holding out his hands as I approached, steel cables writhing behind him in a hypnotic dance. Tall and elegant, his long silver hair rippling like liquid mercury, he watched me with eyes as black as night. "I have been waiting for you."

"Machina." I shivered, gazing around the empty void, hearing my voice echo all around us. We were alone in the fathomless dark. "Where am I? Why are you here? I thought I killed you."

The Iron King smiled, silver hair glowing in the utter darkness. "You can never be rid of me, Meghan Chase. We are one, now and forever. You just have not accepted that yet. Come." He beckoned me forward. "Come to me, my love, and let me show you what I mean."

I backed away. "Stop calling me that. I'm not yours." He

drifted closer, and I took another step back. "And you're not supposed to be here. Stop lurking around my dreams. I already have someone, and it's not you."

Machina's smile didn't falter. "Ah, yes. Your Unseelie prince. Do you really think you'll be able to keep him once you realize who you really are? Do you think he will even want you anymore?"

"What do you know about that? You're just a dream—a nightmare, really."

"No, my love." Machina shook his head. "I am the part of you that you cannot bring yourself to accept. And as long as you keep denying me, you will never understand your true potential. Without me, you will never be enough to defeat the false king."

"I'll take my chances." Narrowing my eyes, I stabbed a finger at him. "And now, I think it's time you went away. This is *my* dream, and you're not welcome here. Get out."

Machina shook his head sadly. "Very well, Meghan Chase. If you decide you need me after all—and you will—I will be right here."

"Don't hold your breath," I mumbled, and my own voice woke me up.

I BLINKED AND RAISED my head from the pillow. The room was dark, but outside the round loft window, gray light filtered in from a brightening sky. Ash was gone and the space beside me was cold. He'd left sometime during the night.

The scent of bacon drifted up from below, and my stomach grumbled a response. I headed downstairs, wondering who was cooking at such an early hour. The image of Ash flipping pancakes in a white apron came to mind, and I giggled hysterically as I entered the kitchen.

Ash wasn't there, and neither was Puck, but Grimalkin looked up from a table laden with food. Eggs, pancakes, bacon, biscuits, fruit, and oatmeal covered every surface of the tabletop, along with whole pitchers of milk and orange juice. Grimalkin, sitting on the corner, blinked at me once, then went back to dunking his paw in a glass of milk and licking it off.

"What is all this?" I asked, amazed. "Did Dad cook? Or... Ash?"

Grimalkin snorted. "Those two? I shudder to think of the consequences. No, Leanansidhe's brownies took care of this, just like they have cleaned your room and made your bed by now." He observed the opaque white droplets on his paw and flicked them off rapidly.

"Where is everyone?"

"The human is still asleep. Goodfellow has not returned, though I am sure he will sometime in the future, probably with the ire of all the local fey on his heels."

"I don't care what Puck does. He can get eaten by trolls for all I care." Grimalkin seemed unfazed by my hostility and calmly licked a paw. I picked at the scrambled eggs sitting before me. "Where's Ash?"

"The Winter prince left yesterday evening while you were asleep and said nothing about where he was going, of course. He returned a few minutes ago."

"He left? Where is he now?"

A thump from the door drew our attention. Paul wandered into the kitchen, shuffling like a zombie, his hair in disarray. He didn't look at either of us.

"Hey," I greeted softly, but I might as well have saved my breath. Paul acted like he didn't hear me. Staring at the laden breakfast table, he picked up a piece of toast, nibbled a corner, and wandered back out, all without acknowledging my existence.

My appetite fled. Grimalkin eyed the glass of milk perched on the corner and tapped it experimentally. "By the way," he continued as I stared moodily out the door, "your Winter prince wishes you to meet him in the clearing beyond the stream after you have eaten. He implied that it was important."

I grabbed a bacon slice and nibbled half-heartedly. "Ash did? Why?"

"I did not care enough to ask."

"What about my dad?" I glanced in the direction Paul had gone. "Will he be safe? Should I just leave him alone?"

"You are terribly dull this morning." Grimalkin deliberately knocked over the glass of milk and watched it drip to the floor in satisfaction. "The same glamour that keeps mortals out of this place also keeps them in. Should the human go wandering around outside, he will not be able to leave the clearing. No matter the direction he takes, he will only find himself back where he started."

"What if I want to take him away? He can't stay here forever."

"Then you had better take that up with Leanansidhe, not I. In any case, it is no concern of mine." Grimalkin dropped from the table, landing on the wooden floor with a thump. "When you go to meet the prince, leave the dishes as they are," he said, arching his tail over his back. "If you wash them, the brownies will be insulted and might leave the cabin, and that would be terribly inconvenient."

"Is that why you made a mess?" I asked, eying the milk dripping to the floor. "So the brownies would have something to clean up?"

"Of course not, human." Grimalkin yawned. "That was purely for the fun of it." And he trotted from the room, leaving me to shake my head, grab a piece of toast, and hurry outside.

CHAPTER SIX

LESSONS

It was a foggy gray morning, with mist curling along the ground in wispy threads, muffling my footsteps. I hopped over the brook and looked back once I reached the other side. The cabin had disappeared once more, showing only misty forest beyond the stream.

In the center of the clearing, a dark silhouette danced and spun in the mist, his long coat billowing out behind him, an icy sword cutting through the fog like paper. I leaned against a tree and watched, hypnotized by the graceful, whirling movements, the deadly speed and accuracy of the sword strikes, far too quick for a human to ever keep up with. Uneasiness gnawed at me as I suddenly remembered the dream, Machina's soft voice echoing in my head. *Do you think you'll be able to keep him, once you discover who you really are? Do you think he will even want you anymore?*

Angrily, I pushed those thoughts away. What did he know? Besides, that was just a dream, a nightmare conjured from stress and the worry over my dad. It didn't mean anything.

Ash finished the drill and with a final flourish, slammed the blade into its sheath. For a moment, he stood motionless, breathing deeply, the mist curling around him. "Is your father any better?" he asked without turning around. I jumped.

"Hasn't changed." I moved across the damp grass toward him, soaking the hems of my jeans. "How long have you been out here?"

He turned, raking a hand through his bangs, shoving them out of his eyes. "I went back to Leanansidhe's last night," he said, walking forward. "I wanted to get something for you, so I had one of her contacts track one down for me."

"Track...what down?"

Ash strode to a nearby rock, swooped down, and tossed me a long, slightly curved stick. When I caught it, I saw that it was actually a leather sheath with a gilded brass hilt poking from the top. A sword. Ash was giving me a sword...why?

Oh, yeah. Because I wanted to learn to fight. Because I'd asked him to teach me.

Ash, watching me with that weary, knowing look on his face, shook his head. "You forgot, did you?"

"Nooooo," I said quickly. "I just...didn't think it would be this soon."

"This is the perfect place." Ash turned slightly to gaze around the clearing. "Quiet, hidden. We can catch our breath here. It's a good place to learn while you're waiting for your father to come out of it. When we're done here, I have a feeling things will get much more chaotic." He gestured to the sword in my hand. "Your first lesson begins now. Draw your sword."

I did. Unsheathing it sent a raspy shiver across the glen, and I gazed at the weapon in fascination. The blade was thin and slightly curved, an elegant-looking weapon, razor sharp and deadly. A warning tickled the back of my mind. There was something about the blade that was...different. Blinking, I ran my fingers along the cool, gleaming edge, and a chill shot through my stomach.

The blade was made of steel. Not faery steel. Not a fey

sword covered in glamour. Real, ordinary iron. The kind
that would burn faery flesh and sear away glamour. The kind
that left wounds impossible to heal.

I gaped at it, then at Ash, who looked remarkably calm to
be facing his greatest weakness. "This is steel," I told him,
sure that Leanansidhe had made a mistake.

He nodded. "An eighteenth-century Spanish saber. Leanansidhe nearly had a fit when I told her what I wanted, but
she was able to track one down in exchange for a favor." He
paused then, wincing slightly. "A very large favor."

Alarmed, I stared at him. "What did you promise her?"

"It doesn't matter. Nothing that endangers us in any way."
He hurried on before I could argue. "I wanted a light, slashing weapon for you, one with a good amount of reach, to
keep opponents farther away." He gestured to the saber with
his own weapon, a blindingly quick stab of blue. "You'll
be moving around a lot, using speed instead of brute force
against your enemies. That blade won't block heavier weapons, and you don't have the strength to swing a longsword
effectively, so we're going to have to teach you how to dodge.
This was the best choice."

"But this is steel," I repeated, listening to him in amazement. He could teach a class with his knowledge of weapons and fighting. "Why a real sword? I could seriously hurt
someone."

"Meghan." Ash gave me a patient look. "That's exactly
why I chose it. You have an advantage with that weapon
that none of us can touch. Even the most violent redcap will
think twice about facing a real, mortal blade. It won't scare
the Iron fey, of course, but that's where training will come
in."

"But...but what if I hit you?"

A snort. "You're not going to hit me."

"How do you know?" I bristled at his amused tone. "I
could hit you. Even master swordsmen make mistakes. I

could get a lucky shot, or you might not see me coming. I don't want to hurt you."

He favored me with another patient look. "And how much experience do you have with swords and weapons in general?"

"Um." I glanced down at the saber in my hand. "Thirty seconds?"

He smiled, that calm, irritatingly confident smirk. "You're not going to hit me."

I scowled. Ash chuckled, then raised his weapon and stalked forward, all amusement gone. "Although," he continued, sliding into predator mode with no effort at all, "I do want you to try."

I gulped and backed away. "Now? Don't I get a warm-up or something? I don't even know how to hold the thing properly."

"Holding it is easy." Ash slid closer, circling me like a wolf. One finger pointed to the tip of his blade. "The sharp end goes in first."

"That's so not helpful, Ash."

He smiled grimly and continued to stalk. "Meghan, I would love to teach you properly, from the beginning, but that takes years, centuries, even. And since we don't have that kind of time, I'm giving you the condensed version. Besides, the best way to learn is by doing." He jabbed at me with his sword, nowhere near coming close, but I jumped anyway. "Now, try to hit me. And don't hold back."

I didn't want to, but I had asked him to teach me, after all. Bunching my muscles, I gave a feeble yell and lunged, stabbing at him with the tip.

Ash slid aside. In the space of a blink, his sword licked out, slapping my ribs with the flat of the blade. I shrieked as I felt the bite of absolute cold through my shirt, and glared at him.

"Dammit, Ash, that hurt!"

He gave me a humorless smile. "Then don't get hit."

My ribs throbbed. There'd probably be a welt there this evening. For a moment, I was tempted to throw down the blade and stalk back to the house. But I swallowed my pride and faced him again, resolved. I needed this. I needed to learn to defend myself, and the ones I cared about. I could take a few bruised ribs, if it meant saving a life one day.

Ash brandished his sword in an expert manner and cocked two fingers at me. "Again."

For the rest of the morning, we practiced. Or, more accurately, I tried to hit Ash and received more swats that stung and burned their way through my clothes. He didn't do it every time, and he never once cut me, but I became paranoid about getting hit. After several more thwaps that stung my pride as well as my skin, I tried switching to full defense mode, and Ash started attacking me.

I got hit a lot more.

Anger burned, flaring up after each swat, each effortless smack that left my skin tingling with failure. He wasn't being fair. He had years, decades even, of swordplay, and he wasn't even giving me a chance. He was toying with me instead of teaching me how to fend off his attacks. This wasn't a lesson, this was just him showing off.

Finally, my temper snapped. After desperately fending off a series of blindingly quick thrusts, I received a swat to my backside that ignited a rage. Screaming, I flew at Ash, intending to hit him this time, to at least smack that calm efficiency off his face.

This time, Ash didn't dodge or block, but spun and caught me around the waist as I charged past. Dropping his sword, he snatched my wrist in one hand and pulled me to his chest, holding me and the blade still as I cursed and struggled.

"There," he murmured in a voice of weary satisfaction. "That's what I was looking for."

Though still angry, I stopped fighting him. My senses

buzzed and I held myself rigid in his arms. "What?" I snarled. "Me to get so pissed I wanted to stab you in the eye?"

"The moment you'd take this seriously enough to *really* try to hit me." Ash's voice, dark and grim, made me freeze. He sighed, resting his forehead on the back on my skull. "This isn't a hobby, Meghan," he breathed, sending a tingle down my spine. "It isn't a game or a sport or a simple pastime. This is life and death. Any one of those hits could've killed you had I been serious. Putting a weapon in your hands means that, at some point, you're going to have to use it. In a fight like this, you're going to be hurt. Make a single mistake, and you'll be dead. And I'll lose...you."

His voice trailed off at the end, as if that last part just slipped out. My throat closed, and all my anger drained away.

Ash pressed his lips to the welt across my shoulder, and my heartbeat stuttered. "I'm sorry," he murmured, genuine regret in his voice. "I didn't mean to hurt you. But I do want you to understand. Teaching you to fight means you're going to be in even more danger, and I may be hard on you sometimes because I don't want you to lose." He released my wrist and ran his hand up to my shoulder, smoothing the hair from my neck. "Do you still want to continue?"

I couldn't speak. I just nodded, and Ash kissed the back of my neck. "Tomorrow, then," he said, drawing back even as I wished he would stay there forever. "Same time. Now, let's go put something on those welts."

I HEARD THE PIANO MUSIC as soon as we crossed the stream. My dad was sitting at the piano bench when we walked in, and didn't look up from the keys. But the music today wasn't as dark and frantic as it had been the night before; it was more calm and peaceful. Grimalkin lay atop the piano, feet tucked under him and eyes closed, purring in appreciation.

"Hi, Dad," I ventured, wondering if he would actually look at me today.

The music faltered, and for a split second, I thought he was going to look up. But then his shoulders hunched and he went back to his playing, a little faster than before. Grimalkin didn't bother to open his eyes.

"I guess that's a start," I sighed, as Ash disappeared into the kitchen for a moment. I heard him talking to a few unknown, high-pitched voices—Leanansidhe's brownies?—before he reappeared holding a small tan jar. My dad continued to play. I tried to look calm and hopeful, but disappointment settled heavy on my chest, and Ash saw it, too.

He didn't say anything as he led me upstairs to the loft, sitting me down on the neatly made bed after pulling off the bear rug. Opening the jar released a sharp, herbal scent that was oddly familiar, reminding me of a similar scene in a cold, icy bedroom, with Ash shirtless and bleeding and me binding up his wounds.

Below, the piano music continued, a low, mournful song that pulled at my insides. Ash knelt behind me on the bed and gently tugged the sleeve off my shoulder, just enough to expose the thin line of red slashed across my skin. I caught a flicker of remorse from him, a flash of dull regret, as a cold, tingling salve was spread over the wound.

"I'm still mad at you, you know," I said without turning around. The dark piano chords made me moody and pensive, and I tried to ignore the cool fingers sliding over my ribs, leaving blessed numbness as they passed. "A little warning would've been nice. You couldn't have said, 'Hey, as part of your training today, I'm going to beat you senseless'?"

Ash reached around with both arms and put the jar into my hands, using that motion to pull me back to his chest. "Your father will be fine," he murmured, as my chest ached with bottled-up grief. "It just takes a while for the mind to catch up on everything it has forgotten. Right now, he's

confused and frightened, and taking solace in the one thing
that's familiar. Just keep talking to him, and eventually he'll
start to remember."

He smelled so good, a mix of frost and something sharp,
like peppermint. Lifting my head, I placed a kiss at the hollow
of his neck, right beneath his jawbone, and he drew in a quiet
breath, his hands curling into fists. I suddenly realized we
were on a bed, alone in an isolated cabin, with no grown-
ups—lucid ones anyway—to point fingers or condemn. My
heart sped up, thudding in my ears, and I felt his heartbeat
quicken, too.

Shifting slightly, I went to trace another kiss along his jaw,
but he ducked his head and our lips met, and suddenly I was
kissing him as if I were going to meld him into my body.
His fingers tangled in my hair, and my hands slid beneath his
shirt, tracing the hard muscles of his chest and stomach. He
groaned, pulled me into his lap, and lowered us back onto
the bed, being careful not to crush me.

My whole body tingled, senses buzzing, my stomach twisting with so many emotions I couldn't place them all. Ash was
above me, his lips on mine, my hands sliding over his cool,
tight skin. I couldn't speak. I couldn't think. All I could do
was *feel*.

Ash pulled back slightly, his silver eyes bright as he stared
at me, his cool breath washing over my heated face.

"You are beautiful, you know that, right?" he murmured,
all seriousness, one hand gently framing my cheek. "I know
I don't say…things like that…as often as I should. I wanted
to let you know."

"You don't have to say anything," I whispered, though
hearing him admit it made my pulse flutter wildly. I could
feel the emotion swirling around us, auras of color and light,
and closed my eyes. "I can feel you," I murmured, as his
heartbeat picked up under my fingers. "I can almost feel your
thoughts. Is that very strange?"

"No," Ash said in a strangled voice, and a tremor went through him. I opened my eyes, staring into his perfect face.

"What's wrong?"

"Nothing. Just…" He shook his head. "I never thought…I could feel like this again. I didn't know if it was possible." He sighed, giving me a pleading look. "I'm sorry, I'm not explaining it very well."

"It's all right." I laced my hands behind his head, smiling. "Right now, talking isn't what I was hoping for."

Ash smiled faintly, lowering his head again.

And froze.

Frowning, I arched my neck, looking behind us upside down, and let out a squeak.

Paul stood at the top of the stairs, staring at us with wide, blank eyes. Even though he didn't say a word and probably didn't understand what was happening, my cheeks flamed and I was instantly mortified. Ash rolled off me and stood, his face shutting into that blank, expressionless mask as I tried gathering the frayed strands of my composure long enough to speak.

Rolling upright, smoothing down my tangled hair and clothes, I glared at my father, who stared back in a daze. "Dad, what are you doing here?" I asked. "Why aren't you downstairs with the piano?" *Where you're supposed to be,* I added sourly. Not that I wasn't happy to see my dad actually looking at me for the first time since we got here, but his timing absolutely sucked.

Paul blinked, still staring at me in a fog, and didn't say anything. I sighed, shot an apologetic look at Ash, and started to lead him back down the stairs. "Come on, Dad. Let's go look for a certain cat I'm going to kill for not warning us."

"Why?" Paul whispered, and my heart jumped to my throat. He looked straight at me with wide, teary eyes. "Why am I…here? Who…who are you?"

The lump in my throat grew bigger. "I'm your daughter." He stared at me blankly, and I gazed back, willing him to recognize me. "You were married to my mom, Melissa Chase. I'm Meghan. The last time you saw me, I was six years old, remember?"

"Daughter?"

I nodded breathlessly. Ash watched silently from the corner; I could feel his gaze on my back.

Paul shook his head, a sad, hopeless gesture. "I don't... remember," he said, and drew away from me, backing down the stairs, eyes clouding over once more.

"Dad—"

"Don't remember!" His voice took on a pensive note, and I stopped as all sanity fled from his face. "Don't remember! The rats scream, but I don't remember! Go away, go away." He ran to the piano and started pounding the keys, loud and frantic. I sighed and peered over the railing, watching him sadly.

Ash's arms wrapped around me seconds later, drawing me back to his chest. "It's a start," he said, and I nodded, turning my face into his arm. "At least he's talking now. He'll remember eventually."

Cool lips pressed against my neck, a brief, light touch, and I shivered. "Sorry about that," I whispered, wishing, selfishly, that we hadn't been interrupted. "I'm sure that's never happened to you before." Ash snorted, and I wondered if we could somehow reclaim that lost moment. I reached back and buried my fingers in his silky hair, pulling him closer. "What are you thinking about?"

"That this has put things in perspective," he said, as the rumbling piano chords vibrated around us, dark and crazy. "That there are more important things to think about. We should be concentrating on your training, and what we're going to do about the false king once it's time. He's still out there, looking for you."

I pouted, not liking that statement. But Ash chuckled and ran his fingers up my arm. "We have time, Meghan," he murmured. "After this is over, after your father regains his memories, after we deal with the false king, we'll have the rest of our lives. I'm not going anywhere, I promise." He held me tighter and brushed a kiss across my ear. "I'll wait. Just tell me when you're ready."

He released me then and walked downstairs. But I stood on the balcony for several minutes, listening to the piano music and letting it take my thoughts to forbidden places.

CHAPTER SEVEN

SUMMER AND IRON

The days settled into a safe, if not comfortable, routine. At dawn, before the sunlight touched the forest floor, I went out to the little clearing to practice sword drills with Ash. He was a patient yet strict teacher, pushing me to stretch beyond my comfort zone and fight like I meant to kill him. He taught me defense, how to dance around an enemy without getting hit, how to turn my opponents' energy against them. As my skill and confidence grew and our practice scuffles became more serious, I began to see a pattern, a rhythm in the art of swordplay. It became more like a dance: a tempo of spinning, darting blades and constant footwork. I was still nowhere near as good as Ash, and never would be, but I was learning.

Afternoons were spent talking to my dad, trying to get him to come out of his crazy-shell, feeling as if I was repeatedly bashing my head against a wall. It was a slow and painful process. His moments of lucidity were few and far between, and he didn't recognize me half the time. Most of our days progressed with him playing the piano while I sat on the nearby armchair and spoke to him whenever the music stopped. Sometimes Ash was there, lying on the couch reading a book; sometimes he disappeared into the forest for hours at a time. I didn't know where he was going or what he was doing, until rabbit and other animals started showing up on the plates for dinner and it occurred to me that Ash might be impatient with the lack of progress, too.

One day, however, he came back and handed me a large, leather-bound book. When I opened it, I was shocked to find pictures of my family staring back at me. Pictures of my family...before. Paul and my mom, on their wedding day. A cute, mixed-breed puppy I didn't recognize. Me as an infant, then a toddler, then a grinning four-year-old riding a tricycle.

"I called in a favor," Ash explained to my stunned expression. "The bogey living in your brother's closet found it for me. Maybe it will help your father remember."

I hugged him. He held me lightly, careful not to push or respond in a way that might lead to temptation. I savored the feel of his arms around me, breathing in his scent, before he gently pulled away. I smiled my thanks and turned to my father at the piano again.

"Dad," I murmured, carefully sitting beside him on the bench. He shot me a wary look, but at least he didn't flinch or jerk away and start banging on the piano keys. "I have something to show you. Look at this."

Opening the first page, I waited for him to look over. At first, he studiously ignored it, hunching his shoulders and not looking up. His gaze flickered to the album page once, but he continued to play, no change in his expression. After a few more minutes, I was ready to give up and retreat to the sofa to page through it myself, when the music suddenly faltered. Startled, I looked up at him, and my stomach twisted.

Tears were running down his face, splashing onto the piano keys. As I stared, transfixed, the music slowly stumbled to a halt, and my father began to sob. He bent over, and his long fingers traced the photos in the book as his tears dripped onto the pages and my hands. Ash quietly slipped from the room, and I put an arm around my dad and we cried together.

From that day on, he started to talk to me, slow, stuttering conversations at first, as we sat on the couch and thumbed through the photo album. He was so fragile, his sanity like spun glass that a breath of wind could shatter at any moment. But slowly, he began to remember Mom and me, and his old life, though he could never connect the little kid in the album with the teenager sitting beside him on the couch. He often asked where Mom and baby-Meghan were, and I had to tell him, again and again, that Mom was married to someone else now, that he had disappeared for eleven years, and she wasn't waiting for him anymore. And I had to watch the tears well in his eyes every time he heard it.

It made my soul ache.

Evenings were the hardest. Ash was as good as his word and never pushed, keeping all interactions between us light and easy. He never turned me away; when I needed someone to vent to after an exhausting day with my father, he was always there, quiet and strong. I would curl into him on the couch, and he would listen as I poured out my fears and frustrations. Sometimes we did nothing but read together, me lying in his lap while he turned the pages—though our tastes in books were vastly different, and I usually dozed off in the middle of a page. One night, bored and restless, I found a stack of dusty board games in a closet, and bullied Ash into learning Scrabble, checkers and Yahtzee. Surprisingly, Ash found that he enjoyed these "human" games, and was soon asking *me* to play more often than not. This filled some of the long, restless evenings and kept my mind off certain things. Unfortunately for me, once Ash learned the rules, he was nearly impossible to beat in strategy games like checkers, and his long life gave him a vast knowledge of lengthy, complicated words he staggered me with in Scrabble. Though sometimes we'd end up debating whether or not faery terms like *Gwragedd Annwn* and *hobyahs* were legal to use.

Regardless, I cherished our time together, knowing this peaceful lull would come to an end someday. But there was an invisible wall between us now, a barrier only I could break, and it was killing me.

And, even though I didn't want to, I missed Puck. Puck could always make me laugh, even when things were at their bleakest. Sometimes I'd catch a glimpse of a deer or a bird in the woods and wonder if it was Puck, watching us. Then I'd become angry at myself for wondering and spend the day trying to convince myself that I didn't care where he was or what he was doing.

But I still missed him.

One morning, a few weeks later, Ash and I were finishing up our daily practice session when Grimalkin appeared on a nearby stone, watching us.

"You're still telegraphing your moves," Ash said as we circled each other, blades held up and ready. "Don't look at the spot you're trying to hit, let the sword go there on its own." He lunged, cutting high at my head. I ducked and spun away, slashing at his back, and he parried the blow, looking pleased. "Good. You're getting faster, too. You'll be a match for most redcap thugs if they tried to start anything."

I grinned at the compliment, but Grimalkin, who had been silent until now, said, "And what happens if they use glamour against her?"

I turned. Grimalkin sat with his tail around his feet, watching a yellow bumblebee bob over the grass in rapt fascination. "What?"

"Glamour. You know, the magic I tried to teach you once, before I discovered you had no talent for it whatsoever?" Grimalkin swatted at the bee as it came closer, missed, and pretended no interest at all as it zipped away. He sniffed and looked at me again, twitching his tail. "The Winter prince does not just use his sword when fighting—he has glamour at his disposal as well, as will your enemies. How are you planning to counter that, human?" Before I could answer, he perked up, his attention riveted on a large orange butterfly flitting toward us, and leaped off the rock, vanishing into the tall grass.

I looked at Ash, who sighed and sheathed his blade. "He's right, unfortunately," he said, raking a hand through his hair. "Teaching you the sword was supposed to be only half of your training. I wanted you to learn how to use your glamour, as well."

"I know how to use glamour," I argued, still stinging from Grimalkin's casual statement about my lack of talent. Ash raised an eyebrow, a silent challenge, and I sighed. "Fine, then. I'll prove it. Watch this."

He backed up a few steps, and I closed my eyes, reaching out to the forest around me.

Instantly, my mind was filled with all manner of growing things: the grass beneath my feet, the vines slithering along the ground, the roots of the trees surrounding us. In this clearing, Summer held full sway. Whether through Leanansidhe's influence or something else, the plants here had not known the touch of winter, or cold, or death, for a long time.

Ash's voice cut through my concentration, and I opened my eyes. "You do have a lot of power, but you need to learn control if you're going to use it." He bent down, plucked something from the grass, and held it up. It was a tiny flower, white petals still tightly closed, curled into a ball.

"Make it bloom," Ash ordered softly.

Frowning, I stared at the little bud, mind racing. *Okay, I can do this. I've pulled up roots and made trees move and knocked a barrage of arrows from the air. I can make one teensy little flower bloom.* Still, I hesitated. Ash was right; I could feel the glamour all around me, but I was still unsure how to actually wield it.

"Would you like a hint?" Grimalkin asked from a nearby rock, startling me. I jumped, and he twitched an ear in amusement. "Picture the magic as a stream," he continued, "then a ribbon, then a thread. When it is as thin as you can possibly make it, use it to gently tease the petals open. Anything more forceful will make the bloom split apart and cause the glamour to scatter." He blinked sagely, then a butterfly near the stream caught his attention and he bounded off once more.

I looked at Ash, wondering if he was irritated at Grimalkin for helping me, but he only nodded. Taking a breath, I held the glamour in my mind, a swirling, colorful vortex of emotion and dream. Concentrating hard, I shrank it down until it was a shimmering rope, then even further, until it was only a shining, oh-so-delicate thread in my mind.

Sweat beaded and rolled down my forehead, and my arms started to shake. Holding my breath, I carefully touched the flower with the glamour thread, coiling magic into the tiny bud and expanding gently. The petals shivered once and slowly curled open.

Ash nodded approval. I smiled, but before I could celebrate, a bout of dizziness hit me like a tidal wave, nearly knocking me down. The world spun violently, and I felt my legs give out, as if someone had pulled a plug and let all my magic drain away. Gasping, I pitched forward.

Ash caught me, holding me upright. I clung to him, feeling almost sick with weakness, frustrated that something so natural was this hard. Ash lowered us both to the ground, pulling back to watch me with troubled silver eyes.

"Is…is it normal to be this tired?" I asked, as feeling slowly returned to my legs. Ash shook his head, his face dark and grim.

"No. That little amount of glamour should have been

nothing for you." He stood, crossing his arms over his chest, regarding me with a worried expression. "Something is wrong, and I don't know enough about Summer magic to help you." Holding out his hand, he pulled me to my feet with a sigh. "We're going to have to find Puck."

"What? No!" I let go of him too fast and stumbled, nearly falling again. "Why? We don't need Puck. What about Grimalkin? He can help, right?"

"Probably." Ash looked over to where Grimalkin was stalking butterflies through the grass, tail twitching in excitement. "Do you really want to ask him?"

I winced. "No, not really," I sighed. Stupid, favor-collecting cat. "Fine. But why Puck? Do you really think he'll know what's going on?"

Ash lifted one lean shoulder in a shrug. "I don't know. But he's been around longer than me and might know more about what's happening to you. The least we can do is ask."

"I don't want to see him." I crossed my arms, scowling. "He lied to me, Ash. And don't tell me that faeries can't lie—omitting the truth is just as bad. He let me believe my dad abandoned us, and he knew where he was all along. Eleven years, he lied to me. I can't forgive him for that."

"Meghan, believe me, I know what it's like to hate Puck. I've been at it for longer than you, remember?" Ash softened his words with a rueful smile, but I still felt a stab of guilt. "Trust me, I don't particularly want to go begging for his help, either." He sighed, raking a hand through his hair. "But if anyone is to teach you Summer magic, it should be him. I can only show you the basics, and you're going to need more than that."

My anger deflated. Of course, he was right. My shoulders sagged and I glared at him. "I hate it when you're reasonable."

He laughed. "Someone has to be. Come on." He turned and held out a hand. "If we're going to find Goodfellow, we should get started now. If he's hiding, or if he doesn't want to be found, we could be searching awhile."

Taking his hand, I resigned myself as we crossed the meadow and slipped into the thick forest surrounding it.

IN THE END, PUCK FOUND US.

The woods surrounding the cabin were sprawling and vast, mostly pine and big, shaggy trees with furry trunks. It made me think we were high in the mountains somewhere. Ferns and pine needles littered the forest floor; the air was cool and smelled of sap.

Ash slipped through the woods like a ghost, following some invisible path, keen hunter instincts showing the way. As we hiked, ducking branches and scrambling over needle-covered rocks, my insides churned angrily. Why did Puck have to help us? What would he know? My dad's face swam before me, tears shining from his eyes as I told him, once again, that Mom was married to someone else, and I clenched my fists. Whether my dad's abduction was planned or not, Puck had a lot to answer for.

Ash brought us to a grotto surrounded by pine trees and stopped, gazing around. I joined him, taking his hand as we searched the trunks and shadows. It was very quiet. Threads of sunlight slanted in through the trees and dappled the forest floor, covered in mushrooms and pine needles. The trees here were old, thick creatures, and the air seemed filled with ancient magic.

"He's been here," Ash said, as a breeze stirred the branches, ruffling his dark hair. "In fact, he's very close."

"Looking for something?"

The familiar voice echoed from somewhere above us. I turned, and there was Puck, lying on an overhead branch, smirking at me. His shirt was off, showing a lean, bronzed chest, and his red hair was all over the place. He looked more...I don't know...*fey* out here, something wild and unpredictable, more like Shakespeare's Robin Goodfellow, who turned Nick Bottom into a donkey and wreaked havoc on the humans lost in the forest.

"Rumor going round these parts is that you're looking for me," he said, tossing an apple in one hand before biting into it. "Well, here I am. What do you want, *your highnesses?*"

I bristled at the implied insult, but Ash stepped forward. "Something is wrong with Meghan's glamour," he said, brief and to the point as usual. "You know more about Summer magic. We need to know what's happened to her, why she can't use glamour without almost passing out."

"Ah." Puck's emerald eyes sparkled with glee. "And so they come crawling back for Puck's help after all. Tsk tsk." He shook his head and took another bite of the apple. "How easy it is to forget grudges when someone has something you need."

I swelled indignantly, but Ash sighed, as if he'd expected this. "What do you want, Goodfellow?" he asked wearily.

"I want the princess to ask me," Puck said, switching his gaze to mine. "I'll be helping *her,* after all. I want to hear it from her own frosted pink lips."

I pressed my pink lips together to keep back a nasty reply. *Glad to see at least one of us is being mature about this,* I wanted to say, which wouldn't have been very mature at all. Besides, Ash was watching me, all solemn and serious, and a little bit pleading. If he could swallow his pride and ask his archnemesis for help, I guess I could be the grown-up here, too.

For now.

I sighed. "Fine." *But there will be repercussions later, believe me.* "Puck, I'd really appreciate it if you helped me out a little." He raised an eyebrow, and I grit my teeth. "Please."

He flashed me a smug grin. "Help you out with what, princess?"

"My magic."

"What's wrong with it?"

I was sorely tempted to fling a rock at his head, but he wasn't flashing me that stupid grin anymore, so maybe he was being serious. "I don't know," I sighed. "I can't use glamour anymore without getting either really tired or really sick. I don't know what's wrong with me. It didn't used to be like this."

"Huh." Puck jumped down from the tree, landing as lightly as a cat. He took two steps toward us and stopped, peering at me with intense green eyes. "When was the last time you used glamour, princess? Without getting sick or tired?"

I thought back. I'd used Summer magic on the spider-hags and nearly thrown up with the effort. Before that, my glamour had been sealed by Mab, so... "The warehouse," I answered, remembering the battle with another of Machina's old lieutenants. "When we fought Virus. You were there, remember? I stopped her bugs from swarming all over us."

Puck bobbed his head, looking thoughtful. "But that was *Iron* magic, wasn't it, princess?" he asked, and I nodded. "When was the last time you used Summer glamour, normal glamour, without feeling sick or tired?"

"Machina's realm," Ash said softly, looking at me. Understanding was beginning to dawn on him, though I had no idea where this was leading. "You pulled up the roots to trap the Iron King," he went on, "right before he stabbed you. Right before he died."

"That's where you got your Iron glamour, princess," Puck added, nodding thoughtfully. "I'd bet Titania's golden mirror on it. You somehow got stuck with Machina's Iron magic— that's why the false king wants you, I'd wager. It has something to do with the power of the Iron King."

I shivered. Glitch had said as much, but I hadn't wanted to think about it. "So what does that have to do with my glamour problems?" I asked.

Ash and Puck shared a look. "Because, princess," Puck

said, leaning back against a tree, "you have two powers inside you right now, Summer and Iron. And, simply put, they're not getting along."

"They can't exist together," Ash put in, as if he'd just figured it out. "Whenever you try, one glamour reacts violently to the other, the same way we react to iron. So the Summer glamour is making you sick because it touched Iron magic, and vice versa."

Puck whistled. "Now that's a Catch-22."

"But…but I used Iron glamour before this," I protested, not liking their explanations at all. "In the factory with Virus. And I didn't have any problems then. We'd all be dead otherwise."

"Your regular magic was sealed then." Ash frowned, deep in thought. "When we went to Winter, Mab put a binding on you, sealing away your Summer magic. She didn't know about the Iron glamour." He looked up. "After the binding shattered, that's when you started having difficulty."

I crossed my arms in frustration. "This is so not fair," I muttered, as Ash and Puck looked on with varying degrees of sympathy. I glared at them both. "What am I supposed to do now?" I demanded. "How am I supposed to fix this?"

"You'll have to learn to use them both," Ash said calmly. "There has to be a way to wield both glamours separately, without one tainting the other."

"Maybe it'll get easier with practice," Puck added, and that irritating smirk came creeping back. "I could teach you. How to use Summer glamour at least. If you want me to."

I stared at him, searching for a hint of my former best friend, for a spark of the affection we'd had for each other. The obnoxious smirk never wavered, but I saw something in his eyes, a glimmer of remorse, perhaps? Whatever it was, it was enough. I couldn't do this alone. Something told me I was going to need all the help I could get.

"Fine," I told him, watching his smile turn dangerously

close to a leer. "But this doesn't mean we're okay. I still haven't forgiven you for what you did to my family."

Puck sighed dramatically and glanced at Ash. "Join the club, princess."

CHAPTER EIGHT

UNDERSTANDING MEASURES

So, there we were again, the three of us: me, Ash, and Puck, together once more but not really the same. I practiced sword drills with Ash in the morning, and Summer magic with Puck in the afternoon, usually around the hottest part of the day. In the evenings, I listened to the piano or talked to my dad, while trying to ignore the obvious tension between the two faeries in the room. Paul was doing better, at least, his moments of confusion fewer and farther between. The morning he made breakfast, I got teary-eyed with relief, although our resident brownies threw a fit and nearly left the house. I was able to woo them back with bowls of cream and honey, and the promise that Paul wouldn't intrude on their chores again.

My glamour use didn't get any better.

Every day, when the sun was at its zenith, I'd leave the lunch table and wander down to the meadow, where Puck waited for me. He showed me how to call glamour from plants, how to make them grow faster, how to weave illusions from nothing, and how to call on the forest for help. Summer magic was the magic of life, heat, and passion, he explained. The new growth of Spring, the lethal beauty of fire, the violent destruction of a summer storm—all were examples of Summer magic in the everyday world. He demonstrated small miracles—making a dead flower come back to life, calling a squirrel right into his lap—and then instructed me to do the same.

I tried. Calling the magic was easy; it came as naturally as breathing. I could feel it all around me, pulsing with life and energy. But when I tried to use it in any way, nausea hit and I was left gasping in the dirt, so sick and dizzy I felt I would pass out.

"Try again," Puck said one afternoon, sitting cross-legged on a flat rock by the stream, chin in his hands. Between us, a mop handle stood upright in the grass like a naked tree. Puck had "borrowed" it from the broom closet earlier that morning, and would probably incur the wrath of the brownies when they discovered one of their sacred tools missing.

I glared at the mop handle, taking a deep breath. I was supposed to make the stupid thing bloom with roses and such, but all I'd done was given myself a massive headache. Drawing glamour to me, I tried again. *Okay, concentrate, Meghan. Concentrate…*

Ash appeared at the edge of my vision, arms crossed, watching us intently. "Any luck?" he murmured, easily breaking my concentration.

Puck gestured to me. "See for yourself."

Annoyed with them both, I focused on the mop. *Wood is wood,* Puck had said that morning. *Be it a dead tree, the side of a ship, a wooden crossbow, or a simple broom handle, Summer magic can make it come alive again, if only for a moment. This is your birthright. Concentrate.*

Glamour swirled around me, raw and powerful. I sent it toward the mop, and the sickness descended like a hammer, making my stomach clench. I doubled over with a gasp, fighting the urge to vomit. If this is what faeries experienced every time they touched something made of iron, it was no wonder they avoided it like the plague.

"This isn't working," I heard Ash say. "She should stop before she really gets hurt."

"No!" Pulling myself upright, I glared at the mop, wiping sweat from my eyes. "I'm going to get this, dammit." Ignoring my roiling stomach, the sweat that ran into my eyes, I took another deep breath and concentrated on the glamour swirling around the mop. The wood was alive, pulsing with energy, just waiting for the push that would make it explode with life.

The wooden pole trembled. Nausea crawled up my stomach. I bit my lip, welcoming the pain. And suddenly, roses burst into bloom along the handle, red and white and pink and orange, a riot of color among the leaves and thorns. As quickly as they had bloomed, the petals shriveled and fell off, littering the ground around the mop handle, bare and naked once more. But it was a clear victory, and I whooped in triumph—right before I collapsed.

Ash caught me, kneeling in the grass. How he knew exactly where to be whenever I fell was mystifying. "There," I panted, struggling upright, bracing myself against his arms. "That wasn't so hard. I think I'm getting the hang of this. Let's do it again, Puck."

Puck raised an eyebrow. "Uh, let's not, princess. Judging by the glare your boyfriend is shooting me, I'd say our lesson is officially over." He yawned and stood, stretching his long limbs. "Besides, I was about to die of boredom. Watching flowers bloom isn't exactly riveting." He glanced at us, at Ash's arms around me, and sneered. "See you tomorrow, lovebirds."

He hopped the stream and vanished into the woods without looking back. I sighed and struggled to my feet, leaning on Ash for balance.

"You all right?" he asked, steadying me as the last of the nausea faded.

Anger flared. No, I wasn't all right. I was a freaking faery who couldn't use glamour! Not without fainting, throwing up, or getting so dizzy I was practically useless. I was allergic to myself! How pathetic was that?

Peevishly, I turned and kicked the mop handle, sending the pole clattering into the bushes. The wrath of the brownies would be swift and terrible, but at that moment I didn't care. What good was having Iron glamour if all it did was make me sick? At this point, I was ready to *give* the false king his stupid Iron magic, for all the good it did me.

Ash raised an eyebrow at my show of temper but didn't say anything beyond, "Let's go inside." A little embarrassed, I followed him across the clearing, over the stream and up the stairs to the cabin, where Grimalkin lay on the railing in the sun and ignored me when I waved.

The cabin was strangely quiet as we walked in, the piano empty and still. I looked around and saw Paul sitting at the kitchen table, bent over a mess of scattered papers, pen scribbling furiously. I hoped he hadn't fallen into creative insanity. But he glanced up, gave me a brief, noncrazy smile, and hunched over the paperwork once more. So today was one of his saner days; at least that was something.

Groaning, I collapsed to the couch, my fingers numb and tingly with leftover glamour. "What's wrong with me, Ash?" I sighed, rubbing my tired eyes. "Why does everything have to be so hard? I can't even be a normal half-faery."

Ash knelt and tugged my hands down, pressing my fingers to his lips. "You were never normal, Meghan." He smiled, and my fingers went tingly for an entirely different reason. "If you were, I wouldn't be here now."

I freed my fingers and stroked his cheek, running my thumb over the smooth, pale skin. For a moment, he closed his eyes and leaned into my hand before brushing a kiss to my palm and standing up. "I'm going to find Puck," he announced. "There must be something we're missing, something we're overlooking. There has to be an easier way."

"Well, if you find it, that would be great. I'm sick of being…sick…every time I make a flower grow." I tried for a grateful smile, but think I just grimaced at him. Ash placed a hand on my shoulder, squeezed gently, and left the room.

Sighing, I wandered over to the kitchen table, curious to see what Dad was working on so vigorously. He didn't look up this time, so I perched on the edge beside him. The table was covered with sheets of paper, scribbled with lines and black dots. Looking closer, I saw they were hand-drawn sheet music.

"Hey, Dad." I spoke softly, not wanting to distract or startle him. "What are you doing?"

"Composing a song," he replied, glancing at me briefly and smiling. "It just hit me this morning, and I knew I had to write it down quickly before I lost it. I used to write songs all the time for…for your mother."

I didn't know what to say to that, so I watched the pencil move, scribbling dots along five simple black lines. It didn't look like music to me, but Dad would stop and close his eyes, swaying the pencil to an invisible tune, before adding more dots to the lines.

My vision went fuzzy for a moment, and the dots seemed to move on the paper. For just a second, the entire song shimmered with glamour. The strict, straight lines gleamed like metal wires, while the various notes, once black and solid, sparkled like drops of water held up to light. Startled, I blinked, and the scribbles became normal again.

"Weird," I muttered.

"What's weird?" Paul asked, looking up.

"Um." Quickly, I searched for a safer topic. Dad didn't have a high regard for glamour, seeing it as nothing more than faery tricks and deception. With everything he'd gone through, I couldn't blame him. "Um," I said again. "I was just wondering...what all those little dots and lines are for. I mean, it doesn't look like music to me."

Paul smiled, eager to talk about his favorite subject, and pulled a full sheet of paper from a stack. "They're measures," he explained, placing the sheet between us. "See these lines? Each line represents a musical pitch. Every note on a scale is represented by its position on the line or in the spaces between. The higher the note is on the lines, the higher the pitch. Follow me so far?"

"Ummm..."

"Now, notice the different dots, or notes," Dad went on, as if I understood anything he just said. "An open dot plays longer than a closed dot. The little stems and flags you see cut the time in half, and in half again. The appearance of the notes tells the player how long to hold them, and what note to play. Everything is measured by time, pitch, and scale, written in perfect harmony. One note or measure in the wrong place will throw off the entire song."

"Sounds very complicated," I offered, trying to keep up with his explanation.

"It can be. Music and math have always been tied closely together. It's all about formulas and fractions and such." Paul stood abruptly with the sheet of music and walked over to the piano. I trailed behind him and perched on the couch. "But then, you put it all together, and it sounds like *this*."

And he played a song so beautiful it caught in my throat, making me want to smile and laugh and cry all at the same time. I'd heard his music before, but this was different, as if he'd put his entire heart and soul into it, and it had grown a life of its own. Glamour flared and swirled around him, a vortex of the most gorgeous colors I'd ever seen. No wonder the fey were attracted to talented mortals. No wonder Leanansidhe had been so reluctant to let him go.

The piece was short and ended abruptly, as if Paul just

ran out of notes. "Well, it's not finished yet," he murmured, lowering his hands, "but you get the idea."

"What's it called?" I whispered, the echo of the song still ebbing through me. Paul smiled.

"Memories of Meghan."

Before I could say anything, the door banged open and Ash stepped through with Puck close behind him. I jumped up as Ash crossed the room, his face tight and severe, and Puck stood in front of the door with his arms crossed, glaring out the window.

"What's going on?" I asked as Ash drew close, looking like he wanted to sweep me up and rush out the door. I glanced at my dad to see how this was affecting him, relieved to see he looked wary and alarmed but not crazy. Ash took my arm and drew me away.

"The Seelie and Unseelie Courts," he muttered, low enough that my father couldn't hear. "They're here, and they're looking for you."

CHAPTER NINE

A KNIGHT'S VOW

I blinked at Ash, and my stomach squirmed weirdly, both in excitement and fear. "Both of them?" I whispered, glancing at my dad, who had wandered back to the table and was hunched over his music again. He tended to ignore the faeries whenever they were in the room, never speaking to them, barely looking their way, and the boys were content to return the favor. It made for some awkward evenings, but I think Paul was terrified that if he drew their attention, he would go mad once more.

Ash shrugged. "They wouldn't talk to me or Puck, except to say that Leanansidhe already gave them permission to come here. They want to speak with you. They're in the clearing now."

I walked to the window and peered out. At the edge of the trees, I could just make out a pair of sidhe knights each holding a banner, one green and gold and emblazoned with the head of a magnificent stag, the other black with a white, thorny rose in the center.

"The emissary said he had a message specifically for you, princess," Puck said, leaning against the door with his arms crossed. "Said it was from Oberon himself."

"Oberon." The last time I saw my biological father, he had banished me to the mortal realm after Mab had done the same to Ash. I thought we had severed all ties; he'd made that quite clear when we parted, that I was on my own and Faery would never welcome me again. What did the King of the Summer Court want with me now?

Only one way to find out. "Dad," I called, turning toward the table, "I'm leaving now, but I'll be right back. Don't leave the house, okay?"

He waved at me without looking up, and I sighed. At least Paul would be too busy to worry about the unexpected party in the meadow. "All right," I muttered, walking toward the door, which Puck opened for me. "Let's get this over with."

We crossed the stream, where Grimalkin was grooming himself on a flat rock, unconcerned with the arrival of the courts, and headed toward the far side of the meadow. It was late afternoon, and fireflies winked over the grass. Ash and Puck walked beside me, protective auras glowing strong, and any fear I had vanished instantly. We had been through so much, the three of us. What was left, that we couldn't face together?

The two knights bowed as we approached. I caught a glimmer of surprise from both Ash and Puck, amazement that two warriors from opposite courts could be in the presence of the other without fighting. I found it amusingly ironic.

Between the knights, almost hidden in the tall grass, a potato-faced gnome stepped forward and bent forward at the waist. "Meghan Chase," he greeted in a surprisingly deep voice, stiff and formal like a butler. "Your father, Lord Oberon, sends his greetings."

I felt a flicker of annoyance. Oberon had no right to claim me as his daughter. Not after disowning me in front of the entire freaking court. Crossing my arms, I glared down at the gnome. "You wanted to see me. Here I am. What does Oberon want now?"

The gnome blinked. The knights exchanged a glance. Puck and Ash stood tall beside me, silent and protective. Even though I wasn't looking at them, I could sense Puck's gleeful amusement.

The gnome cleared his throat. "Ahem. Well, as you know, princess, your father is at war with the Iron Kingdom. For the first time in centuries, we have created a mutual alliance with Queen Mab and the Winter Court." His gaze flicked to Ash before focusing on me again. "An army of Iron fey crouches at our doorstep, eager to taint our land and kill everyone in it. The situation has become most dire."

"I know that. In fact, I think I was the one to first tell Oberon about it. Right before he exiled me." I held the gnome's gaze, trying to keep the bitterness from my voice. "I warned Oberon about the Iron King ages ago, him and Mab both. They didn't listen to me. Why are you telling me this now?"

The gnome sighed and, for a moment, lost his formal tone. "Because, princess, the courts cannot touch him. The Iron King hides deep within his poisonous realm, and the forces of Summer and Winter cannot penetrate far enough to strike at him. We are losing ground, soldiers, and resources, and the Iron fey continue to advance on both courts. The Nevernever is dying faster than ever, and soon there will be no safe place for us to go."

He cleared his throat again, looking embarrassed, and became proper once more. "Because of this, King Oberon and Queen Mab are prepared to offer you a deal, Meghan Chase." He reached into his bag and drew forth a scroll tied with a green ribbon, unrolling it with a flourish.

"Here we go," muttered Puck.

The gnome frowned at him, then turned to the scroll and announced in a grand, important voice, "Meghan Chase, by

order of King Oberon and Queen Mab, the courts are willing to lift your exile, as well as the exiles of Prince Ash and
Robin Goodfellow, abolishing all crimes and rendering full
pardons."

Puck drew in a sharp breath. Ash stood silently; no expression showed on his face, but I caught the briefest flicker
of hope, of longing. They wanted to go home. They missed
Faery, and who could blame them? They belonged there, not
in the mortal world, with its vast skepticism and disbelief in
anything but science. Small wonder the Iron fey were taking
over the world; so few people believed in magic anymore.

But, because I knew faery bargains never came without a
price, I kept my expression blank and asked, "In return for
what?"

"In return..." The gnome dropped his hands, averting his
eyes. "For journeying into the Iron Realm and eliminating
its king."

I nodded slowly, suddenly very tired. "That's what I
thought."

Ash moved closer, drawing wary looks from the gnome
and the two guards. "By herself?" he said quietly, masking
the anger beneath. "Oberon isn't offering any help? Seems a
lot to ask, if his own armies can't get through."

"King Oberon believes that a single person could move
unseen through the Iron Realm," the gnome replied, "and
thus have a better chance of finding the Iron King. Both
Oberon and Mab agree that the Summer princess is the best
choice—she is immune to iron's effects, she has been there
before, and she has already taken down one Iron King."

"I had help then," I muttered, feeling a tightness spreading
through my stomach. Memories rose up, bleak and terrifying,
and despite myself, my hands started to shake. I remembered
the awful wasteland of the Iron Kingdom: the blasted desert,
the acid, flesh-eating rain, the imposing black tower, rising
into the sky. I remembered killing Machina, driving an arrow

through his chest, as the whole tower crumbled into shrapnel. And I remembered Ash, his body cold and lifeless in my arms, and clenched my fists so hard that my nails dug into my palms.

"I'm not ready," I said, looking to Ash and Puck for reassurance. "I can't go back there yet. I still have to learn to fight and to use glamour, and…and what about my dad? He can't stay here by himself."

The gnome blinked, looking confused, but Puck spoke up before he could say anything. "She'll need some time to think about it," he said, stepping forward with a disarming grin. "I assume Oberon doesn't need an answer right this very second, does he?"

The gnome regarded him gravely, yet spoke to me. "He did say time was of the essence, your highness. The longer you remain here, the farther the corruption spreads, and the stronger the Iron King becomes. Lord Oberon cannot wait. We will return at dawn for your answer." He bowed, and the knights stepped back, preparing to leave. "This is a onetime offer, highness," the gnome cautioned. "If you choose not to accept Oberon's offer and return to the Nevernever with us, none of you will ever see it again." He rolled up the paper with a flourish, and disappeared into the woods with the guards.

I walked back to the cabin in a daze, sinking onto the couch. Dad wasn't in the room, and the brownies hadn't started dinner yet, so we were alone. "I'm not ready," I said again, as Puck perched on the other arm and Ash stood, watching me gravely. "I barely took down the first Iron King, and that was with the Witchwood arrow. I don't have anything like that now."

"True," came Grimalkin's voice beside my head, making me jump. The cat blinked at my glare and settled comfortably onto the back cushions. "But that was specifically for

Machina. You do not know if that is needed for the false king."

"It doesn't matter," I said. "I don't have anything this time. I still can't use glamour well, I don't know how I'll do in a fight and—" I paused, nearly whispering the words "—I can't do it alone."

"Whoa, whoa, whoa." Puck stood and joined Ash in glaring at me. "What are you talking about, doing it alone? You know we're going to be right there with you, princess."

I shook my head. "Ash nearly died last time. The Iron Kingdom is deadly to fey, that's why Oberon and Mab can't beat it. I can't lose you both. If I do this, I have to do it alone."

I felt Ash's gaze sharpen, cutting into me. His fury was a cold, icy color, and it pricked my skin even as I felt my own anger rise up to meet it. He should know. Out of everyone, Ash knew how lethal the Iron Kingdom was to normal fey. What right did he have to be angry? I was the one who had to go into the Iron Kingdom. There was no way I'd put either of them through that torture again. I'd refuse Oberon's so-called deal, if it came to that.

And yet, if I refused, Ash and Puck would be stuck with me in the mortal realm, forever. This was their chance to go home. I couldn't deny them that, even if it meant I had to journey into the blasted land of the Iron fey once more and face the false king by myself.

"You know that's not going to work, princess," Puck said, reading my thoughts. "If you think you can keep me or ice-boy from following you into the Iron Realm—"

"I don't want you there!" I burst out, finally looking up. He blinked at me in astonishment, though Ash continued to stare at me with ice-cold eyes. "Dammit, Puck, you didn't see the Iron Realm. You don't know what it's like. Ask Ash!" I continued, pointing at the Ice Prince, knowing I was pushing him dangerously and not caring. "Ask him how just breathing the air was killing him from the inside. Ask him how I felt, watching him get worse and worse and not being able to do anything."

"And yet, I'm still here." Ash's voice was like brittle frost, his eyes darkened to black. "And it seems my promise means nothing to you. Will you release me from it now, when it is convenient to do so?"

"Ash." I looked up at him, hating that he was angry, but needing him to understand. "I can't watch you suffer again, not like that. If you follow me into the Iron Kingdom again, you could die, and that would kill me, too. You can't ask me to do that."

"It…" Ash stopped, closed his eyes for a moment. "It wasn't your choice, Meghan," he continued in a forced, even voice. "I knew the risks when I made that deal, and I know what will happen if I follow you into the Iron Realm. I would go with you, regardless." His voice grew sharper. "But that is beside the point. I *cannot* leave you now, unless you officially release me from my vow to stay."

Release him? Unmake a vow so he wasn't forced to follow me? "I didn't know you could do that," I murmured, feeling a brief regret and a little anger. "So, all that time in Machina's realm, I could have released you, and you wouldn't have had to help me?"

Ash hesitated, as if he didn't want to talk about it any longer, but Grimalkin spoke up from the back of the couch. "No, human," he purred. "That was a contract, not a *promise*. You both agreed to something, and you both got something out of it. That is the way of most bargains." Ash looked down, running a hand through his hair as Grimalkin licked a front paw. "A vow is made willingly, is self-inflicted, and places no requirements upon the recipient. No expectations whatsoever." He sniffed and scrubbed the paw over his ears. "Leaving the one trapped, completely at the mercy of the other…unless they decide to release him, of course."

"So…" I glanced at Ash. "I could release you from your promise, and you'd no longer have to keep it, right?"

Ash looked stricken, but only for a heartbeat. Then the air around him turned frigid, and frost crept over the wooden floor slats. Without a word, he turned and left the room, gliding through the front door and vanishing into the night.

Puck let out an explosive breath. "Ouch. You really know how to tear a guy's heart out, don't you, princess?"

I stared at the front door, feeling my heart sink. "Why is he so angry?" I whispered. "I'm just trying to keep him alive. I don't want him following me because he's being *forced* to by some stupid vow."

Puck winced. "That *stupid* vow is the most serious declaration we can make, princess," he said, and the edge in his voice surprised me. "We don't make promises lightly, if ever. And incidentally, releasing a faery from a vow is the worst insult in the world. You're basically telling him you don't trust him anymore, that you believe he's incapable of carrying it out."

I stood up. "That's not true at all," I protested, as Grimalkin slid from the back cushions to curl up in the spot I'd vacated. "I just don't want him staying with me because he *has* to."

"Jeez, you're thick sometimes." Puck shook his head as I gaped at him. "Princess, Ash would never have made that vow if he wasn't planning on following you anyway. Even if he never spoke it, do you think you could force him to stay behind?" He sneered. "I know you couldn't force *me*—I'm going with you whether you like it or not, so you can stop glaring. But, by all means…." He waved a hand at the door. "Go find ice-boy and free him from his silly promise. You'll never see him again, that's for certain. That's basically what releasing a faery means—you don't want them around any longer."

I slumped in defeat. "I just…I only wanted…I can't watch

either of you die," I muttered again, a weak excuse that sounded lamer by the second. Puck snorted.

"Come on, Meghan. A little faith, please?" He crossed his arms and gave me an annoyed look. "You're writing us off before we even get started. Me and ice-boy both. I've been around a long time, I intend to be around awhile longer."

"I didn't think it would come this soon." I started to sink back onto the couch, but stood up quickly as Grimalkin hissed at me. "I mean, I knew I had to face him eventually, the false king. But I thought I'd have more time to get ready." I scooted over a few feet, away from the cat, and perched on the arm. "All this time, I've felt that I've just been floundering, getting lucky again and again. That luck's going to run out someday."

"It got us this far, princess." Puck walked over and put an arm around me. I didn't shrug it off. I was tired of fighting. I wanted my best friend back. Leaning against him, I listened to the brownies scuttle back and forth in the kitchen. The smell of baking bread wafted into the room, warm and comforting. Our last meal, perhaps?

Way to think positive, Meghan.

"You're right," I said. "And I have to do this. I know that. If I ever want a normal life, I have to face the false king or he'll never leave me alone." I sighed and walked over to the window, brooding into the coming twilight. "It's just...this time it feels different," I said, seeing my reflection in the glass, staring back at me. "I have so much more to lose. You and Ash, the Nevernever, my family, my dad." I stopped, resting my forehead against the glass. "My dad," I groaned. "What am I going to do with my dad?"

There was a thump from the hallway, and I closed my eyes. Well, that was just about perfect timing. I sighed and straightened up. "How long have you been standing there, Dad?"

"From about the time you were talking about luck." Paul

came into the room, sitting across on the piano bench. I watched him in the glass reflection. "You're leaving, aren't you?" he asked softly.

Puck stood and discreetly wandered out the door, leaving me and Dad alone except for the snoozing Grimalkin. I hesitated, then nodded. "I hate to leave you alone like this," I said, turning around. "I wish I didn't have to go."

Paul's brow was furrowed, as if he was struggling to understand, but his eyes remained clear as he slowly nodded. "This is...important?" he asked.

"Yeah."

"Will you be back?"

My throat closed. I swallowed and took a deep breath to open it. "I hope so."

"Meghan." Dad hesitated, fighting for words. "I know...I don't understand a lot of things. I know you're...part of something beyond me, something I won't ever understand. And I'm supposed to be your father, but...but I know you can handle yourself just fine. So, you go." He smiled then, the wrinkles around his eyes creasing. "Don't say goodbye, and don't worry about me. You do what you have to do. I'll be here when you come back."

I smiled at him. "Thanks, Dad."

He nodded, but then his eyes went glassy, as if he'd used up his allotment of sanity with that conversation. Sniffing the air, he perked up, his face brightening like a little kid's. "Food?"

I nodded, feeling suddenly old. "Yeah. Why don't you go back to your room, and I'll call you when dinner is ready, okay? You can...work on your song until then."

"Oh. Right." He beamed at me as he rose, walking back to the hallway. "It's almost done, you know," he announced over his shoulder, swelling with pride. "It's for my daughter, but I'll play it for you tomorrow, okay?"

"Okay," I whispered, and he was gone.

Silence filled the room, broken only by the ticking of the clock on the wall and the occasional scuffle from the kitchen. I walked back to the couch and sank down next to Grimalkin, uncertain what to do next. I knew I should find Ash and apologize, or at least explain why I hadn't wanted him to come. My stomach was in knots, knowing he was angry with me. I had only wanted to spare him more pain; how was I supposed to know releasing a faery from his promise was such a breach of trust?

"If you are so worried about him," Grimalkin said into the quiet, "why not ask him to be your knight?"

I blinked at him. "What?"

His eyes cracked open, slitted and gold, watching me in amusement. "Your knight," he said again, slower this time. "You do understand the word, do you not? It has not been that long for humans to forget."

"I know what a knight is, Grim."

"Oh, good. Then it should be easy for you to understand the significance." Grimalkin sat up and yawned, curling his tail around his legs. "It is an old tradition," he began. "Even among the fey. A lady asks a warrior to become her knight, her chosen protector, for as long as they both draw breath. Only those with royal blood can enact this ritual, and the choosing of a champion is something only the lady can do. But it is the ultimate show of faith between the lady and the knight, for she trusts him above all others to keep her safe, knowing that he would lay down his life for her. The knight still obeys his queen and court, to the best of his ability, but his first and only duty is to his lady." He yawned again and stuck one hind leg into the air, examining his toes. "A charming tradition, to be sure. The courts love such dramatic tragedies."

"Why is it a tragedy?"

"Because," came Ash's voice from the doorway, making me jump, "should the lady die, the knight will die, as well."

I stood quickly, heart pounding. Ash didn't enter the room, continuing to watch me from the frame. His glamour aura was hidden, carefully concealed, and his silver eyes were cold and blank. "Walk with me outside," he ordered softly, and when I hesitated, added, "please."

I glanced at Grimalkin, but the cat was curled up once more with his eyes closed, purring in content. *Wretched cat,* I thought, following Ash down the stairs into the warm summer night. *He wouldn't care if Ash cut me down or turned me into an icicle. Probably has a bet going with Leanansidhe to see how long that will take.*

Shocked and feeling guilty that I could think that, about both Ash and Grimalkin, I trailed the Winter prince across the stream and through the meadow in silence. Fireflies hovered over the grass, turning the clearing into a tiny galaxy of winking lights, and a breeze ruffled my hair, smelling of pine and cedar. I realized I would miss this place. Despite everything, it was the closest to normal I'd come in a long time. Here, I wasn't a faery princess, I wasn't the daughter of a powerful king, or a pawn in the eternal struggles of the courts. Tomorrow at dawn, that would all change.

"If you're going to release me," Ash murmured, and I heard the faintest tremor beneath his voice, "do it now so that I can go. I'd rather not be here when you return to the Nevernever."

I stopped, which made him stop, though he didn't turn around. I gazed at his back, at the strong shoulders and midnight-dark hair, at the proud, stiff set of his spine. Waiting for me to determine his fate. *If you really cared for him,* a voice whispered in my mind, *you would set him free. You'd be apart, but he would still be alive. Letting him follow you into the Iron Realm could kill him, you know that.* But the thought of him leaving punched a hole in my heart that left me gasping inside. I couldn't do it. I couldn't let him go. Gods forgive me if I was being selfish, but I wanted nothing more than to stay with him forever.

"Ash," I murmured, which made him flinch, bracing himself. My heart pounded, but I ignored my doubts and hurried on. "I...will..." Closing my eyes, I took a deep breath and whispered, "Will you be my knight?"

He spun, eyes widening for the briefest of moments. For a few heartbeats, he stared at me, surprise and disbelief written across his face. I gazed back, wondering if it had been a mistake to ask, if I had only bound him further and he would resent being forced into another contract.

I shivered as he approached, coming to stand just a few inches away. Slowly, he reached for my hand, barely holding my fingers as his eyes met mine. "Are you sure?" he asked, so quietly the breeze might've blown it away.

I nodded. "But, only if you want to. I would never force—"

Releasing my hand, he took a half step back, and then lowered himself to one knee, bowing his head. My heart turned over, and I bit my lip, blinking back tears.

"My name is Ashallyn'darkmyr Tallyn, third son of the Unseelie Court." Though his voice was soft, it never wavered, and I felt breathless at hearing his full name. His True Name. "Let it be known—from this day forth, I vow to protect Meghan Chase, daughter of the Summer King, with my sword, my honor, and my life. Her desires are mine. Her wishes are mine. Should even the world stand against her, my blade will be at her side. And should it fail to protect her, let my own existence be forfeit. This I swear, on my honor, my True Name, and my life. From this day on..." His voice went even softer, but I still heard it as though he whispered it into my ear. "I am yours."

I couldn't stop the tears anymore. They clouded my vision and rolled down my cheeks, and I didn't bother to wipe them away. Ash stood, and I threw myself into his arms, feeling him tremble as he crushed me close. He was mine now, my knight, and nothing would come between us.

"Well," Puck sighed, his voice drifting over the grass. "I was wondering how long it would take to get to that."

I turned, and Ash released me, very slowly. Puck sat on a rock near the stream, fireflies buzzing around him, alighting in his hair and making it glow like embers. He wasn't smirking or sneering at us. Just watching.

A flicker of alarm rippled through me as he hopped up and approached, trailing fireflies. How long had he been there, watching us? "Did you hear…?"

"Ice-boy's True Name? Nah." Puck shrugged, lacing his hands behind his head. "Hard as it is to believe, I wouldn't intrude on something that serious, princess. Especially since I know you'd kill me later." One corner of his lip twitched, just slightly, nowhere near his usual wide grin. He glanced at Ash and shook his head, his expression one of amusement and…could it be respect? "Mab is going to love that, you know."

Ash gave a faint smile. "I find I no longer care what the Winter Court thinks of me."

"It's liberating, isn't it?" Puck snorted, then sat down in the grass, turning his face to the sky. "So, this is our last night as exiles, huh?" he mused, leaning back on his elbows. Fireflies rose from the grass in a blinking cloud. "It seems weird, but I might actually miss this. No one pulling my strings, no one bossing me around—except irate brownies demanding their brooms back, putting spiders in my bed. It's…relaxing." Glancing at me, he patted the ground.

I lowered myself into the cool, damp grass as blips of amber and green buzzed around us, landing on my hands, in my hair. Looking at Ash, I took his hand and tugged him down, as well. He settled behind me, lacing his arms around my waist, and I leaned against him and closed my eyes. In another life, perhaps, it would've been the three of us: me, my best friend, and my boyfriend, just hanging out under the stars, maybe breaking curfew, worried about nothing except school and parents and homework.

"What are we doing, here?" came Grimalkin's voice as the cat slipped through the grass beside me, bottlebrush tail in the air. A firefly landed on the tip, and he flicked it off irritably. "This looks remarkably close to relaxing, if I did not know a certain prince is far too uptight to relax."

Ash chuckled and drew me tighter against him. "Feeling left out, cait sith?"

Grimalkin sniffed. "Do not flatter yourself." But he minced his way across the grass and curled up in my lap, a warm heavy weight with soft gray fur. I scratched behind his ear, and he vibrated with purrs.

"Do you think my dad will be all right?" I asked, and Grimalkin yawned.

"He will be safer here than he would be in the real world, human," the cat replied in a lazy voice. "No one enters this place without Leanansidhe's permission, and no one leaves unless she allows it. Do not worry overmuch." He flexed his claws, looking content. "The human will still be here when you return. Or even if you do not. Now, if you would attend to the other ear, that would be nice. Ah...yes, that is quite satisfactory." His voice trailed off into rumbling purrs.

Ash laid his cheek against the back of my head and sighed. It wasn't a sigh of irritation or anger or the melancholy that seemed to plague him at times. He sounded...content. Peaceful, even. It made me a little sad, knowing we couldn't have more time, that this could be our last night together, without war and politics and faery laws coming between us.

Ash brushed the hair from my neck and leaned close to my ear, his voice so soft not even Grimalkin could've heard it. "I love you," he murmured, and my heart nearly burst out of my chest. "Whatever happens, we're together now. Always."

We sat there, the four of us, talking quietly or just bask-
ing in the silence, watching the night sky. I didn't see any
falling stars, but if I had, I would've wished my dad be kept
safe, that Ash and Puck would survive the coming war, and
that somehow, we all would come out of this okay. *If wishes
were horses.* I knew better. Fairy godmothers didn't exist,
and even if they did, they wouldn't wave a magic wand and
make everything better. (Not without a contract, anyway.)
Besides, I had something better than a fairy godmother; I
had my faery knight, my faery trickster, and my faery cat,
and that was enough.

In the end, it didn't matter. A simple wish wouldn't save us
from what we had to do, and my mind was made up. When
dawn turned the sky pink and the envoys came for us again,
I already had my answer.

PART TWO

CHAPTER TEN

THE EDGE OF IRON

Faery was not how I remembered.

I recalled the first time I stepped into the Nevernever through the door in Ethan's closet. I remembered the enormous trees, so close and tangled that their branches shut out the sky, the mist writhing along the ground, the perpetual twilight that hung over everything. Here in the wyldwood, neither court held sway; it was a fierce, neutral territory that cared nothing for the medieval customs of Summer or the vicious society of Winter.

And it was dying.

It was a subtle thing, the taint that had sunk deep into the land and forest, corrupting them from the inside. Here and there, a tree was empty of leaves, and a rosebush had steel thorns that glinted in the light. I walked into a spiderweb, only to discover it was made of hair-thin wires, much like the net the spider-hags had used on me. Outwardly, the change was faint, almost invisible. But the beating heart of the Nevernever, which I felt all around me in every tree, every leaf and blade of grass, was pulsing with rot. Everything was touched with Iron glamour, and it was slowly eating away the Nevernever, like paper held above a flame.

And, judging from the twin looks of horror on the faces of Ash and Puck, they felt it, too.

"It's awful, isn't it?" said the gnome envoy, gazing around solemnly. "Not long after you were…ahem…banished, the Iron King's army attacked, and wherever they went, the Iron Realm spread with them. The combined forces of Summer and Winter were able to drive them back, but even after they were gone, the poison remained. Our armies are camped on the edge, where the wyldwood meets the Iron Kingdom, to try to halt the Iron fey that keep pouring from the breach."

"You're only defending the line?" Ash turned his cold gaze on the gnome, who shrank from him. "What about a frontal assault, to close it completely?"

The gnome shook his head. "It doesn't work. We've sent numerous forces into the breach, but none of them have ever come back."

"And the Iron King has never once showed his ugly face in battle?" Puck asked. "He just sits back like a coward and lets the army come to him?"

"Of course he does." Grimalkin sniffed, wrinkling his whiskers in distaste. "Why would he endanger himself when he has all the advantages? He has time on his side—the courts do not. Oberon and Mab must be desperate if they are willing to lift your exile. I cannot think of another time when they have been willing to retract their orders." He blinked and looked at me, narrowing his eyes. "Things must indeed be serious. It appears you are the final hope to save the entire Nevernever."

"Thanks, Grim. I certainly needed that reminder." I sighed, pushing bleak, terrifying thoughts to the back of my mind, and turned to the emissary. "I suppose Oberon is waiting for me?"

"He is, your highness." The gnome bobbed his head and pattered off. "This way, please. I will take you to the battlefront."

FROM THE TOP OF THE RISE, I looked down into the valley where the Summer and Winter armies were camped.

Tents were set up in a loose, haphazard pattern, looking like a small city of colored cloth and muddy streets. Even from this distance, I could see the distinction between the Seelie and Unseelie: the Seelie preferred lighter, summer-colored tents of brown and green and yellow, while the Unseelie camp was marked by shades of black, blue, and dark red. Even though they were on the same side, Summer and Winter did not mingle, did not share the same space or even the same side of the valley. In the center, however, where the two camps seemed to converge, a larger structure rose into the air, flying the banners of the two courts side by side. At least Mab and Oberon were trying to get along. For now, anyway.

Beyond the camps, a twisted forest of glimmering steel marked the entrance into the realm of the Iron King.

Beside me, Ash scanned the battlefront with narrowed eyes, taking everything in. "They've had to fall back several times," he murmured, his voice low and grave. "The entire camp looks ready to get up and move at a word. I wonder how fast the Iron Realm is spreading."

"Guess we're about to find out," Puck added, as the gnome emissary beckoned us forward and we descended into the camp.

The city of tents was much larger and sprawling up close, renewing my uneasiness for walking through a large group of fey, seeing their glowing, inhuman eyes follow my every move. Thankfully, we only had to walk through the Seelie camp to get to the large tent in the middle, though Puck and Ash stayed very close as we navigated the narrow streets. Elegant Summer knights, clad in armor stylized to look like thousands of overlapping leaves, watched us stonily, their eyes never leaving the Winter prince at my side. A pair of sylphs, razor dragonfly wings scraping together, scurried out of our way, staring at me with unabashed curiosity. A tethered griffin raised its head and hissed, flaring a colorful mane of feathers. One of its wings had been damaged, and it dragged along the ground as the griffin limped back and forth.

"This place smells like blood," Ash murmured, his eyes darting about the camp. A swamp-green troll hobbled by, one arm burned black and oozing fluid, and I shuddered. "Looks like the war isn't going well for us."

"That's what I like about you, prince. You're always so cheerful." Puck shook his head, gazing around the camp, and wrinkled his nose. "Although I will say, this place has seen better days. Does anyone feel like they're about to hurl, or is it just me?"

"It is the iron." Grimalkin picked his way over a puddle, then leaped atop a fallen tree, shaking out his paws. "This close to the false king's realm, his influence is stronger than ever. It will be worse once you are actually within its borders."

Puck snorted. "Doesn't seem like it's affecting you much, cat."

"That is because I am smarter than you and prepare for these things."

"Really? How would you prepare for me tossing you into a lake?"

"Puck," I sighed, but at that moment, two Summer knights approached us, their faces haughty and arrogant even as they bowed. "Lady Meghan," one said stiffly, after a venomous glare in Ash's direction. "His majesty King Oberon will see you now."

"You go ahead," Grimalkin purred, sitting down on the log. "I have no business with Lord Pointy Ears today. I will not be joining you."

"Where *will* you be, Grim?"

"Around." And the cat vanished from sight. I shook my

head and followed the knights, knowing Grimalkin would
reappear when we needed him.

We approached the large tent, ducking through the flaps
as the guards pulled them aside, and entered a forest clearing
draped in shadow. Giant trees stretched above us, tiny pin-
pricks of light glimmering through their branches. Will-o'-
the-wisps danced on the air, swarming around me, laughing,
until I waved them away. An owl hooted close by, adding
depth to the complex illusion surrounding us. If I looked at
the trees from the corner of my eyes, not really focusing on
them, I could see the cloth walls of the tent and the wooden
poles holding them up. But I could also feel the heat from
the humid summer night and smell the earthy scents of pine
and cedar all around us. As far as illusions went, this one was
near perfect.

On two thrones in the center of the clearing, as ancient
and imposing as the forest itself, the rulers of the Summer
Court waited for us.

Oberon was dressed for battle in a suit of mail that glittered emerald-gold under the illusionary stars. A dappled
cape rippled behind him, and his antlered crown cast clawed
shadows over the forest floor. Tall, lean, and elegant, his
long silver hair braided down his back and a sword at his
side, the Erlking watched us approach with alien green eyes
that betrayed no emotion, even when they flickered to Ash
and Puck, standing beside me, and dismissed them just as
quickly.

Titania sat beside him, and her expression was much easier
to read. The faery queen radiated hate, not just for me, but
for the Winter prince, as well. She even stabbed a disdainful
glare at Puck, but the brunt of her loathing was directed at
me and Ash.

Seeing Titania sent a flare of anger through me. She was
ultimately responsible for the whole situation with my real
dad. It was her jealousy that led Puck to have Leanansidhe

take him away, for fear the Summer Queen would hurt or kill him to spite Oberon. Titania saw my expression, and her lips curled into a nasty smirk, as if she'd discerned my thoughts. It made me very afraid for Paul; if Titania knew he was still alive, she might still hurt him to get to me.

"You have come," Oberon said, making the ground tremble. "Welcome home, daughter."

So I'm family again, now that you need something from me, is that it? I wanted to tell him not to call me daughter, that he had no right. I wanted to tell him that he couldn't just disown me and then call me back like nothing had happened. I didn't. I only nodded, gazing at the Erlking with what I hoped was a confident expression. Forget bowing and scraping; I was done with that. If the faeries wanted something from me now, they were going to have to work for it.

Oberon raised an eyebrow at my silence, but that was the only outward sign of surprise. "I take it you found the terms of our contract acceptable?" he continued, his voice low and soothing, washing over me like thick syrup, making it suddenly hard to think. "We will raise your exile, and the exile of Robin Goodfellow, in return for your service in destroying the Iron King. I believe that is a fair bargain. Now…" Oberon turned to Puck, as if the matter were already settled. "Tell me what you have learned about the Iron fey in the time of your exile. You disobeyed my direct orders when you left Faery and went after the girl—it must have been very important."

"Not so fast." I shook off the glamour making my thoughts heavy and glared at Oberon. "I haven't said 'yes,' yet."

The Erlking stared at me in surprise. "You do not agree this is fair?" His voice rose at the end, sounding truly shocked that I would turn him down, or maybe that was just more faery glamour. "The offer is most generous, Meghan Chase. I am willing to overlook your blasphemous relationship with the Winter prince and give you a chance to come home."

"I'm still considering." I felt both Ash and Puck staring at me and hurried on. "Thing is, this isn't my home. I already have one, waiting for me back in the mortal world. I already have a family, and I don't need any of this."

"Enough." Titania rose and stabbed a glare of pure poison at me. "We do not need the half-breed, husband. Send her back to the mortal world she is so fond of."

"Sit down. I wasn't finished."

The look on Titania's face was as priceless as it was terrifying. I continued quickly before I lost my nerve or she turned me into a spider. "I'm willing to bargain with you, but there have to be a few add-ons. My family. Leave them out of this war. Leave them alone, period. And that's *all* family members, including the man Leanansidhe stole when I was six." I leveled a piercing glare at Titania, who stared back at me with murder in her eyes. "I want your word that you'll let him be."

"You dare tell me what to do, Meghan Chase?" The queen's voice was soft, low, and held the ominous threat of an approaching storm. A season ago, I would've been afraid. Now, it only made me more determined.

"You need me," I said, refusing to back down, feeling Ash and Puck press close. "I'm the only one who has a chance of stopping the false king. I'm the only one who can go into that hellhole and come out alive. Well, these are my terms—your word that my family will never see another faery for as long as they live, and that Ash and Puck will be able to return home once this is all over, like you promised they would. I want to hear it firsthand, right now. That's my bargain for stopping the false king. Take it or leave it."

The Erlking was silent a moment, his green eyes blank and mirrorlike, reflecting nothing. Then, he smiled, very faintly, and nodded once. "As you wish, daughter," he mused, ignoring Titania as she whirled on him. "I will promise that no harm will befall your mortal family from *anyone* in my court. The Winter Court and the denizens of Tir Na Nog are not mine to order, but that is the best I can offer."

Titania made a strangled noise of rage and stalked out of the clearing, leaving me victor of the field. I breathed deep to calm my pounding heart and turned to Oberon again.

"What about Ash and Puck?"

"Goodfellow is free to return to Faery as he pleases," Oberon said with a brief glance at Puck. "Though I am certain he will do something else that will raise my ire in the next century or two." Puck gave Oberon an innocent look. The Erlking did not seem appeased. "However," he continued, turning back to me, "I am not the one who issued Prince Ash's exile. You will have to take that up with the Winter Queen."

"Where is she?"

"Meghan." Ash moved closer, putting a hand on my arm. "You don't have to confront Mab on my account."

Ignoring Oberon, I turned, meeting his gaze. "You don't care about going home?"

He paused, and I saw it in his eyes. He did care. Cut off from the Nevernever, he would eventually fade away into nothingness; we both knew that. But all he said was, "My only duty is to you now."

"Mab is in the Winter camp," Oberon said, after a long, piercing stare at Ash. Turning to me, he fixed me with a solemn gaze. "There is a war council tonight, daughter, between all the generals of Summer and Winter. It would do well for you to attend."

I nodded, and the Erlking waved dismissal. "I will have someone show you your quarters soon," he murmured. "Now, go."

We'd started to retreat when Oberon's voice stopped us halfway to the door. "Robin Goodfellow," he said, making Puck wince, "you will remain here."

"Damn," Puck muttered. "That was quick. One minute

back in the Nevernever and he's already pulling my strings. You guys go ahead," he said, waving us off. "I'll meet you as soon as I can." Rolling his eyes, Puck sauntered back toward Oberon, and we left the clearing.

"That was impressive," Ash said quietly as we walked through the maze of tents. Summer fey parted for us, scurrying out of sight as we headed deeper into camp. "Oberon was throwing all the mind-altering glamour he could at you, trying to get you to agree to his terms quickly and not question him. Not only did you resist, you turned the contract to your advantage. Not many could have done that."

"Really?" I thought back to the thick, sluggish feeling in the Erlking's tent. "So that was Oberon trying to manipulate me again, huh? Maybe I could resist since I'm family. Half Oberon's blood and all that."

"Or you're just incredibly stubborn," Ash added, and I smacked his arm. He chuckled, taking my hand, and we continued on to Winter's territory.

The Unseelie camp sat closer to the edge of the Iron Realm, and the tension here was definitely high. Winter knights stalked the camp's borders, grim and dangerous in their black ice armor. Ogres glowered at me from their guard posts, drool dripping from their tusks, their eyes blank and menacing. A wyvern screeched from where it was tied to several stakes, flapping its wings and trying to yank free, snapping angrily at its handlers. I shivered, and Ash's hand tightened on mine. We encountered no resistance, even among the many goblins, redcaps, and boggarts wandering the rows. The Unseelie gave us a wide berth, staring at Ash with a mixture of fascination, fear, and contempt—the wayward prince who'd turned his back on them all to be with the half-breed human. They never went further than to glare at me stonily, or shoot me a suggestive grin, but I was extremely glad for both the Winter prince and the steel blade at my side.

Just beyond the camp, the entrance to the Iron Realm loomed, metallic trees and twisted steel branches glinting in the dim light. I paused to stare at it, feeling ice form in my stomach as I remembered what it was like; the burning wasteland of junk, the corrosive, flesh-eating rain sweeping over the land, Machina's black tower stabbing into the sky.

"Well, look who's back."

I turned to see a trio of Winter knights blocking our path, armored and dangerous looking, blue icicle shards stabbing up from their shoulders and helms.

"Faolan." Ash nodded, moving subtly in front of me.

"You've got some nerve to come back here, Ash," the middle knight said. His eyes glittered beneath his helm, glassy-blue and filled with loathing. "Mab was right to exile you. You and the half-breed Summer whore should have stayed in the mortal realm where you belong."

Ash drew his sword, sending a raspy screech across the field. The knights tensed and quickly backed up, hands dropping to their own blades. "Insult her again, and I will cut you into so many pieces they'll never find them all," Ash stated calmly. Faolan bristled and started forward, but Ash leveled the tip at him. "We don't have time to play with you now, so I'm going to ask you to move."

"You're not a prince any longer, Ash," Faolan growled, drawing his own blade. "You're just an exile, lower than goblin dung." He spat at our feet, the spittle crystallizing in the grass, turning to ice. "I think its time we taught you your place, *your highness.*"

More knights appeared, drawing their swords and hemming us in. I counted five in all, and my heart hammered. As the circle started to close, I drew my sword and stood back-to-back with Ash, raising the blade so the light gleamed off its metal edge. "Stop right there," I told the knights, feigning a bravado I didn't feel. "This is *iron,* as I'm sure you can tell." I sliced at the air with a satisfying *whuff,* and pointed at my assailant. "You want to go through with this, go right ahead. I've been dying to see what this can do to fey armor."

"Meghan, get back," Ash muttered, his gaze never leaving his opponents. "You don't have to do this. They're not here for you."

"I'm not going to let you fight them by yourself," I hissed back.

A crowd was gathering, peering at us from the rows of tents, curious and eager to see a fight. A few goblins and redcaps shouted *"Fight!"* and *"Kill 'em!"* from the sidelines.

Bolstered by the mob and the cries for blood, Faolan grinned and raised his sword. "Don't worry, Ash," he smiled. "We won't rough your human up *too* badly. Unfortunately, I can't say the same for you. Attack!"

The knights charged. Balanced on the balls of my feet, as Ash had taught me, I focused on the two coming in from behind and let instinct take over. The knights were sneering as they approached, their stances loose and sloppy. Obviously, they didn't think I was much of a threat. One sword swept up in a lazy arc toward my head, and I raised my own blade to parry, knocking it aside. I saw the knight's look of shock that I had blocked his attack, and saw an opening. Reacting solely on instinct, my arm shot out, faster than I thought it could, and the tip of my sword pierced his armored thigh.

The knight's scream snapped me out of my fighter's trance, and the stench of burned flesh tainted the air, making my stomach churn. I had fully expected him to leap aside or parry, as Ash always did. Instead, I watched my opponent stagger away, clutching his leg and howling, and my rhythm stuttered to a halt. Giving me a furious glare, the other knight raised a huge blue greatsword and lunged with a snarl. I backed away frantically, barely avoiding him. He was pissed now, coming at me fast, and fear churned my insides.

"Meghan! Focus!"

Ash's voice snapped me out of my terrified daze, and I

instinctively jerked to attention, raising my sword. "Remember what I taught you," he growled somewhere to my left, clipped and breathless from fighting his own assailants. "This is no different."

The knight attacked savagely, teeth bared in a fearsome snarl, his greatsword sweeping through the air in a lethal arch. *His weapon,* I thought, dodging away. *It's heavier than mine, slowing him down. Always use your enemy's weakness to your advantage.* I danced around him, keeping just out of reach, watching him pant and grit his teeth as he followed, swatting at me like a pesky fly.

With a frustrated bellow, the knight slammed the edge of his sword into the earth, and a spray of grit and icy shards flew at my face. I turned quickly to shield my eyes, feeling the ice sting my cheek and exposed skin, and heard the knight lunge for me. On instinct, I ducked, nearly going to my knees, feeling the blade whoosh overhead. Coming up blind, I let my sword arm lead me forward and stabbed with all my might.

A jarring impact rocked my shoulder back, and the knight screamed. Glancing up, I found myself standing in front of the knight, the iron blade jammed into his stomach.

The knight choked and dropped his sword, clutching his middle as he staggered back, the sudden stench of burned flesh rising on the breeze. Face tight with fury and pain, the knight turned and vanished into the crowd, and I breathed a ragged sigh.

Shaking with adrenaline, I looked around for Ash and saw him leveling his sword at the throat of a kneeling Faolan. The other knights sprawled nearby, groaning.

"Are we done here?" Ash said softly, and Faolan, eyes blazing with hate, nodded. Ash let him up, and the knights limped off, to the jeers and taunts of the Winter fey.

Sheathing his sword, Ash turned to me. I was still shaking with adrenaline, replaying every moment of the fight in my head. It didn't seem quite real, like it happened to someone else, but the thrill coursing through my veins said different.

"Did you see that?" I grinned at Ash, my voice trembling with excitement and nerves. "I did it. I actually won!"

"Indeed," mused a familiar, terrifying voice, one that turned my blood to ice and made the hairs on my neck stand up. "It was *quite* amusing. I do believe I'm going to need some new guards, if they can't even defeat one scrawny half-blood."

It's amazing how quickly a bloodthirsty mob can clear out, but the Queen of the Winter Fey had that effect on people. In seconds, the crowd had fled, fading back into the camp until it was just me and Ash in the middle of the path. The temperature dropped sharply, and frost spread over the blades of grass at our feet, which could mean only one thing. A few yards away, flanked by two unsmiling knights, Queen Mab watched us with the stillness of a glacier.

As usual, the Winter Queen was stunning in a long battle-gown of black and red, her ebony hair a dark cloud behind her. I shivered and pressed closer to Ash as she raised one pure-white hand and beckoned us forward. The Unseelie monarch was as unpredictably dangerous as she was beautiful, prone to trapping living creatures in ice or freezing the blood in their veins, making them die slowly and in agony. I'd already felt the brunt of her legendary temper, and I had no desire to do so again.

"Ash," Mab crooned, paying no attention to me. "I heard the rumors that you were back. Have you had enough of the mortal world yet? Are you ready to come home?"

Ash's face was shut into that blank, empty mask, his eyes cold and expressionless. A self-defense mechanism, I recognized, to shield himself from the cruelty of the Winter Court. The Unseelie preyed on the weak, and emotions were considered a weakness here. "No, my Queen," he said, quiet but unafraid. "I'm no longer yours to command. My service to the Winter Court ended last night."

Silence for a few heartbeats.

"You." Mab's depthless black eyes shifted to me, then back to Ash. "You became her knight, didn't you? You swore the oath." She shook her head in disbelief and horror. "Foolish, foolish boy," she whispered. "You are truly dead to me now."

Fearing she might turn and walk away, I eased forward. "You'll still lift his exile, though, won't you?" I asked, and Mab's gaze snapped to me. "When this is over, when we take care of the false king, Ash is still free to return to the Nevernever, right?"

"He won't," Mab said in a lethally calm voice, and goose bumps rose on my arms from the sudden chill. "Even if I raise his exile, he'll stay in the mortal realm with you, because you were foolish enough to ask for that oath. You've damned him far worse than I ever could."

My stomach twisted, but I took a deep breath and continued to speak firmly. "I still want your word, Queen Mab. Please. When this is done, Ash is free to return to Tir Na Nog if he chooses to."

Mab stared at me, long enough for sweat to trickle down my back, then gave us both a cold, humorless smile. "Why not? You are both going to die anyway, so I don't see how it will matter." She sighed. "Very well, Meghan Chase. Ash is free to return home if he wants, though he said it himself—his service to the Unseelie Court is done. His oath to you will destroy him faster than anything else."

And without waiting for a reply, the Unseelie Queen whirled and stalked away from us. Though I couldn't see her face as she left, I was almost sure she was crying.

CHAPTER ELEVEN
THE FAERY WAR COUNCIL

A swollen crimson moon hovered over the camp that night, rust-red and ominous, bathing everything in an eerie, bloody tint. Snow flecks drifted from a nearly clear sky, rusty flakes dancing on the wind, like the moon itself was tainted and corroding away.

I left my tent, which was small and musty and lacked an illusionary forest clearing, to find Ash and Puck waiting for me on the other side of the flaps. The eerie red light outlined their sharp, angular features, making them seem more inhuman than before, their eyes glowing in the shadows. Behind them, the camp was quiet; nothing moved beneath the harsh red moon, and the city of tents resembled a ghost town.

"They've called for you," Ash said solemnly.

I nodded. "Then let's not keep them waiting."

Oberon's tent loomed above the others, twin banners flapping limply in the breeze. A fine dusting of snow lay on the ground, marred by boots and clawed feet and hooves, all heading toward the center of the camp. Flickering yellow light spilled from the cracks in the tent flaps, and I pushed my way inside.

The forest clearing was still there, but this time a massive stone table sat in the middle, surrounded by faeries in armor. Oberon and Mab stood at the head, imposing and grim, flanked by several sidhe gentry. A huge troll, ram horns curling through his bony helmet, stood quietly with his arms folded, watching the proceedings, while a centaur argued with a goblin chief, both of them stabbing fingers at the map on the table. An enormous oakman, gnarled and twisted, crouched low to hear the voices at his feet, his weathered face impassive.

"I'm warning you," the centaur said, the muscles in his flank quivering with rage, "if your scouts are going to set traps at the edge of the wasteland, let me know so *my* scouts don't walk right into them! I've had two break their legs stepping into a pit, and another nearly die from one of your poison darts."

The goblin chief snickered. "Ain't my fault yer scouts don't watch where they tromp," he sneered, baring a mouthful of crooked fangs. "Besides, what're yer scouts doin' so close to our camp, hmm? Stealin' secrets, I'd wager. Jealous that we've always been the better trackers, I bet."

"Enough." Oberon broke in before the centaur could leap across the table and strangle the goblin. "We are not here to fight each other. I wished only to know what your scouts have reported, not the silent war between them."

The centaur sighed and gave the goblin a murderous look. "It is as the goblins say, my lord," he said, turning to Oberon. "The skirmishes we have fought with the Iron abominations seem to be advance units. They are testing us, probing our weaknesses, knowing we cannot follow them into the Iron Realm. We have yet to see the full army. Or the Iron King."

"Sire," said one of the sidhe generals, bowing to Oberon, "what if this is a ruse? What if the Iron King intends to attack elsewhere? We might be better served defending Arcadia and the Summer Court than waiting at the edge of the wyldwood."

"No." It was Mab who spoke then, cold and unyielding. "If you leave to return to your home court, we will be lost. If the Iron King taints the wyldwood, Summer and Winter will soon follow. We cannot retreat to our homes. We must hold the line here."

"Agreed," said Oberon in a voice that was final. "Summer will not retreat from this. The only way to protect Arcadia, and all of the Nevernever, is to stop the advance here. Kruxas," he said, looking at the troll. "Where are your forces? Are they on their way?"

"Yes, your majesty," growled the troll, nodding his huge head. "They will be here in three days, barring any complications."

"And what of the Ancient Ones?" Mab looked at the general who had spoken. "This is their world, even if they slumber through it. Have the dragons heeded our call to arms?"

"We do not know the state of the few remaining Ancients, your majesty." The general bowed his head. "Thus far, we have only been able to find one, and we are unsure if she will help us. As for the rest, they either sleep still or have retreated deep into the earth to wait this out."

Oberon nodded. "Then we will do without them."

"Forgive me, your majesty." It was the centaur who spoke again, giving Oberon a pleading look. "But how do we stop the Iron King if he refuses to engage us? He still hides within his poisoned land, while we waste lives and resources waiting for him. We cannot sit here forever, while the Iron abominations pick us off one by one."

"No," said Oberon, and looked directly at me. "We cannot."

All eyes turned to me. I swallowed and resisted the urge

to shrink back as Puck let out a puff of breath and gave me a wry glance. "Well, that's our cue."

"Meghan Chase has agreed to go into the wasteland and find the Iron King," Oberon said as I edged up to the table, followed by Ash and Puck. Curious, disbelieving, and disdainful stares followed me. "Her half-human blood will protect her from the poison of the realm, and without an army she has the chance to slip through unnoticed." Oberon's eyes narrowed, and he stabbed a finger into the map. "While she is there, we must hold this position at all costs. We must give her the time she needs to discover the location of the Iron King and kill him."

My gut clenched, and my throat felt dry. I really didn't want to have to kill again. I still had nightmares about sticking an arrow through the chest of the last Iron King. But I'd given my word, and everyone was counting on me. If I wanted to see my family again, we had to end this now.

"Your majesty." It was a Winter sidhe who spoke this time, a tall warrior in icy armor, his white hair braided down his back. "Forgive me, sire. But are we really entrusting the safety of the realm, the entire Nevernever to this…half-breed? This *exile* who flouts the laws of both courts?" He shot me a hostile glare, his eyes glittering blue. "She is not one of us. She will never be one of us. Why should she care what happens to the Nevernever? Why should we even trust her?"

"She is my daughter." Oberon's voice was calm, but had the tremor of an approaching earthquake. "And you do not need to trust her. You need only to obey."

"But he raises a good point, Erlking," Mab said, smiling at me in a way that made my skin crawl. "What are your plans, half-breed? How do you expect to find the Iron King, and if you do, how do you expect to stop him?"

"I don't know," I admitted softly, and disgusted growls went around the table. "I don't know where he is. But I will find him, I promise you that. I took down one Iron King—you'll just have to trust I can do it again."

"You are asking a great deal of us, half-breed," said another faery, a Summer knight this time, regarding me with a dubious, acid-green gaze. "I cannot say I like this plan of yours, such as it is."

"You don't have to like it," I said, facing them all. "And you don't have to trust me. But it seems to me that I'm the best chance you've got at stopping the false king. I don't see any of *you* volunteering to go into the Iron Realm. If anyone else has a better idea, I'd love to hear it."

Silence for a long moment, broken only by a faint snicker from Puck. Angry, sullen glares were leveled my way, but no one rose to challenge me. Oberon's face was expressionless, but Mab watched me with a cold, frightening gaze.

"You are correct, Erlking," she said at last, turning to Oberon. "Time is of the essence. We will send the half-breed into the wasteland to slay the abomination called the Iron King. If she succeeds, the war will be ours. If she dies—" Mab broke off to look at me, her perfect red lips curling into a smile "—we lose nothing."

Oberon nodded, still expressionless. "I would not send you alone unless it was of gravest circumstances, daughter," he continued. "I know I ask much of you, but you have surprised me before. I only pray you surprise me again."

"She won't be alone," Ash said softly, startling everyone. The prince moved beside me to face the war council, his face and voice firm. "Goodfellow and I are going with her."

The Erlking gazed at him. "I thought as much, knight," he mused. "And I admire your loyalty, though I fear it will destroy you in the end. But...do what you must. We will not stop you."

"I still think you a fool, boy," Mab said, turning her cold glare on her youngest son. "Were it up to me, I would have torn out your throat to keep you from speaking that oath.

But if you insist upon going with the girl, the Unseelie Court has something that might help."

I blinked in surprise, and Oberon turned to Mab, raising an eyebrow. Obviously, this was news to him, too. But the Winter Queen ignored him, her black eyes shifting to me, dark and feral.

"Does this surprise you, half-breed?" She sniffed in disdain. "Believe what you will, I have no desire to see my last son dead. If Ash insists on following you into the Iron Realm again, he will need something that will protect him from the poison of that place. My smiths have been working on a charm that could possibly shield the bearer from the Iron glamour. They tell me it is almost ready."

My heart leaped. "What is it?"

Mab smiled, cold and brittle, and turned to the watching fey. "Leave," she hissed. "All of you, except the girl and her protectors, get out."

The Winter faeries straightened immediately and left, exiting the clearing without a backward glance. The Summer knights looked questioningly at Oberon, who dismissed them with a curt nod. Reluctantly, they drew back, bowed to their king, and followed the Winter fey out of the tent, leaving us alone with the rulers of Faery.

Oberon gave Mab a level stare. "Hiding things from the Summer Court, Lady Mab?"

"Do not take that tone with me, Lord Oberon." Mab narrowed her eyes at him. "You would do the same, as well. I look out for my own, no others." She raised her hands and clapped once. "Heinzelmann, bring in the abomination."

The grass rustled as three small men with lizardlike features melted from the shadows and padded up to the table. Smaller than dwarves, they barely came up to my knee, but they weren't gnomes or brownies or goblins. I shot a questioning look at Ash, and he grimaced.

"Kobolds," he said. "They're the smiths for the Unseelie Court."

The kobolds carried a cage between them, made of interlocking branches that glowed with Summer glamour, trapping whatever was inside. Peering out at us, hissing and snarling and shaking the bars of its cage, was a gremlin.

I couldn't help but cringe when I saw the creature. Gremlins were Iron faeries, but so chaotic and wild, not even the other Iron fey wanted them around. They lived in machines and computers and would often congregate in huge swarms, usually where they could do the most damage. They were spindly, ugly little creatures, sort of a cross between a naked monkey and a wingless bat, with long arms, flared-out ears, and razor-sharp teeth that glowed neon-blue when they smiled.

I understood now why Mab wanted everyone else gone. The gremlin might not have survived its trek to the table, as one or more knights would probably have cut it down as soon as they saw it. Oberon watched the hissing faery with the look of someone observing a particularly disgusting insect, but did nothing more than blink.

The kobolds heaved the cage onto the table, where the gremlin snarled and spat at us, flitting from one side of the container to the next. The largest kobold, a yellow-eyed creature with bushy hair, grinned, flicking his tongue like a lizard. "It isss ready, Queen Mab," he hissed. "Would you like to perform the ritual?"

Mab's smile was thoroughly frightening. "Give me the amulet, Heinzelmann."

The kobold handed her something that flashed briefly in the dim light. Still smiling, the Winter Queen turned back to the gremlin, watching it with a predatory gleam in her eyes. The gremlin snarled at her. Raising her fist, the queen began chanting, words I didn't understand, words that rippled with power, swirling around her like a vortex. I felt a pull on the inside, as if my soul was straining to leave my body and fly into that whirlwind. I gasped and felt Ash take my hand, squeezing it tightly as if he feared I would fly away, as well.

The gremlin arched its back, mouth gaping, and gave a piercing wail. I saw a dark, ragged wisp, like a dirty cloud, rise up from the gremlin's mouth and get pulled into the vortex. Mab continued to chant, and like a tornado being sucked down a drain, the vortex vanished into whatever she held in her hand. The gremlin collapsed, twitching, sparks jumping off its body to fizzle on the stone. With a final shudder, it was still.

My mouth was dry as Mab turned back to us, a triumphant look on her face. "What did you do to it?" I demanded hoarsely.

Mab raised her hand. An amulet dangled by a thin silver chain, flashing like a drop of water in the sun. It was a tiny thing, shaped like a teardrop, held in place by prongs of ice. The teardrop was as clear as glass, and I could see something writhing like smoke on the inside.

"We have found a way to trap the Iron creature's life essence," Mab purred, sounding horribly pleased with herself. "If the amulet works, it will draw the Iron glamour from the wearer into itself, cleansing and protecting him from the poison. You will even be able to *touch* iron without being burned. Severely, anyway." She shrugged. "At least, that is what my smiths tell me. It has not been tested yet."

"And was that the only one?" Ash nodded to the lifeless gremlin, his face uncertain. The creature seemed even smaller in death than in life, as fragile as a pile of twigs. Mab gave a cruel laugh, shaking her head.

"Oh no, my dear." She let the amulet dangle, spinning slowly on its chain. "Many, many abominations went into the making of this charm. Which is why we could not hand them

out to just anyone. Capturing the creatures alive proved...
difficult."

"And—" I stared at the writhing mist within the glass, feeling faintly ill "—you have to *kill* them to make it work?"

"This is *war,* human." Mab's voice was cold and remorseless. "It is either kill or be destroyed ourselves." The queen sniffed, gazing contemptuously at the twisted body of the gremlin. "The Iron fey are corrupting our home and poisoning our people. I think this fair exchange, don't you?"

I wasn't sure about that, but Puck cleared his throat, drawing our attention. "Hate to sound greedy and all," he said, "but is ice-boy the only one who gets a shiny piece of jewelry? Seeing as there are three of us going into the Iron Realm."

Mab gave him an icy glare. "No, Robin Goodfellow," she said, making Puck's name sound like a curse. "The creature that showed us how to make these insisted you get one, too." She gestured, and Heinzelmann the kobold approached Puck with a grin, handing out another amulet on a chain. This one had vines curled around the glass instead of ice, but they were otherwise identical. Puck grinned as he looped it around his neck, giving Mab a slight bow, which she ignored.

Beckoning Ash forward, Mab draped the amulet around his neck as he bowed. "This is the best we can do for you," she said as Ash straightened, and for a moment, the Winter Queen looked almost regretful, staring at her son. "If you cannot defeat the Iron King, then we are all lost."

"We won't fail," Ash said softly, and Mab placed a palm on his cheek, gazing at him like she would not see him again.

"One last thing," she added as Ash stepped back. "The magic in the amulet is not permanent. It will weaken and corrode over time, and eventually it will shatter altogether. The smiths also tell me that any use of glamour will hasten the charm's destruction, as will direct contact with anything made of iron. How long that will take, they are not sure. But they do agree on one thing—it will not last forever. Once you enter the Iron Realm, you have a limited time to find your target and kill him. So, I would hurry if I were you, Meghan Chase."

Oh, of course, I thought, as my gut twisted and sank down to my toes. *This impossible situation also comes with a time limit. No pressure.*

"Queen Mab!"

The shout, high-pitched and gravelly, echoed from beyond the clearing, and a moment later a leafy bush scurried into the tent and danced around at Mab's feet. It took me a moment to realize it was a goblin with leaves and twigs glued to its clothes, making it blend perfectly into a forest environment.

"Queen Mab!" it rasped. "Iron fey! Snigg spotted many Iron fey camped at the edge of the wasteland! Sound alarm! Ready weapons! Run, run!"

Mab swooped down and in a blindingly quick gesture, grabbed the frantic goblin by the throat, lifting it into the air.

"How many of them are there?" she asked softly, as the goblin choked and kicked weakly in her grip, his leafy camouflage bobbing.

"Um." The goblin gave a last twitch and calmed down. "Few hundred?" it croaked. "Many lights, many creatures. Snigg didn't get a good look, so sorry."

"And are they approaching, or stationary?" Mab continued in what would have been a calm, reasonable voice, if the glassy look in her eyes hadn't betrayed her scariness. "Do we have time to prepare, or are they right at our door?"

"Few miles out, your majesty. Snigg ran all the way back when he saw them, but they had camped, camped for the night. Snigg's guess is they'll attack at dawn."

"So we have a little time, at least." Mab tossed away the goblin like she was throwing out an empty soda can. "Go inform our forces that battle is nigh. Tell the generals to attend me, to discuss our strategy for the morning. Go!"

The goblin fled, a leafy bush scrambling out of the tent. Mab whirled on Oberon. "It is terribly convenient," she hissed, scowling, "for your daughter to appear and we are immediately attacked. It is almost as if they are coming for her."

Sheer black fright washed through me. One or two opponents I could handle, but not an entire army. "What can I do?" I asked, trying to keep the tremor from my voice. "Do you want me to leave now?"

Oberon shook his head. "Not tonight," he said firmly. "The enemy is at our doorstep, and you could walk straight into their jaws."

"I could sneak around—"

"No, Meghan Chase. I will not risk your discovery. Too much is at stake for you to be captured and killed. We will fight them tomorrow and when they are defeated, you will have a clear path into the Iron Realm."

"But—"

"I will not argue with you, daughter." Oberon turned and fixed me with unyielding green eyes, his voice going deep and terrible. "You will remain here, where we can protect you, until the battle is won. I am still king, and that is my final word on the matter."

He glared at me, and I didn't protest. Despite our family ties, he was still Lord of the Summer Fey; it would be dangerous to push him any further. Mab sniffed, shaking her head disapprovingly. "Very well, Erlking," she said, drawing herself up. "I must ready my troops for the battle. Excuse me."

With a last chilly smile at me, the Queen of the Winter Fey left the clearing. I watched her swoop out of the tent, and turned back to Oberon. "So, what now?"

"Now," Oberon replied, "we make ready for war."

CHAPTER TWELVE

THE TRAITOR KNIGHT

The camp celebrated that night. Once word of the impending attack got out, excitement and anticipation spread like wildfire, until it could no longer be contained to a few stuffy tents. Faeries swarmed the streets like revelers after a hockey game, drudging up food and alcohol and other, more questionable things. Drums and pipes, primal and dark, echoed over the wind, pounding out a savage rhythm. On each side of the camp, massive bonfires were lit, roaring up like phoenixes in the night, as the armies of Summer and Winter danced and drank and sang the night away.

I hung back from the main fires, avoiding the dancing and the drinking and the other acts going on in the shadows. From where I stood, a mug of black tea warming my hands, I could see both Summer and Winter fires and the dark silhouettes dancing around them. On the Unseelie side, goblins and redcaps chanted dark, vulgar battle songs, usually about blood and meat and body parts, while dryads and tree nymphs swayed a mesmerizing dance around the Seelie camp, moving like branches in the wind. A sylph fluttered by, chased by a satyr, and an ogre hefted a whole ale keg above his open mouth, bathing his face in dark liquor.

"You wouldn't think there's a fight tomorrow," I muttered to Ash, who was leaning against a tree, a green bottle held lightly between two fingers. Every so often, he'd raise the glass and take a single swallow from the neck, but I knew better than to ask him to share. Faery wine is potent stuff, and I had no desire to spend the rest of the night as a hedgehog, or holding a conversation with giant pink rabbits. "Isn't it traditional to celebrate *after* you win?"

"And what if there is no tomorrow?" Ash turned his gaze toward the Unseelie bonfire, where the goblins were singing, something about fingers and meat cleavers. "Many of them won't live to see another dawn. And once we die, there is nothing left. No existence beyond this one." Though his voice was matter-of-fact, a shadow hovered in his eyes. He took a swig of wine and glanced at me, one corner of his lip turned up. "I think you mortals have a phrase—eat, drink, and be merry, for tomorrow we may die?"

"Oh, that's not morbid at all, Ash."

Before he could reply, something stumbled into our little space, tripped, and went sprawling at my feet. It was Puck, his shirt off, his red hair in disarray. He grinned up at me, a crown of daisies woven through his hair, a bottle clutched in one hand. A group of nymphs crowded around him a second later, giggling. I drew back as they swarmed all over him.

"Oh, hey, princess!" Puck waved inanely as the nymphs pulled him to his feet, still giggling. His hair gleamed, his eyes gleamed, and I barely recognized him. "Wanna play ride the phouka with us?"

"Um. No thanks, Puck."

"Suit yourself. But you only live once, princess." And Puck let himself be pulled away by the nymphs, vanishing into the crowd by the fire. Ash shook his head and took a swig from his bottle. I stared after them, not knowing what to feel.

"That's a side of him I haven't seen before," I muttered at last, hunching my shoulders against the wind. Ash chuckled.

"Then you don't know Goodfellow as well as you think." The dark faery pushed himself off the tree and came to stand beside me, lightly touching my shoulder. "Try to get some rest. The revel will only get wilder as the night goes on, and you might not want to see what happens when faeries get extremely drunk. Besides, you'll want at least a few hours of sleep before the battle tomorrow."

I shivered as I rose, my stomach clenching as I thought of the impending war. "Will I have to fight, too?" I asked as we fell into step back toward my tent. Ash sighed.

"Not if I have anything to say about it," he said, almost to himself. "And I don't think Oberon will want you in the midst of it, either. You're too important to risk being killed."

I was relieved, but at the same time, guilt gnawed at me. I was tired of people dying while I stood by, helpless. Maybe it was time I started fighting my own battles.

We reached my tent and I hesitated, my heart suddenly fluttering like crazy. I could feel his presence at my back, quiet and strong, making my skin tingle. The darkness beyond the flaps beckoned invitingly, and words danced on the tip of my tongue, held back by nervousness and fear.

Just spit it out, Meghan. Ask him to stay with you tonight. What's the worst that could happen? He says no? I cringed inwardly with embarrassment. *Okay, that would suck. But would he really refuse? You know he loves you. What are you waiting for?*

I took a breath. "Ash...um..."

"Prince Ash!" A Winter knight marched through the line of tents and bowed when he reached us. I wanted to kick him, but Ash looked amused.

"So, I'm a prince again, am I?" he mused softly. "Very well. What do you want, Deylin?"

"Queen Mab has requested your presence, your highness," the knight continued, ignoring me completely. "She wishes you to meet her in her tent on the Winter side of the camp. I will remain here and guard the Summer princess until—"

"I no longer answer to Queen Mab," Ash said, and the knight gaped at him. "If my lady wishes me to go, I will honor her request. If she does not, then I would ask you to send the queen my apologies."

The Winter knight continued to look dumbstruck, but Ash turned to me, serious and formal, though I could sense a secret triumph deep within. "If you want me to stay, you only have to say the word," he stated quietly. "Or I can go see what Mab wants. Your will is my command."

I was tempted, so very tempted, to ask him to stay. I wanted to pull him into my tent and make us both forget about the war and the courts and the looming battle, just for a night. But Mab would be even more furious, and I really didn't want to piss off the Winter Queen any more than I already had.

"No," I sighed. "Go see what Mab wants. I'll be all right."

"Are you sure?"

I nodded, and he drew back. "I'll be close," he said. "And Deylin will be right outside. You can trust him, but if you need me, just call."

"I will," I replied, and watched him walk away until he disappeared into the shadows, my skin buzzing with thwarted desire. Deylin gave me a jerky bow and turned away, positioning himself in front of my tent. Sighing, I ducked inside and flopped down on my bed, covering my heated face with a pillow. My head swirled with forbidden thoughts and feelings, making it impossible to relax. For a long time, I could think only of a certain dark knight, and when I finally dropped off to sleep, he continued to invade my dreams.

SOMETHING CLAMPED DOWN over my mouth in the darkness,

muffling my startled yelp. I jerked, but found myself pinned on my back, my arms crushed under the body straddling my waist. An armored knight loomed over me, a full helm and visor concealing his face.

"Shhhhhh." The knight pressed a finger to his lips through the helm. I could feel him smiling behind the visor. "Relax, your highness. This will be much easier if you don't fight."

I bucked desperately, but the gauntlet over my mouth slammed me back, squeezing until tears formed in my eyes. The knight sighed. "I see you want to do this the hard way."

The gauntlet grew icy cold on my skin, burning like fire. I thrashed and kicked, but couldn't dislodge the weight on my chest or the hand over my face. Ice formed on my skin, spreading over my cheeks and jaw, freezing my lips shut. The knight chuckled and removed his hand, leaving me panting through my nose against the ice gag. My face felt like it had been splashed with acid, vicious cold eating into my bones.

"That's better." The knight sat back, settling his weight more fully, and gazed down at me. "Wouldn't want dear Ash to come running just yet, would we?"

I jerked in recognition. I knew that smug, arrogant voice. The knight saw my reaction and chuckled.

Reaching to his helm, he flipped up the visor, confirming my suspicions. My heart pounded, and I shivered violently, struggling to control my fear.

"Miss me, princess?" Rowan smiled, his diamond-blue eyes gleaming in the darkness, and I would've gasped in revulsion if I could. Ash's older brother looked different now; his once-handsome, pointed face resembled a crater of raw flesh and ugly burns. Open, gaping wounds seeped fluid down his cheeks, and his nose had fallen off, leaving ugly holes behind. He reminded me of a grinning skull, glassy eyes sunk deep into his head, bright with pain and madness.

"Do I disgust you?" he whispered, as I fought the urge to

gag. "This is merely a trial, princess, my rite of passage. The iron burns away the weak, useless flesh, until I am reborn as one of them. I must merely endure the pain until I am complete. When the Iron King takes over the Nevernever, I will be the only one of the oldbloods to withstand the change."

I shook my head, wanting to tell him he was wrong, that there was no rite of passage, that the false king was merely using him like all the others. But of course, I couldn't speak through the ice, and Rowan suddenly pulled a dagger, the onyx blade thin and serrated like the edges of a shark's tooth.

"The Iron King wants to do the honors himself," he whispered, "but all you have to be is slightly alive when you get there. I think I'll cut off a few fingers and leave them behind for Ash to find before we go. What do you say, your highness?"

He shifted his weight to free one of my arms, grabbed my wrist, and pinned it to the ground despite my wild thrashing. "Oh, keep squirming, princess," he cooed. "It makes this so erotic." Picking up the knife, he positioned it above my hand, choosing a finger.

I took a deep breath to calm my panic and tried to think. My sword was close, but I couldn't move my arm. Using glamour would either exhaust or sicken me, but I had no choice this time. As Rowan prodded my exposed fingers with the tip of the knife, drawing tiny blood drops and extending the torment, I focused on the hilt.

Wood is wood. Puck's voice echoed in my mind. *Be it a dead tree, the side of a ship, a wooden crossbow or a simple broom handle, Summer magic can make it come alive again, if only for a moment. Concentrate.*

A surge of glamour, and gleaming thorns erupted from the hilt, stabbing through the gauntlet and into Rowan's flesh. The room swirled as dizziness came almost immediately, and I broke the connection as Rowan howled, jerking back and releasing my arm. Exactly as I hoped. With an internal yell, I surged up, ignoring the clinging nausea, and thrust my freed hand under his visor, clawing at his hideous, burned face.

This time, Rowan's scream shook the cloth walls. Dropping the knife, he went to cover his face and I shoved him off with all my might. Scrambling upright, I whirled and drew my sword with one hand, clawing at my frozen face with the other. Ice broke off in chunks, feeling like they took flaps of skin with them. I blinked away tears as Rowan got to his feet, his expression murderous.

"You really think you're going to beat me?" Drawing his sword, which was ice-blue and serrated like the knife, Rowan stepped forward. Blood ran down the side of his face, and one eye was squeezed shut. "Why didn't you run, princess?" he mused. "Run to Ash and your father—I can't chase you through the whole camp. You should have run."

I ripped the last of the ice from my lips and spat on the ground between us, tasting blood. "I'm through with running," I said, watching his one good eye narrow. "And I'm not about to let you stab me in the back, either. I want you to take a message to the false king."

Rowan smiled, teeth shining like fangs in his ravaged face, and eased closer. I held my ground, sinking into a defensive stance like Ash taught me. I was still afraid, because I'd seen Rowan fight Ash before, and I knew he was far better than me. But anger overshadowed fear now, and I pointed at Rowan with my sword. "You tell the false king he doesn't have to send anyone to get me," I said in the firmest voice I could manage. "I'm coming for him. I'm coming for him, and when I find him, I'm going to kill him."

With a shock, I realized that I really meant it. It was either him or my family now, both mortal and faery. For everyone else to live, the false king had to die. As Grim once prophesied, I had become an assassin of the courts.

Rowan sneered, unimpressed. "I'll be sure to tell him,

princess," he mocked. "But don't think you're getting away from me unscathed." He took another step forward, and I eased backward, toward the tent flaps. "I think I'll take an ear for a trophy, just to show the king that I didn't fail him."

He lunged, a blindingly quick move that took me by surprise. I jerked back, sweeping my blade up to parry, managing to deflect his sword, but I wasn't quite fast enough. The tip grazed my skin, slicing a line of fire across my cheek. I stumbled back, tripped over something in the doorway, and fell backward out of the tent.

Deylin's lifeless, frozen body stared up at me, his eyes wide with shock. As I watched, the faery's body rippled, then dissolved like an ice cube in the microwave, until nothing was left but a puddle of water in the dirt.

Cursing, I scrambled to my feet, backing away from the opening. My cheek burned, and I could feel something warm trickling down my face. "Ash!" I yelled, gazing around wildly. "Puck! It's Rowan! Rowan is here!"

The camp was dark, silent. Faeries lay passed out on the ground, snoring where they'd fallen, mugs and bottles scattered everywhere. Smoke curled lazily into the air from charred timbers, embers flickering weakly in the darkness.

Rowan exited the tent, pushing aside the flaps and brazenly stepping into the open, sneering all the while. Still smiling, he put two fingers to his mouth and blew out a piercing whistle that carried over the trees. "Running away now, princess?" he asked, as faeries began to groan and stir, blinking and confused. "How do you expect to kill the Iron King when you can't even get past his knight?"

"I'll find a way," I told him, keeping my sword pointed at his chest. "I did before."

Rowan chuckled. "We'll look forward to it then, princess. Say hello to Ash for me."

"Rowan!"

Ash's shout of fury echoed through the camp. The dark

prince appeared beside me from nowhere, anger swirling around him in a black-and-red cloud. The look in his eyes when he faced his brother was terrifying—that blank, glassy killing stare that promised no mercy.

Rowan laughed and threw up an arm.

An answering bellow rang overhead, and two tons of scaly brown wyvern crashed into our midst, roaring and lashing out with its tail. I saw the gleaming, poisoned barb coming toward me and slashed wildly with my blade, cutting through the tip. The barb and the end of its tail fell, writhing, in the dirt, though the force of the blow knocked me off my feet. In the same second, Ash's sword lashed out, slicing across one bulbous yellow eye.

The wyvern screeched and drew back, and in one swift motion, Rowan leaped atop the scaly neck as it lunged skyward, beating the air with tattered, leathery wings. Rising above our heads, the huge lizard streaked toward the edge of the trees and vanished through the gap that led to the Iron Realm, Rowan's mocking laughter echoing in its wake.

Panting, Ash sheathed his sword and helped me to my feet. "Meghan, are you all right?" he asked, his gaze flicking over my face, resting on my cut cheek. "I'm sorry I wasn't here sooner. Mab wanted a full report from the time we were exiled. What happened?"

I winced. Talking hurt now; my lips were raw and bloody, and the left side of my face felt like someone had pressed it to a lit stove. "He showed up in my tent bragging that he was going to become an Iron faery, and that the false king was waiting for me. He was going to cut off my fingers and leave them for you to find," I continued, looking at Ash, seeing his eyes narrow, "but that was before I clawed his eyes out. Ow." I gingerly probed my cheek, grimacing as my fingers came away stained with blood. "Bastard."

"I will kill him," Ash muttered in that soft, scary voice.

It sounded like a promise, though he didn't say the words. The murderous look in his eyes spoke loud enough.

"Princess!" Puck appeared then, still shirtless, his hair looking like a vulture had nested in it. "What happened? Was that *Rowan* that just beat the hell out of here? What's going on?"

I scowled at him, barely stopping myself from asking what he'd been doing all night. Flowers were still woven into his hair, and I couldn't tell if those were scratches on his bare skin or not. "That was Rowan," I told him instead. "I don't know how he snuck through the camp, but he did. And you can be sure he's off to tell the false king I'm here."

Ash narrowed his eyes. "Then we should be ready for them."

The sharp blast of a horn echoed over the trees then, loud and sudden. It was followed by another, and another, as faeries jerked awake or emerged from their tents, blinking in alarm. Ash raised his head and followed the sound, the ghost of a vicious smile crossing his face.

"They're coming."

The camp erupted into organized chaos. Fey leaped to their feet, snatching weapons and armor. Captains and lieutenants appeared, barking orders, directing their squads to form ranks. Gryphon and wyvern handlers ran to get their beasts ready for combat, and knights began saddling their fey steeds, while the horses tossed their heads and pranced with anticipation. For a moment, I had the surreal feeling of being in the center of a medieval fantasy film, *Lord of the Rings* style, with all the knights and horses rushing back and forth. Then the full realization hit, making me slightly nauseous. This wasn't a movie. This was a real battle, with real creatures that would do their best to kill me.

"Meghan Chase!"

A pair of female satyrs trotted toward me, ducking and weaving through the crowd, their furry goat legs skipping over the mud. "Your father sent us to make sure you were suitably attired for the battle," one of them told me as they drew close. "He had something designed especially for you. If you would follow us, please."

I winced. The last time Oberon had had something designed especially for me, it was a horribly fancy dress that I'd refused to wear. But Ash released my arm and gave me a gentle nudge toward the waiting satyrs.

"Go with them," he told me. "I have to find something for myself, as well."

"Ash…"

"I'll be back soon. Take care of her, Goodfellow." And he jogged away, vanishing into the crowds.

The satyrs beckoned impatiently, and we followed them to a strange white tent on the Summer side of the camp. The material was light and gauzy, draped over the poles in wispy strands that reminded me uncomfortably of spiderwebs. The satyrs ushered me through the flaps, but I turned and stopped Puck at the entrance, firmly telling him he would have to wait outside while I dressed. Ignoring his stupid leer, hoping he wouldn't turn into a mouse so he could sneak in and watch, I went inside.

The interior of the tent was dark and warm, the walls covered with webbing that rustled and slithered, as if hundreds of tiny creatures were scurrying through it. A tall, pale woman with long dark hair waited for me in the dim room, her eyes gleaming-black orbs in her pinched face.

"Meghan Chase," the woman rasped, huge black eyes following my every move. "You have arrived. How fortuitous that we meet again."

"Lady Weaver." I nodded, recognizing the Seelie Court's head seamstress, and stifled the urge to rub my arms. I'd met her before on my first trip into Faery, and like before, her presence made me feel itchy, as if thousands of bugs were crawling over my skin.

"Come, come," Lady Weaver said, beckoning me with one pale, spiderlike hand. "The battle is about to commence, and your father wished for me to design your armor." She led me toward the back of the tent, where something shimmered in the gloom, held up by thin white strands. "It is my best work so far. What do you think?"

At first glance, it looked like a long coat of some sort, fastened at the waist and split to flare out behind the legs. Looking closer, I saw that the material was made up of tiny scales, flexible to the touch, yet impossibly strong. The back was strewn with intricate designs that looked almost geometric in nature. Gauntlets, greaves, leggings, and boots, made of the same scaly material, completed the outfit.

"Wow," I said, drawing closer. "It's beautiful."

Lady Weaver sniffed.

"As usual, my talents are underappreciated," she sighed, snapping her fingers at the two satyrs, who hurried forward. "Here I am, the greatest seamstress in the Nevernever, reduced to weaving dragon-scale armor for unrefined half-breeds. Very well, girl. Try it on. It will fit perfectly."

The satyrs helped me into the suit, which was lighter and more flexible than I'd thought it would be. Except for the gauntlets and greaves, I didn't even feel like I was in armor. Which I guessed was kind of the point.

"Nice," came a voice at the door, and Puck strolled in. I blinked in surprise. He was dressed for battle, too, in a leather breastplate over a suit of silvery-green mail, dark leather gauntlets, and knee-high boots. A green cloth hung from his belt, decorated with curling vines and leaves, and thick shoulder plates jutted out from his collarbone, looking like rough, spiky bark.

"Surprised, princess?" Puck shrugged, causing his shoulder spikes to jerk up. "I don't normally wear armor, but then, I don't normally have to face an army of Iron fey, either. Figured I might as well have some protection." He scanned my outfit and nodded with appreciation. "Impressive. Real dragon-scale—that'll hold up to almost anything."

"I hope so," I murmured, and Lady Weaver snorted.

"Of course it will, girl," she snapped, pursing her bloodless lips at me. "Who do you think designed this suit? Now, shoo. I have other things to work on. Out!"

Puck and I fled, ducking out of the tent. The camp was nearly empty now, ranks upon ranks of Summer and Winter fey lining the edge of the metal forest. Waiting for the battle to begin.

I shivered and rubbed my arms. As if reading my thoughts, Puck moved closer and put a hand on my elbow. "Don't worry, princess," he said. And though his voice was light, there was a hard edge to his smile. "Any Iron bastard that wants you will have to get past *me,* first." He rolled his eyes. "And of course, the dark knight over there."

"Where?" I followed his gaze, just in time to see Ash appear from behind a tent and walk toward us. His armor gleamed under the sun, black marked with icy silver, a stylized wolf head on the breastplate. He looked incredibly dangerous, the black knight out of legend, a tattered cape fluttering behind him.

"Oberon has called for you," he announced, taking in my suit with a single, approving nod. "He wants you to stay near the back, where the fighting won't reach you. He has a platoon of bodyguards stationed there to protect—"

"I'm not going."

Both Ash and Puck blinked at me. "I'm fighting," I said in the firmest voice I could manage. "I don't want to hang back and watch everyone die for me. This is my war, too."

"Are you sure that's a good idea, princess?"

I glanced at Puck and smiled. "Are you going to stop me?"

He held up his hands. "Wouldn't dream of it." He grinned

and shook his head. "I just hope you know what you're doing."

I looked at Ash, wondering what he thought of this, if he would try to talk me down. He gazed back with a solemn expression, teacher to student, sizing me up. "You've never fought in a real war," he said softly, and I caught the trace of worry in his voice. "You don't know what real battle is like. It's nothing like a one-on-one duel. It will be violent and bloody and chaotic, and you won't have any time to think about what you're doing. The things you've seen, the things you've experienced—nothing will have prepared you for this. Goodfellow and I will protect you as best we can, but you *will* have to fight, and you *will* have to kill. Without mercy. Are you sure this is what you want?"

"Yes." I raised my chin and stared back, meeting his eyes. "I'm sure."

"Good." He nodded once, and turned toward the looming forest. "Because here they come."

CHAPTER THIRTEEN

THE CREEPING IRON

"Get ready," Ash muttered, and drew his sword.

My hand shook as I followed his example, the blade awkward and clumsy in my grasp. Ahead of us, light glinted off swords, shields, and armor, a menacing wall of bristling faery steel. Trolls and ogres shifted impatiently, gripping their spiked clubs. Goblins and redcaps licked their pointed teeth, bloodlust shining from their eyes. Dryads, hammadryads, and oakmen waited silently, their green and brown faces tight with hate and fear. Out of all the fey, the slow corruption of the Nevernever affected them most of all and reminded me what was at stake.

I gripped the hilt of my sword, feeling the metal bite into my palm. *Come on, then,* I thought, as a great rustling sounded just beyond the hole—hundreds of feet, marching toward us. Branches snapped, trees shook, and the armies of Summer and Winter howled in reply. *You won't beat me. The false king isn't going to win. Your advance stops right here.*

"Here we go," Ash growled, as with the screeching of a million knives, the Iron fey broke from the forest and came into view. Wiremen and Iron knights, clockwork hounds, spider-hags, skeletal creatures that looked like the Terminator, all shiny and metallic, and hundreds more of different shapes and sizes, pouring out of the forest in a huge, chaotic swarm. For a moment, the two armies stared at each other, hate and violence and bloodlust shining from their eyes. Then, a monstrous armored knight, horns bristling from a steel helm, stepped to the front of the army and swept an arm forward, and the Iron fey charged with hair-raising shrieks.

The Seelie and Unseelie roared in response, surging forward to meet them. Like ants, they spilled onto the battlefield, the space between them growing smaller and smaller as they closed on each other. The two armies met with the deafening screech and clang of weapons, and then everything dissolved into madness.

Ash and Puck pressed close, refusing to advance, only engaging an enemy if it attacked first. The front lines held off the worst of the battle, but gradually the Iron fey began slipping through the holes and pushing toward the back. I gripped my weapon and tried to focus, but it was hard. Everything was happening so fast, bodies whirling by, swords flashing, the shrieks and howls of the wounded. A giant praying mantis–thing lunged at me, bladed arms sweeping down, but Ash stepped in front of it and caught the edges with his sword, shoving it back. An Iron knight, dressed head to toe in plate mail, rushed me, but tripped as Puck kicked him in the knee and sent him sprawling.

Another armored knight broke through the back ranks, slicing at me with his weapon, a serrated, two-handed broadsword. Reacting on instinct, I dodged the blow and stabbed at him with my sword. It screeched off his breastplate, leaving a shiny gash in the armor but not hurting him. The knight bellowed a laugh, confident in his victory, and lunged again, sweeping his blade across at my head. Ducking the blow, I stepped forward and plunged my sword through his visor, feeling the tip strike the back of his helm.

The knight dropped like his strings had been cut. My

stomach roiled, but there was no time to think about what I'd just done. More Iron fey were pouring from the woods. I saw Oberon charge into the fray on a huge black warhorse, glamour swirling around him, and sweep a hand toward the thickest of the fighting. Vines and roots erupted from the ground, coiling around the Iron fey, strangling them or pulling them beneath the earth. Atop a rise, Mab raised her arms, and a savage whirlwind swept across the field, freezing fey solid or impaling them with ice shards. The armies of Summer and Winter howled with renewed vigor and threw themselves at the enemy.

And then, something monstrous broke through the trees, lumbering onto the field. A huge iron beetle, the size of a bull elephant, plowed into the chaos, crushing fey underfoot. Four elves with metallic, shimmering hair sat atop a platform on its back, shooting old-style muskets into the crowd. Summer and Winter fey fell under a hail of musket fire as another beetle broke through the trees. Swords and arrows bounced off the dark, shiny carapaces as the tanklike bugs waddled farther into the camp, leaving death in their wake.

"Fall back!" Oberon's voice boomed over the field as the beetles continued their rampage. "Fall back and regroup! Go!"

As Summer and Winter forces began drawing back, a ripple of Iron glamour washed over me, coming from the bugs. Narrowing my eyes and peering through the madness, I looked closer. It was as if the bugs came into clear focus through a blurry background; I could see the Iron glamour shimmering around them, cold and colorless. The thick, bulky carapaces were near invulnerable, but the beetle's legs were thin and spindly, barely strong enough to hold the monsters up. The joints were weak and spotted with rust… and the ghost of an idea floated through my mind.

"Ash, Puck!" I whirled on them, and their attention

snapped to me. "I think I know how to take down that bug, but I need to get closer! Clear me a path!"

Puck blinked, looking incredulous. "Uh, running toward the enemy? Isn't that like the opposite of what *fall back* means?"

"We have to stop those bugs before they kill half the camp!" I looked at Ash, pleading. "I can do this, but I need you to guard me when I get up there. Please, Ash."

Ash stared at me a moment, then nodded curtly. "We'll get you there," he muttered, raising his sword. "Goodfellow, back me up."

He lunged forward, against the tide of retreating fey. Puck shook his head and followed. We fought our way through the center of the field, where bodies of faeries—or what had been faeries—littered the ground. The fighting was much thicker here, and my bodyguards were hard-pressed to keep the enemy off me.

A roar of musket fire rang out, and a wyvern screeched and crashed to the ground a few yards away, flapping and thrashing. The bulk of the beetle loomed overhead, shiny black carapace blocking out the sun.

"Is this…close enough, princess?" Puck panted, locked in battle with a pair of wiremen, their razor-wire claws slashing at him. At his side, Ash snarled and crossed swords with an Iron knight, filling the air with the scream of metal.

I nodded, heart racing. "Just keep them off me for a few seconds!" I called, and turned back toward the iron bug, staring at its underside. Yes, the legs were jointed, held together by metal bolts. As a spindly leg swept by, I dodged and closed my eyes, drawing Iron glamour from the air, from the bug and the trees and the corrupted land around me. Musket fire boomed, and the screech of swords and faeries rang in my head, but I trusted my guardians to keep me safe and kept concentrating.

Opening my eyes, I focused on one of the insect's joints,

on the tiny bolt that held it together, and *pulled*. The nut trembled, shaking with rust, and then flew out like a cork, a brief glint of metal under the sun. The insect lurched as the leg crumpled and fell off into the mud, and then the whole beetle started to tip like an off-balanced bus.

"Yes!" I cheered, just as the wave of nausea hit. A stab of pain ripped through my stomach, and I fell to my knees, fighting the urge to vomit. A shadow engulfed me, and I looked up to see the enormous bulk of the insect falling sideways, scattering Iron fey and faeries alike, but I couldn't move.

A blur of darkness, and then Ash grabbed me by the arm, yanking me upright. We leaped forward, as with a mighty groan, the beetle crashed to the ground and rolled over, crushing the musket elves beneath it and nearly killing me in the process. On its back, the beetle's remaining legs kicked and flailed uselessly, and I giggled with slight hysterics. Ash muttered something inscrutable and pulled me into a brief, tight embrace.

"You enjoy making my heart stop, don't you?" he whispered, and I felt him shaking with adrenaline or something else. Before I could form a reply, he released me and stepped back, a stoic bodyguard once more.

Panting, I gazed around to see the Iron fey drawing back, vanishing into the metal forest again. The other beetle seemed trapped under a writhing mess of vines, tangling its legs and dragging it down. The musketeers on its back had been impaled with huge spears of ice. Mab and Oberon's doing, probably.

"Is it over?" I asked as Puck joined us, also breathing hard, his armor spattered with some icky black substance, like oil. "Did we win?"

Puck nodded, but his eyes were grim. "In a matter of speaking, princess."

Puzzled, I looked around, and my stomach twisted. Bodies

from both sides lay scattered about the field, some moaning, some still and lifeless. A few had already turned to stone, ice, dirt, branches, water, or had faded away entirely. Sometimes it happened instantly, sometimes it took hours, but faeries didn't leave physical bodies behind when they died. They simply ceased to exist.

But, more disturbing, as I looked closer, I saw that the Iron forest had crept even closer, so much that it had spread to the center of the camp. As I watched in horror, a young green sapling turned shiny and metallic, gray poison creeping up its trunk. Several leaves snapped off and plummeted down to stick in the earth, glimmering like knives.

"It is spreading even faster now." A shadow fell over us, and Oberon swept up on his warhorse, eyes glowing amber beneath his antlered helm. "Every battle, we are forced to fall back, to give more ground. For every Winter or Summer faery that falls, the Iron Kingdom grows, destroying all in its path. If this keeps up, there will be nothing left." Oberon's voice took on a sharper edge. "Also, I thought I told you to stay out of the battle, Meghan Chase. And yet, you fling yourself into the heart of danger, despite my attempts to keep you safe. Why do you continue to defy me?"

Ignoring the question, I looked to the dark forest where the last of the Iron fey were disappearing. Just beyond the tree line, I felt the Iron Kingdom crouched at the edge, eager to creep forward again, watching me with its poisoned glare. Somewhere out there, safe in his land of iron, the false king waited for me, patient and assured, knowing the courts couldn't touch him.

"He knows I'm here now," I murmured, feeling Oberon's eyes on me, as well as the twin gazes of Puck and Ash, and swallowed the tremor in my voice. "I can't stay—he'll send everything he has at you trying to get to me."

"When will you leave?" Oberon's voice held no emotion.

I took a quiet breath and hoped I wasn't sending Ash and Puck straight to their deaths.

"Tonight." As soon as I said it, I shivered violently and crossed my arms to hide my terror. "The sooner I go, the better. I guess it's time."

CHAPTER FOURTEEN

INTO THE IRON REALM

I folded the blanket carefully and placed it in the pack, next to the packages of dried fruit and nuts and the goatskin of water. Water, food, blanket, bedroll…was there anything else I needed for the camping trip to hell? I could think of a few purely human conveniences I'd kill to have right then— flashlight, aspirin, toilet paper—but Faery refused to humor my half-mortal side, so I'd have to do without.

Behind me, the tent flap opened, and Ash stood there, silhouetted against the tent wall and the eerie red light of the moon. "Ready?"

I flipped the bag shut and fumbled with the ties, cursing softly as my hands shook. "As ready as I'll ever be, I suppose," I muttered, hoping he wouldn't catch the tremor in my voice. The ties slipped from my fingers again, and I growled a curse.

The tent flaps closed, and a moment later his arms were around me, covering my shaking hands with his own. Closing my eyes, I relaxed into him as he bent close, his breath cool on my neck.

"I don't want to be their assassin," I whispered, leaning into him. He didn't say anything, only fisted his hands over mine, drawing me closer. "I thought...when I killed Machina...I wouldn't have to do anything like that ever again. I still have nightmares about it." Sighing, I buried my face in his arm. "I'm not backing out. I know I have to do this, but...I'm not a killer, Ash."

"I know," he murmured against my skin. "And you're *not* a killer. Look." Opening his fists, he held my hands in his, stroking my palms with his thumbs. "Perfectly clean," he said. "No stains, no blood. Trust me, if you could see mine..." He sighed and closed his fists again, curling his fingers around my own. "I would save you from my fate, if I could," he said, so soft I barely heard him, even as close as we were. "Let me kill the false king. I have so much blood on my hands, it wouldn't matter."

"You would do that?"

"If I can."

I thought about it, content to feel his arms around me. "I guess...as long as the false king dies, it doesn't matter who kills him, right?" Ash shrugged, but I felt uncomfortable with that decision. This was *my* quest. *I* had agreed to kill the false king. The responsibility was mine, and I didn't want anyone to have to kill for me again, especially Ash.

Although, I still didn't know how I was going to accomplish any of this when we got there. We didn't have a magic Witchwood arrow this time. We just had...me. "Let's not worry about it now," I said, not wanting to think about it anymore. "We have to *reach* him first, anyway."

"Which we'll never do if you two keep groping each other every two seconds," Puck announced, entering the room with a swooshing of tent flaps. Blushing, I stepped away from Ash and pretended to check my pack. Puck snorted. "If you two are quite ready," he said, pushing back the cloth, "we're all waiting on you."

We left the tent, stepping into the cold, still night. My breath clouded the air, and sooty flakes landed on my face and hands. On each side, lining the way to the forest, the armies of Summer and Winter watched us leave, hundreds of fey eyes glowing in the darkness. Somewhere in the camp, a wyvern screeched, but other than that, everything was silent.

Mab and Oberon stood at the edge of the crowd, both as still as the trees themselves. Beyond the rulers, the glimmering forest of steel stretched away into darkness.

"We have given you everything we can," Oberon said as we approached, his solemn voice echoing over the crowds. "From here on, we can only wish you luck, and wait. Everything is up to you now."

Mab raised a hand, and a goblin stepped out of the crowd to stand before us, dressed in that leafy camouflage that made him look like a bush. "Snigg will take you to the edge of the forest where it becomes the Wasteland proper," she rasped, her gaze lingering on Ash. "Beyond that, you're on your own. None of our scouts have ever returned from venturing deeper."

Oberon was still watching me, his green eyes unreadable in the shadows of his face. It seemed to me that the Erlking looked tired and haggard, but that could simply be a trick of the light. "Be careful, daughter," he said in a voice meant only for me.

I sighed. That was as much fatherly affection Oberon was going to dole out. "I will," I told him, shifting my pack to my other shoulder. "And we won't fail, I—" I barely stopped myself from saying "I *swear*," not knowing whether I could keep that promise. "I won't give up," I finished instead.

He gave me a brief nod. Ash bowed to his queen, and Puck grinned at Oberon, defiant to the end. I looked down at the goblin.

"Let's go, Snigg."

The goblin bobbed and shuffled away into the trees, becoming nearly invisible in the brush. With Ash and Puck at my side, I stepped into the forest, following the bobbing mound of vegetation through the trees, and the camp soon faded behind us.

"I RECOGNIZE THIS," Ash muttered after several minutes of walking. Following the goblin scout, we ducked and wove around trees whose trunks looked like they'd been covered in mercury, shiny and metallic in the dappled light. "I think I know where we are."

"Really." Puck sounded sarcastic. "I was wondering when you'd figure it out, prince. Granted, none of the masses knew how close they were, either, so props for knowing your history." He snorted. "You can bet both Oberon and Mab knew it, and deliberately didn't let on. Typical."

"Why?" I glanced around, seeing nothing unusual—beyond the strangeness of a completely metal forest, anyway. "Where are we?"

"This is Fomorian territory," Ash said, narrowing his eyes. "We're heading right for Mag Tuiredh."

I blinked at Ash. "What's Mag Tuiredh? What are Fomorians?"

"An ancient race of giants, princess," Puck answered, ducking a low-hanging branch. "Semiaquatic, clannish and the ugliest bastards you'd ever have the misfortune of seeing. Deformed and twisted, the lot of them. I'm talking one-armed, one-eyed terrors with hooves growing out of their heads, limbs in places they're not supposed to be. One of their queens even had a set of teeth on each of her—"

"Okay, I think I got it." I shuddered, skirting a bush with metal thorns growing out of it like needles. "So, are these giant things hostile? Do you think they've been killed by the iron?"

"Oh, they were definitely hostile," Puck continued cheerfully. "In fact, they were so hostile, we had a war with them, long, long ago. I think it was the *only* other time Summer and Winter cooperated, right prince? Oh, wait, you weren't even around yet, were you?"

"They're extinct, Meghan," Ash said, ignoring Puck. "They've been extinct for centuries. Summer and Winter completely wiped them out. Mag Tuiredh was their city. It's nothing but ruins now, and generally everyone avoids it. It's an evil place, full of curses and unknown monsters. One of the darker places of the Nevernever."

"And the perfect place for the new Iron King," I mused.

We fell silent then, for the trees abruptly fell away and the Iron Kingdom stretched out before us.

I remembered the heart of Machina's realm, the flat, cracked plateau, spiderwebbed with lava, and the endless railroad that led to the black tower. This was different, a blasted, rocky desert with huge, jagged outcroppings and uneven hills. Looking closer, I saw that some of the hills were huge piles of junk: tires, pipes, smashed cars, rusty barrels, satellite dishes, broken computers and laptops, even the wing of an airplane. Street lamps grew out of the rocky ground or atop distant outcroppings, glimmering faintly in the haze. The corroded red moon, balanced atop two pointed ridges, seemed closer than ever.

"Interesting," Puck remarked, crossing his arms to his chest. "You know, I used to say Fomorian territory couldn't get any worse than it was. Nice to know I can still be proven wrong once in a while."

Ash stepped forward, gazing around the wasteland in silence. His back was to me, so I couldn't see his face, but he was probably remembering our last trip into the Iron Kingdom. I wondered if he was already regretting his promise.

Snigg the goblin gave a feeble cough, muttered an apology, and scurried back into the forest the way we'd come, leaving us to our fate. Suddenly alarmed, I looked harder at Ash and Puck, cursing myself for not realizing sooner. We were deep in the Iron Realm now; Ash and Puck would be feeling the effects of the land, the poison that would kill them if those amulets didn't work.

"Are you two all right? Ash? Look at me." I grabbed the prince's arm and turned him toward me, peering into his face. His skin seemed paler than usual, and my stomach twisted. "The amulets aren't working, are they? I knew it. We should go back."

"No." Ash put his hand over mine. "It's fine, Meghan. They're working well enough. I can still feel the iron, but it's bearable. Not like before."

"Are you sure?" When he nodded, I looked from him to Puck. "What about you?"

Puck shrugged. "It's no Shiatsu massage, princess, but I'll live."

I glared at them. "I know faeries can't lie, but you two better not be saying that just so I won't worry." Neither of them said anything, and my anger rose. "I mean it, you two."

"Relax, princess." Puck shrugged defensively. "They're working, okay? I know I'm not supposed to feel great, but I don't feel like my insides are about to crawl up my throat, either. I'll live. I've been through worse."

"And it doesn't matter." Ash faced me with an air of stubborn calm. "We'd still be here, regardless. We can't go back now. Besides, we're wasting time."

"I agree," came another voice, deeper in the Iron Realm. "The protective qualities of your amulets are limited, after all. The longer you stand around doing nothing, the shorter your time becomes."

Somehow, I wasn't surprised. "Grimalkin," I sighed, turning around. "Stop hiding. Where are you?"

The cat glanced up from a nearby rock, where nothing had been a second ago. "You," he purred, regarding us lazily, "are late. Again."

"Why are you here, Grim?"

"Is it not obvious?" Grimalkin yawned and looked at each of us in turn. "The same reason I am always here, human. To keep you from falling down a dark hole or wandering into a giant spider's nest."

"You can't stay here," I told him. "The iron will kill you and you don't have an amulet."

Grimalkin sniffed. "Really, human, you are incredibly dim at times. Who do you think told Mab about the amulets in the first place?" He raised his chin, just far enough for me to catch a glint of crystal beneath his wavy fur.

"*You* have one? How?"

The cat sat down and licked his forepaw. "Do you really wish to know, human?" he asked, giving me a sideways glance. "Be careful of your answer. Some things are better off a mystery."

"What kind of answer is that? Of course I want to know, especially now!"

He sighed, vibrating his whiskers. "Very well. But, keep in mind, you insisted." Putting his paw down, he sat up and curled his tail around himself, regarding me with a grave expression. "Do you remember the day Ironhorse died?"

A lump caught in my throat. Of course I did. I could never forget that night. Ironhorse charging the enemy alone so we could have a distraction; Ironhorse shielding me from a fatal blow; Ironhorse, shattered and broken on the cement floor of the warehouse. His last words. I teared up, thinking about it.

And then, I remembered Grimalkin, sitting beside the noble Iron faery just before he died, leaning close to his head. I'd thought my eyes were playing tricks on me, for I'd caught only a split-second glance before the cat was gone, but now it seemed extremely important that I remember.

My stomach felt cold. "What did you do to him, Grim?"

"Nothing." Grimalkin faced me with an unblinking stare.

"Nothing that he had not already agreed to. I knew I would have to go into the Iron Realm sooner or later, and Ironhorse knew he could very well die on his quest to help you. He was prepared for it. We came to...an understanding."

"Oh my God." The realization hit me like a hammer, and I gaped at the cat. "That's him in there, isn't it? You used Ironhorse for your amulet." I felt sick and staggered away from the cait sith, bumping into Ash. "How could you?" I whispered, actually beginning to shake. "Is *everything* a contract to you? Ironhorse was our friend, I would have died without his help. Or don't you care that you're using him like a battery?"

"Ironhorse was prepared to give up everything for you, human." Grimalkin narrowed his eyes to golden slits, staring me down. "He wanted this. He wanted a way to protect you if he were no longer here. You should be grateful. I would not have done the same. Because of his sacrifice, the quest can continue." The cat rose and leaped from the rock, turning to stare at us over his shoulder.

"Well?" he asked, waving his tail. "Are you coming or not?"

I scowled and took a few steps forward. "Where do you think you're taking us?"

He twitched an ear. "Ironhorse told me, should I ever find myself in the Iron Realm with you, to look for an old friend of his. The Clockmaker, I believe was his name. And he is fairly close. Lucky for us."

"Why go to the Clockmaker? Why not just look for the false king?"

"Ironhorse implied that this was important, human." Grimalkin blinked and sat down, thumping his tail impatiently. "But, if you do not think so, by all means go wandering about until the amulets lose their power and you are completely lost. Or, was that your plan all along?"

I glanced at the boys. They both shrugged. "Seems as good

a plan as any," Puck said, rolling his eyes. "If the cat knows where he's going, that is. I'd hate to get lost in here."

Grimalkin sniffed, curling his whiskers in disdain. "Please, do not insult me. Lost? Since when have I ever led you wrong?"

I sighed. "Here we go again."

AFTER A NIGHT OF WALKING, I realized just how *big* the Fomorian city was.

I'd imagined Mag Tuiredh as a city of sprawling ruins: crumbled stone walls, half-erect buildings, and just a scattering of large rocks where a castle once stood. And perhaps, if it had been in the real world, that's all it would have been. But in the Nevernever, where age and time didn't exist and even the structures resisted the concept of decay, Mag Tuiredh loomed tall and threatening in the hazy distance, black towers belching smoke into the mottled yellow sky.

"How old is this city?" I asked, shielding my eyes to peer across the barren landscape. Even through the mottled yellow-gray clouds, the light still glinted off a thousand metallic things, flashing in the sun and blinding me. Puck and Grimalkin had seen some movement in the rocks, and were scouting around to find the source of it.

"No one really knows," Ash replied, his gaze sweeping over the landscape. "The Fomorians were here before us, and their city was already massive. Back then, Mag Tuiredh sat half in and half out of the mortal realm, in a place known today as Ireland. Because humans still worshipped us as gods and the Nevernever was still very young, many faery races preferred to live in the mortal realm. The Fomorians had already enslaved several lesser races, and tried to do the same to us. Naturally, we didn't take very kindly to that."

"So there was a war."

"One that rocked the foundations of both realms. In the end, Mag Tuiredh was pulled completely into the Nevernever, and the Fomorians were driven into the sea. That was the last anyone saw of them. At least, that's the story I've heard."

"But if they're gone…" I looked back to the city and the dark smoke boiling into the sky "…why are those things still smoking?"

"I don't know." Ash shifted his gaze to the distant towers. "Mag Tuiredh supposedly sat empty for thousands of years, but who knows what it's been turned into now. Judging from that smoke, I would say Mag Tuiredh is no longer uninhabited."

"Bad news." Puck suddenly dropped from an overhead slab, landing beside us with a poof of dust. "We're being followed. Grim and I saw something that looked like a giant metal insect, buzzing along behind us. I tried to catch the little bastard, but it saw me coming and booked it."

"You think there are more of them?" Ash tensed and dropped his hand to his sword, probably remembering the gremlin hoard swarming him in the mines on our first trip here. Puck's eyes darkened, and he shook his head.

"Dunno. But I think someone knows we're here."

Grim popped into view on a rock, twitching his tail. His wispy gray fur stood on end like he'd just come out of a dryer with horrible static cling. "There is a storm coming. We should seek cover."

No sooner were the words out of his mouth than a flash of lightning lit the sky and the air filled with the tang of ozone.

The hairs on my neck stood up. "Grim," I gasped, whirling on the feline, "get us out of here! We have to find shelter now!"

Whether it was my terrified look or the panic in my voice, the cat didn't dawdle this time. We fled, scrambling over dirt and rock, while above us the sky turned from yellow-gray to black in a matter of seconds. Sharp-smelling wind whipped at our clothes and made my eyes water, and the air around us felt charged with electricity. A thread of green lightning slashed the sky, and the first drops began to fall.

A searing pain stabbed me in the thigh, and I clenched my teeth to keep from screaming, knowing one of the acidic drops had just hit me. Somewhere behind us, Puck yelped in shock and surprise. My stomach churned, and I could no longer see the cat in the darkness and rising wind.

"Grimalkin!" I yelled in desperation.

"This way!" The cat's yowl cut through the growing storm, and two glowing eyes suddenly appeared at the mouth of a cave in the side of a cliff. The cave was so well hidden, blending perfectly into the landscape, that had Grimalkin not been there I never would've seen it.

Another drop hit my forehead, sliding down my cheek, and this time I did scream as a line of fire slashed down my skin. I could hear the hiss of the rain striking all around us, and I threw myself into the cave, followed by Ash and Puck, just as the sky opened with a roar and the rain poured down.

Gasping, I lay on my back on the sandy floor, watching the storm sweep the land, while Ash and Puck leaned against the cave wall, panting.

"Well, that was...different," Puck gasped. "What the hell is that anyway?"

"Acid rain," I said, not having the will to push myself off the floor just yet. My face throbbed, and the sand was cool against my cheek. "We ran into it on our first trip here, too. Not fun."

"Welcome to the wonders of the Iron Kingdom," Ash muttered, and pushed himself off the wall, coming to kneel beside me. I took his hand and let him pull me into a sitting position.

"Are you all right?" he asked, brushing the hair from my face, lifting it away from the burn. His fingers hovered over the wound, and I flinched despite myself, causing him to sigh. I saw Puck watching us over Ash's shoulder, and blushed self-consciously, suddenly desperate to break the tension.

"So, tell me the truth," I said, only half joking. "Will it scar? Will I have to wear a mask like the Phantom of the Opera, to hide my hideous face?"

Ash shrugged off his pack, and a moment later a cool, familiar-smelling salve touched my cheek, soothing the fiery pain. "I think you'll be fine," he said, smiling faintly. "No battle scars for you, at least not today." His hand lingered on my face a moment more before he rose, drawing me to my feet. Puck snorted and walked away, pretending to examine the cave.

Grimalkin strutted by, tail in the air, oblivious to the rising tension. "The rain will not let up anytime soon," he said as he passed, "so I suggest you get some rest while you can. I also suggest one of you take watch. We do not want to be surprised if the owner of this cave returns while we are asleep."

"Good idea," Puck echoed from the back of the cave. "Why don't you take first watch, prince? You could actually be doing something that doesn't make me want to gouge my eyes out with a spork."

Ash's lips curled in a smirk. "I would think you're better suited to the task, Goodfellow," he said without turning around. "After all, that's what you're best at, isn't it? Watching?"

"Oh, keep it up, ice-boy. You're gonna have to sleep sometime."

I rolled my eyes at them. "Fine. You two fight it out—I'm going to try to get some sleep." Unshouldering my pack, I stalked to a corner, dumped out the contents, and unrolled my sleeping bag. Lying on the sandy floor, I listened to Ash and Puck's back-and-forth banter as they set up camp, throwing out insults and challenges. Strangely, it seemed more normal than it had been until now, and I fell asleep to their voices and the sound of the rain.

HE WAS WAITING FOR ME in my dreams again.

I sighed. "Machina," I said, facing the Iron King, my voice nearly lost in the surrounding void, "why are you here? I thought I told you to leave me alone. I don't need you."

"No," he murmured, smiling as his cables cloaked him in a cage of glimmering steel. "That is not true. You've come far, but you're still not there yet, Meghan Chase. You still need me."

"I don't." I didn't move as he approached, the cables reaching out to snake around me. "I'm stronger now than when we first met. I'm learning to control the magic you left me with." With a thought, I pushed the cables away, causing them to rear back in surprise.

"You still don't understand." Machina withdrew his extensions, folding them like shimmery wings behind his back. "You use the magic like a tool, like a sword that you swing in awkward circles, cutting wildly at those around you. If you are to win, you must embrace it fully, make it a part of you. If you would only let me show you how."

"You've given me enough," I said bitterly. "I didn't ask for this. I didn't want it. If you were alive, I would be happy if you took it back."

"I could not." Machina regarded me with depthless black eyes. "The power of the Iron King can be given, or it can be lost. It cannot be taken."

I frowned. "Then...why is the false king trying to kill me? If the power can only be given away, why is he trying to take it by force?"

Machina shook his head. "The false king has never learned how a king is chosen. Believing he can wrench the power from you by force, he has become blind in his obsession. He does not realize his actions only make him less worthy."

"If I die...then the power is lost?"

Machina nodded. "Unless you give it away yourself, or it chooses a new successor."

"Can't I just give it away now?"

"No," Machina said flatly. "If the power is to be given, it must be given at the moment of death. When the bearer knows they are going to die, only then will the power leave the body. If the bearer dies without choosing a successor, the power will lie dormant, waiting, until someone comes along who is worthy to bear it. But no, you cannot just give it away whenever you please." Machina sounded faintly insulted at the thought. "Besides, Meghan Chase, who would you give it to? Who would you find worthy enough to carry that burden?"

"I suppose that means you somehow found me worthy," I muttered, "though I really wish you wouldn't have bothered."

The Iron King only smiled.

"I will be here," he murmured, fading away, his brightness becoming less and less, though his voice still echoed in the void. "You cannot win without me, Meghan Chase. Until we are one, you are destined to lose this war."

I OPENED MY EYES TO SILENCE. The rain had stopped, and a warm furry weight was pressed against my ribs, vibrating with purrs. Careful not to disturb Grimalkin, I rose and pushed back the covers, gazing around the cave. Puck lay on his back in the corner, tangled in blankets, one arm flung over his eyes. A jackhammer snore echoed from his open mouth, and I grimaced.

Ash stood at the cave mouth, silhouetted black against the cloudy sky, gazing out at the distant city. From the sickly light coming in, I guessed it was mid to late afternoon. By the subtle tilt of Ash's head, I knew he'd heard me, but he didn't turn around.

Padding up behind him, I slipped my arms around his waist. His hands folded over mine, lacing our fingers together, and we stood like that for a moment, breathing in tandem, me listening to his heart through his armor.

"Are you all right?" His deep voice vibrated in my ear, pressed against his back.

"Fine." I pulled back to stare at the back of his head. "Why? Reading my emotions again, are you?"

"You were talking in your sleep," he continued solemnly. "I wasn't listening, but you said 'Machina' once or twice." He paused, and my heart flip-flopped in my chest. "It's the Iron Kingdom, isn't it?" Ash went on. "Being back here, it's making you remember."

"Yeah," I lied, pressing my face to his back. I didn't want to tell him about my conversations with the old Iron King, whom we had killed on our last trip here but who was supposedly lurking inside me. "It was just a nightmare, Ash. Don't worry about me."

"That's my job now," he replied, so soft I barely heard it. "Meghan, don't be afraid to ask for help. You're not alone. Remember that."

I squirmed uncomfortably, hoping he wouldn't pick up on my feelings of guilt. "So, this knight-and-lady thing," I said to change the subject. "Do you have to do what I say? Or is it more of a strong suggestion? If I ordered you to...I don't know...stand on your head, would you do it?"

I wasn't trying to be serious, but he hesitated, and I wondered if I touched on a sore subject. "You know my True Name now," he said after a moment. "Technically, yes, if you order me by use of my full name, I would be forced to obey. But..." He paused again. I'd never heard him sound so unsure. "The understanding is that it will never come to that. That...the lady trusts the knight enough to..."

"Ash," I interrupted. "Turn around."

He obeyed, spinning slowly to face me, his expression

carefully guarded. Lacing my hands behind his neck, I pulled
him down and kissed him. For just a moment, he was stiff
and unyielding, but then he relaxed and his arms slid around
my waist, drawing us closer.

"I'm sorry," I whispered when we pulled back. "I don't
want you to regret…being here with me, being my knight
and all."

He ran his fingers through my hair, brushing it from my
cheek. "If I'd thought I would regret it," he said calmly, "I
never would have made that oath. I knew what becoming a
knight would mean. And if you asked me again, the answer
would be the same." He sighed, framing my face with his
hands. "My life…everything I am…belongs to you."

My eyes prickled as Ash leaned in and kissed me.

A particularly loud snore came from the cave, and the lump
in the corner rolled toward us suspiciously. Ash sighed again,
drawing back after giving the "sleeping" Puck a resigned
look. "We should leave soon," he murmured, glancing toward
the city. "If we go now, we can reach Mag Tuiredh before
nightfall. Also, I saw Puck's metal insect, flying around out
there. It's definitely following us. And if it does attack, I'd
rather be able to see it coming than have to fight it in the
dark."

I shivered and dropped my gaze, staring at the amulet on
his chest. The crystal was no longer perfectly clear. Inside,
the swirls were silvery and metallic, like the mercury inside
a thermometer. It gave me a chill, like staring at the falling
grains of an hourglass, reminding me that his time in the Iron
Realm was limited. "Right," I said, breaking away. "Let's get
going then. Puck, I know you're awake. We're leaving."

"Oh, thank God." Puck snorted and hopped to his feet.
"I was afraid I'd have to listen to you two slobber all morning. I'm already feeling slightly sick—please don't make it
worse."

"Indeed," Grimalkin added from the mouth of the cave,

though he had been sleeping on my blanket a second before. "Let us go. We are running out of time."

Quickly, we gathered our supplies and set out again. The looming Fomorian city beckoned in the distance.

As we left the cave, following Grim and Puck over the rocks, I caught a shimmer from the corner of my eye, like a heat wave, darting behind a boulder. I stopped and glanced back, but empty sand and rock greeted me when I turned my head.

"Did you see it?" Ash muttered as we started down the dusty path again.

Frowning, I glared around the landscape, wincing as the sun flashed off the random metallic objects scattered every-where. "I don't know. I thought I saw...something. Like a shimmer almost, but a clear one. You saw it?"

He nodded, his hunter's gaze never still, constantly scan-ning. "Something is tracking us," he said in a low voice. "Goodfellow knows it, too. Keep alert. We could run into trouble soo—"

It attacked from the top of a boulder, leaping at us with a scream. One second, there was nothing. The next, that strange shimmer rippled through the air again, and something slammed into me, raking my armor with invisible claws that screeched against the dragon-scale. I staggered back as a long feline shape, large as a cougar and translucent as glass, leaped away from Ash's sword and darted into the rocks again.

I drew my sword with a raspy screech as Puck pulled his daggers, his eyes darting around the empty landscape. "Anyone wanna tell me what *that* was?" he said, just as a second transparent cat-thing leaped at him from the oppo-site direction. I yelled and he ducked, the cat barely missing him. Landing in a spray of dust, it bounded into the rocks and vanished.

We moved to stand back-to-back, weapons out in front of us, searching for a glimpse of our invisible assailants. *No, I*

thought, *not invisible,* that didn't make sense, not in the Iron
Kingdom. Grimalkin could become invisible, using normal
glamour to do so—in fact, he had already disappeared. Regular glamour was the magic of illusion and myth, things the
Iron fey could not work with, so how were they hiding their
presence? What was the logical explanation?

There was a blur as the monster cats attacked again, rushing in from opposite sides. I didn't see them until one was
right on top of me, and I felt hooked claws raking my side.
They were frighteningly quick. Thankfully, the dragon-scale
armor held, screeching and sparking in protest, but the cat
darted away again before I could react.

Puck snarled a curse, swiping at empty air as the second
cat flashed behind the rocks once more and was gone. Blood
dripped down his arm to spatter in the dust; he hadn't been
as lucky, and my desperation grew.

Think, Meghan! There had to be an explanation. Iron fey
couldn't use regular glamour, so how could a solid creature appear invisible? I could feel the Iron glamour circling
around us, cold, patient, and calculating, and suddenly I
understood.

"They're cloaking," I said, as the pieces clicked into place.
"They're using Iron glamour to twist the light around themselves so they appear invisible." I felt a thrill of discovery, of
knowing I was right. All those years of watching *Star Trek*
had finally paid off.

Ash spared me a split-second glance. "Can you use it to
see which direction they're coming from?"

"I'll try."

Closing my eyes, I reached out, searching for our attack-
ers, expanding my senses until…there. I could feel them in
my mind, two clear, cat-shaped blobs of glamour, creeping
forward along the ground just a few yards away. One was
edging up on Ash, muscles quivering, and leaped forward
with a shriek.

"Ash, high left! Seven o' clock!"

Ash whirled, exploding into motion. I heard a yowl, and the cat shape in my mind split in two just before something hot and wet splashed over my face.

Not stopping to think or gag, I saw the second cat leap straight at me, claws extended, aiming for my neck this time. My sword came up, and the monster slammed into my chest, its leap carrying it right onto the blade. The cat's weight knocked me backward to sprawl in the dust, driving the air from my lungs with a painful gasp.

For a few seconds, I could only lie there with my mouth gaping, crushed under the body of the killer feline. Up close, the dead cat was a strange metallic gray, its fur short and shiny like a mirror. But its teeth were the same yellow ivory of all big cats, pointed and lethal, and its breath stank of rotten meat and battery acid. That was all I noticed before Ash dragged the huge feline off me and Puck pulled me to my feet.

"Well, that was fun." Puck wore one of his sarcastic grimaces. "You okay, princess?"

"Yeah." I gave Ash a quick smile to ease the worry on his face, and turned to Puck again. "I'm fine—but you're bleeding, Puck!"

"What, this?" Puck grinned. "It's just a scratch." His grin turned into a grimace as I sat him down on a rock and started tearing off his sleeve. His arm was a mess, blood everywhere, and I could see the four nasty claw marks that ran from his elbow to wrist. I winced in sympathy.

"Ash, I'm going to need some of that salve you brought," I muttered, dabbing away the blood. When he didn't move, I turned on him, narrowing my eyes. "All right, I'm tired of this. I know you two don't get along, but you need to figure something out or we're never going to make it out of here alive."

I received a rather cold stare, but he opened his bag and

dug out the jar, handing it to me stiffly. Puck settled back on the rock, grinning as I bent over his arm.

"You're good at this, princess," he purred, shooting Ash a smug grin over my shoulder. "Been watching ice-boy, or are you just a natural caretaker? I could get used to—ow!"

He glared as I tied off the bandage with a jerk.

"Don't push your luck," I warned him, and he gave me a huge, doe-eyed look full of innocence. It was the first glimpse of the old Puck I'd seen in a long time, and it made me smile.

As I was gathering the medical supplies, Grimalkin appeared again, wrinkling his nose at the dead cats. "Barbarians," he sniffed, leaping down from the rock, giving the bodies a wide berth as he trotted up. "Human, you might want to know that there are certainly other creatures that will be attracted by the commotion. I would advise you to hurry."

CHAPTER FIFTEEN

THE CLOCKMAKER

We reached the Fomorian city just as the sun was going down.

Mag Tuiredh was enormous. Not just sprawling, but *huge.* As in *I-feel-like-I've-been-shrunk-to-the-size-of-a-mouse* huge. Like Jack-in-the-Beanstalk huge. Everything was giant-size: doorways were twenty feet tall, streets were wide enough to drive a plane through, and steps were *my* height. Whomever the Fomorians were, I hoped that they were really gone as Ash said.

The city was ancient; I could feel it as we made our way through the mossy ruins, which towered like broken giants overhead. The original buildings were made of rough stone, but the Iron Realm's corruption was everywhere. Broken street lamps popped up at odd intervals, grown right out of the ground and flickering erratically. Cables and computer wires snaked up walls, spread across the streets, and coiled around everything, as if trying to choke the life from the old city. In the distance, near the center of Mag Tuiredh, black smokestacks loomed over everything, belching smog into the hazy sky.

"So, where do we find this Clockmaker?" Puck asked as

we walked through a square filled with strange metallic trees. The trees were in full bloom, not with flowers or fruit, but with lightbulbs that glowed with eerie brightness. A fountain in the middle of the square bubbled a thick, shiny black liquid that might've been oil.

Grimalkin looked back at us, eyes shining in the gloom. "The most obvious place possible," he said, and turned his gaze skyward.

Over the tops of the buildings, rising up toward the clouds like a dark needle, a giant clock tower peered down on the city with a face like a numbered moon.

"Oh." Puck craned his neck back, staring at the huge timepiece. "Well, that's…ironic." He scratched the back of his head and frowned. "I hope the Clockmaker is still awake. He probably doesn't get a lot of visitors after nine p.m."

Something about that statement put me on edge, even more so when I looked at Ash, who was staring at the clock in growing horror. "It shouldn't be here," he murmured, shaking his head. "How is it even working? Time doesn't exist in the Nevernever, but that thing is recording the passing of it, keeping track. With every second it records, the Nevernever gets older."

I remembered the way my watch stopped on my first trip to Faery, and looked at Grim in alarm. "Is that true?"

The cat blinked. "I am not an expert on the Iron Realm, human. Even I cannot give you the answers to everything." Raising a hind leg, he scratched inside an ear, then contemplated his back toes. "But, remember this—nothing lives forever. Even the Nevernever has an age, though no one can remember what it is. That clock is not recording anything new."

"It should be destroyed," Ash muttered, still glaring at it.

"I would refrain from angering its keeper until we secure his help." Grimalkin stood, stretched, then suddenly went rigid. Ears twitching, he stood motionless for a moment, listening for something beyond the circle of trees. The hair slowly rose along his back, and I gulped, knowing he was seconds away from disappearing.

"Grim?"

The cat's ears flattened. "They are all around us," he hissed, just before he vanished.

We drew our weapons.

Thousands of green eyes pierced the darkness, razor grins shining like neon-blue fire, as a huge hoard of gremlins poured into the light. Like ants, the swarm flowed over the ground, buzzing and hissing in their static voices, to surround us. We stood back-to-back, a tiny circle of open ground in a sea of little black monsters with grinning fangs and glowing eyes.

Thousands of voices chattered at me, like a hundred radios turned on all at once. The noise was deafening, nonsensical, high buzzing voices grating in my ears. But the gremlins didn't attack. They stood there, dancing or hopping in place, teeth flashing like razors, but they moved no closer.

"What are they doing?" Puck asked. He had to yell to be heard.

"I don't know!" I replied. The cacophony was giving me a headache; my ears were ringing, and it seemed the noise got even worse at the sound of my voice. Without even think-ing about it, I raised my head and yelled *"Shut up!"* into the hoard of gremlins.

Silence descended instantly. You could've heard a cricket chirp.

Wide-eyed, I shared a glance with Ash and Puck. "Why are they listening to me?" I whispered. Ash narrowed his eyes.

"I don't know, but can you do it again?"

"Back off," I tried, taking a step forward. A whole section of gremlins scooted backward, keeping the same distance between us. Another step, and they did the same thing. I blinked.

"Okay, this is creepy. Go away?" I asked, but this time the gremlins didn't move, and some of them hissed at me. I backed up. "Well, I guess I can only push them so far."

"Don't ask them to leave," Ash murmured behind me. "Tell them."

"Are you sure that's a good idea?"

He nodded. I swallowed and faced the hoard again, hoping they wouldn't decide to swarm me like angry piranhas. "Get out of here!" I told them, raising my voice. "Now!"

The gremlins hissed and crackled and screeched in protest, but withdrew, flowing backward like the tide, until we were alone in an empty square.

"How…interesting," Grimalkin mused, back to being visible again. "It is almost as if they were waiting for you."

"That was weird," I agreed, rubbing my arms, where I could still feel the vibrations of the gremlins buzzing on my skin. The gremlins were listening to me now, just like they had with Machina. Since I had the power of the Iron King, they probably thought I was their new master, disturbing as that was. I certainly didn't want a hoard of creepy little monsters following me around, laughing and causing trouble. The whole incident put me on edge, and I was eager to get out of the city. "Come on," I said. "I think we should keep moving."

WE CONTINUED, HEADING TOWARD the tower where the huge clock kept watch over the city. Everywhere we went, I could feel the gremlins' eyes on me and hear them skittering in the shadows. Did they want something from me? Or were they just curious? Apart from the gremlins, Mag Tuiredh seemed devoid of life. But that didn't explain the smoking towers in the distance, or the flashes of Iron glamour I felt all around me.

The farther we ventured into Mag Tuiredh, the more "modern" the city became. Rusty steel buildings sat among the ancient ruins, thick black wires ran over our heads, and neon lights glimmered from the tops of roofs and corners. Smog writhed along the streets and sidewalks, adding an eerie, creepy feel to the dead city. I wondered where all the Iron fey were. Not that I wanted to run into any, but in a city this big, you would think there'd be at least a few.

When we reached the base of the clock tower, I was amazed at how huge it was; a tower of steel and glass and metal, sitting among ancient ruins that were gigantic themselves, looming over them all. But the door to the tower was human-size, bronze and copper and covered with gears that clanked and spun as I wrenched it open.

An endless staircase ran the length of the walls, spiraling up into blackness. Ropes and pulleys dangled from thick metal beams, and monstrous gears spun lazily in the huge expanse of the middle. It was, obviously enough, like being inside a giant clock.

"This way," came Grimalkin's voice, and we followed the cat up the twisting staircase until he vanished somewhere above us. The stairs had no railings, and I hugged the wall as we went higher into the clock, the floor just a shrinking stone square far, far below.

Finally, the staircase ended in a balcony that overlooked the long drop to the bottom. Directly overhead was the wooden ceiling, and in the center of the balcony, a ladder led up to a square trapdoor, the kind you would push on to get into the attic. Puck climbed the ladder, jiggled the trapdoor, and when he discovered it wasn't locked, eased it open so he could peer through the crack. A moment later, he pushed it back all the way and motioned the rest of us up.

A cozy, cluttered room greeted us as we eased through the trapdoor, being careful not to make any noise. The floors and walls were all made of wood, with the far wall showing the back of the enormous clock face. Several tables ran through the room, every square inch of them taken up by timepieces of various sizes and designs. The walls were also covered with them. Cuckoo clocks, grandfather clocks, wooden clocks, sleek metal clocks—you name it, this place had it. All the clock faces showed a different time; none of them were the same. An endless ticking filled the air, and the occasional tweet, chime, or dong echoed throughout the room. If I stayed here long enough, I would go insane in a very short while.

The Clockmaker, whoever he was, was nowhere to be seen. A stuffed green chair sat in the corner, an island of comfort in the sea of clutter, though at the moment it was far from empty.

A huge, mirror-coated feline lay curled up on the cushion, breathing deeply as if asleep. Definitely not Grimalkin; I recognized the same type of creature that had attacked us on our way to the city. Before I could decide what to do, slitted emerald eyes opened and the cat bolted upright with a snarl.

We drew our swords, the screech of blades nearly drowned out by the sudden booming of a grandfather clock in the corner. The cat hissed and immediately rippled out of sight. I quickly reached for my own magic, trying to see where the cat went, ready to yell out instructions to Ash and Puck. But instead of attacking, the cat-shaped spot of glamour leaped onto a table, miraculously avoiding the many clocks that littered the surface, and bounded from the room, vanishing though a small entrance in the back.

"There you are," said a voice. "Right on time."

A small, hunched creature pushed aside a curtain and came waddling down the rows of tables. He was half my height and wore a bright red vest with several pocket watches adorning the fabric. His head was a cross between human and mouse, with large round ears, bright beady eyes, and a mustache that looked suspiciously like whiskers. A thin, tufted tail swayed behind him as he walked, and a pair of tiny gold glasses perched on the end of his nose.

"Hello, Meghan Chase," he greeted, hopping onto a stool and pulling a watch out of his vest, observing it sagely. "It is very good to meet you at last. I would put on a pot of tea, but I'm afraid you have no time to stay and chat. Pity." He blinked at my silence, then must've noticed the wary looks of my companions. "Oh, don't mind Ripple. I keep him around for the gremlins. Nasty little things, gremlins, always getting into the gear heads, throwing everything off. Now, Meghan Chase…" He put his watch away and folded his long fingers to his chest, gazing up at me. "Our time is fading fast. Why have you come?"

I gave a start. "What…don't you know? You already knew my name, and when I was coming."

"Of course." The Clockmaker twitched his whiskers. "Of *course* I knew what time you would get here, girl. Just as I know what time Goodfellow will knock over my nineteenth-century French mantle clock." Puck jerked up at this, bumping a table and sending a clock crashing to the floor. "To the second," the Clockmaker sighed, closing his eyes. Opening them again, he observed me with a piercingly bright gaze, ignoring Puck as he quickly put the clock back on the table, trying to piece it together again. "I see how everything starts, and the exact moment its time runs out. But that was not my question, Meghan Chase. I know why you are here. The question is, do you?"

I shared a look with Ash, who shrugged. "I'm looking for the false king," I said, wincing as Puck dropped something small and shiny with a curse, sending it rolling across the floor. "Ironhorse said you might be able to help."

"Ironhorse?" The Clockmaker's whiskers trembled, and he hopped down from the stool, waddling across the room. "I saw when his clock stopped, when his time finally ran out. He was one of the great ones, though his fate was tied directly to King Machina. When Machina's seconds trickled away, it was only a matter of time before Ironhorse stopped, too."

I swallowed the lump in my throat at the thought of Ironhorse. "We need to find the false king," I said. "Do you know where he is?"

"No." The Clockmaker sniffed, picking up a bolt and frowning at it. "I do not."

I blew out my breath in a huff. "Then why are we here?"

"All in good time, my dear. All in good time." Shooing Puck away from the table, the Clockmaker turned to his work. His long fingers flew over the clock, barely distinguishable blurs, like he was typing something in fast-forward. "I told you, girl, I know the *time* things happen, and when they end. I do not know the reasons why. Nor do I know the location of the false king." He straightened, fishing in his vest to pull out a white cloth, which he used to polish the once-broken clock. "However, I do know this. You will find him, and find him soon. Your destiny, and the destiny of many others, are shown in the faces of the clocks, ticking away together. So, you see, girl." He picked up the clock and hopped from the stool, pausing to stare at me with beady eyes. "You already know everything you need to find him."

I bit down my impatience. This was useless. And every second we wasted here, Puck and Ash's amulets were corroding, succumbing to the poison of the Iron Realm. "Please," I told the Clockmaker, "we don't have much…time. If you say you can help us, do it now so we can be on our way."

"Yes," agreed the Clockmaker, turning to face me fully. "*Now* it is time."

He reached into his vest, and pulled out a large iron key on a silk ribbon. "This is yours," he said solemnly, handing it over. "Keep it safe. Do not lose it, for you will need it soon."

I took the key, watching it spin and dangle in the light. "What is it for?"

"I do not know." The Clockmaker blinked at my frown. "As I said, girl; I only know the *when* of a thing. I do not know the *hows* and *whys*. But I do know this: in one hundred and sixty-one hours, thirteen minutes, and fifty-two seconds, you will need that key."

"A hundred and sixty hours? That's several *days* from now. How am I supposed to keep track?"

"Take this." The Clockmaker reached into the other side of his vest and drew forth a pocket watch, spinning hypnotically on a gold chain. "Everyone should have a time device," he stated as he handed it to me. "I do not know how the oldbloods do it, never worrying about time. I would find it simply maddening. So, I give this to you."

"I…um…appreciate it."

His whiskers twitched. "I am sure you do. Oh, and one last thing. That watch you hold, Meghan Chase? Its life span is drawing to a close. Thirty-two minutes and twelve seconds from the time you use that key, it will cease to run."

I felt a chill in the warm, cozy room. "What does that mean?"

"It means," the Clockmaker said, his beady eyes never blinking as they stared at me, "that in one hundred and sixty-one hours, forty-five minutes, and fifty-eight seconds, something will happen to make that watch stop.

"Now." He smiled at me—at least, I think he did—beneath his whiskers and gave me a slight bow. "I believe our time together has come to an end. Good luck to you, Meghan Chase," he said as he waddled out of the room. "Remember, it ends at the beginning. And give my regards to the first lieutenant, when you see him." He pushed aside the curtains over the door, slipped through, and was gone.

I sighed. Threading the key through the watch's chain, I looped the whole thing around my neck. "Just once, I'd like it if a faery could give me a straight answer," I muttered as Ash pulled up the trapdoor again. "Seems to me this whole trip was a waste of time, time we don't have. And where the hell is Grimalkin? Maybe he could make some sense of everything, if he didn't keep disappearing every time I turn around."

"I am right here, human." Grimalkin appeared on the chair, curled up much as the larger cat had been. His tail thumped the cushion irritably. "Where I was for much of the conversation. It is not my fault you cannot see past the end of your nose." With an offended air, the cat leaped from the cushion and slipped out the trapdoor, not stopping to look back.

Great, now the cat was mad at me. Knowing Grimalkin, I'd have to beg and plead for him to tell us what he knew, or offer up my firstborn son or something.

Frustrated, I stomped back down the stairs, Ash and Puck trailing behind. Outside, the city glittered with lights, both natural and artificial, but except for the gremlins, chattering and buzzing in the shadows, the streets themselves were empty. I wondered how much time we had lost, coming here. I wondered, despite Grimalkin's assurances, if it had really been necessary.

"Where to now?" Ash mused, looking at me. "Do we have a destination?"

"Yes," I said decisively, almost relieved to be back on track. "The tower."

"The tower? *Machina's* tower?"

I nodded. "That's the only place I know of to find the false king. The Clockmaker said so himself—it ends at the beginning. Everything started with *him*. Machina's tower is where we have to go."

"Sounds good to me," Puck said, crossing his arms. "We

have a plan. Finally. So, uh…how do we get there? I don't see any information booths selling maps."

I closed my eyes, trying to remember the Iron King's tower and the path we took to get there. I saw the railroad, cutting straight through a flat obsidian plain, lava pools and smokestacks littering the ground. I remembered walking down that road with Ash, the sun glaring in our faces, toward the stark black monolith rising in the distance.

"East," I muttered, opening my eyes. "Machina's tower is in the very center of the Iron Realm. If we head east, we should be able to find it."

CHAPTER SIXTEEN
ECHOES OF THE PAST

We walked for nearly two days, stopping only to catch a few hours of exhausted sleep before heading eastward again. Following the rising sun, we traveled through a marsh of bubbling oil, where the rusty hulls of cars lay rotting in the sludge, through a forest of street lamps and telephone poles, where strange electrical birds flitted from wire to wire, leaving sparks in their wake. We walked past "the Valley of Worms," as Puck called it, a gully filled with thousands of discarded computers, crawling with huge worms, some bigger than pythons, their metallic blue hides lit with hundreds of blinking lights and sparks. Thankfully, they seemed blind to, or uncaring of, our presence, but my heart was still pounding against my ribs miles after we left the Valley of Worms behind.

As we traveled, I began to feel a strange pulse from the land, faint at first, but growing stronger the farther we went. As if something was calling to me, drawing me close like the pull of a magnet. And the eerie thing was, if I closed my eyes and really concentrated, I could *feel* the center of the Iron Realm, like an invisible bull's-eye in my mind. I didn't mention it to Ash and Puck, unsure if it was just a crazy hunch, but I caught Grimalkin watching me once or twice, glowing cat eyes serious and thoughtful, as if he knew something was going on.

On the second day, we reached the edge of a vast desert, a sea of sand dunes, rising and falling with the wind. I'd never seen the ocean, but I imagined it must be something like this, only with water instead of sand, sprawling and endless, stretching away into the horizon. To our left, a wall of sheer black cliffs soared up over the dunes, and wind-pushed waves crashed against the jagged rocks, spraying dust into the air like sea foam.

"Are you sure we're still going the right way, princess?" Puck asked, shielding his eyes from the glare of the sun. I gazed out over the dunes, squinting in the harsh light, and felt a pulse somewhere on the other side, the beacon that was calling me.

"Yes." I nodded. "We're still on track. Let's keep moving."

The desert and the cliffs seemed to go on forever. Just walking through the sand proved challenging; though it held our weight, we still sank into the dunes, up to our knees sometimes, as if the desert wanted to swallow us whole. Every so often, the sand hills would be swept away by the wind, revealing what lay beneath. Strange items rose to the surface, like driftwood bobbing in the waves. Everything from socks to pens, forks and spoons, keys, earrings, wallets, Matchbox cars, and an endless amount of coins, were unearthed for just a moment, glinting in the light, before the sand curled over them once more, hiding them from view.

Once, out of curiosity, I bent and scooped a bright pink cell phone out of the sand, flipping it open. Of course, the batteries were long dead, and the screen was dark, but there was a faded sticker on the front, a Hello Kitty with Japanese kanji beneath. I wondered how it got here. It obviously had belonged to somebody at one time. Had they simply lost it?

"Thinking of making a call, princess?" Puck asked as he caught up to me and raised an eyebrow at the phone in my hand. "Reception out here probably sucks. Though, if you do get a signal, try ordering for pizza. I'm starving."

"I see," I said abruptly, making Puck frown in confusion. Gesturing around at the dunes, I continued. "I know where we are, sort of. I'll bet all of these items were lost at one time, in the mortal world. Look at this stuff: pens, keys, cell phones. This is where it all comes, where the lost things finally end up."

"The Desert of Lost Things," Puck said dramatically. "Well, that's appropriate. *We're* here, aren't we?"

"We are *not* lost," I told him firmly, tossing the cell phone away. It hit the sand and was swallowed immediately. "I know exactly where I'm going."

"Oh, good. And here I thought we were taking the scenic route."

"We've got trouble." Ash's curt voice interrupted us. The Winter prince came striding up the dune with Grimalkin trotting behind him, his long fur standing on end. A sudden blast of hot wind tossed his hair and made his cloak snap around him. "There's a storm coming," Ash said, and pointed across the desert. "Look."

I squinted over the dunes. On the horizon, shimmering in the heat, something was moving. As the wind began to howl, filling the air with grocery lists, homework sheets, and baseball cards, I saw a wall of swirling, glittering sand, eating up the ground as it flowed toward us like an unleashed flood.

"Sandstorm!" I gasped, stumbling backward. "What'll we do? There's nowhere we can really go."

"This way," Grimalkin said, sounding much calmer than I was feeling. A gust of wind tossed sand over his back, and he shook himself impatiently. "We have to get to the cliffs before the main storm arrives, or it could become unpleasant. Follow me."

We headed for the cliffs, fighting the sand and wind that shrieked around us, ripping at clothes and stinging exposed flesh. As the storm drew closer, heavier items began to fly through the air, as well. When a pair of scissors hit me in the chest, skittering off the dragon-scale armor, my blood ran cold. We had to get to shelter quickly, or we'd be sliced to pieces.

The edge of the dust storm roared over me like a tidal wave, screaming in my ears, pelting me with sand and other things. With my eyes squinted nearly closed, I couldn't see where I was going, and dust clogged my nose and mouth, making it hard to breathe. I lost sight of Grimalkin and the others and struggled blindly through the maelstrom, one arm covering my face, the other held out in front of me.

Someone took my hand, pulling me forward. I peeked up and saw Ash, head and shoulders hunched against the wind, dragging me toward the looming cliff wall, a dark curtain in the middle of a stormy sea. Puck was already crouched behind a jagged outcropping, huddled against it as streams of sand flowed around him, bouncing odds and ends off the stones.

"Well, this is fun," Puck said as we ducked behind the rock, huddled together as wind and sand shrieked around us. "It's not every day I get to tell someone I was attacked by a pair of flying reading glasses. Ow." He rubbed his forehead, where a bruise had started to form.

"Where's Grimalkin?" I yelled, peering into the raging wind. A plastic doll head struck the rock inches from my face and went bouncing into the storm, and I cringed back.

"I am here." Grimalkin materialized behind the rock, shaking sand from his coat in a dusty cloud. "There is a small opening in the cliff wall a few yards down," he announced, peering up at me. "I am going there now, if you care to follow. It is more comfortable than cringing against a rock."

Hugging the wall, arms raised to shield our eyes from sand and flying objects, we trailed Grimalkin along the cliff until we reached a narrow crack, a corridor that snaked away into the rock. The opening was tight and narrow, and there wasn't much room to do more than stand, but it was better than being out in the storm.

I squeezed into the corridor, sighing in relief. My ears rang from the shrieking wind, and sand clung to everything: hair, lips, eyelashes. Taking off one gauntlet, I wiped my face, wishing I had a towel, and tried combing the sand from my hair.

"Ugh." Puck shook his head like a dog, sending dust and grit flying. Ash glared at him and moved away from the shower, standing beside me. "Ack. Blech. Oh, great, I'm already starting to itch. I'm going to have sand in every crack for months now."

Grinning at Puck's statement, I reached up and ruffled Ash's hair, sending a rain of dust to the ground. He winced and gave me a rueful look. "I wonder how long the storm will last," I mused out loud, watching sand hurl past the opening. Catching sight of Grimalkin, grooming rigorously on a nearby rock, I called out to him. "Grim? Any ideas?"

The cat didn't even slow down. "Why do you ask me, human?" he asked, licking himself as though his fur was on fire and not just covered in sand. "I have never been here." He shook his head, then moved on to his paws and whiskers. "We could be here for minutes or days—I am no expert of the sand and wind cycles in the Desert of Lost Things." His voice was thick with sarcasm, and I rolled my eyes. "Although," he continued, furiously scrubbing his face, "it might interest you to know there is a tunnel around the corner to the right, half-hidden behind a bush. Perhaps you should see to it that it is empty, and not filled with Iron spiders or something equally unpleasant."

We drew our weapons. Talk about a rock and a hard place. The last thing we wanted was to be trapped in a narrow corridor with an enemy bearing down on us and the storm at our backs. With Ash in front of me and Puck bringing up the rear, we edged forward until we found the tunnel Grim was talking about, a gaping slash in the rock wall, dark and uninviting, like the open mouth of a beast.

Cautiously, Ash poked his sword through the opening, and when nothing immediately leaped out, I eased forward to peer inside.

At first, as my eyes adjusted to the darkness, it looked like an ordinary stone tunnel, maybe to a cave system or something similar. But then I saw that the tunnel had been carved out of the rock, that a clump of familiar white mushrooms grew on the wall near the entrance, and an old metal lantern hung on a nail farther in. This wasn't a random cave. Someone had been using these tunnels, and recently.

And suddenly, I knew where we were.

"Princess, wait," Puck warned as I stepped in farther. "What are you doing?"

"I know what this is," I muttered, taking the lantern off the nail. It still had oil, and I coaxed a tiny flame to life, lifting it up. The light glinted off a toy fire engine lying next to a rock, and I had to smile. "Yes," I murmured, bending down to pick up the toy truck. "This is a packrat tunnel. I'm sure of it."

"Pack what?" Puck frowned as he ducked through the opening, still keeping his daggers out as he glared around uneasily. "Rats? Giant iron rats? Oh, thank goodness, that's so much better than spiders."

"No." I glared at him as Ash sheathed his sword and stepped into the tunnel, gazing around cautiously. "Packrats. Little Iron fey that carry mounds of junk on their backs. We met them on our first trip through the Iron Realm, when I was looking for Machina. These tunnels should lead right to their nest."

"Oh. Awesome. That makes me feel *so* much better."

"Will you stop it? They're harmless. And they helped us before." I put down the truck and stepped farther into the tunnel, raising the lantern as high as I could. The burrow snaked away into pitch blackness, but I felt that same odd pull, coming from the dark.

"Where are you going, human?" Grimalkin appeared on a nearby rock, watching me intently. "Do you know the way through these tunnels? It would be highly annoying if we became lost following you."

"I know the way," I said softly, taking a few steps forward, deeper into the burrow. "And if we can find the packrats, they'll be able to help us." Turning around, I saw all three hanging back with varying dubious expressions, and sighed. "I know what I'm doing, guys. Trust me, okay?"

Ash and Puck shared a brief glance, and then Ash pushed himself off the wall to stand beside me. "Lead the way," he said, nodding into the darkness. "We'll be right behind you."

"For the record," Grimalkin stated as we ventured, single file, into the black, "I do not think this is a good idea. But, as no one listens to the cat anymore, I will have to wait until we are completely lost to say 'I told you so.'"

THE TUNNELS WENT ON. Like a giant rabbit warren or termite nest, they twisted and curled their way through the mountain, leading us deep underground. I followed the strange pull, letting it guide me through the seemingly endless maze of burrows, Ash, Puck, and Grim trailing behind. The stone-worked tunnels all looked the same, except for the odd broken toy or piece of junk scattered among the rocks. Several times, we passed through a nexus where multiple channels broke off in different directions. But I always knew which way to go, which tunnel to follow, and didn't even think much about it, until Grimalkin gave a sudden, irritated hiss.

"*How* are you doing this, human?" he demanded, lashing his tail in agitation. "You have been here only once, and it is impossible for mortals to memorize directions so quickly. How do you know you are going the right way?"

"I don't know," I muttered, taking us down yet another side passage. "I just do."

Puck's bark of laughter startled me. "See?" he crowed, pointing at Grimalkin, who flattened his ears at him. "You see how irritating that is? Remember that, next time you— hey!" he called as Grimalkin disappeared. "Yeah, I can't see you, but I know you can still hear me!"

We were getting closer to the packrats' nest, a fact I knew because of the amount of junk that started appearing in random places: a broken keyboard here, a bicycle horn there. Soon the tunnels were strewn with it, making us watch where we put our feet. Unease gnawed at me; this far in, we should've run into a packrat or two. I had been looking forward to meeting them again, wondering if they remembered me. But the tunnels felt empty and cold, abandoned. And they had been that way for a while.

Abruptly, the tunnel fell away, and we stepped into a huge cavern, with mountains of junk piled farther than we could see. Making our way past the enormous trash heaps, I strained my eyes and ears, hoping to catch a glimpse of the packrats, hear them babble in their funny language. But, in my heart, I knew it was futile. I couldn't sense any spark of life in this place. The packrats were long gone.

"Hey," Puck said suddenly, his voice echoing about the cavern. "Is that…a throne?"

I drew in a sharp breath. A chair made entirely of junk sat atop a smaller mound of rubbish in the center of the room.

On a whim, I walked over to the mound and crouched at the foot of the throne, and began sifting through the debris.

"Um...princess?" Puck asked. "What are you doing?"

"Aha!" Straightening, I raised my hand in triumph, brandishing my old iPod. Ash and Puck both gave me confused looks as I tossed the broken device on the mound again. "I just wanted to see if it was still here. We can go now."

"I take it you've been here before," Ash said quietly, nodding to the chair. "And that throne wasn't empty the first time, was it? Who sat there?"

"His name was Ferrum," I replied, remembering the old, old man with silver hair that nearly touched the floor. "He said he was the first Iron King, the one Machina overthrew when he took over. The packrats still worshipped him as king, even though he was terrified of Machina." I felt a faint prick of sadness, staring at the empty seat. "I guess he finally died, and the packrats left when he was gone. I wish I knew where they went."

"There is no time to wonder about that now," Grimalkin said, appearing on the throne cushion, looking disturbingly natural gazing down at us. "This room still stinks of powerful Iron magic. It is corroding your amulets faster than normal. We must press on, or they will stop working right here."

Alarmed, I looked at Ash's crystal and saw he was right. The amulet was nearly black. "Hurry," I said, jogging from the throne room with the boys at my heels, back into the endless labyrinth of stone. "I think we're halfway there."

A FEW HOURS PASSED, or at least I thought they did—it was so hard to tell time underground—and the fuel in the lantern burned low. We stopped to rest a couple of times, but I found it difficult to stay in one place, becoming restless and antsy until we started moving again. Puck joked that something must be summoning me again, and I didn't know if he was wrong. Certainly *something* was drawing me, growing stronger and stronger the closer we got, making it impossible to rest or think until we reached our destination.

And when the tunnels finally ended, dropping away into a monstrous precipice spanned by a narrow stone bridge, I knew I was almost there.

"Machina's fortress," I said softly, gazing across the chasm, "is on the other side of the bridge. This is the way I took to reach it. We're almost directly underneath the tower."

Puck whistled, the sound bouncing off the walls. "And, you think the false king will be here, princess?"

"He has to be," I said, hoping my convictions were right. *"It ends at the beginning.* Machina is the one who started it all."

I hoped. Back when I first came here with the packrats, the area below the tower was known as the Cogworks, due to the massive iron gears, cogs, and pistons that clanked and ground their way along the walls and ceiling, making the ground vibrate. The noise had been deafening, as some of the larger gears had been three times my size. Now, everything was silent, the giant gears cracked and broken and strewn about, as if the entire Cogworks had collapsed on itself. Some lay smashed under huge boulders, evidence that the ceiling had fallen in, as well. When Machina died, his tower had crumbled, destroying everything beneath it. I wondered what it would look like on the surface, how much of the Iron King's influence had survived.

Not much, I was afraid.

We made our way over the bridge, where the stone turned to iron grating, and started picking our way through the smashed clockwork, searching for a way up. As I made my way through the rubble, I noticed strange gnarled roots that hadn't been here before, coiled around the gears and dangling from the ceilings. I could feel them pulsing with life.

"Over here," Ash said, waving us over. A bent iron staircase spiraled up from the rubble, ascending toward a metal grate in the ceiling.

I felt a surge of excitement and apprehension. Whatever had been calling me was somewhere overhead. Probably it was the false king and we were walking right into his trap, but I had to see what was up there. The boys drew their weapons, and I pulled my blade, feeling my heart pound in my chest, whether in nervousness or excitement, I couldn't tell. With Ash leading the way and Puck close at my back, we ascended the stairs to Machina's tower.

CHAPTER SEVENTEEN

THE RUINS OF THE IRON KING

The last time I pushed open the trapdoor to Machina's tower, I'd been blasted by the heat of a dozen furnaces as I entered the boiler room. In the fiery red glow, dwarves in baggy suits and oxygen masks had shambled back and forth, wielding wrenches and checking leaky pipes. Now, everything was silent, the great furnaces dark and cold. Beams had fallen from the ceiling, pipes were bent and broken, and ash coated everything with a fine gray powder. Those strange roots were also everywhere, snaking in from the ruins above. Through the holes in the ceiling, I could see a section of the tower walls, shiny and metallic.

"Place looks abandoned to me," Puck said, tracing a finger through the dust, drawing a smiley face with the tongue sticking out. "I sure hope this is the right spot, princess."

I glanced up through the ceiling, following the roots until they vanished from sight. "Whatever we're looking for, it's up there. Come on."

Using roots and the pile of rocks, we climbed up one last floor. On solid ground again, I straightened and gazed around at what had been Machina's tower.

It was a mess, a maze of iron beams, broken glass, and

crumpled walls. Gears lay scattered about, rusting and broken, wires and cables dangled overhead, and shattered pipes dripped water and oil onto the floor. Numerous suits of armor, bearing the symbol of a barbed-wire crown on the breastplate, were scattered throughout the ruins like toy soldiers. I shivered, imagining rotting skeletons within those metal suits, but Ash kicked a helmet open and found it empty. It seemed Machina's Iron knights followed the same rule as the rest of Faery: when they died, they simply ceased to exist.

Everything was still, as if the very ruins were holding their breath.

"Looks like nobody's home," Puck said, turning in a slow circle. "Hellooooooooo? Anybody here?"

"Be quiet, Goodfellow," Ash growled, peering into the shadows with narrowed eyes. "We're not alone."

"Yeah? How do you figure that, prince? I don't see anyone."

"The cait sith has disappeared."

"…crap."

Meghan Chase, this way.

A faint glow emitted from the center of the ruins, drawing me to it like a moth to a flame. Without saying anything, I started walking toward it, ducking under beams and around half-standing walls, heading deeper into the maze.

"Princess! Dammit, hold up!"

They scrambled after me, muttering curses, but I barely heard them. It was here, whatever was calling me. It was just ahead…

And then, the walls, ruins, and rubble fell away, revealing an enormous tree in the center of the tower.

The oak soared into the air, massive and proud, the trunk so wide four people couldn't wrap their arms around it. Its huge branches spread over the tower like a roof, blocking out the open sky. The whole tree glimmered like the edge of a blade, metallic and shiny, leaves flashing in the dim light like tinsel.

"Machina," I whispered, and stared at the tree in amazement as Puck and Ash finally caught up. "Is it really...could it be?" Easing forward, I walked to the roots of the oak, gazing up at the trunk. Several feet overhead, a stick jutted out of the metal, straight, thin, and—unlike the rest of the tree—made of wood. "There's the arrow! Oh...oh, wow. This really is him."

"Wait, Machina was a tree?" Puck scratched the back of his neck. "I'm a little lost here, princess."

"He turned into a tree when I stabbed him with the Witchwood arrow." I was close to the former Iron King now, so close I could see my distorted reflection in the trunk. "I never imagined it would survive the tower's collapse." On impulse, I reached out and touched it, pressing my palm to the shiny surface.

This is no longer the Iron King, Meghan Chase. I wasn't really surprised to hear his voice in my head again, though I could feel the power thrumming below my hand. Though the tree was infused with iron all the way to its heart, it wasn't dying. In fact, it was flourishing. *This oak is only the physical remains of his power, and yours. As I told you before, I am with you now.*

"Meghan," Ash said, his tone full of warning. I stepped back from the tree, breaking the connection, and turned to find we were surrounded.

Iron fey stared back at us from every corner of the ruins, their eyes glowing in the shadows. From what I could tell, most of them had weapons—mostly iron swords and crossbows, but a few had guns pointed at us, as well.

"Meghan Chase," said a familiar voice, and Glitch stepped out from behind the crowd, the spines on his head crackling with electricity as he shook his head at me. "What the hell are you doing here?"

I STARED AT GLITCH, confusion and disappointment spreading through my chest. "Glitch?" I said, and the rebel leader arched an eyebrow. "Why are you here? I thought…this was where the false king lived."

Glitch snorted. "Are you kidding? The false king wouldn't come within a hundred yards of this place. This is Machina's domain still, and everyone knows it." He crossed his arms, glaring at me with shimmering violet eyes. "But I believe I asked you first, princess. Why are you here? Don't tell me you came looking for the false king."

"Yes," I said. "I came here to kill him."

Glitch choked, and his spines crackled as the lightning threads flared wildly. "Excuse me?" he burst out. "Let me get this straight. You're the one thing the false king needs to become unstoppable, and instead of hiding in the mortal world like a sane person, or better yet, letting us guard you and keep you safe, you want to go assault the false king's forces and take him out yourself." He shook his head with a snapping sound. "You're even crazier than I thought."

"We can do it," I insisted. "I just need to know where he is."

"Uh, no, you can't," Glitch shot back. "There's no way I'm telling you his location so you can march happily off to get yourself killed. This is what we're *going* to do. You and your boyfriends will stay here, safely out of the false king's reach, while he attacks the Nevernever and depletes his forces a bit. Then we can think about planning a counterstrike, but he's too powerful to take on right now."

"We can't wait," I insisted. "I can't let him attack the Nevernever and destroy any more of it. We have to act now."

"Sorry, your highness, but I don't think you're in any position to be giving orders," Glitch said firmly. "This is my base, and these are my forces. And I'm afraid I can't let you leave. Like I said before, it would be like handing the victory to the false king. And I tend to be a sore loser. You and the two oldbloods will stay right here."

"Think you can keep us here by force?" Ash mused in his soft, dangerous voice, scanning the army spread around us. "I can promise you'll lose a lot of rebels that way, and you need every one you can get."

"Don't take me so lightly, prince," Glitch replied, and his own voice had gone quietly lethal. "There's a reason I was Machina's first lieutenant, and you're in my house now."

"Really?" Puck pulled his daggers before I could stop him. "Well, I'm placing my bet on the visiting team." Around us, the rebels tensed, raising their weapons, and Puck shot Ash a savage grin. "Odds are stacked just the way I like 'em. You ready, ice-boy?"

"Stop right there!" My voice echoed around the room, startling everyone, myself included. "This will not, under any circumstances, turn into a fight. We're on the same freaking side, dammit. Put your weapons away, now."

Puck blinked at me, astonished, but Ash straightened and calmly slid his sword back in its sheath, diffusing the tension. A collective sigh seemed to go through the chamber as the rebels relaxed and lowered their weapons, as well.

I sighed and turned to Glitch again, who was watching me with an unreadable expression on his face. "Look," I said, stepping forward, "I know you don't think I should go anywhere near the false king, but you don't have to worry. I was the one who defeated Machina, remember? I snuck into this very tower, faced the last Iron King, and stuck an arrow through his heart. That's why I'm here. Oberon and Mab sent me to deal with the false king—they think I'm the only one who has a chance. I don't want to fight you, but one way or another, I have to face him. You can either help me, or get out of my way."

Glitch sighed and scrubbed a hand through his hair, making the lightning sizzle. "You have no idea what you're doing," he snapped, shaking neon threads from his fingers. "You think you're ready to take on the false king? All right, then." He stepped away from the tree, beckoning us with a hand. "Come with me. Not you two!" he barked, pointing to Ash and Puck. "They can stay here. We're going for a little ride."

"I don't think so," Ash said calmly, dropping his hand to his sword hilt. I shot him a warning look. Glitch snorted.

"Come off it, prince," he said in a weary voice. "You really think I would hurt her? I'm the one who doesn't want her running off on a suicide mission. Now that she's exactly where I wanted her to be in the first place, you think I'd jeopardize that? Your princess will be perfectly safe under my care. And trust me, she's going to want to see this."

"I have no reason to trust anything you say," Ash stated flatly. The rebel leader threw up his hands.

"Fine," he snapped. "You want an oath out of me, is that it? Here it is, then. I, Glitch, last lieutenant of King Machina, promise to keep Meghan Chase safe from harm, and to bring her safely back to the paranoid care of her guardians. Is that good enough for you?"

"What about Puck and Ash?" I added.

"Nor will my forces do them any harm, as well. Are we quite done here?" Glitch shot me an exasperated look. "I would think you'd want to see this, princess, since you're so eager to get to the false king."

I glanced at Ash and Puck. "I'll be all right," I said, raising a hand to cut off Puck's protest. "If Glitch says this is important, I should go."

"I don't like it." Puck crossed his arms and gave the rebel leader a dubious glare. "It's not that I don't trust the guy, but...no, wait—that's *exactly* the reason. Are you sure you want to do this, princess?"

I nodded. "I'm sure. You two stay here, I'll be back as soon as I can."

"One more thing," Ash said in his dangerous, soft voice as we turned away, and Glitch shot him a wary look. "If you do not return with her," Ash continued, staring him down, "if she comes to any harm while she is with you, I will turn this entire camp into a bloodbath. That is *my* promise, lieutenant."

"I'll bring her back, prince," Glitch snapped, and there was the faintest hint of fear in his voice now. "I gave you my word, and I'm bound to uphold it, same as you. Try not to slaughter any of my people while we're gone, okay?"

"Where are we going?" I asked as we turned away. Glitch gave me a humorless smile.

"I'm going to show you what you're up against."

HE TOOK ME UP A FLIGHT of stairs to a part of the tower that hadn't completely crumbled, where an open landing trembled and swayed in the wind. Far below, the flat obsidian plain stretched away into the horizon, spiderwebbed with orange lava and dotted with metallic trees. Overhead, the sky was clear save for a few ragged clouds, and the crimson moon winked at us like an evil red eye.

Glitch walked to the edge of the landing, gazing out over the Iron Realm, his face turned to the sky. "Sky's clear, good." He spun to face me, smirking. "No clouds now, but a storm can sweep in quickly, so we have to move fast. Don't want to be caught in the rain without an umbrella, I can tell you that."

"How are we going to get there?" I asked, peering cautiously over the edge at the blackened plain stretched out below us.

Glitch smiled at me. "Fly."

A buzzing filled the air. I looked straight up to see a pair of long, segmented creatures spiraling down at us, and leaped back as they perched on the edge of the landing.

I tried not to cringe, but it was hard. The creatures looked like a cross between a hang glider and a dragonfly, with bulging insect eyes and six copper legs that gripped the railing with tiny claws. Their bodies were thin and shiny, though their wings looked more batlike than insect, made for gliding instead of speed. And they had propellers on their rear ends.

Glitch looked annoyingly pleased with himself. "These are gliders," he told me, enjoying my uneasiness. "Just walk to the edge of the platform and spread your arms and they'll crawl into position. You steer them by pulling on their front legs and shifting your body weight. Easy enough, right?" I stared at him in disbelief, and he chuckled. "After you, your highness. Unless you're scared, of course."

"Oh, of course not," I drawled sarcastically, taking a cue from Puck. "Big giant insect thing holding me several hundred feet in the air? What's there to be nervous about?"

Glitch leered and offered no comment. Taking a deep breath to calm my pounding heart, I walked to the edge and looked down. That was a mistake. Steeling myself for the inevitable, I spread my arms.

A moment later I felt creepy jointed legs gripping my clothes as one of the insects crawled up my back, shockingly light for something that big. I clenched my teeth and tried not to flail as the legs curled under me, forming a kind of hammock. Overhead, the wings buzzed and fluttered, awaiting takeoff, but we didn't move. I looked down at the dizzying drop, and my stomach spun so violently I was afraid I'd throw up any second.

"Uh, you're going to have to fall forward, princess," Glitch said helpfully. I would've turned to glare at him if I hadn't been terrified to move.

"Yeah, I'm getting to that." Closing my eyes, I took deep short breaths, preparing for the drop. I would never take up bungee jumping, that much was certain. "Okay," I whispered, trying to psyche myself up. "On three. Here we go. One… two…three!"

Nothing happened. My mind said jump, but my body refused to fall. I teetered on the edge of the landing, the wind whipping my hair, and felt sick. "I don't know if I can do this," I said, as my glider gave an irritated buzz. "Hey, don't judge me. How do I even know this is sa—ahhhh!"

Something nudged me from behind, just enough to make me lose my balance. Shrieking like a bean sidhe on a roller coaster, I fell forward.

For a moment, I couldn't open my eyes, certain I was going to die. The wind whipped around me, howling in my ears as I seemed to plummet straight to my death. Then the glider curved upward, leveling out as it caught the wind currents. As my heart slowed and my death grip on the glider's legs eased a bit, I cautiously opened my eyes and looked around.

The land stretched out before me, flat and infinite, fractured with glowing threads of lava vanishing into the horizon. From this height, the Iron Realm didn't look quite so ominous. The wind shrieked in my ears and whipped at my hair, but I wasn't afraid. Experimentally, I tugged on the glider's front leg, and it instantly swerved to the right. I pulled on the other leg and it swooped to the left, sending a thrill coursing through me. I wanted to go faster, higher, to find a flock of…something…and race them into the sun. How had I been afraid of this? This was easy; this was awesome! The glider buzzed in excitement, as if sensing my mood, and I would've sent it into a steep dive if a voice hadn't stopped me.

"Exhilarating, isn't it, princess?" Glitch had to shout to be heard as his glider swooped down next to mine. The lightning in his hair snapped wildly, trailing threads of energy behind him. "First time on a glider, and you'll never want to walk again."

"You couldn't have let me jump on my own?" I yelled, glaring at him. He laughed.

"I could have. But we would've been standing there till the sun came up." Glitch pulled on his glider's legs, and the insect swooped skyward, rolled, and came down on my other side. "So, your highness, you seem to be getting the hang of this, no pun intended. Want me to show you what these can really do? That is, if you're not afraid of a little challenge."

My adrenaline was pumping, and the thrill of flying made my blood soar. I was annoyed at the Iron faery and up for a challenge, little or not. "You're on!"

Glitch grinned, and his eyes sparked. "Follow me, then. And try to keep up!"

His insect shot skyward, his whoop ringing out behind him. I yanked my glider's front legs back, and it followed instantly, shooting up like a bottle rocket. Glitch banked sharply to the right; I pulled the glider's right leg, and it performed the same maneuver, sweeping around in a lazy arc. We chased Glitch across the open sky, through a series of loops, arcs, curves, and dives, all at top speed. The ground rushed beneath me, the wind howled in my ears, and my blood raced faster than it ever had before. I pushed my glider into a steep, vertical dive, pulling up at the last second. My adrenaline surged, and I whooped with sheer, unrestrained joy.

Finally, we caught up to Glitch again, back to flying in a normal, straight line. He shot me a grudging look as I joined him, still panting from the thrill of stunt gliding an insect. "You're a natural," he said, shaking his head. "The gliders don't perform that well for just anyone. You have to bond for it to really give you its all. Guess you made an impression."

I was absurdly pleased at the compliment, and had the strange impulse to pat my glider on the head. "How much longer to where we're going?" I asked, noticing that the huge red moon above us was beginning to set. Glitch sighed, and his playful mood vanished.

"We're almost there. In fact, you should start to see it... now."

We soared over a rise, the land dropping away into a shallow basin, and I saw the forces of the false king for the first time.

They covered the ground in a glimmering carpet, a small city's worth of Iron fey, marching forward in perfectly square sections. The army was massive, easily twice the size of the forces of Summer and Winter. Great iron beetles, like the ones we saw in the earlier attack, lumbered forward like tanks, overshadowing the ranks of smaller fey. I counted at least three dozen of them, and remembered how hard it was to bring down just one of the massive bugs. But that wasn't the worst of it.

Behind the army, creeping forward at an impossible rate, was a massive iron fortress. I blinked, rubbing my eyes, wondering if I was hallucinating. It was impossible. Something that size should not be able to move. But yet, there it was, rolling after the army, a huge structure of iron and steel. It was lopsided and uneven, looking cobbled together from whatever was lying around, but somehow shaped into a monstrous moving citadel.

"He's been gathering his forces for a while," Glitch said as I stared at the fortress, unable to take my eyes from it. "Those skirmishes at the edge of the Nevernever? Just a distraction, something to weaken the other side while he gathers his strength. At the rate he's going, he'll reach the edge of the Iron Kingdom in a little under a week. And when he plows through the Nevernever with that fortress and the full might of his army behind it, none of the oldbloods will be able to stop him. First he'll take out the courts, and then he'll plant that castle in the middle of your precious Nevernever to finish it off. Faery will be converted to Iron in a matter of days.

"So, your highness," Glitch said, as we wheeled our gliders around, retreating from the army and the fortress of death that followed. My excitement had fled, replaced with sheer fright and a nagging despair. "What do you expect to do against *that?*"

I had no answer for him.

THE REBELS HAD CONVERTED part of Machina's tower into their underground base. Though much of it still remained a ruin, enough had been cleared out for us to be given separate quarters. Glitch showed us a set of rooms we could use— small and windowless, with a rough stone floor—and said he would leave them unlocked for the time being.

"You can roam the tower grounds all you like, but I'd prefer it if you didn't leave the ruins," he said, pushing open the door to another identical room, furnished with only a cot, a lamp, and an upside-down barrel that served as a table. "You're our guests, of course, but be warned that I've given specific orders to keep you from leaving the tower, by force if necessary. Not that I want a fight. I'd much rather things be civil between us."

"Yeah, good luck with that, socket-head," Puck sneered, and I was too tired to argue. Glitch needn't have worried; I wasn't planning any grand escape. There was no place for us to go. We couldn't get to the false king through that huge army, and even if we did, we'd have to somehow find a way into that moving fortress, which would certainly be heavily guarded. I was at a loss. Asking Glitch and the rebels to charge the false king's forces would be suicide, but if we didn't do something quickly, that castle would reach the battlefront and then it would be game over.

Ash moved close, putting a hand on my shoulder, his eyes bright with concern. "Don't worry about Glitch, or the castle," he said in a low voice, so that only I could hear. I'd told him about the army and the Iron fey and the moving fortress the moment I came back with Glitch, and the Winter prince had nodded grimly but didn't seem terribly concerned about it. "Nothing is impenetrable. We'll think of something."

"Really? 'Cause I'm feeling a bit outgunned at the moment." I sighed and leaned into him, closing my eyes. Puck and Glitch were throwing insults and challenges at each other a few yards away, but it didn't seem terribly serious so I wasn't going to worry about it. "How are we supposed to get in that thing?" I whispered. "Or even get close? There's no force big enough to stand against that huge army. And by the time they reach the wyldwood it'll be too late."

"We have a little time." Ash's voice, low and soothing, flowed over me. "And you haven't really slept since we left Leanansidhe's. Get some rest. I'll be right outside the door."

"You're always—" the statement was interrupted by a huge yawn "—telling me to rest," I finished, deliberately ignoring the irony. Ash snorted, and I frowned, poking him in the chest. "I can take care of myself, you know."

"I know," he replied, steering me toward the room. "But you also have this tendency to push yourself beyond the limits of your endurance, and you don't notice until you fall over from exhaustion." He escorted me over the threshold, smiling as I glowered at him. "As your knight, I'm entitled to point these things out. Part of the job description when you asked me."

"Yeah, right," I muttered, crossing my arms. Ash smiled.

"I don't lie, remember?" He stepped into the room, bent down, and brushed a featherlight kiss to my lips, making my insides melt. "I'll be close. Try to get some rest." He closed the door, leaving me with a growing ache that wouldn't go away.

CHAPTER EIGHTEEN

RAZOR

Tired as I was, it was hard to sleep. I lay on the lumpy, uncomfortable cot and stared at the ceiling, my thoughts swirling too furiously to rest. I thought about the false king and his moving fortress, of the armies of Summer and Winter camped on the edge of the Iron Realm, oblivious to the danger. I tried formulating ways to stop the moving citadel and the huge army bearing down on the camps, but my plans looped in crazy, complicated circles or were too suicidal to take seriously.

But mostly, I thought of Ash, who kept invading my thoughts every few seconds. I wanted him here with me, alone in this little room with the door locked, but at the same time I didn't know if I was ready. Several times, I thought about opening the door and dragging him back inside with me, but would that be too forward? Would he think it inappropriate, considering where we were? Or was he waiting for me to make the first move? He had said he would wait for me, right?

I must've drifted off, because the next thing I knew, something landed on my stomach, and I bolted upright with a yelp, throwing it off.

"Ouch," exclaimed a raspy voice, and a gremlin leaped from the floor to the edge of the cot, regarding me with electric green eyes. "Found you!" it exclaimed, and I yelled.

Ash burst into the room a millisecond later, sword already drawn, ready to attack whatever had ambushed me. Seeing the gremlin, he tensed, and I threw my hand up, stopping him before he could lunge.

"Ash, wait!" He paused, scowling, and I turned to the gremlin, which was now in a defensive crouch, hissing and baring its teeth at Ash. "Did...did you just talk?" I stammered. "You spoke, right? I didn't just imagine it?"

"Yes!" it exclaimed, bouncing up and down, its ears flapping like sails. "Yes, you hear me! Razor found you! Found girl and funny dark elf."

"Razor," I repeated, as Ash stared at us in complete bewilderment. "Is that your name?"

"You can understand it?" Ash said, frowning at the gremlin, who snarled and scuttled up the wall, hanging there like an enormous spider. "The creature is actually talking to you?"

I nodded and looked back at the gremlin, which was now gnawing on one of its huge ears and still glaring at Ash. "When did you guys learn to talk?"

The gremlin blinked at me. "We talked," it stated, cocking its head as if confused. "Always talked. No one hears us, though. Except the Master."

I winced. Even though I had suspected for a while now, to have a gremlin actually confirm it was disturbing. They listened to me because they thought I was their new master. I was at a loss. Not long ago, I thought the gremlins mindless and animalistic, cunning but lacking any sort of language or society. To hear one speak was more than a little surprising.

I looked down at Razor, beaming up at me, hanging on

my every word. I certainly had no idea what to do with a gremlin. "How did you get in here?" I asked instead.

"Followed!" The spindly creature grinned, flashing his neon-blue, razor-sharp teeth. Its voice buzzed like a bad radio station. "Brothers say they see you at old city. Razor followed. Followed you here. Found you!"

"What does it want?" Ash muttered, frowning as the gremlin cackled and scurried to the ceiling, hanging upside down as it swayed from side to side.

"I don't know." I looked up at the gremlin. "Razor, why did you follow me? What do you want?"

"Food!" the gremlin crowed. "Razor smells food! Hungry!" Hissing, he scuttled across the ceiling, zipped out the open door and vanished into the ruins.

Ash sighed and sheathed his blade. "Are you all right?" he asked. "It didn't hurt you, did it?"

I shook my head. "I can understand them," I said, wondering what to do with this new revelation. Standing, I walked to the door, peering out at the ruins. Lights flickered erratically, and a faint hum filled the air, the buzz of machines and electricity. "They think I'm their master now, Ash," I said, leaning against the door frame. "Like Machina was. I guess…because I have his power, they think they should follow me."

"Interesting." Ash's thoughtful voice made me glance back. I was half expecting him to be worried or disgusted with the whole talking to gremlins thing. But the look in his eyes was one of intrigue, not contempt. "I wonder what you could do," he mused, "with all the gremlins under your command."

A sudden commotion somewhere in the ruins drew my attention. "Gremlin!" someone shouted, accompanied by much cursing. "We have a gremlin! Get away from those wires, you little—hell." The lights sputtered and went out, plunging the ruins into blackness. "Glitch! It just ate through the electrical cables!"

"Get the backup generator going!" Glitch's voice cut through the commotion. "Diode, see if you can reconnect the lights. And someone catch that gremlin!"

Puck appeared, fading out of the shadows, yawning and scrubbing his hair. "Sounds like they've got a little pest problem." He grinned as the lights flickered and struggled to come back on. Ash glared at him.

"Where've you been, Goodfellow?"

"Me? Oh, I've been scouting the compound, chatting to the natives, exploring possible escape routes, you know, useful stuff." Puck scratched his nose and leered at Ash. "What've *you* been doing all night, ice-boy?"

"Wouldn't you like to know."

I sighed, loudly, before they could start insulting each other. "Has anyone seen Grimalkin yet?"

"Nope, but you know our furry friend." Puck shrugged and leaned against the wall. "He'll show up when we least expect him, being all cool and mysterious. I wouldn't worry about the furball." The lights flickered once and finally stayed on. Puck rolled his eyes. "You know, if we ever wanted to cause a lot of havoc, we'd just have to find a dozen gremlins and turn them loose. Those things make more trouble than me. Almost. So, princess." He turned to me, and his voice dropped to a murmur. "Any idea of when we're getting out of here?"

"I don't know, Puck." I shook my head. "I don't exactly have a plan, yet. We have to somehow get around that huge army, sneak into the castle, find the false king, and take him out, all before he reaches the wyldwood."

"Sounds pretty impossible to me," Puck grinned. "When do we start?"

"Start what?" And Glitch came around the corner, eyes narrowed suspiciously. "I hope you're not planning to start anything with the false king, because if you are, let me say again how stupid and impossible that is. Also, I'm not going to let you deliver yourself right into his hands, princess. You'll have to get through me before you go off on any suicide missions. Just letting you know. So please…" He smiled at me, though it didn't quite reach his eyes. "Behave yourselves. For all our sakes."

"What do you want, Glitch?" I asked, before Ash and Puck said anything that would get us thrown in rebel jail. Not that I didn't doubt our ability to fight our way free, but I didn't want needless bloodshed from those who were supposedly allies. Even though I knew it would probably come to that eventually. Neither of the boys did well in forced captivity, and we would have to go after the false king soon, planned or not. I couldn't let him reach the wyldwood and destroy everything.

"Just wanted to let you know, if you haven't guessed already, that there's a gremlin running around the base. They're not dangerous, usually, but they'll make a nuisance of themselves by chewing on wires and short-circuiting any equipment we have. So if the lights flicker, or if something stops working abruptly, you can thank our little friend."

Puck snickered. "It gives me all kinds of hope knowing your highly trained forces can't track down one teensy little gremlin."

"You think you can do better, you try finding the thing." Glitch glared at Puck, and his spines bristled, before turning to me. "Anyway, here." He handed me a bag. "Thought you might be hungry. Since you're our guests, it would be impolite if we didn't share our food with you. That's your rations for the week. Try to make it last." At my surprised look, he rolled his eyes. "Not all of us live on oil and electricity, you know."

"What about Ash and Puck?"

"Well, I'm *pretty* sure eating our food won't melt their insides to gooey paste. But you never know."

"Thanks," I said dryly.

The lights flickered again, and a voice yelled for Glitch somewhere overhead. Sighing, Glitch excused himself and hurried away, calling instructions. I wondered if I should be helping the rebels try to catch the gremlin, since it was my fault Razor was here, but then decided it was Glitch's problem now. He wasn't willing to help us or let us go, so he could deal with the trouble it caused.

At the mention of food, I realized I hadn't eaten anything since the night before, and my stomach grumbled. Opening the bag, I found several cans of processed meat, beans, fruit cocktail, a tube of squeezy-cheese with crackers, and a six-pack of diet soda. There was also a stack of paper bowls and a handful of plastic spoons.

Peering into the bag over my shoulder, Puck made a disgusted noise. "Of course, all their food would be wrapped in those stupid cans. What's so great about preservatives, I ask you? Why can't humans just be happy with an apple?"

I glanced over my shoulder and sighed. "I take it you're not going to eat anything while we're here?"

"I didn't say that."

"Well, stop griping then, and let's find a place to eat." Closing the bag, I started down the hallway, looking for some privacy. My room was the logical place, but I felt cramped and claustrophobic in that tiny space and wanted to see the open sky.

"Fine, princess." Ash and Puck followed me up the stairs into the ruins above. "But if I get sick, I expect you to wait on me hand and foot."

"If you get sick, I'll just have Ash put you out of your misery."

"I'm touched that you care."

The tower was buzzing tonight as scores of rebels scurried back and forth, trying to repair the damage one lone gremlin had caused. I felt a nasty glow of satisfaction as I watched them, and a strange pride that I had caused this. Well, that my gremlin had caused this. What good were they, these rebels, if all they did was hide from the false king in the hopes that someone else cleaned up the mess?

And when did I start thinking of the gremlin as mine?

Despite the activity in the tower, the space around the great oak was quiet and still. I felt drawn to it, just as I was the first night we came here. Beneath the towering limbs, nestled in a circle of roots at the base of the trunk, I sat down and started pulling out rations.

Ash and Puck looked on warily until I waved a plastic spoon at them. "Sit," I ordered, pointing to the roots. "I know this isn't faery wine, but it's all we've got and we have to eat something." Dumping a can of fruit cocktail into a paper bowl, I passed it to Ash. He took it and perched gingerly on the edge of a root.

Puck sat and gazed mournfully into the bowl I handed him. "Not an apple slice to be found," he sighed, picking through the gooey mess with his fingers. "How can mortals even pass this off as fruit? It's like a peach farmer threw up in a bowl."

Ash picked up the spoon, gazing at it like it was an alien life form. Dropping it back into his untouched food, he placed the bowl on the ground and stood.

"Ash." I looked up from my cold beans. "What are you doing?"

"It's watching us." Very casually, his hand went to his sword hilt. "Very close this time. It feels—" he closed his eyes, and I saw a shimmer of glamour around him "—like it's right above us."

He whirled, blindingly quick. There was a flash of blue light as he hurled something at the tree, and a second later a high-pitched squeal rang out as something dropped from the branches, nearly landing in my lap.

I jumped up. It was a big metal insect of some sort, shiny and wasplike, its wings still buzzing faintly as it died. Our

mysterious stalker, finally brought into the open. An ice
shard had gone clean through its body, ripping it apart, but
its hooked legs clutched something long and slender. Bending
down, avoiding the needlelike stinger on the end, I wrenched
the object from the creature's grasp.

It was a stick, a branch with several leaves sprouting along
the wood. The wood was still alive, though the leaves were
flecked with iron, and shiny threads ran along the length.
A note was wrapped around the stick, and as I pulled it off,
Ash gently took the branch from me, narrowing his eyes.

"Do you know what this is?" he murmured.

Puck smirked. "Uh, yes, actually. In most circles, it's called
a stick. Used for starting fires, poking large insects, and playing fetch with your dog."

Ash ignored him. "It's the branch from a rowan tree,"
he said, meeting my gaze. "And, given the circumstances, I
don't think it's a coincidence. He knows we're here. He sent
this directly to you."

My blood ran cold. "You think he's out there?"

"I'm sure of it. Read the message."

I unrolled the note, feeling my stomach clench as I scanned
the words. *The Iron King has a proposal for you. Find me.*

Peering at the note upside down, Puck scowled. "Find
him? Like we're going to drop everything and tromp all
over the Iron Realm looking for him? You're not thinking
of actually meeting him, are you, princess?"

"I think I should," I said slowly, looking at Ash. "He might
know of something that we can use against the false king.
Or, maybe the false king is offering to end the war."

"Or it could be a trap, and Rowan will betray us like he
did all of Faery." Ash's voice was cold.

"That might be, but I still think we should see what he
wants. What he's offering." I looked around at the dozens of
rebels moving about the ruins. "But first, we need to find a

way out of here. You heard Glitch—he's not going to let us walk out the front door."

"Finally." Puck grinned, rubbing his hands together. "I thought we were never going to get out of here. So what's your pleasure? Diversion? Fight? Sneaking out the back door?"

"Before we bring the entire camp down on our heads," Ash said, handing me the branch, "perhaps we should figure out where Rowan is first."

"Oh, right. That would make sense, wouldn't it?" I stared at the note, wishing yet again that faeries would just say what they meant without making it into a riddle. "I wish Grim were here. He'd know where to find Rowan." I felt a sudden stab of guilt for not thinking of the cat until now. "You think he'll be all right? Should we try to get him a message?"

"Too risky." Ash shook his head. "We could draw suspicion to ourselves, and besides, no one but us knows the cait sith is here. That might prove useful later on, having an ally no one else is aware of."

"Grim can take care of himself, princess," Puck agreed, eager to get started. "It's what he's best at, after all. So, the question is, how do we figure out where the stick came from?"

I looked around and saw a skinny hacker elf walking through the ruins, carrying an armful of keyboards and wires. "Easy. We just ask."

"Excuse me!" I called, jogging up to the elf, who jumped and gave me a nervous look over the tangle of computer wires. His huge black eyes, with lines of green numbers scrolling across, whirled anxiously. "Diode, right? I was wondering if you could help me."

The hacker blinked, shuffling his feet. "Glitch has informed us that we are not to engage you oldbloods in verbal communication," he said in a nasal voice.

"I just have a question." I smiled at him, hoping to make

him less nervous. It only succeeded in making him squirm more. Sighing, I held up the rowan branch. "I found this by the oak tree. Do you know what it is?"

Diode narrowed his eyes. "That is a *sorbus aucuparia,* more commonly known as a European mountain ash, or rowan tree. Yes, most of the natural flora and fauna has since been overtaken by ferrous influences, but there are a few places where you can find them still clinging to their natural state."

I understood only half of what he was saying, but got the general idea. "Where?" I asked, and Diode blinked again.

"The nearest stand of *sorbus aucuparia* is two point seven miles due west from the tower," he said, nodding in the general direction. "Of course, you won't be able to see it, being forbidden to leave the compound and all. Oh my!" He stepped back from me, and his eyes whirled. "You're not planning to escape, are you? Glitch will find out, and the trail would lead back to me, and I'd be an accomplice to a crime. Please tell me you're not planning an escape."

"Relax, I'm not planning an escape." Not entirely a lie, since he just told me to tell him that, rather than asking me if I was. But it must've worked, because he breathed a relieved sigh and relaxed.

"Well, that's nice, but I have to get back to work." The hacker elf backed up, nearly tripping over his own feet, and gave me a shaky smile. "I have to...be somewhere else now. It was...um...goodbye." Clutching his cables, he fled into the ruins.

"Did you two hear that?" I asked as Puck and Ash appeared behind me. Ash made a thoughtful noise and crossed his arms.

"Three miles due west," he murmured, gazing after the fleeing elf. "Not far, but do you think it's wise to let him go? He might run straight to Glitch."

"Then we should move fast." I checked my sword and my

armor, making sure all were in place. "We're getting out of here, now."

Puck's eyes gleamed. "Need a spectacular diversion of some sort, princess?" he asked.

"No, let's not burn any bridges before we have to." I started into the ruins, looking for a certain flight of stairs that would take us where we needed to go. "We might want to come back here, and I don't want to fight a horde of angry rebels because you blew up their base or something. We're sneaking out nice and quiet."

"Um, but if we're sneaking out, shouldn't we be looking for the back door?"

"Hide." Ash suddenly grabbed my arm and pulled me behind a pillar, crushing me to his chest, as Puck dove behind a rock pile. A split second later, Glitch appeared on the far side of the room, with Diode at his heels.

"I don't know, sir," Diode was saying. "But it seemed suspicious. You don't think she's planning an escape, do you? She told me she wasn't."

"That doesn't mean anything," Glitch said. I could feel Ash's heart against my palm, though he had gone perfectly still, hardly breathing. "You haven't met a human in your life, Diode, so you don't know that they're all capable of lying through their teeth."

Diode gasped, and Glitch blew out a long breath, running his hands through his spines. "It might not be anything," he said, as they continued walking. I held my breath as they passed behind our pillar. "But go ahead and find her, all the same. The last thing we want is that girl throwing herself under the false king's wheels."

"Of course, sir." Their voices faded as they continued into the ruins and out of sight.

Puck popped up from behind the rubble. "If we're gonna leave, we should do it soon. Like, now. Before socket-head figures it all out."

"This way," I hissed, and we hurried on.

After a few more close calls, I finally saw the base of the stairs to the tallest landing, the one that gazed out over the plateau. Unfortunately, it was also guarded by a burly dwarf with a mechanical arm and an iron-tipped spear. Several hacker elves crouched nearby, repairing wires and other electronics.

"Want me to take them out?" Ash muttered as we crouched in the shadows.

"Yeah, that wouldn't be noisy at all," Puck whispered back. I glared at the dwarf and the Iron fey, the only obstacles to reaching our destination.

And then, I saw the glint of a glowing green eye in the ruins above, the curve of a neon smile. *Razor! He would distract them, I bet. If I could just make him hear me...*

As if reading my mind, the gremlin suddenly turned and looked right at us.

I caught my breath. *Well, why not? Razor, if you can hear this, I need to get past that dwarf onto the stairs. Could you maybe cause a diversion or someth—*

The gremlin grinned madly, and then with a screech that sounded almost maniacal, scuttled from his hiding place in a flurry of sparks, drawing the attention of everything in the room. Laughing, he dangled overhead, seeming to mock them all, before zipping out of sight. Shouts and curses filled the ruins as the rebels, dwarf included, dropped everything to pursue the gremlin.

"Well, that's convenient," Puck mused. "I really need to get a few of those things."

"Come on," I snapped, and we bolted up the stairs, still hearing the shouts of the rebels below as Razor led them on a wild-goose—or gremlin—chase. We reached the landing without opposition, the wind whipping my hair as we stepped onto the ledge.

Puck gave me a look of mock-alarm as I gazed up the tower

wall, searching for our way out. "Um, how exactly were you planning on getting out this way, princess? Fly?"

"Yes." I finally spotted what I was looking for, hanging off the wall near the very top, a cluster of gliders sleeping in the sun. I whistled softly, and they roused themselves, turning their insect heads to peer down at us.

Puck, following my gaze, made a revolted noise in the back of his throat. "You're kidding me. You want us to fly out of here on those things? Um…how about I just turn into a bird and follow you—"

"No. You heard what Mab said." I beckoned to the gliders, and they buzzed sleepily. "Using glamour could shatter your amulet. We want to conserve it as much as possible."

Puck grimaced. "I think I might make an exception for this, princess. Not that I don't enjoy the thought of being carried around by a big metal bug, but…" He backed up a step as the gliders began crawling down the wall. "Oh, wonderful. They're looking at me weird, princess."

"What's the matter, Goodfellow?" Ash smirked, crossing his arms as the gliders landed on the platform, watching us with huge, multifaceted eyes. "Afraid of a few bugs?"

"Bugs are creepy." Puck made a face at one of the gliders, wincing as it buzzed at him. "Giant metal bugs that look at me weird belong in horror flicks." He sneered at Ash. "Besides, I don't see *you* stepping up to the plate, prince."

"I just want to make this moment last as long as I can."

"Guys! There's no time for this!" I glared at them, and they stopped, looking guilty. "This is our only way out. Just follow my lead and do what I do."

I walked to the edge of the landing and looked down. Yesterday, gazing at that vast drop made my stomach want to crawl up my throat. Now, my heart raced with excitement, and I spread my arms.

For a moment, nothing happened, and I was afraid the gliders wouldn't respond, after all. But then I heard the familiar buzz of wings, and a second later the glider landed on my shoulders, curling its copper legs around me.

"Creeeeeepy," Puck sang. I turned to glare at him.

"Shut up and listen. You use the front legs to steer. Try to relax and you'll be fine." I ignored Puck's dubious look and faced forward again. "Here we go," I muttered, and dove off the edge.

The wind caught the glider's wings and sent us both shooting upward, and my adrenaline soared in response. I thought I heard Puck's yell of disbelief as I spiraled up, and grinned wildly, imagining his face if I showed him what the glider could really do. But there was no time for the crazy dives and aerial maneuvers of the night before, though I could feel the glider's excitement as well, like a flighty racehorse eager to run. I did a couple of backward loops, just to get it out of our systems, before circling back to see if the boys needed further encouragement. To my surprise both Puck and Ash had managed to take off, and both were gliding toward me, though Puck did look a bit green as I pulled alongside them.

"Are you two all right?" I called, trying not to grin. Puck gave me a weak thumbs-up.

"Fabulous, princess!" His glider buzzed loudly, and he winced. "Though I'd much rather be flying on my own wings. This isn't natural. Which way from here?"

Ash pointed toward the distant horizon. "Due west is that way," he said, and I nodded. Without even waiting for me to steer it, my glider abruptly veered off to the right, and we set a course for Rowan and the setting sun.

CHAPTER NINETEEN

ROWAN'S PROPOSAL

After several minutes of flying, I spotted a dark blot shimmering like a mirage on the otherwise flat landscape. As we drew closer, I saw that it was a stand of trees, still alive, an oasis in the middle of the blasted wasteland. But circling overhead, I also saw that they were dying, their trunks streaked with metal and most of their leaves already bright and metallic. A few sparse limbs bore leaves that were still alive, and they matched the branch I'd found at the rebel base. This was our rowan stand, all right. If the note was to be trusted, Ash's traitor brother was here.

We landed our gliders, which buzzed anxiously about being left, and entered the grove cautiously, weapons drawn. The trees shivered in the wind, metallic branches scraping together like knives, making chills run up my spine.

Rowan stepped out of the trees ahead, a lean figure in white, his horribly burned face making my stomach clench. Two Iron knights flanked him, their jointed, segmented armor bearing a new symbol. Instead of a barbed-wire crown, the symbol of an iron fist now adorned their breastplates, punching up toward the sky. One of the knights was a stranger, unfamiliar to me. But I recognized the second immediately; the face above the breastplate could've been Ash's, except for the scar marring his cheek and the deadness in his gray eyes.

"Whoa, I'm seeing double," Puck muttered, blinking rapidly. "Long-lost brother of yours, ice-boy? Were you separated at birth or something?"

"That's Tertius," I whispered as we continued to approach. "He was with Ironhorse the first time we went into the Iron Realm. I saw him again at the Winter Palace, when he stole the Scepter of the Seasons and killed Sage." Ash clenched his fists at that, the air around him turning cold. "Don't underestimate him. He might look like Ash, but he's an Iron knight through and through."

"Yeah, but…" Puck looked from Tertius to Ash and back again. "That doesn't tell me why he looks like ice-boy's clone."

"Because," Rowan answered, his smooth voice carrying through the trees, "he *is* a clone of my dear little brother. The former king, Machina, created his knights to be his elite guard, so he fashioned them in the images of those at court. You should have seen my double—ugly bastard. I did him a favor and put him out of his misery. Sage's twin, unfortunately, was gone before we could ever meet." He stopped a few yards away and bowed, the two knights stopping just behind each shoulder. "Hello, again, princess. I'm very glad you could make it. And with your two lapdogs in tow, as well. I'm impressed. That must have taken some serious magic." His blue eyes flickered to Ash, gleaming dangerously, and he smiled. "That's a lovely necklace, little brother, but it won't save you in the end. The only way to survive the Iron Realm is to become part of it. You're only buying yourself some time with that bauble. Once it breaks, as I'm sure it will, this realm will swallow you whole."

"It will buy me enough time to kill you," Ash replied. "Which I'm happy to do right now, if you like."

"Now, now." Rowan waggled a finger at him. "None of that. We're not here to fight. I come here to offer a proposal that could potentially end this war. Don't you want to stop the war, Meghan Chase?"

I was instantly suspicious and crossed my arms. "That's why you brought me here? So you can bargain for the false king?"

"Of course," Rowan soothed. "But first, I'll need an agreement from you, princess. One that says we agree not to kill each other while standing on neutral ground. We wouldn't want my dear little brother to forget himself and attack, now would we?"

I narrowed my eyes. "I'm more worried about you double-crossing us and having an ambush waiting right outside. Why should I trust you?"

"You wound me, princess." Rowan put a hand over his heart. "I can assure you, all we want to do is talk, but if you're *not* interested in hearing our proposal, I guess we'll leave with our tails between our legs and continue our march on the Nevernever."

"Oh, fine." I could do this dance with Rowan forever, but it would get us no closer to the proposal. Still, I'd learned my lesson with faery deals and bargains, and I chose my words carefully. "We'll agree to a truce if your side honors it, as well. As long as we stand on neutral ground—" I gestured to the grove around us "—neither side will attack the other. Agreed?"

"Agreed. There now, that wasn't so bad, was it?" Rowan smiled at me, infuriatingly smug. "And you're going to want to hear this, princess. In fact, I think you'll find this deal very interesting." He leaned back and watched me, taking his time. I didn't answer, refusing to rise to the bait. Rowan grinned. "Your side is done, princess," he said. "We all know that you can't win—the Iron King's army is far greater than either Summer's or Winter's, and his fortress is impenetrable.

In a few days, Faery will be consumed by the Iron Realm, unless Meghan Chase steps up to save it."

"Get to the point, Rowan."

Rowan leered at me, reminding me of a grinning skull. "The Iron King is prepared to stop his advance on the Nevernever, call back all his forces, and halt his fortress where it stands today, if you agree to his proposal."

"Which is?"

"To marry him." Rowan's smile grew wider, matching my look of horror. "Join your power to his. Wed Summer to Iron, and the Iron King will cease his war on the Nevernever for as long as you remain his bride. That way, no one else gets hurt, no one else dies, and most important, the Nevernever as you know it will survive. But you must agree to become his queen, or he will hit the courts of Summer and Winter with everything at his disposal. And he will destroy them."

My hands were shaking, and I clenched my fists to stop them. "That's his deal? Marriage?" My stomach recoiled in disgust, and I took a breath to hide the sickness. "What *is* it with all these Iron Kings wanting to marry me?"

"Not a bad offer, if you ask me," Rowan said, smirking. "Become a queen, save the world… Of course, you would be married in name only—the Iron King has no interest in your…erm…body, just your power. I'm sure he would even let you keep your pet lapdogs, if you want. Think of all the lives you would save, just by saying yes."

I felt ill, but…if I could stop the war without anyone dying… Was marrying the Iron King worth saving the entire Nevernever? The lives I could save, Ash and Puck and everyone else… I glanced at Ash, and found him looking as sick and horrified as I felt. "Meghan, no," he said, as if reading my thoughts. "You don't have to do this."

"Of course, she doesn't *have* to," Rowan called. "She can simply refuse, and the Iron King will march into the Nevernever and destroy everything. But, maybe she *doesn't* care about saving Faery, after all. Maybe all those lost lives have no meaning to her. If that's the case, then please, carry on and forget this conversation ever happened."

I closed my eyes, my mind spinning with choices and possibilities. *If I agree, can I get close enough to the false king to stab him? Would that break the terms of the proposal? I have to try. This might be our only chance to get close. But...* I opened my eyes and looked at Ash, at the fierce protectiveness on his face, the fear that I would say yes. *I'm so sorry, Ash. I don't want to betray you. I hope you can forgive me for this.*

Something in my expression must've tipped him off, for he went pale and took a step forward, clutching my upper arms, fingers digging into my skin. "Meghan..." His voice was hard, but I could hear the despair below the surface. "*Don't.* Please."

Rowan laughed, cruel as the edge of a blade, enjoying our torment. "Ooh, yes, beg her again, little brother," he taunted. "Beg her not to save Faery—let her see you for what you really are, a soulless creature consumed with your own selfish desires, uncaring of anything but what you consider yours. Make sure you tell her how much you love her, enough to destroy your entire court and everything in it."

"Hey, corpse-breath, why don't you do everyone a favor and sew your lips shut?" Puck drawled, his eyes narrowed in anger. "It'll match the rest of your face *and* be an improvement. Don't listen to him, princess," he continued, turning to me. "These kinds of marriage proposals *always* have some hidden agenda or loophole."

Something Puck said jogged my memory, and I gently freed myself from Ash to face Rowan. "Let's hear that proposal again," I said. "From the beginning. Just his offer, word for word."

Rowan rolled his eyes. "Do I look like a parrot?" he sneered. "Fine, princess, but I grow impatient, and so does the king. Last time, so do your best to follow, yes? The Iron

King wishes you to become his queen. Wed Summer to Iron, and he will cease his war with the Nevernever for as long as you remain his bride—"

"As long as I remain his bride," I repeated. "Till death do us part, I suppose?"

"That is the traditional wedding vow, I believe."

"So, what's to stop him from killing me as soon as I say 'I do'?"

Rowan stiffened, and the two Iron knights shared a glance. "You assume the Iron King would do such a thing?"

"Of course he would!" Puck added, nodding as if it all made sense. "If Meghan 'weds her power to his,' he won't need her anymore. She will have already given him what he wants. So, on their wedding night, off with her head."

"*'He will cease his war with the Nevernever as long as she remains his bride,'*" Ash continued thoughtfully, narrowing his eyes. "Which means he'll resume his march as soon as she's dead."

"And he'll be more powerful than ever," I finished.

Rowan laughed, but it sounded rather forced. "Fascinating theory," he taunted, though it lacked the usual bite. "But it doesn't change the fact that the Iron King is ready to destroy the Nevernever, and this is your only chance to stop him. What's your answer, princess?"

I looked at Ash, smiled faintly, and turned to Rowan. "The answer is no," I said firmly. "I refuse. Tell the false king he doesn't have to offer a marriage proposal to get me to come to him. I'll be there soon enough, when it's time to kill him."

Rowan's lips curled in a nasty smile. "How very predictable," he mused, backing up. "I thought you might say that, princess. That's why I've already sent forces to destroy your little rebel base. Better hurry back—they should almost be there by now."

"*What?*" I stared at Rowan, wishing I could punch the

smirk right off his face. "You bastard. They weren't even a threat. You couldn't have left them alone?"

"Glitch is a traitor to the Iron King, and his rebels are a blight that must be eliminated," Rowan said smugly. "Besides, I would have destroyed them anyway, just to see the look on your face when you realized more people will die because of you. Of course, the longer you stay here talking, the more time you waste to warn your little friends. I would start running now, princess."

I dug my nails into my palms, anger burning my chest. We couldn't fight them; the terms of the truce prevented it, and we had to get back quickly to help Glitch. If it wasn't already too late. Rowan smiled at me, knowing our position, and waved cheerfully.

I glared at him, backing away with Ash and Puck. "When I come for the false king," I told Rowan, "I'll be coming for you, too. I promise you that."

The traitor prince ran a blackened tongue along his lips. "Oh, I'm looking forward to it, princess." He grinned, and we sprinted out of the grove.

CHAPTER TWENTY

IRON AGAINST IRON

I heard the battle even over the howl of the wind.

Pushing my glider as fast as it could possibly go, I swooped over a rise and saw the tower ruins swarming with enemy forces. Iron knights clashed with armored dwarves, silvery praying mantises with scythelike arms swiped at frantic hacker elves, and metal clockwork hounds hurled themselves into the fray. In the distance, a huge beetle tank lumbered toward the base, crushing everything in its path as musket elves blasted their guns into the crowds.

"We should take out that bug first," Ash called, drawing alongside me. "If I take care of the gunners on top, can you bring it down?"

I nodded, ignoring the persistent fear in my gut. "I think so."

"You two go on," Puck shouted, wheeling his glider away. "I'll hold the line at the entrance, make sure nothing gets through. See ya when we win, princess!" he called as he swooped away.

I took a breath and glanced at my knight. "Ready, Ash?"

He nodded. "Let's go."

I pushed the glider's legs and sent it into a steep dive, swooping toward the huge black insect. Far below, the screech of metal rang in my ears. The boom of gunshots echoed over the field, and the screams of the wounded and dying made my skin crawl.

Something small and fast zipped by us, hitting the glider's leg in a burst of sparks and making it veer sharply to the left. Wheeling around, I looked back to see several birdlike creatures, their beaks and the edges of their wings gleaming like a sword edge, spiraling up for another dive-bomb attack.

"Split up!" I yelled to Ash, who had seen them, as well. "We're sitting ducks otherwise. I'll try to draw off their attacks." Without waiting for a reply, I yanked on the glider's leg and sent it wheeling in another direction, looking back for the bombers. Two broke from the flock and streaked toward me with high-pitched cries.

I banked left, missing them, but barely. They shot past me like falling stars, viciously fast. One of the bird's razor-edged wings hit my poor glider again, nearly making me lose control as the bird darted away. Straightening out again, I looked up to see the birds coming around once more, and clenched my jaw.

Okay, birds. You wanna play? Come on, then.

I pushed the glider into a steep dive, aiming for the battle below. The birds followed, their hunting cries echoing behind me. As we zipped by Ash, I spared him a split-second glance, just in time to see icy-blue light burst from the front of his glider and the shattered form of a bird drop away. I felt a stab of alarm as we passed; he was using glamour! But then the ground came swooping up insanely fast, filling my vision, and I had no time for other thoughts.

I pulled up, barely missing the top of a knight's head, and heard a shriek of dismay as the closest dive-bird slammed into the Iron knight with a loud crunch, sending them both tumbling over the field. Weaving and dodging, I skimmed along the ground, soldiers and rebels whipping by me like telephone poles as I headed for the tower.

"This might not have been such a great idea," I muttered, but then it was too late, and we flew straight into the ruins.

Beams and walls loomed up in front of me. I dodged and ducked frantically, yanking madly on the poor glider's legs as we avoided crashing by a hairbreadth again and again. I didn't dare look back to see how our remaining pursuer was doing, but I didn't hear any crash or screech of metal, so I assumed it was still following us.

As I ducked under a beam, the ruins fell away and the tree rose up in the center, huge and magnificent. With the bird's angry scream still on my tail, I hurled myself at the trunk.

A shudder went through the glider, and I gritted my teeth. "Come on, just give me one more trick," I muttered. The trunk loomed before us, filling my vision. At the last possible second, I yanked sharply, and the glider swooped straight up, missing the tree by inches. The bird was not so fortunate and slammed beak-first into the trunk, making several leaves tumble to the ground. I couldn't pause to celebrate, though, as we were skimming vertically along the tree, so close I could've reached out and touched it, and the branches were zooming down at us. With one last effort, we dodged and wove our way through the top of the tree until finally bursting through the canopy in an explosion of silver leaves, into open sky.

The glider sagged, its whole body trembling, and I reached up to pat its chest. "You did good," I panted, shaking myself. "It's not over yet, though."

The glider gave a tired buzz but roused itself and shot forward toward the battle again. Ash came swooping toward us, his expression and even the way he flew his glider determined and angry.

"Why do you insist on hurling yourself into battles where

I can't follow?" he snarled, wheeling his glider next to mine. "I can't protect you if you're constantly running away from me."

His words stung, and my adrenaline-soaked brain responded in turn before I thought better of it. "I made the call—it was a split-second decision, and I don't need your approval, Ash! I don't need you to protect me from everything!"

Shock, hurt, and disbelief flickered across his features. Then, his expression closed, his eyes turning blank and stony as the mask of the Unseelie prince dropped across his face.

"As you wish, lady," he said in a stiff, formal voice. "What would you have me do?"

I shivered, hearing him speak like that. The cold, unreachable Ice Prince… But there was no time to talk, as a scream from the fighting below and the roar of gunfire jerked me back to the situation. Talking would have to wait.

"This way," I said, and pushed my glider into a steep dive, Ash following on my tail. The fighting was still fast and furious, but the numbers were fewer now on both sides. The monstrous iron beetle still plodded forward relentlessly, scattering waves of rebels before it, their weapons bouncing off its metal hide.

"We have to take that bug down, now!" I yelled to Ash, hoping he could hear me. "If I can get on top of it, I might be able to stop it!"

As I circled the beetle, the musket elves perched on its broad back looked up and spotted me. Swinging their guns around, there was a roar of musket fire, and I felt the wind from several iron balls go zinging past my face. The glider jerked violently, shuddering in the air, and I fought to keep it upright.

Then Ash's glider swooped by overhead, and the Unseelie knight dropped right into the cluster of elves. Sword flashing, he whirled and spun in a blue circle of death, and the elves fell away, tumbling off the beetle to the unforgiving ground.

Standing alone on the back of the huge insect, Ash gave his blade a final flourish and slammed it back in its sheath. His cold gaze met mine, defiant and unyielding, a silent challenge. Avoiding his icy glare, I swung close enough to drop onto the beetle's carapace, letting my poor, gallant glider fly off to recuperate.

Okay, I was on the bug's back. Now what? I looked around, wondering if there was a steering wheel or reins or something that controlled this giant thing.

"The antennae," Ash said flatly, breaking through my thoughts. I blinked at him.

"What?"

The Ice Prince gave me one of his hostile stares and gestured toward the front of the beetle, where a pair of stiff black antennae, each as thick as my arm, stuck over the bug's carapace. Ropes, dangling from the tips of the antennae, swept down and were tied to a platform behind the beetle's head. "There's your saddle," Ash pointed out, still in that same cold, flat voice. "Better get this thing under control before it plows straight into the tower."

I swallowed the lump in my throat and hurried to the steering platform, arms spread to balance against the swaying of the giant bug. Grabbing the reins, I peered out over the beetle's head, seeing the remaining forces of knights and rebels scurrying away before me. I saw Glitch, locked in battle with a huge clockwork golem, roll under the giant's blow and touch the golem's knee as he passed. The golem spasmed, froze in place, and toppled to the ground, threads of lightning crawling over its body. An Iron knight rushed Glitch from behind, but Puck suddenly leaped over the golem and slammed his foot into the knight's face, knocking him back. They were fighting bravely, but the false king's forces had backed the rebels against the base of the tower and were steadily closing in. They needed the cavalry, right *now*.

"Okay, bug," I muttered, gripping the reins. The beetle's antennae twitched, and it cocked a massive black eye back to stare at me. "I hope you like me better than every horse I've ever been on. Now, charge!"

The bug lurched forward, nearly throwing me from the platform, and gave a bellow that shook the earth. Iron knights and soldiers glanced back in alarm as the huge bug plowed into them, crushing them underfoot or sweeping them aside with its armored head. As we broke through the lines, tossing the enemy like leaves, the reenergized rebels gave a savage roar and charged, swarming over the soldiers with desperate abandon.

Moments later, beaten back, demoralized, half their army killed by rebels or trampled under the huge bug, the remaining enemy forces broke away and retreated, fleeing over the cracked ground to vanish over the horizon.

I pulled the rampaging beetle to a stop, tying off the reins as a cheer went up from Glitch's remaining forces. I was wondering how I would get off the giant bug, when the beetle, sensing the battle was done, folded its legs and sank down with a rumbling groan, making the ground tremble. Sliding down the smooth carapace, I landed with a grunt and straightened quickly, looking around for Glitch.

Ash dropped beside me, making no sound, his features still distant and cold like a stranger's. Guilt stabbed me like a blade when I saw him, but even now, I couldn't talk to him like I wanted. Now more than ever, I knew we couldn't sit here doing nothing. Not when the false king was almost to the front lines. We had to act now.

I fought my way through the crowd, shouldering rebels aside as they surrounded me, laughing and cheering, congratulating me on a brilliant counterstrike.

"Where's Glitch?" I called, my voice nearly lost in the cacophony. "I need to speak to him! Where is he?"

Suddenly, I saw him, standing over a body on the ground, arms crossed to his chest and face grim. A hacker elf knelt over the prone figure, prodding him with long fingers. My heart stopped when I saw who it was.

"Puck!" I shouldered my way through the crowd, rushing up to his still form. My heart pounded. Blood smeared his face, oozing out beneath his hair, and his skin was pale. One hand still gripped his curved dagger. I shoved the elf out of the way, ignoring his protests, and knelt beside Puck, taking his hand. He was deathly still, though I thought I could see the faint rise and fall of his chest, and tears rose to my eyes.

"He fought bravely," Glitch murmured. "Threw himself at a squad of Iron knights that would've killed me. I've rarely seen such courage, even among the Iron fey."

Rage burned, hot and furious, searing away the tears. I suddenly had to fight the urge to leap up and stab Glitch with Puck's dagger. "You," I said in a low voice, anger burning my throat. "You have no clue of what courage is. You say you oppose the false king, but all you do is sit here and cower, hoping he won't notice you. You're cowards, all of you. Puck was hurt fighting *your* war, and you don't even have the guts to do the same."

Angry murmurs went through the crowd. I felt Ash step up beside me, silently challenging anyone to come close. Glitch was quiet for a moment, but the lightning in his hair snapped angrily.

"And what would you have us do, your highness?" he challenged. "Throw my people at the feet of the false king, knowing that they will die? You saw his army. You know we wouldn't stand a chance."

"You don't really have a choice," I replied, still searching Puck's face, hoping for a flicker of life, a sign that he would be all right. "You can't stay here. The false king knows where you are now. He'll come after you again, and he won't stop until he kills every last one of you."

"We can move," Glitch said. "We can evacuate to a safe place again—"

"For how long?" I stood and turned on Glitch, glaring at him furiously. "How long do you think you can hide before he finds you again?" I raised my voice, staring around me at the rest of the fey. "How long are you willing to cower like sheep while he destroys everything? Do you think you'll *ever* be safe while he's out there? If we don't stand against him now, he'll only get stronger."

"Again, what would you have us do, princess?" Glitch snapped, his spines snapping furiously. "Our forces are too small! There's nothing we can do to stop him."

"There is." I stared at him, keeping my voice level and calm. "You can join forces with Summer and Winter."

Glitch barked a laugh as the crowd exploded with noise. "Join the oldbloods?" he mocked. "You *are* delusional. They want to destroy us as much as the false king. You think Oberon and Mab will happily let us march in and shake hands and everything will be fine? They won't let us across the border without trying to kill us all."

"They will if *I* lead you there." I stared him down, refusing to give. "They will if there is no other way to beat the false king. Come on, Glitch! You all want the same thing, and this is the only way we stand a chance. You can't hide from him forever." Glitch didn't say anything, refusing to meet my gaze, and I threw my hands up in frustration. "Fine! Stay here and shake like a coward. But I'm going. You can try to keep me here by force, but I can tell you, it's not going to be pretty. As soon as Puck is well enough, we're leaving, with or without your consent. So either help me or get out of my way."

"All right!" Glitch yelled, startling me. Running his hands through his hair, he sighed and gave me an irritated look.

"All right, princess," he said in a softer voice. "You win. You make a good point. The enemy of my enemy is my friend, right?" He sighed again, shaking his head. "We can't stay hidden forever. It's only a matter of time before he comes for us again. If I'm going to die, I'd rather die in battle than be hunted down like a rat. I only hope your oldblood friends don't try to kill us as soon as the battle is done. I can see Oberon conveniently letting that little detail slip in any deal we make with them."

"He won't," I promised, relief blossoming through me. "I'll be there. I'll make sure of it."

"You tell 'em, princess," Puck murmured from the ground.

I whirled, my heart leaping, as Puck opened his eyes and grinned up at me weakly. "Now that," he said as I knelt beside him, "was a rousing speech. I think I shed a few tears."

"You idiot!" I wanted to smack and hug him at the same time. "What happened? We thought you might be dying."

"Me? Nah." Puck grabbed my arm and eased himself up-right, wincing as he gingerly prodded the back of his head. "Took a nasty whack to the skull that put me out for a few minutes, that's all. Would've said something sooner, but you were on a roll and I didn't want to interrupt."

The urge to hit him increased, especially since he was shooting me that old, stupid grin, the one that reminded me of my best friend, who'd looked after me in school, who was always there no matter what happened. I pulled him to his feet, punched him in the shoulder, and threw my arms around him, hugging him tightly. "Don't scare me like that," I hissed. "I couldn't bear losing you a second time."

Releasing him, I turned to Glitch, who was watching us with a bemused, uncomfortable expression on his face. "Didn't you say something about helping us?"

"Sure, princess. Whatever you say." Glitch looked more resigned than convinced, but turned to his rebels and raised his voice. "Evacuate the camp!" he called, his voice carrying over the field. "Pack up and take only what is necessary! Healers, gather our wounded and take care of them as best as you can! Anyone who can still fight needs to be ready to travel by morning! The rest of you, suit up and be ready to march! Tomorrow, we go to join forces with Oberon and the oldbloods! Anyone who has a problem with that, or who is too weak or hurt to fight, should leave right now! Get going!"

The camp exploded into action. Glitch watched the rebels scurry about for a moment, then turned to me with a weary look.

"Well, it's done. I hope you know what you're doing, your highness. We leave before dawn." Then, someone called to him, and he left, vanishing into the dispersing crowd and leaving me alone with Puck and Ash.

I was suddenly aware of Ash, standing a few yards away, regarding me and Puck with the expression of a granite wall. I hadn't forgotten him, but that cold, silvery glare, blank as a mirror's surface, brought a rush of emotions flooding back. Before I could say anything, Ash turned to me and gave a stiff, formal bow. "My lady," he said in a calm, flat voice, meeting my gaze. "I must tend to my injuries before the night is out. Will you please excuse me?"

That same cool, formal tone. Not mocking or vicious, just overly polite, without emotion. My stomach clenched, and words froze to the back of my mouth. I wanted to talk to him, but the coldness in his eyes sliced into me, making me pause. Instead, I simply nodded, and watched my knight turn on his heel and stride toward the tower without looking back.

Puck gave a very exaggerated shiver and rubbed his arms.

"Whew, is it cold in here, or is it just me? Trouble in paradise, princess?" I felt my face heat, and Puck shook his head. "Well, don't drag me into it. I learned long ago that you don't get in the middle of a lover's spat. Nothing *ever* goes as planned—people fall in love with the wrong person, someone ends up with a donkey head, and then it's a whole big mess." He glanced at me and sighed. "Let me guess," he muttered, leading me back toward the tower. "You did something mildly crazy during the last battle, and ice-boy freaked out."

I nodded, a lump rising to my throat. "He was angry that I went off without him," I said. "But then I got mad because he didn't trust me to handle things myself. I mean, I can't always have him watching over my shoulder, right?" Puck raised his eyebrows, and I sighed. "Okay, it was reckless and stupid. I could've been killed, and a lot of people are counting on me to stop the false king. Ash knew that."

"And...?" Puck prodded.

"And...I might have...told him that I didn't need him anymore."

Puck winced. "Ouch. Well, you know what they say—you always hurt the one you love. Or is that the one you hate? I can never remember." I sniffled, and he put an arm around me as we ducked into the ruins. "Well, don't worry about it too much, princess. Let ice-boy cool off for the night and then try to talk to him tomorrow. He won't stay angry with you too long, I bet. Ash isn't one to hold a grudge."

I pulled back and frowned at him. "What are you talking about? He's held a grudge against you for centuries!"

"Oh. Right." Puck half grimaced as I slapped his chest. "But it's different with you, princess. Ash is just afraid you *don't* need him. That whole ice-prince song and dance?" He snorted. "It's just a device he uses to protect himself, so he doesn't get hurt when someone stabs him in the back. That happens a lot at the Winter Court, as I'm sure you know."

I did know. I'd seen the cold, callous nature of the Unseelie Court, and the royal family was the worst, with Mab pitting her own sons against each other to earn her favor. Ash had grown up among those who knew only violence and betrayal, where emotion was considered a weakness to be exploited, and love was a virtual death sentence.

"But I know Ash," Puck continued. "When he's with you…" He hesitated, scratching the back of his head like he did when he was nervous. "The only time I've seen him like that was when he was with Ariella."

"Really?"

He nodded. "I think you're good for him, Meghan," he said, smiling in a small, sad way that was completely different from the Puck I knew. "I see the way he looks at you, something I haven't seen in him since the day we lost Ariella. And…I know you love him in a way you can't love me." He looked away, just for a moment, and took a deep breath. "Jealousy isn't something we deal with well," he admitted. "But some of us have been around long enough to know when to let go, and what is most important. The happiness of my two best friends should be more important than some ancient feud." Stepping close, he placed a palm on my cheek, brushing a strand of hair from my face. Glamour flared up around him, casting him in a halo of emerald light. In that moment, he was pure fey, unbound by shallow human fears and embarrassment, a being as natural and ancient as the forest. "I have always loved you, princess," Robin Goodfellow promised, his green eyes shining in the darkness. "I always will. And I'll take whatever you can give me."

I looked down, unable to meet his open stare, human fears and self-consciousness coming to the surface. "Even if all I can offer is friendship? Will that still be enough?"

"Well, not really." Puck dropped his hand, his voice turning light and carefree again, more like the Puck I knew. "Damn not being able to lie. Princess, if you suddenly decide ice-boy is a first-class jerk and that you can't stand him, I'll always be here. But, for now, I'll settle for being the best friend. And as the best friend, it's my duty to inform you not to lose sleep over Ash tonight." We came to my room, and Puck paused, turning to me with his hand on the doorknob. "Also, don't bother trying to find him. If Ash says he wants to be left alone, he wants to be left alone. Intruders might get an icicle at the head for bothering him." He winced and pushed the door open. "Trust me on that."

A pair of sleepy golden eyes turned to us as we entered the room, and Grimalkin sat up on the cot. "There you are." He sighed, yawning to show off his bright pink tongue. "I was afraid you would never get here."

"Where have you been, Grimalkin?" I burst out, crossing the room to glare down at him. He blinked at me calmly. "Everyone is about to leave, and we couldn't find a trace of you."

"Mmm. You must not have looked very hard." The cat blinked at me calmly. "So, you actually convinced Glitch to join with the courts, did you? That will be interesting. You *do* know that even with the combined forces of the rebels, our side is still comparatively smaller in number to the false king's army? I believe that is why Mab and Oberon sent you specifically after the false king—if the head is cut off, the body will follow."

"I know." I faced the cat, feeling self-conscious under that disapproving gaze. "But I have to go through the army to get to the head. At least this way I'll have a chance of getting into that fortress. Right now I can't even get close."

"And letting the false king march his army into the Nevernever is a better choice."

"What am I supposed to do, Grimalkin? This is our only chance. I don't have another option."

"Perhaps. Or perhaps you all go to your deaths. I am continuously amazed with the lack of preparation around here." Grimalkin scratched his ear and stood, waving his tail. "By the way, I believe someone was looking for this earlier."

He moved aside, revealing the limp, crumpled form of a

gremlin lying on the cot. I gasped and looked at Grim, who seemed ridiculously pleased with himself.

"Grimalkin! You didn't...is he...?"

"Dead? Of course not, human." The cat's whiskers twitched, offended. "Although, it could be slightly dizzy when it wakes up. I do advise you to keep it more under control, however, as it seems inordinately drawn to mischief. Perhaps you could put it on a leash."

"Looks like it's coming to," Puck noted.

I knelt beside the cot as Razor's ears twitched and the spindly body stirred, raising his head. For a moment, he stared at me, blinking in confusion. Then his gaze slid to Grimalkin and he shot up with a hiss, leaping for the wall.

He missed, tumbling back onto the cot in a tangle of ears and limbs. Spitting in confusion and fury, he staggered to his feet, wobbling and flailing at the air. I grabbed for him, but he darted away, lightning quick, and leaped off the cot.

Puck's hand shot out, grabbing him by his enormous ears, holding him at arm's length as he squirmed and struggled. Razor hissed and cursed and spat, sparks flying from his mouth, his gaze not on Puck but on the cait sith beside me.

"Bad kitty!" he screeched, snarling and baring his fangs at Grimalkin, who yawned and turned away to groom his tail. "Evil, evil, sneaky kitty! Bite your head off in your sleep, I will! Hang you by your toes and set you on fire! Burn, burn!"

"Uh, princess," Puck said, wincing as the gremlin clawed and flailed, sparks flying everywhere, "this isn't exactly fun for me. Should I drop this thing or have Grim knock it out again?"

"Razor!" I snapped, clapping my hands in front of his face. "Stop it, right now!"

The gremlin stopped, blinking up at me with an almost

hurt expression. "Master punish bad kitty?" he said in a pitiful voice.

"No, I'm not going to punish the bad kitty," I said, and Grimalkin snorted. "And you aren't, either. I want to talk to you. Will you stay and not run off if we let you go?"

He bobbed his head, as best he could while his ears were gripped tightly by Puck. "Master wants Razor to stay, Razor stay. Not move until told. Promise."

"All right." I glanced at Puck and nodded. "Let him go."

Puck raised an eyebrow. "You sure, princess? All I heard was static buzz and chipmunk chatter."

"I can understand him," I said, earning a dubious look from Puck and a gleam of keen interest from Grimalkin. "He promised not to move. Let him go."

He shrugged and opened his fist, dropping the gremlin to the cot again. Razor hit the mattress and instantly froze; not even his ears vibrated as he gazed up at me with expectant green eyes.

I blinked. "Uh, at ease," I muttered, and the gremlin plopped into a sit, still watching me intently. "Look, Razor, I think it's best if you leave. The camp is being evacuated right now. You can't stay here by yourself, and I don't think you'll be welcome where we're going."

"No leave!" Razor leaped up, his face eager. "Stay with Master. Go where Master goes. Razor can help!"

"You can't," I said, hating the way his ears drooped like a scolded puppy. "We're marching to war, and it'll be dangerous. You can't help us against the false king's army." He buzzed sadly, but I kept my voice firm. "Go home, Razor. Go back to Mag Tuiredh. Isn't that where you really want to be? With all the other gremlins?"

Grimalkin sighed loudly, causing me to look back and Razor to hiss at him. "Am I the only one here who has any insight at all?" he said, looking to each of our faces. We stared at him, and he shook his head. "Drawing a blank, are you? Think about what you just said, human. Repeat that last phrase, if you would."

I frowned. *"Isn't that where you want to be?"*

He closed his eyes. "The next phrase, human."

"With all the other gremlins." He stared at me expectantly, and I raised my hands. *"What?* What are you getting at, Grim?"

Grimalkin thumped his tail. "It is times like these I am ever more grateful that I am a cat," he sighed. "Why do you think I brought you that creature, human? To keep up my stalking skills? I assure you, they are quite adequate already. Please attempt to use the brain I know is hidden somewhere in that head. There are thousands of gremlins in Mag Tuiredh, perhaps hundreds of thousands. And who is the only person in the entire realm who can communicate with them?"

"Me." Suddenly what he was implying hit me full force. "The gremlins. There are thousands of them out there. And…and they listen to me."

"Bravo," Grimalkin deadpanned, rolling his eyes. "The lightbulb finally comes on."

"I can ask the gremlins to help us," I said, ignoring Grimalkin, who lay down and curled his tail around himself, his work apparently done. "I can go to Mag Tuiredh and…" I stopped, shaking my head. "No. No, I can't. I have to be there when we reach the Nevernever, or Oberon and Mab will try to kill Glitch and his army. They would think it's just another attack by the false king."

"You're probably right about that," Puck mused, crossing his arms. "Mab wouldn't hesitate, and even Oberon would chop first and ask questions later when it comes to the Iron fey." He glanced down at Razor, who was still watching me intently and cocking his head like a dog trying to understand.

"What about Buzzsaw there? Could you send it back with a message to its friends, telling them what you want?"

"I guess I could try. What do we have to lose?" I turned to the gremlin, who sat up and flared his ears, ready and eager. "Razor, if I asked the other gremlins to help me, do you think they would come?"

"We help!" Razor bounced in place, grinning. "Razor help! Help Master, yes!"

I didn't know if that meant all the gremlins would help or just him, but I went on anyway. "I want you to take a message back to Mag Tuiredh. This is for all gremlins. Gather everyone who is willing to fight and meet us at the edge of the Iron Realm, where it meets the wyldwood. We have to stop the false king's moving tower before it hits the battle-front. Can you do that, Razor? Do you understand what I'm asking?"

"Razor understands!" the gremlin crowed, and leaped to the wall, flashing his neon grin. "I help! Meet Master in funny elf lands! I go!" And before I could call him back, he scurried up the corner, slid through the slats in the vent, and disappeared.

Puck raised an eyebrow and glanced at me. "Do you think he really understood what you wanted?"

Grimalkin raised his head and gave me an annoyed look, as if I had just blown something he'd spent hours setting up. "I don't know," I murmured, watching the vent. "I guess we can only hope."

I DIDN'T SEE ASH all that evening, though I ignored Puck's advice and looked for him. The ruins, bustling with activity at first, eventually died down into a somber quiet as scores of faery rebels prepared to march to battle. Armor was cleaned, blades were sharpened, and Glitch vanished behind closed doors with several of his advisers and hacker elves, probably to discuss strategy. Puck, forever curious and viewing all private meetings as a personal challenge, told me he would find out what was going on and disappeared. Restless, nervous, and annoyed that I couldn't find Ash, I retreated to my room, where Grimalkin was curled in the middle of my bed and refused to scoot over so I could lie down.

"Grimalkin, move!" I snapped after trying and failing to ease him over. He rumbled a growl as I pushed at him, flexing his very sharp claws, and I quickly pulled my hand back. Golden eyes slitted open and glared at me.

"I am rather weary, human," Grimalkin warned, flattening his ears in a rare but dangerous show of temper. "Considering I spent all night tracking down that gremlin, I would politely ask that you let me sleep before we go trekking down the same path we just came from. If you are looking for the Winter prince, he is up on the balcony with the insect things." Grimalkin sniffed and closed his eyes. "Why not go pester him for a while?"

My heart leaped. "Ash? Ash is on the balcony?"

Grimalkin sighed. "Why do humans deem it necessary to repeat everything that is told them?" he mused, but I was already out the door.

CHAPTER TWENTY-ONE

FERRUM'S PAST

The rebels shot me curious, annoyed looks as I jogged through the base, dodging hacker elves gathering up their computers, stammering apologies as I wove my way through the crowds. Reaching the stairs to the balcony, I took them two at a time but slowed when I came to the landing. Remembering what Puck said about intruders and hurled icicles, I peeked cautiously around the corner.

Ash stood on the edge of the landing, his back to me, the wind tugging at his hair and cloak. Overhead, dark red clouds blotted out the moon, and tiny flakes of gray danced on the breeze, dissolving to powder when they touched my skin. A fine coating of dust covered the balcony, muffling my footsteps as I eased through the arch. I knew Ash heard me from the tilt of his head, but he didn't turn around.

"It's unbelievable," he whispered, his eyes gazing out over the landscape. In the distance, a thread of poisonous green lightning crawled under the belly of the clouds, and the air turned sharp and chemical. "To think this was once the Nevernever. To know that it could all turn into this…" He slowly shook his head. "It would be the end of us. Faery would be extinct forever. Everything I knew, places that have stood since the beginning of time, gone."

"We won't let that happen," I said firmly, joining him at the edge. "The false king will be stopped, and this will go back to normal. I'm not going to let everything disappear."

He didn't say anything to that, continuing to gaze over the landscape. Silence fell, thick and uncomfortable. The wind whipped at my hair, howling across the distance between us. I could sense both of us wanting to speak, to break the awkwardness of unspoken apologies, until the quiet grew more than I could bear. "I'm sorry, Ash," I murmured at last. "For what I said earlier. I didn't mean it."

He gave his head a small shake. "No. You shouldn't apologize." With a sigh, he raked a hand through his hair, still not looking at me. "I'm the one who taught you to fight, to take care of yourself. I have no right to be angry when you prove yourself capable of every lesson I gave you."

"I had a pretty good teacher."

He smiled, very faintly, though his eyes remained dark, his gaze on the clouds sweeping the horizon. "You're not the same girl I met when you first came to the Nevernever, searching for your brother," he said softly. "You've grown... changed. You're stronger now, like she was." He didn't say her name, but I knew whom he meant. Ariella, the love he lost to a wyvern attack long before we ever met. "She was always the strong one," Ash continued, his voice barely above a murmur. "Even the Winter Court couldn't crush her spirit, turn her spiteful and cruel. She was better than all of us. But I couldn't save her." He closed his eyes, clenching his fists with the memory. "She died because I failed to protect her. I can't..." His voice trembled, just a little, and he took a quiet breath. "I can't watch that happen to you."

"I'm not her," I said, slipping my arm through his. "You're not going to lose me, I promise."

He shivered, glancing at me from the corner of his eyes.

"Meghan," he began, and I could sense his unease. "There's something...I haven't told you. I should have explained before but...I was afraid it would be a self-fulfilling prophecy if you knew." He paused a moment, as if waiting for me to say something. When I didn't, he took a deep breath. "Long ago," he began, "someone told me that I would be cursed in love, that those I came to cherish would be torn from me, that as long as I remained soulless, I would lose everyone I truly cared for."

My heart stopped for a moment, then picked up again, faster than before. "Who told you that?"

"A very old druid priestess." He seemed hesitant now, and I caught a flicker of dark blue regret from the corner of my eye. "This was before Ariella, back in the ancient times, when humans still feared and worshipped the old gods and had all sorts of rituals for keeping us out, which of course only challenged us to find ways around them. I was much younger then, and my brothers and I would play our cruel games with the mortals, particularly with the young, silly females we came across." He paused, tilting his head back slightly, gauging my reaction.

"Go on," I murmured.

He sighed, and very gently freed himself from my hand, turning to face me. "There was a girl," he said, choosing his words very carefully, "barely sixteen in mortal years, and as innocent as they came. Her favorite pastime was picking flowers and playing in the creek at the edge of the forest. I knew, because I watched her from the trees. She was always alone, carefree, so naive to the dangers in the woods." A hint of bitterness crept into his voice, a dark loathing for the faery in the story. I felt cold as he continued in a soft, flat voice. "I lured her into the forest with pretty words and gifts and promises of affection. I made sure she fell in love with me, that no other human male would ever make her feel what I could, and then I took it all away. I told her that mortals were nothing to the fey, that she was nothing. I told her that it was a game, nothing more, and that the game was now over. I broke more than her heart; I broke her spirit, broke her. And I reveled in it."

I had been waiting for it, but it still made me sick, the knowledge that Ash could be that heartless, just another capricious fey toying with human emotion. This girl, sixteen, lonely, eager for love, had been like me once. If I had been at the edge of the woods that day, instead of her, Ash would've done the same to me.

"What happened to her?" I asked when he fell silent again. Ash closed his eyes.

"She died," he said simply. "She couldn't eat, couldn't sleep, couldn't do anything but pine away, until her body grew so weak it simply gave out."

"And you felt horribly guilty about it?" I guessed, trying to glean some sort of moral from this tale, a lesson learned or something like that. But Ash shook his head with a bitter smile.

"I didn't think twice about her," he said, dashing my hopes and making my gut twist. "Not having a soul frees us from any sort of conscience. She was only a human, and a foolish one at that, to fall in love with a faery. She wasn't the first, nor would she be the last. But her grandmother, the high priestess of the girl's clan, was not so foolish. She sought me out, and told me what I just told you—she cursed me, promised that I would be destined to lose everyone I truly cared for, that it was the price for being soulless. Of course, I just laughed it off as the superstitions of a weakling mortal...until I fell in love with Ariella." His voice grew even softer. "And now, with you."

He turned away and gazed out over the edge again. "When Ariella was taken from me, I suddenly understood. We don't have a conscience, but falling in love changes things. I understood what I had put that girl through, the pain she suffered because of me. I told myself I wouldn't make the mistake of caring for someone again." He gave a bitter chuckle and shook his head. "And then you came along and ruined all that."

I couldn't answer. I kept seeing that girl, and the dark, handsome stranger she fell for, died for. "Why are you telling me this?" I whispered.

"Because, I want you to understand what I am." Ash looked down at me, solemn and grim. "I'm not a human with pointed ears, Meghan. I am and will always be Fey. Soulless. Immortal. Because of my actions that day, someone I loved died. And now, here we are, on the brink of war and—" He stopped and looked down, his voice dropping to a near whisper. "And I'm afraid. I'm afraid I'll fail you like I did Ariella, that the crimes of my past will ruin any chance we have at a future. That you'll realize who I really am, what I really am, and when I turn around you'll be gone."

He stopped, the wind whipping at his hair and clothes, swirling ashes into the silence. A glider on the wall turned its head and buzzed sleepily. Ash's posture was stiff, his back and shoulders rigid, steeled for my reaction. Bracing himself to hear footsteps walking back down the stairs. I saw his shoulders tremble and caught the faint aura of fear before he could hide it.

I stepped close and slipped my arms around his waist, hearing his quiet intake of breath as I pulled him against me. "That was a long time ago," I murmured, pressing my cheek to his back, listening to his thudding heart. "You've changed since then. That Ash wouldn't protect a silly human girl with his life, or become her knight, or walk into exile with her. Every step of the way, you've always been there, right beside me. I'm not letting you go now."

"I'm a coward." Ash's voice was subdued. "If I cared for you as much as I should, I would end my life and the curse along with it. My existence puts you in danger. If I were no longer here—"

"Don't you dare, Ashallyn'darkmyr Tallyn." I held him tighter, even as he flinched at the sound of his True Name. "Don't you dare throw your life away for an unknown superstition. If you die—" My voice broke, and I swallowed thickly. "I love you," I whispered, fisting my hands against his stomach. "You can't leave. You swore you wouldn't."

Ash's hands came to rest over mine, twining our fingers together. "Even if the world stands against you," he murmured, bowing his head. "I promise."

WE STAYED ON THE BALCONY that night, sitting against the wall, watching the storm sweep over the outlying hills. We didn't say much, content just to be near each other, lost in our own thoughts. When we did speak, it was of the war and the rebels and other, present-day things, staying far from the past…or the future. I dozed several times, waking with his arms around me and my head against his shoulder.

The next thing I knew, he was shaking me awake. The night had moved on, and a pinkish light glowed against the distant horizon.

"Meghan, wake up."

"Hmm?" I yawned, rubbing my eyes. Sleeping in armor while leaning against a wall, I realized, was proving to be a bad idea, as my backside throbbed with pain. "Time to go already?"

"No." Ash stepped to the edge of the balcony. "Come look at this. Hurry."

I peered out over the edge. At first, I couldn't see anything, but then the light gleamed off something shiny and metallic on the horizon. I squinted, shielding my eyes with my hand. Could that be the glint of metal armor? Or the shiny top of an iron beetle? My blood ran cold.

"They're coming," Ash muttered, and I stumbled back from the edge.

"We have to tell Glitch!"

I scrambled back from the landing, Ash close behind me. As we flew down the stairs, it quickly became clear that Glitch already knew. The camp was in chaos, rebels rushing back and forth, grabbing weapons and throwing on armor. Those who had been wounded the day before hurried out with freshly bandaged wounds, limping or carrying those who couldn't walk.

"There you are!" Puck met us at the foot of the stairs, rolling his eyes as we came charging down. "Another army on the way and you two are playing kissy-face on the balcony. Suit up. Looks like there's going to be another fight."

"Where's Glitch?" I said as we hurried through the ruins, dodging rebels. "What is he thinking? We can't fight another army now! Too many are hurt, and another fight could crush them."

"Doesn't seem like we have much choice, princess," Puck said as I spotted the rebel leader arguing with Diode under the limbs of the giant tree. Glitch's face was strained, and the hacker elf's eyes whirled and spun as he gestured frantically.

"Glitch!" I sprinted up to him, dodging a hound, which snarled as I barely avoided a collision. "Hey, I need to talk to you!" Glitch looked up and winced when he saw who it was.

"What do you want, your highness? I'm a little busy at the moment."

"What are you doing?" I asked as I caught up, Diode scrambling aside. "You can't make your people fight now! We're about to join Summer and Winter and we need everyone we can get. If you fight now, so soon after the last battle, you could lose everyone!"

"I'm aware of that, your highness!" Glitch snapped in

return, his spikes flaring angrily. "But we don't have much of a choice, do we? We can't run—they'll just hunt us down out there. We can't hide—there's really nowhere to go. All we can do is make our stand here. Thankfully, that's not the false king's full army, just a few attack squads. The real army is still on its way to the wyldwood, with the moving fortress I might add, and if we don't take care of this little problem now, we won't have a chance of joining Summer and Winter. Now, get out of my way. I should be at the front when the fighting starts."

"Wait!" I grabbed his sleeve as he brushed past, and he whirled angrily. "There is one more option. We came up through the packrat tunnels beneath the tower. We could escape that way."

"The tunnels?" Glitch shook off my hand. "Those tunnels run for miles. It's a gigantic maze down there. We could wander for days."

"Not me." I still didn't know how I was so familiar with the tunnels, but once I said the words, I knew they were true. "I know the way. I can get everyone through safely."

He looked disbelieving, and my temper flared. "It's either that or lose everyone before the war even starts! Dammit, Glitch, you have to start trusting me!"

"Do it," Ash said softly, locking gazes with the Iron faery. "You know she's right."

Glitch sighed noisily, stabbing his hands through his hair. "You sure you know the way?" he asked me.

"I wouldn't be here if I didn't."

"All right," he said slowly. "Fine. We'll put our lives in your hands once more, your highness. Diode, spread the word. Tell everyone to meet at the central chamber and be ready to march."

"Yes, sir." Diode shot me a relieved look and scampered off. Glitch watched him go, then turned to glare at me with narrowed violet eyes. "This better work. You're a gigantic pain in the ass, you know that, your highness?"

"One who's about to save yours," I returned, earning an appreciative snort from Puck. Glitch rolled his eyes and stalked off, and we made our way to the center of the ruins.

NOT FIFTEEN MINUTES LATER, the entire rebel army was gathered beneath the branches of the great oak, armed and armored, ready to march. I was wondering how quickly we could get all the rebels down into the tunnels when Diode approached and informed us the trapdoor we came through wasn't the only one, that there were several scattered throughout the tower, and one of them was in the center chamber, right below the tree. He was pointing out that it was buried and nearly hidden in the roots of the oak, when Glitch came in, his hair snapping wildly as he leaped onto the trunk.

"They're almost to the tower. We need to go, now!"

Working together, Ash, Puck, and Glitch hauled up the trapdoor, letting it drop open with a ringing clang that echoed throughout the room. Straightening, Glitch looked to me and gestured to the gaping hole, leading down into darkness. "After you, your highness. Diode, go with the princess to make sure everyone knows to follow her."

"What about you?"

"I'm staying topside to make sure everyone is through." Glitch nodded to the stocky dwarf with the mechanical arm, waiting stoically behind us. "When everyone is down, Torque and I will follow and seal the tunnel behind us. We're likely not coming back here again."

"But—"

"I'll worry about blocking our escape, you worry about not getting us lost down there." Glitch handed me a flashlight and pointed to the hole. "Now move, before they're at our door!"

Switching on the flashlight, I descended into the tunnels.

The musty darkness closed around me, smelling of dust, mold, and wet rock, strange and familiar at the same time. Ash dropped next to me, then Puck, and then Diode, his glowing numbered eyes seeming to float in the darkness. I wondered where Grimalkin was, and hoped he got out safely.

The hacker elf swept a nervous gaze around the tunnels, eyes spinning anxiously. "Are you sure you know the way?" he muttered, trying to sound confident, but it came out as more of a squeak. I swept my flashlight around the underground passageway and smiled in relief. Everything was familiar. I knew exactly where to go.

"Diode, start sending them down. Tell everyone to follow me."

I stepped forward, and the rebels began dropping through the trapdoor, lanterns and flashlights swaying in the darkness. At first, it felt strange, being at the head of a huge army, feeling their eyes on my back as I led them through the tunnels. But soon, the crunch of feet and the wavering lights behind me faded into background noise, until I almost didn't notice them.

Several minutes later, a boom rocked the passages behind us, shaking the floor and raining dust on everyone. Diode squawked in fear, Puck braced himself against a wall, and Ash grabbed my arm, holding me steady as I staggered.

"What was that?" the hacker elf cried as the dust finally cleared. Coughing, I waved my hand in front of my face and looked back at the rebels, getting to their feet and looking around nervously.

I shared a glance with Ash and Puck. "Glitch must've collapsed the tunnels," I said, picking up the flashlight I'd dropped. "It was the only way to keep the false king's forces from following us."

"What?" Diode looked back fearfully, eyes whirling. "I

thought he was just going to seal the doors. So, we can't return to base?"

"He never meant to come back here," I murmured, shining the light beam into the maze before us. "There's no turning back now. The only choice is to move on."

TIME HAD NO MEANING in the sunless corridors of the packrat tunnels. We might've been traveling for hours, or days. The tunnels all looked the same: dark, eerie, filled with strange odds and ends, like an abandoned computer monitor, or the severed head of a doll. After the explosion, Glitch would join me at the head of the march every so often, if only to make sure I still knew where I was going. After about the sixth time, he began to get on my nerves.

"Yes, I still know where I'm going!" I snapped as he emerged beside me yet again, cutting him off before he could say anything. Ash walked on my other side, silent and protective, but I caught him rolling his eyes as Glitch came up.

The rebel leader scowled. "Relax, your highness. I wasn't going to ask this time."

"Aw, that's a shame," Puck said, falling into step beside him. "You're gonna make me lose my bet with ice-boy. Come on, be a sport. Say it one more time, for me?"

"What I was going to ask," Glitch continued, ignoring Puck, "is how much longer till we're out? My troops are getting tired—we can't keep this up much longer without a break."

I frowned and looked at Ash. "How long have we been walking?"

He shrugged. "Hard to tell. A day, perhaps. Maybe longer."

"Really?" It didn't seem that long to me. I didn't feel tired. In fact, the longer we traveled, the more energy I had—the same kind of energy that had drawn me to Machina's tree.

But this was a darker power, bitter and ancient, and I suddenly knew where it was coming from.

"We must be getting close to Ferrum's chamber," I muttered, and Glitch's eyebrows rose.

"Ferrum? The old king Ferrum?"

"You know about him?"

"I helped Machina overthrow him." Glitch was staring at me in disbelief. "I led the charge to the throne room with Virus and Ironhorse. You mean to tell me that he's still alive?"

"No." I shook my head. "Not anymore. He was here when I first came to the Iron Realm, on the way to get my brother back. The packrats still worshipped him, but he was terrified Machina would find him again. I think he finally faded away, and the packrats moved on when he died."

"Huh." Glitch shook his head in wonder. "I can't believe the old coot stayed alive for so long. If I had known about him, you can bet I would've searched every tunnel in the Iron Realm until I found him and put him out of his misery."

I looked at him in horror. "Why? He seemed harmless to me. Just a sad, angry old man."

"You don't know what he was like before." Glitch's eyes narrowed. "You weren't there when he was king. Ferrum was paranoid, terrified that someone would try to take his crown away. I was one of the newest lieutenants, but Ironhorse told me that with every new Iron fey that appeared, Ferrum grew more afraid and angry. It would've been best if he had stepped down, handed the throne to a successor. He was old and obsolete, and we all knew it. In this realm, the old move out to make room for the new. But Ferrum refused to give up his power, even though his bitterness was corrupting the land around him. Machina pleaded with him to reconsider his right to rule, to step down gracefully and hand the responsibility to someone else."

"Ferrum told me Machina took his throne out of a lust for power, because he wanted it for himself."

Glitch snorted. "Machina was one of Ferrum's strongest supporters. The rest of us—me, Virus, and Ironhorse—were getting tired of Ferrum's threats, of the constant fear that one of us could be next. But Machina told us to be patient, and we were more loyal to him than our crazy king. Then the day came when Ferrum's jealous paranoia finally got the better of him, and he tried to kill Machina, stabbing at him when his back was turned. His last mistake, I'm afraid. Machina realized Ferrum was no longer fit to rule and gathered his own supporters to take the king off the throne. We were only too happy to comply."

I felt dazed. Everything I thought I knew about Machina was wrong. "But...Machina still wanted to take over the Nevernever," I protested. "He wanted to eradicate the old faeries and make a kingdom of Iron fey."

"Machina was ever the strategist." Glitch shrugged, unconcerned. "He knew Ferrum's way—hiding in fear from the courts and hoping they wouldn't see us—wasn't going to work much longer. The Iron Kingdom was growing faster than ever. We couldn't hide anymore. Sooner or later, the courts would find out, and then what? What do you think would happen when they discovered a whole kingdom of faeries born from the very thing that could kill them? Machina knew there would be a war. He figured it would be best if we struck first."

"Too bad Meghan had to ruin it for you," Puck added, smirking at the back of Glitch's head. Glitch turned to him and matched his sneer.

"It won't matter if the false king conquers the Nevernever now, will it?" he countered. "I'll still be here, and so will all the Iron fey, but you oldbloods will become a thing of the past. And not even her highness will be able to stop it."

"That's not going to happen," I snapped, turning on him. "I'll stop the false king, just like I did Machina."

"Glad to hear it." Glitch leveled a stare at me. "But did you ever think about how you're going to stop the spread of the Iron Realm? Just because the false king is gone doesn't mean we're going away as well, princess. The Iron Kingdom will continue to grow and change the Nevernever, and in the end the courts will come after us anyway. I agree that, right now, we have to stop the false king, but you're only delaying the inevitable."

"There has to be a way," I muttered. "You're all faeries, you use glamour the same way. You're just a little different, that's all."

"We're not," Glitch said firmly, "a *little* different. Our glamour kills oldbloods. Summer magic is deadly to us, as well. If you think we can hold hands and be friends, princess, you're only fooling yourself. But we need to stop soon, or this army will be too exhausted to fight anything."

I shook my head. "No, we have to keep moving. At least until we're out of the tunnels."

"Why?"

"Because…" I closed my eyes. "He's almost there."

All three faeries stared at me. "How do you know?" Ash asked softly.

"I can feel him." Goose bumps rose along my arms, and I hugged myself, shivering. "I can feel the land…crying out where he passes. It feels…" I paused, searching for words. "It feels like someone is dragging a blade across the surface, leaving a scar behind. I've been able to sense him ever since we passed Ferrum's old chamber. The false king…he's getting close to the wyldwood now, and he's waiting for me."

CHAPTER TWENTY-TWO

THE LAST NIGHT

Eventually, we came out of the tunnels.

The night was remarkably clear as we set up camp, a tattered, ragtag army pitching tents on the edge of a bubbling magma lake, the air smelling of sulphur and brimstone. I didn't want to camp so close to the lake but Glitch overrode me, saying the smell would mask our presence, and besides his army was exhausted thanks to my forced march through the packrat tunnels. Even Ash and Puck were tired; they wouldn't say anything, but the gaunt looks and pale faces told me they weren't feeling the best. Their amulets were almost used up. The Iron Realm was finally taking its toll.

"Go lie down," I told them both, once Glitch had left to help the army pitch camp. "You're both exhausted, and we're not doing anything else tonight. Get some rest."

Puck snorted. "My, aren't we bossy today," he said, though it lacked his usual energy. "Give a girl an army and it goes straight to her head." He yawned then, scrubbing his scalp. "Right, then. If anyone needs me, I'll be passed out in my tent, trying to forget where I am. Oh, look, demon fey, lake of liquid hot magma—does this remind you of anything?" He grimaced, giving me a weak grin. "When I said I'd follow you to hell and back, I wasn't trying to be literal, princess. Ah, well." He lifted one hand in a cheerful wave. "See you tomorrow, lovebirds."

"What about you?" Ash asked as Puck sauntered off, whistling loudly. "You've been walking just as long as the rest of us. We won't have another chance to rest before we reach the battleground."

A flash of movement caught my attention. For a moment, I thought I saw a furry gray cat leap onto a boulder near the edge of the lake. But the air around him shimmered with heat, and he was gone. "I know," I said, squinting in the hot, dry air. "And it might sound strange, but I feel fine. You go on," I continued, gazing up at him. "I know you're tired. Get some rest before the battle. I'll be around."

He didn't argue, which showed me just how exhausted he was. Stepping close, he placed a soft kiss on my forehead and walked off toward the ring of tents farthest from the lake. I watched him until he vanished behind an old, twisted monolith, then I wandered down to the lake edge.

This close to the lava, my skin felt like it would peel off my bones if I scratched at it, and I didn't dare venture too close to the edge. One slip or stumble, and it would end very badly. Magma bubbled sluggishly, curling in slow, hypnotic patterns of orange and gold, strangely beautiful in the hellish glow. For a moment, I had the brief, crazy urge to skip a pebble across the glowing surface, then decided that would probably be a bad idea.

"The Molten Pool," said a voice beside me, and Grimalkin appeared atop a boulder, his whiskers glowing red in the light. I was relieved to see him, though I knew he could take care of himself. "In the center of the Obsidian Plains. Ironhorse told me about this. These were his lands, back in the days of King Machina."

"Ironhorse." I leaned back against the rock and gazed out over the pool. The boulder was warm to the touch, even through my armor. "I wish he could've been here to see this," I muttered, imagining the huge, black-iron horse standing proudly at the other side of the lake. "I wish we could've brought him home."

"There is no use in wishing for the impossible, human." Grimalkin sat down, curling his tail around himself, as we both stared out over the lake. "Ironhorse knew what he had to do. Do not let human guilt distract you from your duty, for Ironhorse did not."

I sighed. "Is that what you had to say to me, Grim? Don't feel guilty for a friend's death?"

"No." The cat twitched an ear and stood, facing me directly. "I have come to tell you that I am leaving, and I did not want you worrying about my whereabouts on the eve of battle. There are more important things to focus on. So...I am leaving."

I pushed myself off the rock and turned to face him. "Why?"

"Human, my part here is done." Grimalkin regarded me with what could almost be affection. "Tomorrow, you march into battle with an army of Iron fey at your back. There is no place for me in this fight—I am under no illusion that I am a warrior." He stepped forward, ancient golden eyes staring into mine, reflecting the light of the pool. "I have brought you as far as I can. It is time for you to step forward on your own and claim your destiny. Besides..." Grimalkin sat back, gazing out across the lake, the hot breeze ruffling his whiskers. "I have my own contract to fulfill, before this is all over."

"*You* made a contract?"

He gave me his disdainful look, twitching his tail. "You don't believe Ironhorse asked for nothing in return, do you? Really, human, sometimes I despair. But the night is waning, and I must go." Leaping gracefully off the rock, he began trotting away, bottlebrush tail held straight up and proud.

I swallowed hard. "Grim? Will I see you again?"

The cait sith turned back, cocking his head. "Now, that is a strange question," he mused. "Will you see me again, though I myself am no oracle and know nothing of the future? This I cannot tell you. I will never understand humans, but I suppose it is part of your charm." He sniffed again, waving his plumed tail lazily. "Do try to stay out of trouble, human. I will be terribly annoyed if you manage to get yourself killed."

"Grim, wait. Are you sure you'll be all right?"

Grimalkin smiled. "I am a cat."

And, just like that, he was gone.

I smiled faintly and wiped a stray tear from my face. Grim had always vanished and reappeared at will, but this time it was different. I suddenly knew I wouldn't see him again, not for a long time anyway.

"Goodbye, Grimalkin," I whispered, and in an even softer voice, lest the cunning feline be nearby listening, added, "thank you."

I shivered in the hot wind, already feeling his loss. How many more would I lose before this was over? Somewhere out there, closer than ever, the false king was closing on the armies of Summer and Winter. Tomorrow was the moment of truth. Tomorrow was Judgment Day, where we would either be victorious, or die.

I suddenly wished I could talk to my family. I wanted to see Mom's face again, hold Ethan and ruffle his hair one last time. I even wanted to see Luke, to tell him I forgave him for never noticing me, never seeing me. Mom was happy with him, and if she hadn't met him, I wouldn't have Ethan as a brother. I wouldn't have a family. My throat closed up, and longing twisted my stomach into a painful knot. Would they miss me, if I never came home? Would they stop looking for me eventually, the daughter who vanished one night and never returned?

The wind howled across the plain, lonely and desolate, as the full realization hit me and clutched my heart with icy fingers. I could die tomorrow. This was a war, and there would be numerous casualties on both sides. The false king himself could be too much, if I even figured out a way to get into his fortress. We could very well lose. I could be struck down, and my family would never know what happened, what I was fighting for. If I died, who would tell them? Oberon? No, if I lost, he would fade away, as well. If I lost, it would be over. The end of Faery. Forever.

Oh, God.

I was shaking now, unable to stop myself. This was really it. The last battle, and it all rested on me. What if I failed? If I couldn't beat the false king, they would all die—Oberon, Grim, Puck, Ash...

Ash.

Shivering, I hurried back to the camp, past the cluster of tents set up around the lake. The camp was quiet and still, unlike the wild, prebattle revel of the Summer and Winter camps. I suddenly understood the significance and would have welcomed the distraction tonight. Too many dark thoughts were swirling around my head, so many emotions that I felt I would burst. But, despite everything I felt and the crazy emotions churning inside me, it all came back to him.

I found his tent sitting on the edge of camp, farther out from the rest. I didn't know how I knew it was his; all the tents looked basically the same. But I could feel him, as surely as I felt my own heartbeat. For a moment, I hesitated at the entrance, my hand poised to push back the cloth. What would I say to him, the last night we could be alive?

Gathering my courage, I pushed open the flap and stepped inside.

Ash lay on his back in the corner, one arm flung over his eyes, his breathing slow and deep. He was shirtless, and the amulet gleamed against his sculpted chest, almost completely black now, a drop of ink against his pale skin. I was surprised he hadn't heard me come in; the normal Ash would've been up and on his feet with his sword drawn in the blink of an eye. He must've been truly exhausted from our march through the tunnels. Taking advantage of the moment, I watched him, admiring the lean, hard muscles, gazing at the scars slashed across his pale skin. His chest rose and fell with each quiet breath, and just watching him sleep made me feel a bit calmer.

"How long are you going to keep staring at me?"

I jumped. He hadn't moved, but one corner of his mouth was curved in a slight smile. "How long did you know I was here?"

"I felt you the moment you came to the tent and stood outside, wondering if you should come in." Ash removed his arm and shifted to perch on an elbow, watching me. His expression was solemn now, silver eyes bright in the gloom. "What's wrong?"

I swallowed. "I just...I wanted...oh, dammit..." Blushing, I trailed off, gazing at the floor. "I'm scared," I finally admitted in a whisper. "Tomorrow's the war and we could die and I won't ever see my family again and...and I don't want to be alone tonight."

Ash's gaze softened. Without a word, he shifted back on the cot, making room for me. Heart pounding, I crossed the room and lay down next to him, feeling his arm wrap around my stomach, pulling me close. I felt his heartbeat against my back and closed my eyes, tracing idle patterns on his arm, brushing a faint scar on the back of his wrist.

"Ash?"

"Hmm?"

"Are you scared? Of dying?"

He was quiet a moment, one hand playing with my hair, his breath fanning across my cheek. "Perhaps not in the way you would think," he murmured at last. "I've lived a long time, been in many battles. Of course, there was always that knowledge that I could die, but there have been times I've wondered if I shouldn't give up, let it happen."

"Why?"

"To escape the emptiness. I was dead inside for so long. Not existing didn't seem any different than what I was doing." He buried his face in my shoulder, and I shivered. "It's different now, though. I have something to fight for. I'm not afraid to die, but I don't intend to give up, either." His lips touched my hair, very lightly. "I won't let anything happen to you," he murmured. "You are my heart, my life, my entire existence."

My eyes watered, and my heart thudded in my ears. "Ash," I whispered again, clenching my fists in the quilt to stop the shaking. I knew what I wanted, but I was still afraid, afraid that I wouldn't do it right, afraid of the unknown, afraid that I would somehow disappoint him. Ash kissed the back of my neck, and I felt his arm tighten, fingers digging into my shirt. I saw a flare of color behind me, bright red desire, felt him tremble as he struggled to control himself, and all my doubts melted away.

I shifted in his arms, rolling toward him so that he was propped on an elbow above me, eyes shining in the darkness. And I let him see the need, the longing, rising up like tendrils of colored smoke to dance with his. I didn't have to say anything. He drew in a quiet breath and lowered his head, touching his forehead to mine.

"Are you sure?" His voice was barely a whisper, a ghost in the dark.

I nodded, tracing my fingers down his cheek, marveling as he closed his eyes. "We could die tomorrow," I whispered back. "I want to be with you tonight. I don't want to have any regrets, when it comes to us. So, yes, I'm sure. I love you, Ash."

My voice was lost then, as Ash closed the final few inches and kissed me. And in the quiet stillness before dawn, on the brink of a war that could tear us apart, our auras danced and twined in the darkness, coiling around each other until they finally merged, becoming one.

PART THREE

CHAPTER TWENTY-THREE

THE BATTLE FOR FAERY

When I woke, the tent was still dark, though a faint gray light peeked through the flaps. Ash was already gone, typical for him, but my body still glowed from the aftermath of last night. I could feel him now, stronger than ever. He was close. He was—

Right beside me.

I jumped a bit, and turned to see him sitting beside the cot, fully clothed, his sword across his lap, watching me. He wasn't smiling, but his face was relaxed, his eyes peaceful.

"Hey," I whispered, smiling and reaching out to him. His fingers wrapped around mine and he kissed the back of my hand, before standing.

"It's almost time," he said quietly, tucking his sword into his belt again. And the looming war descended like a hammer, shattering the tranquility. "Better get dressed—Glitch will be looking for us. Or worse—"

"Puck," I groaned and struggled upright, searching for my clothes. Ash silently turned his back while I dressed, facing the door, and I bit down a giggle at his chivalry. Once I shrugged into the dragon-scale armor, I turned to show I was ready to follow him out. But Ash crossed the tiny space between us and drew me close, fingers combing my tangled hair, his expression thoughtful.

"I've been thinking…" he mused as I slid my arms around his neck, gazing up at him. "When this is over, let's disappear for a while. Just the two of us. We can check on your family first, and then we can go. I can show you the Nevernever like you've never seen it before. Forget the courts, the Iron fey, everything. Just you and me and nothing else."

"I'd like that," I whispered. Ash smiled, brushed a kiss to my lips, and pulled away.

"That's all I needed to hear." His eyes gleamed, determined and eager, and filled with something I hadn't see before. Hope. "Let's go win a war."

We stepped out of the tent together, not touching, but I didn't need to touch him to feel him, right beside me. He was part of my soul now, and that somehow made this all the more real. The battle loomed over our heads, close and ominous, made all the more threatening by the eerie red clouds and the ash flakes drifting from them, as if the very sky was falling apart. I gazed up at the sky with a fierce determination. I would win this war. I never wanted anything like this.

"There you are." Glitch emerged from the crowds, dressed for battle with a spear that crackled at the tip, shedding sparks of lightning. "We're almost ready. My scouts have reported the battle has already started, that Summer and Winter have already engaged the false king's forces. The entire army has breached the line into the wyldwood—it looks like this is it."

My blood ran cold. "What about the fortress?"

"Not there yet." Glitch planted the butt of the spear in the ground. "The forest is slowing it down. But it's close. We have to hurry. Where's Goodfellow?"

"Right here." Puck appeared, a smug grin on his face, carrying a long pole beneath his arm. "Been working on something, princess. Last night, I was wondering how the courts were going to tell us apart from the false king's army. Bad Iron fey, good Iron fey—they all look the same to me. Sooooo..." He swept the pole up with a flourish, and a bright green banner snapped open at the top, the silhouette of a great oak splayed proudly across the front. "I wanted to make it a picture of a flower or butterfly," Puck said, smiling at my awed look, "but I didn't think that would strike fear into the heart of the false king."

"Not bad, Goodfellow," Glitch said with grudging respect.

"Oh, so glad you think so, socket-head. My mad crocheting skills finally came in handy for something."

"In any case," Glitch added, rolling his eyes, "we would be proud to carry that into battle for you."

My heart swelled. All these people were willing to follow me, to die to save Faery. I couldn't fail them. I wouldn't.

At that moment, a great commotion came from the edge of the camp, Iron fey shouting in alarm, tents flung aside, and the sound of thundering footsteps. A moment later, the crowds fell back as a group of huge black horses galloped into camp, skidding to a stop before me.

I gasped. They looked like smaller, sleeker versions of Ironhorse, made of black metal with burning crimson eyes and nostrils that breathed flame. As I stared, one of them stepped forward and tossed his head at me.

"Meghan Chase?" he asked in that same regal, noble air, his deep voice accompanied by a blast of cinders. I blinked rapidly and nodded.

"One called Grimalkin sent us." The Ironhorse look-alike nodded to the others. "He carries with him the spirit of our progenitor, the first Iron Horse, and has compelled us to join you and your cause against the False Monarch. Out of respect for the Great One, we have agreed. Do you accept our assistance?"

Ironhorse, I thought sadly. *You're still helping us, even now.* "I accept your offer," I told the first horse, who nodded regally and bent his foreleg, lowering himself into a bow.

"Then, it is done," he said, as the others bent their front legs and did the same. "For this conflict only, we will carry you and your officers into battle. Afterward, our contract is done, and you will release us."

"Oh, goodie," Puck said as I stepped forward. "I'm going to have a rash in the most uncomfortable places."

I swung onto the horse's back, feeling thick iron muscles shift under me as he rose, clanking and groaning. His metallic skin was warm to the touch, especially near my legs, as if a great fire burned inside him. I remembered the flames roaring in Ironhorse's belly, visible through his exposed ribs and pistons, and felt another ripple of sadness at his loss.

Ash, Puck, and Glitch watched me from the backs of the metal horses, who snorted flame and tossed their heads, eager and ready. The banner was hoisted up, the black oak against a background of green flapping in the wind. I gazed out over the solemn, upturned faces and took a deep breath.

"Summer and Winter are not your enemies!" I called, my voice echoing into the silence. "They are different, yes, but they are fighting the enemy that you hate—a tyrant who seeks to destroy everything King Machina stood for. We cannot abandon them now! Peace with the courts is possible, but the false king will corrupt and enslave everyone if he wins. The only thing necessary for evil to conquer is for us and those like us to do nothing, and I will not sit by and let that happen! We will take this fight to the false king, and we will show him what happens when we stand united against him! Who is with me?"

The roar of the army was like a sudden tornado, as hundreds of voices rose up as one. I drew my sword and raised it over my head, adding to the sea of weapons flashing in the light.

"Let's go win a war!"

I HEARD THE SOUNDS of the battle before I saw it. They echoed through the trees that marked the edge of the Iron Realm: shouts and screams, howls of fury, and weapons clashing in the wind. Every so often there was the boom of gunfire, or the thunderous roar of flame. Above the tree line, a huge emerald dragon swooped into the air, paused a moment, then dove out of sight again.

Spikerail, the horse I was riding, snorted and tossed his head. "The battle has already been joined," he announced, nearly prancing with excitement. "Shall we give the order to charge?"

"Not yet," I replied, putting a restraining hand on his shoulder. "Let's get through the trees, at least. I want to see the battle, first."

He pawed the ground impatiently, but kept his pace to a fast walk as we entered the forest. The metal trunks closed around us, dark and twisted, smelling of rust and battery acid. Above the clash of battle, I heard something else in the woods—a great snapping and groaning, as if something huge were pushing through the trees.

"Faster," I told Spikerail, and he broke into a trot, stirring up clouds of ash as we moved through the forest. The sounds of battle drew closer.

And then the trees fell away, and we were gazing down on mass chaos.

I'd seen the fey in battle twice now, but this seemed even more vicious, more desperate, as if hell itself had been released onto the field. Troops swarmed each other like ants, hacking with ancient and modern weapons, blades and armor glinting in the swirling ash storm. Iron beetles lumbered through the mobs, the gunmen on their backs blasting away. Creatures plunged and dove through the air; an icy-blue dragon, its scales streaked with red, landed on the back of an iron bug, blasted the musket elves with a deadly spray of frost before they could react, and swooped away again. A gryphon, darting by with an elfin rider, was snatched out of the air by a

clockwork golem and smashed against a rock. Two metallic
praying mantises double-teamed a Summer knight, slashing
at him with their massive, curved blades, until he slipped in
the ash and was instantly beheaded.

The battle wasn't going well, it seemed. There was a lot
more silver and gray on the field than green and gold, blue
and black.

"Looks like we got here just in time," Puck mused beside me.
"Ready for the 'here comes the cavalry' charge, princess?"

"If we hit their right flank," Ash said, observing the battle
with narrowed silver eyes, "we may surprise them where their
line is thin and tear through them before they can react."

I met both their gazes, fierce, protective, blazing with
determination and love, and felt no fear. Well, maybe a little
fear, but it was swallowed by resolve and the almost painful
need to win this fight. Drawing my blade, I wheeled Spikerail
to face the army—*my* army, truth be told—and looked out
over the taut, waiting forces.

"For Faery!" I called, raising my sword, and the rebels
took up the cry. A few hundred voices rose into the air,
roaring, cheering, stabbing their weapons skyward. My
adrenaline soared as the crescendo echoed around me, and
I howled again, adding my voice to the mix. With a shrill
whinny, Spikerail reared, pawing the air, and plunged down
the slope.

Wind whipped at my hair and ash swirled around me,
stinging my eyes. My ears were filled with pounding hoof-
beats and the roar of the army behind us. We neared the ocean
of battle, the rise and fall of soldiers like waves on the shore,
the scream and clash of weapons, and roared as we came in,
like a hurricane coming to land. The false king's army turned
just as we hit them, their eyes going wide, desperately ready-
ing to meet this new threat, but by then it was too late. We
slammed into them with the force of a tidal wave, swift and
vengeful, and all hell broke loose around me.

Spikerail plunged through the masses, blasting and breathing flame, powerful hooves lashing out at those who got too close. I struck out from his back, stabbing at the false king's army with my sword. Everything was chaos. I was vaguely aware of Ash and Puck fighting close to me, fending off attacks from all sides. I saw Ash stab one Iron knight through the chest and hurl an ice spear through another. I saw Puck throw what looked like a fuzzy golf ball at a group of Iron knights, where it erupted into an angry grizzly. Glitch whirled his spear in a deadly circle, lightning arcing from the tip, stabbing the point through the knights' armor to fry them to blackened husks.

Where's Oberon? I wondered, blocking a spear thrust at my face, kicking the knight away. I had to find him, to tell him that the rebels were not the enemy, that they were here to help. I spotted Glitch through a lull in the fighting and nudged Spikerail in his direction. If Glitch was there as well, to explain himself and his actions, perhaps Oberon would listen.

"Glitch!" I called as we drew close. "Come with m—"

A bellow interrupted us, and a huge clockwork golem plowed through the ranks, swinging its club and sending rebels flying. It caught Glitch by surprise, and the rebel leader tried to dodge, too late. The metal club caught his horse's shoulder and knocked both of them several feet through the air. I screamed, but my voice was lost in the cacophony, and the golem lumbered closer to the motionless Glitch, raising its club for the killing blow.

Ash suddenly wheeled his horse around and charged the golem, hurling an ice dagger that shattered off the metal skull, making its head snap up. Roaring, it swung at Ash, and my heart leaped to my throat as the huge club came swooshing down. But at the last moment, Ash sprang from his mount's back and landed on the golem's arm, running up to its shoulder. As the golem pulled back with a roar, thrashing and flailing, the Ice Prince raised his sword and stabbed it through the construct's neck. There was a flash of blue light, and the golem bellowed, falling to its knees. Ash leaped off the giant, landing on his feet in the grass, as the golem shuddered and collapsed into a hundred pieces of frozen clockwork, rolling through the ashes.

"I'm not impressed, ice-boy!" Puck yelled, kicking away an Iron knight. "Do that again, only this time, make it dance!"

Ignoring Puck, I turned Spikerail and hurried over to where Glitch had fallen. His horse lay in an ash drift, struggling to get up, and Glitch lay a few feet away, his spikes snapping feebly.

"Glitch!" I leaped off Spikerail's back and ran to the prone figure, kneeling beside him in the ashes. "Are you all right? Talk to me." Ash and Puck loomed to either side, protecting us from surrounding chaos. I reached down and shook his limp arm. "Glitch!"

He groaned and cracked open his eyes. "Ow," he moaned. "Dammit, what hit me?" He tried sitting up and winced, grabbing his arm. "Ouch. That's not good."

"Can you stand?" I asked anxiously.

He nodded and tried to get up, but gasped and sank back again, gritting his teeth. "Nope. Ribs broken, as well. Sorry, highness." Glitch swore and shook his head. "I might have to sit this one out."

"That's fine. We just have to get you out of here." I looked around, flinching as Puck leaped between me and a clockwork hound, cutting the dog out of the air. I spotted Glitch's horse, finally on his feet though looking a bit dazed, and gave a shrill whistle. "Coaleater!" I yelled, remembering the horse's name. "Over here!

The horse limped up, and we helped Glitch heave himself onto its back. "Take him to safety," I told the horse, who bobbed his head in consent, seemingly glad to get out of the fight. "Make sure he gets the help he needs. I'll take it from here."

"Meghan." Glitch's voice, though reedy with pain, was firm. The rebel leader gazed down at me and nodded, once. "I was wrong about you. Good luck. Win this war for us."

"I will," I replied, as Coaleater moved carefully but swiftly out of sight, disappearing into the swirling ash. Now it was the three of us, just like before. Puck and Ash pressed close, and I narrowed my eyes, peering through the whirling bodies. "Let's find Oberon, right now."

I threw myself back into the fight, Puck and Ash right beside me. Together, we carved our way through the seemingly endless ranks of Iron fey. Sweat ran into my eyes, my dragon-scale armor took a hundred or so painful bangs and scrapes, and my arms burned from swinging my sword, but we continued to fight, inching our way across the field. I became lost in the dance: block, swing, parry, dodge, stab, repeat, always moving on, always pressing forward. An iron beetle bore down on us, muskets firing, and I drew on the Iron glamour to tear the bolts from its legs at the joints, fighting the nausea that overtook me right after. The beetle crashed to the ground and was quickly overrun. Another clockwork giant stumbled into our midst, and this time both Ash and Puck went after it, Puck turning into a raven and pecking at its eyes, while Ash darted around and leaped onto its back, plunging his blade through its chest. Glamour swirled around me, Iron, Summer, and Winter, though the magic of the Iron fey was much stronger here. I could feel it, pulsing through the land, lending strength to both the rebels and the forces of the false king. I could feel the core of the Iron glamour drawing closer, pulsing and angry, corrupting everything in its path.

For just a moment, I was distracted, and that was long enough for something to slip through my guard. The tip of a spear cut through my defenses and slammed me in the shoulder, not enough to pierce the dragon-scale, but hard enough to rock me back and send a flare of pain up my arm. I dropped my sword, and the knight pulled back for another shot.

A huge, gnarled fist closed over his head, crushing the helmet like a grape and lifting the knight high into the air. I gaped as a monstrous, treelike being with thick, thorny skin and a crown of antlers flung the knight away, then turned to knock back a whole platoon with its treelike limbs. Grasses and flowers bloomed briefly where it stepped, as the great tree creature moved forward with surprising speed and grace, looming above my head, as if to protect me. Then its gaze swept down, and I was staring into the ancient, familiar face of the Summer King.

"You've returned." Oberon's voice shook the ground, deeper and lower than a thunderclap, and just as emotionless. The Seelie King gave no hint as to what he was feeling, if he felt anything when he saw me. "And you have brought more Iron fey to our territory."

"They're here to help us!" I yelled, snatching my sword and glaring up at him. He gazed back with impassive green eyes, and I stabbed a finger in his direction. "Don't you dare turn on them, Father! They want the same thing you do!"

Oberon blinked, and I realized I had just called him *father*. Well, I *was* the Summer princess; it was useless to deny it any longer. "I make no promises," the Seelie King said, and turned away, his giant limbs crushing another pair of Iron knights. "We shall see, after the battle, what to do with the intruders."

Furious, I snarled a curse and turned on the Iron knight trying to rush me from behind. Stupid, unreasonable, uncompromising faeries! He'd better not try anything with the rebels when this was done. I'd given my word that they would be safe from him and Mab.

I stabbed my sword through the chest of an Iron knight,

watched the empty armor clatter to the ground, and looked up for the next enemy. Only to find there wasn't one. I looked around to see the false king's forces pulling back, running away. As a tired cheer rose up from the army around us, I looked up to see Oberon, surrounded by the remains of countless Iron fey, crush a final golem into scrap metal and turn to me. A shiver went through the Summer King. He began shrinking, growing smaller and less…thorny…until he was as I remembered him. But his eyes, and the inflexibility on his face, remained.

"Why have you brought them here?" Oberon demanded, his cold gaze going to the rebels at my back. "More Iron fey to poison the land, more Iron fey that would destroy us."

"No!" I stepped forward, instinctively shielding them behind me. "I told you before, they're here to help. They want the false king gone, just like you."

"And what then? Offer them sanctuary within our courts? Let them go back to the Iron Realm, so that it may continue to spread and corrupt our home?" Oberon seemed to grow in stature, though his size remained the same. The rebels murmured and cringed back as the Seelie King swept his arm over the crowd. "*Every* Iron fey, whether they are hostile or peaceful, is a danger to us. We will *never be safe* while they are alive. This is why we asked you to go into their realm and destroy the Iron King. You have failed us. And now, all of Faery will perish because of you."

"I gave my word that they would be safe here!" I shouted, feeling Ash and Puck step up beside me. "If you attack them, you'll make me your enemy, as well! And I don't think you can afford an attack on two fronts, Father."

"The girl is right." A blast of icy cold, and Mab the Winter Queen swept up, her white battlegown streaked with splashes of red and black. "We waste time arguing here while our home is being destroyed around us. Let the rogue fey fight with us—there will be time later to decide their fate."

I didn't like the sound of that, either, but in another moment, it didn't matter. A loud grinding, ripping sound echoed across the field, coming from the edge of the woods, like thousands of trees were being snapped at once. Branches shook violently, swaying like reeds in the wind, and my heart lurched as the massive bulk of the fortress broke through the edge of the woods, crushing trees beneath it, and dragged itself onto the field.

Up close, the false king's fortress was even larger than I'd thought, casting a looming shadow across the battleground and blocking out the sky. Again, I was struck by how irregular it was, an accumulation of different parts—smokestacks, towers, balconies—thrown into place with no care as to how it looked, yet somehow held together. Smoke leaked from every crevice, billowing into the sky, and the entire thing moved forward with a cacophony of clanks and groans and squeals, sending chills down my spine.

As the armies of Summer and Winter drew back in shock from the monstrous structure, Ash grabbed my arm and pointed to the ground beneath it. "Look!" he said, his voice filled with horror and disbelief. "Look at what's carrying it!"

I gasped, hardly comprehending what I saw. The fortress was being carried on the shoulders of hundreds, maybe thousands, of packrats. They shuffled forward in a daze, their eyes blank and glassy, moving across the field like ants with a giant grasshopper.

"Oh, God," I whispered, stumbling back a step. "They don't know what they're doing. The false king must have enchanted them somehow."

"Uh, enchanted or not, they're not stopping," Puck observed, looking nervous as the huge fortress crawled forward, moving at a slow but steady pace through the falling ash. "If we're gonna get inside that thing and stop the false king, now would be a great time."

"Attack!" roared Oberon, sweeping his arm toward the moving citadel. "All forces, stop that castle! Do not let it cross the lines!"

The armies surged forward again, both my Iron fey and the oldbloods, uncaring that they were suddenly fighting side by side. In the face of a much greater evil, they hurled themselves at the fortress, their battle cries rising into the air as one.

A flash of smoke and fire erupted from the fortress, and a moment later the explosion of a cannonball rocked the ground, sending several flying. Suddenly the air was filled with explosions, as the fortress opened fire on the advancing fey. Howls and screams rose into the air, and from the woods, coming from behind the fortress, another regiment of the false king's swarmed onto the field.

"Reinforcements!" I gasped as the new army slammed into our forces. Drawing my sword, I turned to Ash and Puck. "Let's go. One way or another, we have to get into that fortress."

We charged the field, joining our allies in trying to hold the line. But the false king's army was new and fresh, and most of our forces were already exhausted. More and more of our soldiers fell under the relentless push of the false king's army, and the fortress continued to creep forward, peppering the ground with cannonballs and explosions. We were being pushed back. We were giving ground.

With a roar, the green Summer dragon swooped overhead, its shadow flashing over us, and landed on the castle, talons digging into the side. Snarling, the dragon ripped and tore at the fortress walls, smashing cannons and breathing fire at the faeries manning them. For a moment, my heart leaped with hope.

But then, the metal towers atop the castle glowed blue-white with energy, and an arc of lightning leaped outward, slamming into the dragon. The dragon screeched, going rigid, as more strands of deadly electricity coursed over and through it, lighting up the sky. It finally dropped off the castle, trailing smoke from its blackened scales, and crashed to the ground. It didn't move again.

My spirits plummeted. We couldn't do it. If a freaking *dragon* couldn't get into the fortress, what chance did I have? Shearing through a wireman, I looked around the field and my heart dropped even lower. There didn't seem to be many good guys left. Oberon was back in his tree-giant form, flinging soldiers left and right, and Mab was an icy whirlwind of death, surrounded by frozen corpses and suits of armor, but I couldn't see much of our army through the masses of Iron knights and other false-king soldiers. Worse, they appeared to have us surrounded.

An explosion shook the ground, very close, and I staggered backward, showered with rocks and dirt. Ash and Puck stood back-to-back, fending off attacks from all sides, but they were being pushed back, as well. A cold numbness spread through my body. We were going to lose. I couldn't get into the fortress, couldn't beat the false king. His army was too much for us. We had failed. I had failed.

"Master!"

Something small and fast leaped at me. I reacted instinctively and swatted it from the air, smashing it to the ground.

"Ouch."

"Razor!" I scooped up the gremlin, holding him at arm's length to see him clearly. He buzzed with joy. "What are you doing here? I told you to go to Mag Tuiredh. Why did you follow me?"

"Razor help! Help Master! Wanted to find you!"

"I know, but I needed you to get the others!" Despair rose up like a wave, and I shook him, angry and frustrated. He squeaked. "Why didn't you go to Mag Tuiredh? Why didn't you do what I asked? Now we're all going to die!"

"No die!" Razor squirmed from my grasp, hitting the dirt to bounce around my feet. "No die, no! Razor did what Master wanted! Look!"

He pointed. From the edge of the woods, over the roar of explosions and screams of battle, I saw thousands of tiny green lights. Eyes, all staring at me. I gasped, and as one, they all broke into a smile, neon-blue crescent grins floating in the air.

They spilled from the woods like a rush of ink, black against the ash-covered ground, thousands upon thousands of gremlins, flowing toward the castle. They swarmed over and around the Iron soldiers like rocks in a stream, unhindered and unstoppable. Several fey lashed out at them, and several gremlins fell, left behind by the mass, but there were just too many of them to stop. They scurried up to the fortress and leaped onto its walls, swarming it like army ants or hornets. Lightning flashed, blasting them from the walls, and gremlins fell like rain, but there were always more, hissing and buzzing, and suddenly, the entire fortress shuddered to a halt.

Razor laughed, clamping on to my leg. "See?" he crowed, crawling up to my shoulder. "We help! Razor help! Razor did good?"

I pried him off me and kissed the top of his head, ignoring the rather violent static shock I received. "You did awesome. Now, get to safety. I'll take it from here." He buzzed happily and darted off, vanishing into the crowd.

I took a deep breath and looked around. Ash and Puck had broken away from the main fighting to shield me from the masses coming forward. We were going to have to break through those lines, and quickly.

"Ash! Puck!" They whirled toward me, and I pointed forward. "The fortress defenses are down! I'm going in!"

"Hold!" Mab appeared before us, beautiful and frightening, her hair whipping about like snakes. "I will open a path for you," she said, turning toward the raging battlefield.

"This will take the last of my power, so be sure not to waste it, half-breed. Are you ready?"

Still reeling from the shock that Mab was helping me, I nodded. The Winter Queen raised her hand, and I felt glamour swirling around her, raw and powerful. She swept her arm down, and a blast of freezing, icicle-strewn wind shot forward, ripping into the crowd, pelting them with shards as sharp as razors. Iron fey screeched and fell back, blinded, covering their eyes and faces, and a path opened before us, leading straight to the castle.

"Go," Mab hissed, her voice slightly strained, and we didn't hesitate. Gripping my sword, with Ash leading and Puck close behind, we charged into the hole.

The fortress loomed overhead, still flashing and spitting lightning as the gremlins swarmed over it. The packrats seemed frozen in place, eyes blank, faces slack, unaware of the battle going on around them. They didn't react as we reached the base of the castle and Ash leaped onto the edge.

I held my breath, praying he wouldn't get blasted off like the dragon, but there were so many gremlins scurrying about, the defenses didn't even notice us. Still, lightning flashed all around us, smelling of ozone and burning flesh, as Ash pulled me up and we pressed ourselves against the wall. Gremlins fell around us, charred and blackened, and I pressed my face into his shoulder.

"A door, a door, my kingdom for a door," Puck muttered.

"There," Ash said, pointing to a balcony several yards above us. "Come on. We'll have to climb."

Scaling the walls wasn't difficult, though it was extremely nerve-racking with all the lighting and the shrieks of dying gremlins. But we reached the balcony in a short amount of time. A small iron door stood nestled in an alcove next to the railing, and I started toward it, eager to get out of the lightning storm. But before I was halfway across the balcony, the entire fortress trembled, like a dog shaking off water, and lurched into motion. I stumbled forward, slamming my shoulder into the door. It wouldn't budge, no matter how hard I wrenched the handle or threw myself against it.

"Dammit!" Puck yelped, ducking as a deadly bolt of electricity slashed down nearby, making my skin crawl. "We're gonna have to find another way in, unless someone happens to have a key!"

The key! Reaching up, I yanked the chain from my neck and shoved the iron key into the hole beneath the handle, praying it would work. I heard a soft click, and slammed myself into the door once again, just as the fortress lurched forward. This time, the door flew inward, and I tumbled over the threshold, Puck and Ash close behind me. Then it slammed shut with a clang, trapping us inside the fortress of the false king.

CHAPTER TWENTY-FOUR

THE FALSE KING

Panting, I looked around us, grabbing a pipe to keep steady as the fortress shook and bounced and trembled, trying to buck the intruders off its back. The inside of the false king's fortress looked much like the outside, thrown together with no thought to architectural soundness, or anything that made sense, really. Stairways ran into walls, doors hung from the ceiling, and hallways snaked off to nowhere or curled around themselves. Rooms and floors sat at weird angles, making it difficult to keep your balance, and were filled with strange odds and ends. A tricycle rolled by, banging into a staircase, and a lamp, hanging upside down from the ceiling, flickered erratically.

"Great. The false king's fortress is a giant rabbit hole." Puck ducked as a model plane flew by on a string, barely missing him. "How are we supposed to find anything in this mess?"

I closed my eyes, feeling the dark, Iron glamour pulsing all around me. In Machina's tower, I'd known I would find the Iron King at the very top, close to the sky and the wind, waiting for me. Here, in this crowded, tangled burrow, I could feel him, too. The false king. He knew I was here, an intruder in his private warren. I could feel his glee, his anticipation, as the fortress itself suddenly turned its gaze inward, searching for us. For me.

I shivered and opened my eyes. "He's at the very center," I murmured, looping the chain, the watch, and the lifesaving key around my neck once more. "The heart of the fortress. And he's waiting for us."

"Then let's not keep him," Ash muttered, drawing his sword, which glowed like a beacon in the darkness. Huddled close, we crept forward, into the shadowed, tangled mess of the false king's fortress.

We eased our way between mountains of junk, through rooms that made no sense, dodging trash and low-hanging cables. One time we followed a corridor that led us in a twisted spiral back to where we came. Another time we picked our way through a labyrinth of huge pipes, hissing steam. All the while, the dark glamour I felt grew stronger, more eager, the closer we came to the center.

And then, very suddenly, the close, crowded walls opened up, and we stumbled into a vast open arena. Thick black pipes held up the ceiling, hissing madly, and metal poles stuck out of the roof, threads of lightning arcing between them, causing the whole place to flicker like a strobe light.

In the center of the open space, an iron chair spiked up from the floor, polished and gleaming. Seated motionless on the throne, a body watched us, but under the flickering lights, it was difficult to see it clearly. Then a strand of lightning leaped from the ceiling and slithered rapidly over the throne, lighting it up like a Christmas tree, and I saw the face of the false king for the first time.

"You!" I gasped. My heart lurched, and my stomach dropped to my toes. Of course, it was him. How could I not have seen it before?

"Hello, Meghan Chase," purred Ferrum, smiling at me. "I have been waiting for you."

"FERRUM," I WHISPERED, trying to match the figure of the false king with the sad, angry old man I'd met in the pack-rat tunnels. He was very much the same, withered and bent over, his arms and legs like brittle twigs and his white hair flowing almost to his feet. Voluminous black robes nearly swallowed his frail figure, and a twisted iron crown rested on his forehead, seeming to weigh him down. His skin had that same metallic tone, like he'd been dunked in liquid mercury, and the lightning crawling over his body didn't seem to faze him a bit.

But he glowed with power now, a dark, purplish aura that surrounded him, like it was sucking in all the light. I could feel it pulling at me, trying to drain my life and glamour, suck me dry until I was an empty husk. I shuddered and stepped back, and Ferrum broke into a maniacal grin.

"Yes, you feel it, don't you, girl?" Ferrum raised a claw and beckoned me forward, still smiling. "You feel the void, the vacuum, where my power used to lie. The power of the Iron King. The power you stole from me when you killed Machina!" Ferrum slammed his fist into the chair with a hollow boom, making me jump. I didn't remember him being this strong.

"But now, you are here," he finished, still gazing at me with those crazy, inhuman eyes. "And I will take back what is rightfully mine. For centuries have I waited for this day, when I can reclaim my throne and my right as king!" He leaned forward, speaking fervently, as if to convince us. "It will be different this time. Machina was right to fear the oldbloods. They will destroy us if we do not put them down first. When I kill you and my power is returned, I will take this land and remake it in my own image, where my subjects and slaves can live in peace, and I can rule as I did before, unopposed and unquestioned."

"You're wrong," I said quietly, as his eyes widened, blazing and feverish. "The power of the Iron King was never yours, not since you lost it to Machina all those years ago. It can be earned, and it can be lost, but it can never be taken. Machina gave it to me. Even if you kill me, you won't get back your power. You can't reclaim the past, Ferrum. Let it go. You'll never be the Iron King again."

"Silence!" Ferrum screeched, hitting the throne arm again. "Lies! I have waited for this day too long to listen to your filthy half-truths! Guards, guards!"

Clanking footsteps boomed around us, and a platoon of Iron knights appeared, encircling the arena. Ash and Puck pressed close, and we stood back-to-back, weapons drawn, as the knights came to a stop at the edge, surrounding us in a ring of steel.

Ferrum rose from his throne, floating a few feet from the ground like a spindly wraith, his long hair floating around him. "You will not deny me what is rightfully mine," the false king raged, pointing at me with a long metallic finger. "And your little bodyguards will not stop me from taking it, either. I have some friends of theirs who are dying to see them."

I wasn't surprised when the ranks parted and Rowan stepped out on one side, Tertius on the other. The Iron knight looked bored and cold, but Rowan's grin was inhumanly eager as he drew his sword, spinning it casually as he advanced on Ash.

"Come on, little brother," Rowan sneered, the flickering light washing over his burned, ravaged face. "I've been waiting for this a long time."

"Meghan." Ash eased back a step, torn between protecting me and going after Rowan. I softly touched his arm.

"It's okay." He gave me a desperate, helpless look, and I smiled encouragingly. "I'll be all right. This is what we came here for. Keep Rowan off me, and I'll take care of Ferrum." *I hope.* "Puck, will you be all right?"

"No problem, princess." Puck whirled his daggers, facing

off against Ash's doppelganger. The look on his face scared me a little. It was one of pure, savage zeal as Puck bared his teeth in a fearsome smile. "I think I'm gonna enjoy this."

Ash held my gaze. "I can't protect you this time," he whispered. "And I know you're ready for this but, Meghan...be careful," he finished, and I nodded.

"You, too." I stepped back, but he pulled me forward and kissed me, quick and desperate, before turning to face Rowan.

"Go on, then," he said softly, his voice shaking a bit. "Go save us all."

With my head up and my resolve firmly in place, I turned and walked toward the center of the room. This was it. Ash and Puck couldn't help me now. I had to do this on my own.

Ferrum waited for me before his throne, a skeletal wraith-creature, his robes and hair billowing behind him. The screech and clash of weapons echoed behind me as two of the people I loved most in the world fought for their lives, but I didn't turn back to look. My gaze was only for the false king as I stopped a few yards from the throne, my sword held loosely at my side.

Ferrum watched me for a moment, hanging in the air like a vulture, and he broke into a slow, eager smile. "This can be simple and painless, you know," he whispered. "Kneel before me now, and you will not suffer. Your end will be as peaceful as a lullaby, singing you to sleep."

I gripped my sword, swinging it into a ready position as Ash had taught me. "We both know that's not going to happen."

Ferrum smiled. "Very well," he said, and his arms rose away from his sides. I felt him drawing glamour from the fortress, from the poisoned land and even his subjects, sucking the dark power into himself. His fingers flexed, growing long and pointed, turning into gleaming blades. "I prefer it this way, myself." And he flew at me.

He was insanely fast. I barely had time to see him coming, a blur of silver across the floor, before he was in front of me, swiping at my face. I knocked away the stabbing fingers and slashed at him in return, but he was already gone, zipping to the side. I felt his claws strike my armor, and then a blinding pain as they sliced through the scales like paper, cutting into my arm. I whirled and swiped at him, my blade passing through empty air as Ferrum darted away, clear across the room in a blink.

My arm burned, the silver dragon-scale spattered with red where the false king had cut me. Ferrum drifted closer, slower this time, his mouth twisted in a hungry smile. He knew he was faster than me. I closed out the pain and raised my sword again, and the false king laughed in triumph.

"Is that the best you can do, Meghan Chase? All the power of the Iron King at your fingertips, and you can do nothing. How disappointing." A blink and he was close again, smiling. I threw myself back, but Ferrum didn't press his advantage, shaking his head like a disappointed grandfather.

"You have no idea how to wield that power, do you, girl? It sits, smoldering inside you, an untapped flood. Or are you just saving it for later?" He was mocking me now, confident in his victory, and that pissed me off. I lunged at him with a snarl, slashing at his face, intending to wipe that ugly sneer from his mouth. He dodged, thrust out a hand, and I was hit with a blast of pure Iron glamour. My sword was torn from my hands. The force knocked me back, sent me tumbling to the edge of the arena, gasping and winded at the feet of the Iron knights. Over the ringing in my ears, I heard Ash's howl of fury and the false king's mocking laughter.

"Get up!" he snapped as I staggered to my knees. I tried, but the floor was spinning and my stomach felt like it had been pulled inside out. The false king barked another laugh.

"Pathetic!" he crowed. "You are weak! Weak, to be carrying
the power of the Iron King. I don't know what Machina was
thinking, to waste it on you! No matter. I will cut it out of
your weak human body and use it as it was meant to be used,
for the glory of myself and my kingdom."

He raised his hands, claws smeared with my blood, and
drifted toward me. Dark, poisonous Iron glamour pulsed all
around us, ebbing from the walls and from every shadow of
the fortress, feeding him, empowering him. I couldn't beat
Ferrum like this. I was going to have to fight fire with fire
and hope I wouldn't pass out from the effort.

I gazed across the arena to my sword, lying in the middle
of the floor, flickering under the lights. I remembered how
I had once twisted the shape of an iron ring, made iron
bolts change direction in midair. I remembered how Ferrum
made his own fingers change, becoming deadly and sharp,
and concentrated on my weapon, seeing the Iron glamour
in my mind. The sword glowed white-hot, stretched, and
lengthened, turning from a sword to a spear. Nausea rose up
as my Summer magic reacted violently to the Iron glamour,
cramping my stomach and making the room spin, but I bit
my lip and gave the magic one last, desperate pull.

Ferrum was right over me, his claws poised to end my
life, when the spear flew from the floor, streaked across the
room, and hit him from behind. I saw it erupt from his chest,
striking the armor of one of the knights, and I scrambled
away as Ferrum arched back with a scream, clutching the
spear through his middle.

Staggering to the center of the arena, I collapsed as the
nausea overtook me, gasping and trying not to retch. It was
over. We had won, somehow. Now all we had to do was
get past Rowan and Tertius, and make it back to our side.
Hopefully, the Iron knights would let us go now that Ferrum
was dead—

High-pitched, frantic laughter stopped me in my tracks.

When I raised my head, my blood ran cold. Ferrum was still standing, the spear through his chest, glamour snapping and flaring around him like a thunderstorm. "You think you can defeat me with iron, Meghan Chase?" he howled. "I *am* iron! I was the first Iron fey born into this world—it runs in my veins, my blood, my very essence! Your pathetic use of Iron glamour only makes me stronger!"

Reaching down, he pulled the spear from his chest in one smooth, contemptuous motion. I struggled upright as the false king rose into the air, hair and clothes whipping around him in the gale. "Now," Ferrum droned, lifting the spear above his head, "it is time to end this."

Lightning arced from the ceiling to the tip of the spear, lancing down and crackling around the false king. I felt my hair stand up, rising away from my neck, as Ferrum lifted his other hand and pointed at me.

There was a blinding flash. Something slammed into my chest, and the noise of the world cut out, as abruptly as if someone had switched off a television.

Everything went white.

"You cannot beat him."

Blinking, I squinted against the glare, shielding my eyes as I gazed around. All around me, everything was white. No ground, no shadows, nothing but a blank white void as empty as space.

But I knew he was here, with me.

"Where are you, Machina?" I asked, my voice echoing into the emptiness.

"I have always been here, Meghan Chase," was Machina's reply, coming from everywhere and nowhere. "I was given to you, freely and without constraint. It is you who has rejected me every time."

That didn't make any sense, and I shook my head to clear it, trying to remember where I was. "Where is everyone?

Where is…Ferrum! I was fighting Ferrum. I have to get back. Where is he?"

"You cannot beat him," Machina said again. "Not the way you are fighting. He is the essence of Iron's corruption, feeding off the land like a bloated tick. His power is too great, and you cannot defeat him with Iron glamour alone."

"I'm going to have to try," I said angrily. "I don't have a magic Witchwood arrow to kill him like I did you. I just have myself."

"The Witchwood arrow was only a conduit for your own Summer glamour. It was powerful, yes, but it only worked because you are Oberon's daughter, and his living, healing Summer blood flows through you. In essence, you injected the Iron King with your own Summer magic, and my body could not take it. It is the same with Ferrum."

"Well, I can't do that anymore. Every time I use Summer magic, the Iron gets in the way. I can't use one without the other tainting it. I can't win like that. I can't—" Close to despair, I sank to my knees, burying my face in one hand. "I have to win," I whispered. "I have to. Everyone is depending on me. There must be a way to use my Summer magic. Dammit, my father is the Summer King, there has to be a way to separate—"

And then it hit me.

I remembered my father. Not the Seelie King—my human father, Paul. I could see us sitting at the old piano, while he tried to explain how music worked. I could see the Iron glamour in the notes, the strict lines and rigid rules that made up the score, but the music itself was a vortex of song and pure, swirling emotion. They weren't separate entities, creative magic and Iron glamour. They were one; cold logic and wild emotion, merged together to create something truly beautiful.

"Of course," I whispered, reeling from the understanding. "I was using them separately, of course they reacted to each other. That's what you were trying to tell me, wasn't it? This power—me, you, Summer and Iron glamour—I can't use one or the other. They're useless separated. I have to… make them one."

It was so simple, now that I thought about it. Paul had shown me they could combine; it was nothing new. This was why Machina gave his power to me—I was the only one who could merge them, a half-breed who could wield both Summer and Iron.

I felt a presence behind me, but didn't turn. There would be nothing there if I did. "Are you ready?" Machina whispered. No, not Machina, the manifestation of the Iron glamour, *my* Iron glamour. The magic I had been rejecting, running away from, all this time. Using it, but never really accepting it. That ended today. It was time.

"I'm ready," I murmured, and felt hands on my shoulders, long-fingered and powerful. Steel cables began coiling around me, around us, tightening as they slithered over my skin. About the time they stabbed into me, wiggling under my skin and crawling up toward my heart, I closed my eyes. Machina's presence was fading away, growing fainter and fainter, though right before he vanished altogether, he bent close and whispered in my ear:

"You've always had the power to defeat the false king. He is a corrupter, a life-taker, poisoning everything he touches. He will try to drain your magic by force. You can defeat him, but you must be brave. Together, we can restore this land."

The cables finally reached my heart, and a jolt like an electrical current slammed into my body, as all that was left of the Iron King faded completely and was gone.

I GASPED AND OPENED MY EYES.

I was in Ferrum's chamber, lying on my back, watching the lightning threads dance over the ceiling. Only a few seconds must have passed since Ferrum hit me, as the false

king was still standing in the middle of the arena with his
arm outstretched. Beyond him, I could just make out Ash
and Puck, still locked in battle with their opponents. Ash was
shouting something, but his voice blurred in my ears, coming
from far away. I felt dizzy, numb, and my skin tingled, as if
all my limbs were asleep, but I was alive.

Something light slithered over my neck, tickling my
skin. I reached up and felt cold metal; the pocket watch the
Clockmaker had given me, so long ago. Lifting it up, I saw
immediately that there was no saving it; the electricity had
cracked the glass and melted the edges of the gold casing.
The delicate hands were frozen in place. From the looks of
the damage, it seemed the timepiece had taken the full brunt
of the lightning bolt, one hundred and sixty-one hours from
the time the Clockmaker had given it to me.

Thank you, I told him silently, and unlooped the chain
from my neck, letting the watch clatter to the ground.

Ferrum's eyes widened as I struggled to my knees, then my
feet, fighting to stay upright as the floor lurched and spun.
"Still alive?" he hissed as I shook off the last of the dizziness
and faced him, clenching my fists. Everything was clearer
now. I could feel the Iron glamour of the fortress pulsing all
around me, and the black hole that was the false king, sucking
it all away. I probed further and sensed the glamour of the
Nevernever holding out against the Iron Realm, growing
weaker as the Iron Kingdom pressed forward. I could feel
the heartbeat of both lands, and the creatures dying on either
side.

*The power of the Iron King can be given, or can be lost, but it
cannot be taken.*

I suddenly realized what I had to do.

I trembled, wishing there had been more time—that Ash
and I could've had more time. If I'd known, I might've done
things differently. But beyond that moment of regret, I felt

calm, certain, filled with a resolve that pushed back all fear or doubt. I was ready. There was no other way.

I looked at Ferrum and smiled.

The false king hissed and sent another bolt of lightning at me. I raised my hand, Summer and Iron glamour swirling around me, and knocked it aside, sending it into the wall over Ferrum's head. The energy exploded in a shower of sparks, and Ferrum screeched in rage. For a moment, I held my breath, waiting for the pain and nausea to hit.

Nothing. No pain, no sickness. Summer and Iron glamour had merged perfectly, one no longer tainting the other. I reached out and called my spear to me, ripping it from Ferrum's grasp, grabbing it as it smacked into my palm. Ferrum's eyes bugged, and glamour flared around him like a dark flame. I flourished the spear and sank into a ready stance.

"Come on then, old man," I called, ignoring my pounding heart, the way my hands were shaking. "You throw like a girl. You want my power? Come get it!"

Ferrum rose into the air like a vengeful phoenix, hair and robes snapping behind him. "Insolent child!" he screamed, "I shall not toy with you a moment longer! I will take my power back right now!"

He flew at me, covering the arena floor in a blink, though I saw everything clearly. I watched Ferrum close on me, his face twisted into a mask of rage, lunging forward. I saw those deadly talons, stabbing at my chest. I knew I could block it, step aside…

I'm sorry, Ash.

I closed my eyes instead.

Ferrum hit me square in the gut with the full power of his hate behind it, driving his claws deep into my chest. The force bent me over, punching the breath from my lungs, a moment before fire blossomed through my stomach. The pain was excruciating. I would've gasped, but there was no air left in me. Somewhere far away, I heard Ash scream in rage and fury, Puck's cry of dismay, but then Ferrum stepped forward, pushing his claws in even farther, and everything melted into a red haze of agony.

Bent over the false king's arm, my body shook and convulsed, and I concentrated on not passing out, not giving in to the blackness that crawled at the edge of my vision. It was tempting, so tempting, to give in, to let go of the pain and sink into oblivion. My blood dripped to the floor between us, a growing crimson pool; I could feel my life leaking away, as well.

"Yes," Ferrum whispered in my ear, his breath smelling of rust and rot, "suffer. Suffer for stealing my power from me. For thinking you were worthy to carry it. Now, you will die, and I will become the Iron King once more. The power of the Iron King is mine once again!"

I raised a trembling, blood-soaked hand and grabbed the collar of his robes, raising my head to meet the false king's triumphant gaze. My life was fading fast; I had to be quick. "You want it?" I whispered, forcing the words out, when all I wanted to do was scream or cry. "Take it. It's yours." And I sent my power, the merged glamour of Summer and Iron, into the false king.

Ferrum threw back his head and laughed, swelling with power, his voice ringing through the chamber. Glamour flared around him like a dark fire, and he seemed to swell, to grow as the massive power of the Iron King flowed into him.

Suddenly, it sputtered, the cold black corruption flickering with tongues of green and gold, heat and warmth. Ferrum jerked, eyes going wide with confusion and fear, staring at me in horror.

"What...what are you doing to me? What have you done?" He tried pulling back, but I clamped my fingers around his wrist, holding us together.

"You wanted the Iron King's power," I told Ferrum, whose

eyes were bulging and crazy now, glamour swirling around him like a colorful vortex, "you can have it. Iron and Summer both. Afraid you can't separate them, now." Glamour continued to pour into Ferrum, as I clung to him with my fading strength. "You might've killed me, but I swear, I won't let you touch the Nevernever. Or my family. Or my friends. The Iron King's reign ends right now."

Branches erupted from the false king's chest, twisted and bent, rushing up toward the ceiling, and Ferrum screamed. Ripping his claws from my stomach, he staggered back, clutching at the limbs, trying to tear them out. I fell to my knees, stayed upright for a split second, then collapsed, my head striking the ground with a thump.

Reality blurred, and time seemed to slow. Ferrum writhed and thrashed, his screams filling the chamber as his arms split and turned into branches, his fingers becoming gnarled twigs. I saw Ash, his face frighteningly out of control, slam his brother's sword away, step forward and plunge his blade through Rowan's armor, into his chest. A flash of vicious blue, and Rowan arched back, going stiff as if frozen from inside. Ash yanked his sword up and out, and Rowan shattered, falling to the floor in a million glistening pieces.

A howl from the other side of the room showed two Pucks holding Tertius between them, while a third Puck raised his dagger and plunged it into the knight's chest.

"Damn you." Ferrum's voice was a croak, and my attention flickered back to the false king. He was almost gone now, a tiny, gnarled old tree, bent and withered. Only his face showed through the trunk, hateful eyes boring into me. "I thought I'd seen evil in Machina," he wheezed, "but you are far, far worse. My power, all my power, gone. Wasted." His voice broke, and he made a noise like a sob before turning a last sneer on me. "At least I can take comfort in the fact that neither of us will have it in the end. You will die soon. Not even the power of the Iron King can save you n—" His voice abruptly cut out, or maybe I lost consciousness for a moment, because the next time I opened my eyes, Ferrum was gone. An ugly, skeletal tree was all that remained of the false king.

The pain was still there, but it was a dull, distant thing now, insignificant. Somewhere far away, someone called my name. At least, I thought it was my name. I blinked, trying to focus, but my thoughts were fuzzy and slipped away like smoke, and I was too tired to call them back.

Closing my eyes, I let myself drift, wanting nothing but the chance to rest. Surely I had earned it by now. Defeating a false king and saving all of Faery—there were certainly worse ways to die. But, even as I hovered on the edge of the void, I could still feel the labored heartbeat of the land, the poisoned trail Ferrum had carved on his journey, and the corruption seeping into the Nevernever. Just because Ferrum was gone didn't mean the Iron Realm would disappear. The last of the Iron King's power still flickered inside me, weakly, a candle held up to the wind. It was still my responsibility, this power. What would happen to it when I died? Who would I give it to? Who *could* I give it to, this new glamour of Summer and Iron, without killing them?

"Meghan!" The voice called to me again, and I recognized it now. It was *his* voice, the voice of my knight, frantic and tormented, pulling me back from the void. "Meghan, no!" it pleaded, echoing in the blackness. "Don't do this. Come on, wake up. Please." The last word was a desperate, whispered sob, and I opened my eyes.

Ash peered down at me, silver eyes suspiciously bright, his face pale and wan. Cradled in his arms, I blinked as the sounds of the world came back, the crackle of energy above, the shuffle of metal boots from the Iron knights still surrounding us. I spared a quick glance over, and saw that all the knights had laid down their arms and were now watching us with identical grave expressions, waiting.

I looked back to Ash, seeing Puck standing over his shoulder as well, white and pale. "Ash," I whispered, my voice sounding weak and breathy in my ears. "I'm so sorry. I didn't think…now you'll fade away because of me, because I asked you to take that vow."

He pressed his face to my hair, closing his eyes. "If you are gone," he whispered back, his voice shaking, "then I will welcome nonexistence. There will be nothing left for me to live for." He pulled back, his silver eyes boring into me. "There's still time," he murmured, standing easily with me in his arms. "We have to get you to a healer."

Puck was suddenly there, intense and angry, his hair a stark contrast to his pale face. "Dammit, Meghan," he snapped. "What the hell were you thinking? We have to get you out of here, now!" He eyed the ring of knights and his eyes narrowed. "You think the bucket brigade will let us go, or should I carve a path through them?"

"No," I whispered, clutching Ash's shirt. They both looked at me in surprise. "I can't go to a healer. Take me…" I winced and fought a gasp as a bolt of pain clawed my stomach, and Ash's grip tightened. "Take me to the tree," I forced out. "The ruins. I have to go back…to where it all began."

He stared at me, expressionless, but a tremor went through him. "No," he whispered, but it was more of a plea.

"Princess, there's no time!" Puck stalked forward, desperate. "Don't be stupid! If we don't get you to a healer now, you'll die!"

I ignored Puck, holding Ash's gaze, steeling myself for what I had to do. "Ash," I whispered, tears flooding my eyes. "Please. I don't have…much time left. This is my last request. I have to…get to that tree. Please."

He closed his eyes, and a single tear crawled down his cheek. I knew I was asking him to do the impossible, and it was tearing me apart that Ash was suffering. But at

least I would make it right in the end. I'd promise him
that much.

"Don't listen to her, prince." Puck sounded almost frantic
then, grabbing Ash by the shoulder. "She's delirious. Get to
a healer, dammit. Don't tell me you're going to listen to this
insanity."

"Puck," I whispered, but suddenly noticed the empty silver
chain, dangling from Ash's chest. The amulet was gone.
Where the crystal had once been, only a blackened shard
remained. It must've finally shattered during the fight with
Rowan. My stomach twisted. "Oh, God, Ash," I breathed.
"The amulet. You won't be protected in the Iron Kingdom
anymore. Have someone else take me back."

He raised his head, his eyes bleak but determined, a look
I'd seen before, when he had nothing left to lose.

"I'll take you."

"No, you won't!" Puck stepped in front of us, and suddenly his dagger was pressed against Ash's throat. Ash didn't
move, and Puck leaned in, his face savage. "You'll take her
to a healer, prince, or so help me I will cut out that piece of
ice you call a heart and take her myself."

"Puck," I whispered again, "please." He didn't look at me,
but tears brimmed at the corners of his eyes, and the hand
holding the dagger trembled. "I have t-to do this," I went on,
as Ash and Puck continued their staredown, neither giving an
inch. "This…is the only way to save everything. Please."

He drew in a shaky breath. "How can you ask me to let
you die?" he choked, still keeping the blade at the prince's
throat. A thread of blood formed under the knife, and ran
down to Ash's collar. "I'd do anything for you, Meghan.
Just…not that. Not that."

Gently, I reached up and closed my fingers around the
knife hilt, easing it down and away from Ash's neck. Puck
resisted for a moment, then stepped back with a sob. The
dagger fell from his grip and clanged to the floor.

"Are you sure this is what you want, princess?" His voice was strangled, his eyes begging me to change my mind.

"No," I whispered, as my own tears spilled over, and the arms around me tightened. Of course it wasn't. I wanted to live. I wanted to see my family and finish school and travel to distant places I'd only read about. I wanted to laugh with Puck and love with Ash, and do all those things that normal people took for granted. But I couldn't. I was given this power, this responsibility. And I had to finish what I'd started, once and for all. "No, Puck, it isn't. But, this is how it has to be."

Puck took my hand, gripping it as if he could keep me here just by holding on. I looked into his green eyes, shining with emotion, and saw all his years as Fey, all his triumphs and failures, loves and losses. I saw him as Puck, the devilish, legendary troublemaker, and as Robin Goodfellow, a being as ancient as time, with his own scars and wounds gathered in his immortal life. Puck squeezed my hand, tears running unabashedly down his face, and shook his head.

"Wow," he muttered, his voice choked with tears. "Here we are, the last night and all, and I can't think of anything to say."

I pressed my palm to his cheek, feeling the moisture beneath my fingers, and smiled at him. "How about 'goodbye'?"

"Nah." Puck shook his head. "I make a point of never saying goodbye, princess. Makes it sound like you're never coming back."

"Puck—"

He bent and kissed me softly on the lips. Ash stiffened, arms tightening around me, but Puck slid out of reach before either of us could react. "Take care of her, ice-boy," he said, smiling as he backed up several paces. "I guess I won't be seeing you, either, will I? It was…fun, while it lasted."

"I'm sorry we didn't get to kill each other," Ash said quietly.

Puck chuckled and bent to retrieve his fallen dagger. "My one and only regret. Too bad, that would have been an epic fight." Straightening, he gave us that old, stupid grin, raising a hand in farewell. "See you around, lovebirds."

Glamour rippled through the air, and Puck disintegrated into a flock of screaming ravens, flapping wildly as they scattered to all corners of the room. The knights ducked as the birds swooped over their heads, cawing in their harsh, mocking voices. Then the birds vanished into the darkness, the sound of wings disappeared, and Puck was gone.

THE KNIGHTS LET US THROUGH without a fight, bowing their heads as we passed. Some of them even raised their swords, as if in salute, but I didn't really notice much. Cradled gently in Ash's arms, my body and mind numb to everything, I concentrated on not falling asleep, knowing if I did, I might never open my eyes. Soon I could rest, give in to the exhaustion claiming my body, lie back and forget it all, but I had one last thing to do. And then I could finally let it all go.

Soft flakes touched my cheek, and I looked up.

We were outside the fortress now, standing at the top of a flight of stairs, gazing down at the field. The sounds of battle had ceased, and silence hung over the field as every eye, be it Summer, Winter, or Iron, turned in my direction. Everyone was frozen, staring at me in shock, unsure of what to do.

Ash never stopped, walking deliberately forward, his face unreadable, and the ranks of Summer, Winter, and Iron fey parted for him without a word. Faces passed by me, silent in the falling ash. Diode, his whirling eyes wide with alarm. Spikerail and his herd, lowering their heads as we walked by. Gremlins trailed us, hushed and grim, weaving their way through the crowd.

Mab and Oberon came into view, their eyes at once blank and sympathetic. Ash didn't stop, even for Mab. He marched by the faery rulers without even a glance, continuing through the gray drifts, until we reached the edge of the field and the huge frost dragon waiting for us. The dragon shifted, settling back to stare at the Winter prince with ice-blue eyes.

"Take us into the Iron Realm." Ash's voice was soft, but several degrees below freezing, leaving no room for argument. "Now."

The dragon blinked. Hissing softly, it turned and crouched low, stretching its long neck for Ash to get on. Without so much as a jolt, Ash stepped onto a scaly forearm and leaped up between the dragon's shoulders, settling me in his lap. As the dragon rose up, spreading its wings to launch, Razor let out a buzzing cry, and the gremlins exploded into shrill, high-pitched wailing, leaping up and down and pulling at their ears. Though startled, no one moved to stop them, and their keening voices followed us into the air, until the wind swallowed them up.

I DIDN'T REMEMBER FLYING. I didn't remember landing. Just a soft thump as Ash slid off the dragon's back onto solid ground again. Raising my head from his chest, I gazed around. The landscape was blurred and fuzzy, like a fading, out-of-focus camera, until I realized it was me and not the surroundings. Everything was gray and dark, but I could still make out the tree, the great iron oak, rising from the tower ruins to brush the sky.

Behind us, the dragon made a low rumble that sounded like a question. "Yes, go," Ash murmured without turning around, and there was a blast of wind that signaled the dragon had fled, back to the Nevernever where it wouldn't be poisoned. I noted, in my numb state of mind, that Ash didn't tell it to wait for him.

Because he wasn't planning to leave, either.

Ash's step was firm as he carried me through the tower, drifting through the empty ruins, slipping through the shadows, until we reached the base of the tree. Only when we stepped into the central chamber and the branches loomed above us did he start to tremble. But his voice was steady, and his grip didn't loosen as he approached the trunk and stopped, lowering his head to mine.

"We're here," he murmured. I closed my eyes and reached out with my remaining glamour, feeling the pulsing heart of the tree and the roots, extending deep into the earth.

"Lay me down…at the base," I whispered.

He hesitated, but then stepped beneath the tree and knelt, depositing me gently on the ground between two giant roots. And he stayed there, kneeling beside me, holding my hand in his. Something splashed the back of my hand, cold as spring water, crystallizing to my skin. A faery's tears.

I gazed up at him and tried for a smile, tried to be brave, to show him that none of this was his fault. That this was how it had to be. His eyes glimmered in the darkness, bright and anguished. I squeezed his hand.

"It was…quite a ride, wasn't it?" I whispered, as my own tears ran down my cheek, staining the hard ground. "I'm sorry, Ash. I wish…we had more time. I wish…I could've gone with you…but things didn't quite work out, did they?"

Ash brought my hand to his lips, his eyes never leaving mine. "I love you, Meghan Chase," he murmured against my skin. "For the rest of my life, however long we have left. I'll consider it an honor to die beside you."

I took a deep breath, chasing back the darkness on the edge of my vision. Now came the hardest part, the part I'd been dreading. I didn't want to die, and even more, I didn't want to die alone. The thought made my stomach clench, and my breath come in short, panicked gasps. But Ash would not fade away. I would not let him die because of his vow. This was the last unselfish thing I could do for him. He had been with me every step of the way; now it was my turn to set him free.

"Ash." I reached up and touched his cheek, tracing the line of his jaw. "I love you. Never forget that. And I...I wanted to live the rest of my life with you. But..." And I paused, trying to catch my breath. It was getting hard even to speak, and Ash's outline was fading at the edges. I blinked hard to keep him in focus.

"But I...I can't let you die because of me," I continued, seeing understanding dawn in his eyes, followed by alarm. "I won't allow it."

"Meghan, no."

"It's all right if you hate me," I continued, speaking faster so he couldn't change my mind. "In fact, that might be for the best. Hate me, so you can find someone...someone else to love. But I want you to live, Ash. You have so much to live for."

"Please." Ash gripped my hand, "Don't do this."

"I release you," I whispered. "From your vow of knighthood, and the promises you made. Your service to me is done, Ash. You're free."

Ash bowed his head, shoulders heaving. I swallowed the bitter lump in my throat, my stomach churning painfully. It was done. I hated myself for it, but it was the right thing to do. I'd asked so much of him already. Even if he was prepared to die, I wasn't going to let that happen.

"Now," I said, releasing his hand. "Get out of here, Ash. Before it's too late."

"No."

"Ash, you can't stay. The amulet is gone. If you're here much longer, you'll die."

Ash said nothing. But I knew that stubborn set of his shoulders, the flare of resolve around him, and I knew he would stay with me regardless. And so, I did the only thing I could think of. He would curse the day he met the human girl in the wyldwood, vow to never, ever, fall in love again. But he would live.

"Ashallyn'darkmyr Tallyn," I said, and he closed his eyes, "by the power of your True Name, leave the Iron Realm right now." I turned my head so I wouldn't see him, forcing out the last words. "And don't come back."

I'm so sorry, Ash. But please, live for me. If anyone deserves to come out of this alive, it's you.

A soft noise, almost a sob. Ash rose, hesitated, as if fighting the compulsion to obey. "I will always be your knight, Meghan Chase," he whispered in a strained voice, as if every moment he remained was painful to him. "And I swear, if there is a way for us to be together, I will find it. No matter how long it takes. If I have to chase your soul to the ends of eternity, I won't stop until I find you, I promise."

And then he was gone.

Alone at the base of the giant oak, I lay back, fighting the urge to cry, to scream out my fear and desolation. There was no time for that anymore. The world was getting dark, and I had one last thing I had to do.

Closing my eyes, I reached out with my glamour, feeling both Summer and Iron rise up in response. Cautiously, I probed the roots of the giant oak, following them deep into the cracked, dry earth, sensing the devastation of the land around it. The Iron glamour that was killing one species but sustaining another.

I thought of my family. Of Mom and Luke and Ethan, still waiting for me at home. I thought of my human dad, Paul, and my real father, the Summer King. Of everyone I had met along the way: Glitch, the rebels, Razor. Ironhorse. They were of the Iron Kingdom, but they were still fey. They deserved a chance to live, just like everyone else.

I thought of Grimalkin, and Puck. My wise teacher and my brave, loyal best friend. They would live, I would make certain of that. They would laugh and inspire ballads and collect favors until the end of time. This was for them. And for my knight, who had given everything for me. Who would've been there to the very end, had I let him.

Ash, Puck, everyone. I love you all. Remember me. And in one final, determined push, I gathered the power of the Iron King into a massive, swirling ball and sent it deep into the roots of the giant oak.

A shudder went through the tree, continuing into the land around it, like ripples on a glassy pond. It radiated outward, spreading to the dead trees and vegetation, and the once-withered plants stirred as the new glamour touched their roots. I sensed the land waking up, drinking in the new magic, healing the poison that the Iron glamour had seeped into the land. Trees straightened, unfurling new leaves from steel branches. The hard obsidian plain shuddered as green sprouts pushed their way to the surface. The mottled yellow clouds began to break apart, showing blue sky and sun peeking through the cracks.

A cool breeze blew in from somewhere, cooling my face and causing a rain of leaves to flutter around me. The air smelled of earth and new grass. Lulled into a deep peace, listening to the sounds of growing things all around me, I closed my eyes and finally surrendered to the darkness.

CHAPTER TWENTY-FIVE

THE IRON QUEEN

Machina waited for me on the other side.

"Hello, Meghan Chase," he greeted softly, smiling in the brightness that surrounded us. No longer the black void of dreams, or the harsh whiteness of my mind, I didn't really know where I was. Coiling mist surrounded me, and I wondered if this was just one more test before I reached the afterlife, or whatever lay beyond the fog.

"Machina." I nodded. He was barely discernible in the mist, but every so often the fog would clear and I saw him, though sometimes he appeared as a massive tree. "What are you doing here?" I sighed. "Don't tell me you're guarding the pearly gates. You never struck me as the angelic type."

The Iron King shook his head. His cables, folded behind him, looked almost like glimmering wings, but Machina could not, in any way, be mistaken for something else. I blinked, and for a moment it seemed I stood under the limbs of the great oak again. But the land around it was changed, green and silver, twined together seamlessly. I turned my head and Machina stood before me again, gazing down with what could only be pride.

"I wanted to congratulate you," he murmured, like the

whisper of wind through the leaves. "You've come farther than anyone could have expected. Defeating the false king by sacrificing yourself was phenomenal. But then, you gave your power to the one thing that could save you both—the land itself."

Movement swirled around me, flashes of color, showing a land both familiar and strange. Mountains of junk dominated the landscape, but moss and vines grew around them now, twisted and blooming with flowers. A huge city of stone and steel had both street lamps and flowering trees lining the streets, and a fountain in the center square spouted clear water. A railroad cut through a grassy plain, where a huge silver oak loomed over crumbling ruins, shiny and metallic and alive.

"Summer and Iron," Machina continued softly, "merged together, becoming one. You've done the impossible, Meghan Chase. The corruption of the Nevernever has been cleansed. The Iron fey now have a place to live without fearing the wrath of the other courts." He sighed and shook his head. "If Mab and Oberon can leave us in peace, that is."

"What about the regular fey?" I asked, as the images faded and it was just me and the Iron King once more. "Can't they live here, as well?"

"No." Machina faced me solemnly. "Though you have cleansed the poison and stopped the spread of Iron glamour, our world is still just as deadly to the oldbloods. Iron fey are still everything the regular fey fear and dread; we cannot survive in the same place. The most we can hope for is peaceful coexistence in our separate realms. And even that might be too much for the other rulers of the fey courts. Summer and Winter are mired in their traditions. They need someone to show them another way."

I fell silent, considering this. What Machina said made sense, but he didn't say how he would accomplish this. Who

would step up and be the champion of the Iron fey, the new
Iron King?

Of course. I sighed, shaking my head. "You'd think, after
saving the entire realm of Faery, I could get some sort of
vacation," I muttered, daunted by the huge task before me.
"Why does it have to be me? Can't someone else do it?"

"When you gave away your power, you essentially healed
the land," Machina said, regarding me with a small smile.
"And, because you are connected, the land healed you in
return. You, Meghan Chase, are the living, beating heart
of the Iron Realm. Its glamour sustains you; your existence
gives it life. You cannot survive without each other." He
started to fade, the brightness around us growing dimmer,
becoming a black void. "So," murmured the last Iron King,
his voice barely a whisper in the dark, "the only question is,
what are you going to do now?"

SOMETHING TOUCHED MY FACE, and I opened my eyes.

A small, anxious face stared into mine, eyes glowing green,
huge ears fanning away from its head. Razor squawked as I
blinked at him, then grinned in delight.

"Master!"

I groaned and waved him off. My body felt weak, pounded
on and beaten into submission, but thankfully, there wasn't
any lingering pain. Above me, the metal branches of the great
oak waved gently in the wind, sunlight slanting through the
leaves and dappling the ground. My fingers brushed cool
grass as I carefully eased myself into a sitting position, gazing
around in astonishment.

I was surrounded by Iron fey. Gremlins and Iron knights,
hacker elves and clockwork hounds, wiremen, dwarves,
spider-hags, and more. Glitch stood silently with his arm in a
sling, next to Spikerail and two of his iron horses, watching
me with solemn eyes.

I could feel them, all of them. I could feel every heartbeat, sense the Iron glamour coursing through them, pulsing in time with the land, flowing through me. I knew the edges of my realm, brushing against the Nevernever, not spreading, not corrupting, content to sit within its new boundaries. I felt every tree and bush and blade of grass, spread before me like a seamless patchwork quilt. And, if I closed my eyes and really concentrated, I could hear my own heartbeat, and the pulse of the land, echoing it.

What will you do now, Meghan Chase?

I understood. This was my fate, my destiny. I knew what had to be done. Pulling myself upright, I took a step forward, away from the trunk, standing on my own. As one, every Iron fey, rank upon rank of them, bowed their heads and sank to their knees. Even Glitch, bending down awkwardly, holding on to a kneeling Spikerail for support. Even Razor and the gremlins, burying their faces in the grass. The Iron knights clanked in unison as they drew their swords and knelt, the sword points jammed into the earth.

In the silence, I gazed out over the mass of kneeling fey and raised my voice. I don't know why I said it, but deep down, I knew it was right. My words echoed over the crowd, sealing my fate. It would be a hard road, and I had a lot of work ahead of me, but in the end, this was the only possible outcome.

"My name is Meghan Chase, and I am the Iron Queen."

EPILOGUE

MIDNIGHT AT 14202 CEDAR DRIVE, LOUISIANA

"Are you sure you want to do this?" Glitch asked me, his spines glowing electric-blue in the darkness. We stood at the edge of the trees, looking out over an overgrown front yard and gravel driveway, a battered Ford at the top.

I nodded wearily. The night was warm, humid, and no breeze stirred the branches of the tupelo trees around us. I wore jeans and a white top and it felt strange, being back in normal clothes. "They deserve to know the truth. I owe them that much. They need to understand why I can't come home."

"You can visit," Glitch said encouragingly. "No one's going to stop you. No reason you can't go back from time to time."

"Yeah," I agreed softly, but I wasn't convinced. Time flowed differently in Faery, in the Iron Kingdom I now found myself ruling over. The first few days had been hectic, as I frantically did everything I could to keep Mab and Oberon from declaring another war on the Iron fey, now that Ferrum was gone. Several meetings had been called, new treaties drawn up and signed, and strict rules had been placed on the boundaries between our kingdoms, before the rulers of Summer and Winter were appeased. I had the sneaking suspicion that Oberon was slightly more lenient because we were related, and I had no problem with that.

Puck had been at these meetings, gregarious and unchangeable as always. He made it clear that he would not be treating me any differently just because I was a queen now, and proved it by kissing me on the cheek in front of a squad of angry Iron knights, whom I had to yell at to stand down before they tried skewering him. Puck had flounced off, laughing. Around me, he was cheerful and flippant, but overly so, as if he wasn't quite sure who I was anymore. There was a wariness to him now, an uncertainty that went beyond our easy friendship, making us awkward and uncomfortable with each other. Perhaps it was his very nature, as the incorrigible Robin Goodfellow, to defy kings and queens and make a mockery of those in authority. I didn't know. Eventually, Puck would come around, but I had a feeling it would be some time before I got my old best friend back.

I did not see Ash, ever.

I shook myself, trying to put him from my mind as I had done these past few days. Ash was gone. I'd made sure of that. Even if I hadn't used his True Name, there was no way he could venture into the Iron Kingdom, no way he could survive there. It was better this way.

Now, if I could only convince my heart of that.

"Sure you'll be all right?" Glitch asked, breaking through my thoughts. "I could come with you, if you'd like. They won't even see me."

I shook my head. "Better if I do this alone. Besides, there's one member of that household who *can* see you. And he's seen enough scary monsters to last him a lifetime."

"Begging your pardon, your highness," Glitch smirked, "but who are you calling a scary monster?"

I swatted at him. My first lieutenant grinned, a constant shadow since the day I'd taken over the Iron Kingdom. The Iron fey looked up to him, listened to him, when I couldn't be there. The Iron knights had accepted his position easily, almost relieved to be back under his command, and I didn't question it. "I'll be back before dawn," I said, glancing up at the moon through the trees. "I trust you can handle things until then?"

"Yes, your majesty," Glitch replied, no longer smirking, and I winced, still getting used to the idea of being called "your majesty," by everyone. "Princess" had been bad enough. "Mag Tuiredh will be safe and secure until your return. And your...father...will be well looked after, do not worry."

I nodded, thankful that Glitch understood. After I became queen and set Mag Tuiredh as the site of the new Iron Court, I kept the promise to myself and returned to Leanansidhe's cabin for Paul. My human father was almost recovered, clear-minded most of the time, his memories fully intact. He knew me, and he remembered what had happened to him, all those years ago. And now that his mind was finally his own, he was going to do everything in his power to keep it that way. I made it clear that he was free to leave the faery world at any time, that I wasn't about to keep him here if he wanted to go. For the moment, Paul refused. He wasn't ready to brave the human world, not yet. Too much had changed in the time he'd been away, too much had happened, and he'd been left behind. One day he might rejoin the real world, but for now, he wanted to know his daughter again.

He'd refused to come with me tonight. "Tonight is for you," he'd told me before I left. "You don't need any distractions. One day, I'd like your mother to know what happened, but I hope to explain it myself. If she even wants to see me again." He sighed, looking out the window of his room. The sun was setting behind the distant clock tower, casting his face in a reddish light. "Just tell me this. Is she happy?"

I hesitated, a lump forming in my throat. "I think so."

Paul nodded, smiling sadly. "Then she doesn't need to

know about me. Not yet, anyway. Or not ever. No, you go and see your family again. I really don't have any business being there."

"Majesty?" Glitch's voice interrupted my musings. He'd been doing that a lot lately, bringing me back to the present when I drifted off. "Are you all right?"

"I'm fine." I faced the dark house again, pushing my hair back. "Well, here I go. Wish me luck." And before I lost my nerve, I stepped onto the gravel driveway and forced my steps in the direction of the house.

For as long as I could remember, the middle step of the porch had creaked when trod upon, no matter where you put your foot or how lightly you stepped on it. It didn't creak now, not even a squeak, as I glided up the steps and came to a halt at the screen door. The windows were dark, and moths fluttered around the porch light, flicking shadows over the faded wooden steps.

I could have easily opened the locked door. Doors and locks were no barrier to me now. A few whispered words, a push of glamour, and the door would swing open on its own. I could've entered the living room unhindered, invisible as the breeze.

I didn't glamour the door. Tonight, at least for a little while, I wanted to be human. Raising my fist, I knocked loudly on the faded wood.

There was no response at first. The house remained still and dark. A dog barked, somewhere in the night.

A light flicked on inside, footsteps thumping over the floor. A silhouette against the curtains, and then Luke's face appeared in the window, peering out suspiciously.

At first, my stepfather didn't appear to see me, though I was staring right at him. His brow furrowed and he dropped the curtains, stepping back. I blew out a sigh and pounded the door again.

It swung open this time, quickly, as if whoever was on the other side expected to catch the prankster banging on his door at 12 a.m.

Luke peered at me. He looked older, I thought, his brown eyes wearier than before, his face grizzled. He regarded me with a puzzled look, one hand still on the doorknob. "Yes?" he prompted when I didn't say anything. "Can I help you?"

He still didn't recognize me. I wasn't surprised, or even angry really. I wasn't the same girl who vanished into Faery a year ago. But before I could say anything, the door was yanked open all the way, and Mom appeared in the frame.

We stared at each other. My heart pounded, half-fearful that Mom would turn that blank, puzzled gaze on me, not recognizing the strange girl on the porch. But a second later, Mom let out a small cry and flew through the door.

Another moment and I was in her arms, hugging her tightly as she sobbed and laughed and asked me a thousand questions all at once. I closed my eyes and let this moment swirl around me, holding on to it for as long as I could. I wanted to remember, for just a few heartbeats, what it was like to be, not a faery or a pawn or a queen, but just a daughter.

"Meggie?" I pulled back a bit and, through the open door, I saw Ethan standing at the foot of the stairs. Taller now, older. He must've grown at least three inches while I was gone. But his eyes were the same: bright blue and as solemn as the grave.

He didn't run to me as I entered the living room, didn't smile. Calmly, as if he knew I'd be back all along, he walked across the floor until he was standing a foot away. I knelt, and he watched me, holding my gaze with an expression far too old for his face.

"I knew you'd come back." His voice was different, too. Clearer now, more sure of himself. My half brother was no longer a toddler. "I didn't forget."

"No," I whispered. "You didn't forget."

I opened my arms, and he finally stepped into them, fisting

his hands in my hair. I hugged him to me as I stood, wondering if this was the last time I would hold him like this. He might be a teenager when I saw him next.

"Meghan." Mom's voice made me turn. She stood at the edge of the living room with Luke behind her, watching me with a strange, sad expression. As if she'd just figured something out. "You're…not staying, are you?"

I closed my eyes, feeling Ethan's arms around my neck squeeze tight. "No," I told her, shaking my head. "I can't. I have…responsibilities now, people who need me. I just wanted to say goodbye and…" My breath hitched, and I swallowed hard to clear my throat. "And try to explain what happened to me the night I went back." I sighed and cast a glance at Luke, still standing by the door in confusion, his brow furrowed as he looked from me to Mom and back again. "I don't know if you'll believe me," I continued, "but you should hear the truth. Before…before I have to leave."

Mom walked across the floor as if sleepwalking, sinking on the couch in a daze. But her eyes were clear and determined when she looked at me and patted the cushion beside her. "Tell me everything," was all she said.

And so I did.

Starting from the very beginning. The day I walked into Faery to get Ethan back. I told them about the faery courts, about Oberon and Mab and Puck. I told them about Machina and the Iron fey, about Glitch and the rebels and the false king. I glossed over a few small, terrifying details, parts of the story where I almost died, or that were too scary for Ethan to hear. I left out the parts with Paul, knowing it wasn't my place to tell his story. By the time I reached the end, where I defeated Ferrum and became the Iron Queen, Ethan was asleep on my lap, and Luke's eyes were glazed over in utter disbelief. I knew he wouldn't remember much of the story, if any, that it would slip and fade from his mind, becoming something he heard in a fairy tale.

Mom was silent for several heartbeats when I finished. "So, you're...a queen now." She said the words like she was testing them, seeing how they felt. "A...faery queen."

"Yes."

"And...there's no way for you to stay in the real world. With us. With your family."

I shook my head. "The land is calling me. I'm tied to it now. I have to go back."

Mom bit her lip, and her eyes finally filled with tears. I was surprised when Luke spoke, his deep, calm voice echoing through the room. "Will we see you again?"

"I don't know," I said truthfully. "Maybe."

"Will you be all right?" Luke continued. "Alone with these...things?" As if speaking the word *faery* would make it more real, and he wasn't about to start believing yet.

"I'll be fine." I thought of Paul and wished he could be here tonight. "I won't be alone."

The sky through the windows was lightening. We had talked through the night, and dawn was on its way.

Gently, I kissed Ethan's forehead and eased him onto the couch without waking him, then stood to face Mom and Luke. "I have to go," I said softly. "They're waiting for me."

Mom hugged me again, and Luke enfolded us both in his thick arms. "Be sure to write," Mom sniffed, as if I was going on a long trip, or away to college. Maybe it was easier for her to think that. "Call us if you have the chance, and try to come home for holidays."

"I'll try," I murmured, stepping away. For a moment, I gazed around the farmhouse, reliving old memories, letting them warm me inside and out. No longer home, but it was a part of me that would always be there, a place that would never fade away. I turned to Mom and Luke and smiled through the tears I hadn't realized were falling until now.

"Meghan." Mom stepped forward, pleading. "Are you sure you have to do this? Can't you stay, just a few days?"

I shook my head. "I love you, Mom." Drawing on my glamour, I swirled it around me like a cloak. "Tell Ethan I won't forget."

"Meghan!"

"Goodbye," I whispered, and faded from sight. Both Mom and Luke jumped, looking around frantically, then Mom buried her face in Luke's shoulder and sobbed.

Ethan woke up, blinked at his parents, then looked right at me, still invisible by the front door. His eyebrows rose, and I put my finger to my lips, praying he wouldn't cause a fuss.

Ethan smiled. One small hand rose in a brief wave, then he hopped off the couch and padded up to Mom, still being consoled by Luke. I watched my family, felt their love and grief and support, and smiled proudly.

You'll be fine, I told them, swallowing the lump in my throat. *You'll be fine without me.*

Blinking back tears, I gave my family one last look and swept through the front door into the waiting dawn.

I WAS HALFWAY ACROSS the front lawn, forcing myself to put one foot in front of the other and not turn back, when a bark caught my attention, and I looked up.

Something was bounding toward me over the grass, a shadow in the predawn light. Something large and furry and vaguely familiar. A wolf? No, a dog! A big, shaggy...no, that couldn't be right...

"Beau?" I gasped, as the huge German shepherd slammed into me with the force of a freight train, nearly knocking me down. It *was* Beau. I laughed as his big paws muddied my shirt and his enormous tongue slapped the side of my face.

"What are you doing here?" I asked, rubbing his neck as he panted and wagged his whole body in joy. I hadn't seen our old farm dog since the day Luke had unjustly taken him to the pound, thinking he'd bitten Ethan. "Did Mom decide to bring you home? How—"

I stopped, my fingers brushing something thin and metallic looped around his neck, under his shaggy fur. Wondering if it was a collar with tags, I calmed Beau long enough to pull it free, drawing it over his ears and holding it up for a closer look.

It was a familiar silver chain, on which hung the remains of a shattered amulet, glinting in the predawn light.

My heart skipped a beat. With Beau still dancing at my feet, I looked around, scanning the front yard and the edge of the trees. He couldn't be here. I'd sent him away, released him from his vows. He should hate me.

And yet...here it was.

For a few heart-pounding moments, I waited. Waited for his dark form to slip out of the shadows, for those bright silver eyes to find me. I thought I could feel him nearby, watching. I could almost imagine I sensed his heartbeat, felt his emotions—or maybe that was my own longing. My own sense of loss and grief and regret, and the love I knew could never be.

A weight pressed against my chest, and I smiled sadly. Deep down, I knew he wasn't coming. We were from different worlds, now. Ash couldn't survive in the Iron Realm, and I could not—would not—abandon it. I had responsibilities, to the Iron Realm, to my subjects, to myself. Ash couldn't be a part of that. Better a clean break than to drag it out, wishing for the impossible. He knew that. This was just his final gift; his last farewell.

Still, I hesitated, my stomach in knots, hoping against hope that he would find me, change his mind, and come back. But several silent minutes passed, and Ash did not appear. Finally, as the last of the stars faded from the heavens, I put the chain in my pocket and knelt to scratch Beau behind the ears.

"He's something, isn't he?" I asked the dog, who blinked and thumped his tail solemnly. "I don't know where he found you, or how he brought you here, but I'm glad he did. I wish I could see him one more time…" A lump rose to my throat, and I swallowed it down. "You'll like it in your new home, boy," I went on, trying to be cheerful. "Plenty of room, lots of gremlins to chase, and I think you'll really like Paul." The dog whined, cocking his head. I kissed his long muzzle and stood. "Come on," I said, wiping my eyes, "I'll introduce you."

The sky was now a soft pink. Birds twittered in the branches around me, and a faint wind rustled the leaves. Everywhere, life was stirring, moving on. I took a deep breath and looked to the sky, letting the breeze dry my tears. Ash was gone, but I still had people who needed me, who were waiting for me. I could wallow in my loss, or I could trust my knight and move on. I could wait. Time was on my side, after all. In the meantime, I had a kingdom to run.

"Majesty!"

Glitch's voice shattered the calm of the morning, and my first lieutenant came striding through the trees. Beau growled, flattening his ears, until I touched his neck and he calmed down.

"All you all right?" Glitch asked anxiously, violet eyes wide as he stared at Beau. "What is that…thing? It looks dangerous. Did it hurt you?"

"Beau, this is Glitch," I introduced, and the dog gave a tentative tail wag. "Glitch, this is Beau. Be nice, the both of you. You'll be seeing a lot of each other, I expect."

"Wait. It's coming with us?"

I laughed at his horrified expression. Beau barked happily and wagged his tail, leaning close. I slipped my arm through Glitch's and smiled at the dog pressed against my leg. Life wasn't perfect, but it was as perfect as it could be at the moment. I had a place in the world. I wasn't alone.

"Come on," I told them. "They'll be waiting for us, back at the city. Let's go home."

Ash

He watched her from the fading dark, unseen and invisible, just another shadow in the trees. He wondered if he had been right to come here, to see her one last time, though he knew resisting her was futile. He couldn't leave without seeing her again, hearing her voice and seeing her smile, even though it wasn't for him. He had no illusions about his addiction to her. She had her fingers sunk firmly into his heart, and could do with it what she wished.

He watched her walk away with the Iron faery and the dog, watched them leave to return to her own realm, back to a place he couldn't follow.

For now.

"So." Robin Goodfellow appeared beside him, arms crossed over his chest, also watching the girl and her companions depart. "She's gone."

"Yes."

Goodfellow shot him a sideways glance, wary and expectant. "What now?"

He sighed, raked a hand through his hair. "I have something to do," he murmured. "A promise to keep. I might not be back for a long time."

"Huh." Goodfellow scratched his head, and grinned. "Sounds like fun. Where are we going?"

Now it was his turn to eye the other fey. "I don't recall inviting you."

"Too bad, ice-boy." Infuriating as always, Goodfellow leaned back and smirked at him. "I've had enough of war and killing for a while. Tormenting you is so much more fun. Besides…" Goodfellow sighed and looked back to the now-empty steps. "I want her to be happy, and she's most happy with you. Maybe this will make up for…past mistakes." He shook his head and returned to his normal idiocy. "So, either you say, 'sure, I'd love to have you along,' or you have a big bird dropping things on your head the whole trip."

He sighed, defeated. Perhaps it was best for Goodfellow to trail along. He was a competent fighter after all. And they had been…friends…once. Though this journey would change nothing. "Fine," he muttered. "Just stay out of my way."

The Summer faery grinned, rubbing his hands together, looking gleeful. He felt a brief moment of trepidation, inviting Puck along. Most likely, they would try to kill each other before the trip was through. "So, where are we going?" Goodfellow asked. "I assume you have some sort of plan for this adventure."

An adventure. He didn't think of it that way, but it didn't matter. *I don't care what it's called. I just want to be with her at the end. I'm not giving up. Meghan, I'll be with you soon. Please, wait for me.*

"Hey, ice-boy. Did you hear me? Where are we going? What are we doing?"

"I heard you," he murmured, and turned away, beginning to walk into the trees. "And yes, I have a plan."

"Really. Do enlighten me."

"First, we're going to find a certain cat."

★ ★ ★ ★ ★

How far can love be tested before it breaks?
Look for more dangerous faeries and breathtaking adventures
in THE IRON KNIGHT
Ash's story.
Coming soon from Harlequin Teen.

ACKNOWLEDGMENTS

It occurred to me, as I sat down to write this page, that I have come to the end of book three. Book *three,* and a few years back, I didn't even know if I would publish a single novel. Of course, I couldn't get here without the help of many awesome, wonderful people. Without them, I never could've written *The End* on the final page of the final chapter. I have so many people to be grateful for.

Thanks to my parents, who put up with a daughter who daydreamed her way through school, hid novels behind her math textbooks during class, wrote stories when she was supposed to be taking notes, and generally drove her poor teachers insane. Though you lamented my complete and utter disinterest in math and social studies, you still encouraged me to dream.

Thanks to the people on the inside: my awesome agent, Laurie McLean, who knows the business far better than I, for which I am very grateful. To my wonderful editor, Natashya Wilson, who is probably the strongest and most dedicated person I know. To the entire Harlequin Teen staff, for awesome support, beautiful covers, and making this whole experience completely and utterly amazing.

A huge shout-out to the awesome YA book bloggers of the blogosphere, for taking the time to read, post your thoughts online, and spread the word. You are truly a dedicated, passionate group. To the awesome Tenners, whom I'm pleased to be a part of: thanks for being there to share triumphs and frustrations, to talk about things only other authors can sympathize with. It was nice to be able to vent without people edging away from the "crazy writer lady."

Thanks to all my readers, for Team Ash and Team Puck, for those crazy fights on Twitter that amuse me far more than they should. Thank you for making it fun.

And, as always, my deepest gratitude goes to my husband, Nick, who continues to be my best support and inspiration. Still couldn't have done it without him.

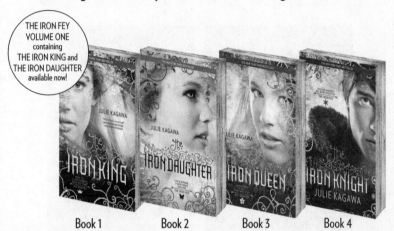

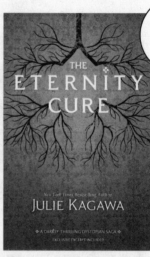
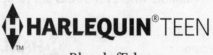